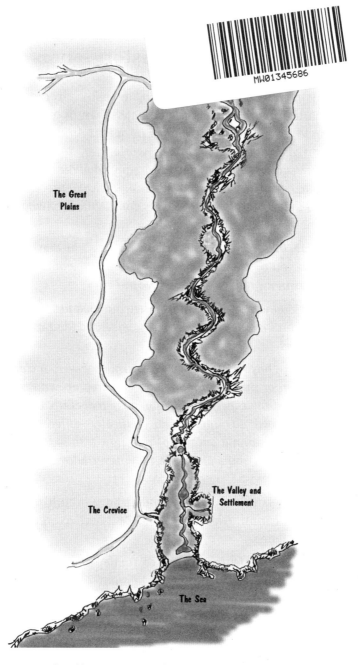

THE VALLEY OF THE RUNNERS AND VICINITY

# In the Beginning God created the Big Bang, and the rest is history—or is it?

Around fifty-thousand years ago, a blink of an eye in evolutionary terms, our ancestors—perhaps as few as one hundred, according to DNA evidence—emerged from East Africa. They were trapped in a brutal and untamed world. Yet, somehow they managed to survive, explore, and eventually populate every corner of the earth, eventually even reconquering Africa, a process which eliminated their hominid kin. This was done while surviving an ice age.

Who were these Cro-Magnon people? How did they appear? And what if you or I were dropped back in time, would we really look just like them? And what would we do?

The Cro-Magnon paradox is that they did look just like us and had our big brains. And they were as savage and kind as the best and worst of us.

Every culture has its creation story, perhaps a seed of truth lies hidden in each of them. Perhaps there is a creator, who reached out and touched the experiment begun on planet earth. Could it be a retrovirus—used to implant dramatically different DNA—transforming a hominid species of ape into a thinking human. Random chance or God's plan? We may never know. But all can agree life is good.

This tale is what the beginning might have been like, with all things human: curiosity, love, benevolence as well as greed, selfish ambition and hate.

And faith versus science? Lawrence Stanley asks why not both? He asks what does it really mean to be human?

# In the Beginning . . .

## Book One of The Runners

### A Novel By

# Lawrence Stanley

WWW.LAWRENCE-STANLEY.COM

# In the Beginning . . .

*Book One of The Runners*

Cover art by Bruce Harman

Copyright © Writers Best Publishing, LLC.
All rights reserved. 2019-2022.

Library of Congress Cataloging-in-Publication Data

ISBN 978-0-9801697-4-4

*East Africa, circa 50,000 BC*

*I have no special talents. I am only passionately curious.*

Albert Einstein

# Good and Evil 1

Eve couldn't believe she was doing this. The ledge was so narrow here it defied belief. So high up on the cliff-face, she had never felt the same rush before in her life. At any moment the platform in her arm could tip and pull her over the edge to the broken rocks far below.

She tried not to focus on that, but on scooting her feet forward an inch at a time as she maneuvered the platform forward towards the gap she hoped to bridge with it.

Her left arm scraped against the cliff. The platform rocked under her right, tugging at her as her heart pounded in her ears. She slowed her pace to that of a snail as her breathing grew ragged. The platform—four bamboo poles lashed together—was just wide enough to walk on and just long enough to bridge the gap.

On her first attempt she had extended the platform hand-over-hand, but then it tipped and slipped out of her grasp. It had fallen through the gap, and crashed to the valley floor below. It was far too heavy to handle that way. Eve could see that now. With a better plan in mind, she stood the platform upright and aligned it with the ledge. She let the platform slowly fall forward. It picked up speed as it dropped. Shocking amounts of speed. Frantic to slow it, she reached out, not thinking as she reacted instinctively trying to break its fall as it crashed down on the opposite ledge. It bounced.

"Bloody bones," she muttered as she watched in dismal horror as it slipped off the ledge. Despite her desperate attempt to hang on, it again fell to the valley floor. Eve scrambled back from the edge. "Bloody, bloody bones." Her plan had not worked as she hoped. *You shouldn't even be out here, you stupid girl.* "I'm getting closer!" she screamed at the voice in her head. She hated how it always called her stupid. It wasn't her fault she had to know what lay beyond the gap and in the crevice hiding in the cliff.

Trekking back down the treacherous rock-face, she retrieved the platform and hauled it up to the ledge. Once again she stood it on end. She aligned it with the opposite side of the ledge. She let it fall. It slammed onto the far end. *Bang!* Just as she thought her plan had worked, the end of the platform closest to her bounced forward from the shock. The platform dropped through the gap.

Eve dove out for it. She managed to touch it, but not grab a firm hold. For a moment she teetered, tingling all over. Her legs jerked involuntarily. Her arms flailed. She scrambled away from the abyss and clung to the cliff wall. "Bloody, bloody bones," she swore. "What are you even doing up here, Eve?" She worried she was out of her bloody mind.

Chest heaving and perspiration beading over her brow, she glanced out over the peaceful valley stretching deadly-far below. Her desire to see what waited for her in the forbidden crevice warred with her fears. She focused on the sun, now low in the west. Her breathing began to slow. As she glanced down at the platform, a joyful-terror washed over her. She thanked the Spirit of the Tree she had not held on firmly. A fall from this height would be the death of her for sure.

*One more try,* she told herself as her desire overcame caution. She climbed back down, and set herself on what she promised was her last attempt of the day.

Back on the ledge, she stood the platform upright. This time she planned to put her own weight on the platform, to keep it from bouncing when it landed. That would be safe enough—she hoped. This way she figured she could keep it from falling off. Still the idea scared her and her hands tingled and shook. Her stomach fluttered with the platform in the breeze. If it fell through the gap this time, she was certain to fall with it.

Tapping the platform with her toe, Eve fine-tuned its position on the ledge. She needed to aim precisely. If too close the platform would hit the wall and bounce out. If she aimed too far out it would rock and fall off again.

A warm breeze stirred and rustled her long brown hair. "If this works, Eve," she said to herself. "You are never calling yourself stupid again." She just needed to think like her father. He was the tribe's chief. She knew if she was to be chief she needed to be just like him. She already had his deep blue eyes and brown hair. Now she just needed to think like him.

She gathered her courage just as she had seen her father gather his. Frowning, she focused on the platform and the gap before her. *This is it. No more tries.*

With the sun setting in the west and the temperature rapidly dropping with it, she knew she would have to let go of the platform soon. She waited for the breeze to subside. When it gentled, she released the platform. It was all or nothing now!

She grabbed the platform near the base as the bamboo poles tipped forward. Throwing her body onto the platform, she quickly squatted on it. She closed her eyes as she fell forward.

The platform hit the opposite ledge. *Clack!* The impact nearly toppled her over the edge, but the platform stabilized.

"Yes! Finally!" she cried, thrilled. The platform was secure! At last, she had access to the forbidden place splitting the cliff.

The large fissure in the cliff-face halfway across the platform called to her. It led somewhere, somewhere otherly, but Eve wasn't sure where. Another world perhaps? Nobody knew. And nobody was allowed to go there. The nagging question of why ate at her. Maybe her father knew but he couldn't speak. If she was to follow in his footsteps then she had to know as well.

She had asked Twig and the other children to come with her, but none of them had joined her quest. They of course wanted to know, but they let their fear rule them. It was fitting she was the bravest. She was also one of the oldest of the speaking children in addition to being the daughter of Blue Eyes, the tribe's leader.

Despite the beauty of the valley, she knew there was an ugliness underneath—or could be at any moment. The storms would come again, even if for the moment the river valley seemed like a wonderful, safe place. It looked so beautiful and serene. And it provided everything she and the others needed. Eve had explored the valley, from the crashing waves of the ocean in the east, to the thundering water falling into the valley from the west. She explored it, and she knew all the plants and all the animals which shared her world. She knew exactly where to find them. In this world, there were only two things forbidden.

One was the sacred tree which grew near the cave where she lived. It bore a special fruit all year around. The overpowering smell of it made people crazy. The tree was special, unique even. It was the only tree like it in the whole world. None of the others had glistening silver bark or two-toned leaves, none like the special tree. She called it the Tree of Life.

The fruit from the Tree of Life was coveted but could not be picked and eaten without approaching the tree. The closer the curious approached, the stronger the tree's power impaired their minds. It instilled fear and made them dream of things they had never seen, or worse, have nightmares of beings they did not know. The tribe worshiped the tree. Exactly why was unclear.

Was it because the fruit healed the sick—if they could make the journey? Eve speculated there was more to it. But what? The old ones revered it like it had saved them from an unspoken evil. Eve couldn't picture what that evil was. Regardless, she wanted to know why the tree was so respected.

Sadly, none of the adults could tell her. Even if they did know, they could not speak. Somehow Eve and her friends could. She was not quite sure how or why it had happened but she and the other kids worked out sounds for everything around them. Eve could not remember learning to speak. It had just happened. And while not all the children who were born could speak, many could. It annoyed her that she could speak but had no answers. And it frustrated her to no end that those who held the answers could not tell her what they were.

The second forbidden thing was completely different. It was clearly evil. It was feared by all. It was the stuff of nightmares.

When Eve was young, her father would often awake, quaking with fear. He would point to the crack in the cliff-wall. Then he would shake his head. Contorting his face and flailing his arms, he would imitate a monster. He would snarl and growl. It had made Eve cry back then. Sometimes she had nightmares too, but bravery was her ally now. This close, she simply had to know what the crevice held.

She stepped onto the bamboo platform lightly. Obvious from a glance, the tribe had destroyed this section of the ledge with heavy rocks, pounding away until it broke. Whatever monster lay trapped in the dark crack, the tribe clearly did not want it to escape.

Eve took several tentative steps onto the platform. Each step brought her closer to the crack. She strained to see inside the two-foot wide fissure in the cliff-face as it ran up into the sky.

A sudden terror gripped her as the platform shifted under her unexpectedly. A shiver ran up her spine and she froze. Her breath grew shallow, and her legs weak. She wiped her brow with clammy hands and considered turning back.

*What am I thinking?* she asked herself. It was getting late. She had gotten the platform up. Wasn't that enough for one day?

And yet Adam and the others would be watching. Adam claimed to be the oldest child who spoke—nobody knew for sure—but he was definitely too afraid to come with her. Eve smiled at the thought of deflating his puffed-up sense of self, even though she knew he would never admit to being afraid. Instead of coming with her, he acted like he didn't care about exploring the crack. His act didn't fool her, nor did it surprise her.

Twig, however, had surprised her. Twig was her best friend and was rarely afraid of anything, but she had not only refused to come, she had tried to convince the gang to stop her. That had been strange, but Eve had already made up her mind.

She left the gang lounging on the riverbank beneath the big tree. She had dared them to come with her, but they had followed Adam's lead and claimed not to care. Eve knew better though. They were watching her right now, hidden by the green jungle far below. Knowing that, Eve couldn't quit now. If she did, she would never hear the end of it.

She stepped forward and gripped the rocky edge. She peered around the corner into the deep shadows. Inky darkness stared back at her. Cold air drifted out of the crack. It felt . . . wrong. Goosebumps rose on her arms. Her stomach felt queasy. *Don't get sick now, Eve. Focus!*

There was no turning back.

*Curiosity is the very basis of education and if you tell me that curiosity killed the cat, I say only the cat died nobly.*

Arnold Edinborough

# A First Look 2

A broken path of rock wandered into the gloom. Climbing over the rocks wedged between the crevice walls, Eve inched her way forward. Her heart pounded as she thought what Adam would say if she were to back out now with no new intelligence. The thought kept her going. She came to a section of loose rock and tiptoed over it. A large rock loomed ahead, blocking her way. She pulled herself up onto the boulder and peered over the top. Nothing prepared her for the terrifying sight which met her gaze.

She froze. Tears clouded her sky-blue eyes. She screamed, willing her paralyzed body to run. But it refused to do anything except keep on screaming. Her body was frozen to the boulder. Her head and eyes were locked with evil itself. After what felt like an eternity, she managed to tear away. Only then did her limbs begin to work as they should. Breaking free, she ran back down the path, crying "Go, go, go!" to herself.

Bursting out onto the platform she almost flew over the edge. She pulled in a ragged breath, relieved, she was back in the safe, happy world she knew so well. Here, the warm air smelled sweet. As Eve breathed deeply, her panic subsided. Setting in the west, the sun tossed shadows along the cliff front and behind.

With hands shaking and knees quivering from one-to-hold-at-a-time, she managed to make the descent. At the bottom the gang all wore concerned looks. Their facades of indifference were gone now.

"We heard the screaming," Monkey shouted.

"Adam said we should come to get you," Bev said, pressing close, protectively. All of them were talking at once.

"What happened?" Art asked.

"What did you see?" Twig inquired more calmly than the rest. She was one of the older girls. As Eve's best friend, she should have been more concerned, but not Twig, not this time.

"Are you okay?" Adam asked.  Concern lined his face.

Tears still streamed down Eve's wide-eyed face.  She did not say anything, but motioned for them to follow her as she ran back towards the river, toward the big tree whose branches hung low over the water.  It was their headquarters, and Eve's refuge from her mother.

The large tree had long been a place of shelter and of safety.  Now the tree was their schoolroom, their workshop, their hangout—their second home.  Here only those who spoke were allowed.  Here Eve and the rest of the gang were safe.

They dashed down the familiar path, their bare feet slapping up puffs of dust.  One-by-one they arrived and dropped into their normal spots.  Eve plopped down on her favorite seat, a massive, low hanging limb which reached out over the river.  It gently swayed as she pulled herself up.

Adam sat at the base of the trunk.  He was the son of Blue Eyes' lieutenant and was tall and muscular with unruly brown hair and a strong face.  It now held a quizzical, or maybe it was a cynical look.  Eve never knew which.  His relaxed posture and casual but intense gaze could have indicated disgust for her, a silly girl who defied the rules.  Or it could have indicated he admired her courage while still being concerned for her safety.  She couldn't read him.  She told herself she didn't care  one way or the other.

Twig skipped to a stop at the tree and pulled her uniquely colored hair, the lightest of anyone's in the tribe, from her eyes. She was, as her name implied, quite thin. Compared to her body, her head seemed oversized. And yet, what Twig lacked in physical strength and beauty, she made up for in brains. She was the mastermind behind speech. Eve had asked her many times why they could speak and where the words came from but Twig did not give a direct answer, dismissing the question with a wave of her hand. Eve was pretty sure Twig had cataloged and named all the plants, animals, and items of daily use. She also tried to teach the gang to express abstract ideas, particularly about the past and future. She was always correcting the speech of others and had set herself in charge of teaching the younger children what she knew of the world. She had no regular seat and preferred to remain unpredictable.

Eve watched as Twig selected a rock opposite her. She seemed eager to hear about what was in the crack.

On Twig's heels was Fish. Eve dismissed him with a glance. He was average in every way, save for his fascination with the water. He could swim like a fish. He was always playing around in the water—making boats, building fish traps, and constructing dams. Eve liked him well enough, like a brother. He was easy to deal with. He took his usual seat on a fallen log at the water's edge.

Eve waited for Art as he puffed in last.  She did not know what she thought about the rotund boy.  He was not as active as the others, but he was cheerful—especially when it came to food.  Yet he was different and strange, and Eve would sometimes catch him staring at her.  In his spare time, Art drew on the walls of the cave—to help record events.  He wanted to keep track of the seasonal weather, like the monsoons and the flooding of the river.  They had discussed counting the days between flooding events, but had quickly run out of numbers.

"We are all who can speak," Eve began.  "Though a small part of our tribe we are our own family.  As such, today I have taken the first step in finding answers as to why we are so different from our parents."

Eve glanced from Fish to Monkey, and from Bev to Twig, then finally to Art and Adam.  They were all outcasts, and as long as they stayed out of sight, they were forgotten.  She still found it amazing they could understand her when none of their parents could.  The adults could mimic their sounds sometimes, but they never connected speech to anything other than the identification of the most basic items.  For her parents a grunt could work, but for her current audience, Eve decided she needed to make her story more exciting, especially after this big buildup.  Timing would be important.

"What about Little Red?" Fish asked. "He can speak too."

"Yes, yes, Fish," Eve said, annoyed at the interruption. "We've been over this before. He is too young, throwing tantrums like a baby any time you tease him about his red hair. That's all we need." Little Red was annoying but he had some virtues. He was idealistic and often stood for justice and defending the innocent, and he probably was old enough. "Now, let me think," Eve added, regretting not having admitted him. Her story would no doubt scare the daylights out of him.

Monkey dropped a branch from above on Fish. "Yeah, shut up, Fish. You are almost too young, yourself."

"Did you learn why only we can talk?" Art asked. "That is what I want to know."

"What I want to know is why the adults hate us so much," Monkey said. "Bloody bones! It's not like I am a real monkey." Eve knew what he meant. Her own mother used to beat her when she spoke.

"How about we let Eve tell us what she saw?" Adam said. "Eve?"

"Let me catch my breath," she said, glancing at the setting sun.

"Well, what did you see?"

"Eve?" Adam asked.

Eve glanced at the ground. *He doesn't think I saw anything!* she thought angrily, but then smiled to herself. If she paced her story so the climax was coincident with dusk, he and the others would jump out of their skin. Waving Adam and the others to silence, she began, taking time to describe her struggle with the platform.

As darkness fell, she described the cold, damp air wafting from the crack, how it assailed her senses, then how she climbed over the enormous boulder. "As I looked over the top, my eyes locked on the Evil One. Hideous sharp teeth! Its sunken black eyes froze me in place!" She glanced around the group. She could barely make out their faces as the sun glowed orange with the last light of day.

Adam leaned forward in anticipation. "Then what?"

Eve continued. "It had me under its power. I couldn't move! Finally, I managed to scream. The sound broke the monsters' hold on me. I pulled back and ran." Then, as if a thought just occurred to her, she said "But—" She opened her eyes wide and spoke in a warning tone. "I didn't remember to take down the platform. The Evil One might have followed me. Even now it might be coming to eat us! Grrrrrr!"

Little Red cried out as he burst from his hiding place behind a nearby tree stump. Monkey fell and caught himself on his branch. The rest all jumped to their feet and ran screaming towards home. Eve followed, triumphant, delighted with herself and the day's exploits. The lucky cry from Little Red, and him bursting out so unexpectedly made her smile.

In the growing darkness, as she followed the gang down the familiar path along the river, she started to have uneasy feelings herself about the platform being left in place. *I probably should have taken it down,* she rebuked herself.

To her delight, the gang ran faster than normal. When they came to the final bend, they crossed the river, hopping from rock to rock through the rapids which marked the way to the cave. They ran over the bamboo bridge they had constructed over the deepest part, and raced along the smaller stream. Here, under a thick section of trees where it was totally dark—always a scary place—they stayed close together as they traveled the final section. Quickly they splashed across the shallow stream next to the little waterfall.

At the top of the rise, on a grassy flat, the silver tree glowed by starlight. Eve shivered. It seemed to point its gnarled limbs at her accusingly. *You have broken the law,* it cried, and Eve wondered if she would be punished for exploring the crevice. She worried she might even die for it.

She stood staring at the tree. Perhaps she could appease it. She could give it a gift in the morning. Maybe if she caught it a fish and tossed it under its silver branches? It would certainly have to forgive her if she brought it several shells of water.  Wouldn't it?  Hopeful, she entered the cave, now quiet and dark.  She felt her way to her mat.  When she stepped on her younger brother who was sprawled on her mat, she shoved him off it.

"Late. Bad girl," he squeaked, taunting her. Eve curled up and ignored him.  He was already talking nonsense, chattering away anytime he could get someone to listen, and often when he couldn't.

In the dark, sleep eluded Eve.  When she closed her eyes, all she could see was the evil, hideous skull.  She had seen monkey skulls, seal skulls, and human skulls, but nothing compared to the one in the crevice.  The Evil One was huge.  It had a raised ridge above its eyes, and its jaw was full of sharp teeth, large enough to eat a man whole.

If only she could ask her father about it.  If only he could teach her all the things he knew.  He could tell her everything she needed to know to be a good chief.  He could take her on adventures. Together they could defeat the Evil One!  It was a beautiful fantasy, but she knew it was only that.

Her father's life was peaceful, and he enjoyed it that way.  There was always plenty to eat, and no Evil One in the valley.  He, like the rest of the tribe, seemed happy to do nothing but eat, sleep, and make babies.

Nothing ever seemed to change.  And yet many of the adults carried scars, proof life was not always easy or safe.  And while most of the adults wore animal skin or woven reed coverings around their waists, they were completely inept at producing them—the speaking children made everyone's clothes.

Some adults would forget to put them on. They did not seem to mind. They never worried about the past or the future. They didn't even make a tool unless they needed it right at the moment.

Eve's mind drifted to the events of the day, then back to the Tree of Life. She pictured her father, strong and brave, kneeling and bowing to the tree. He would do this some nights when he couldn't sleep, or before leaving for a hunt. Eve couldn't understand it. She had to know why. But one thing was clear; she would have to go back into the cliff and explore further.

At some point, she drifted off to sleep. When she awoke birds were singing in the trees outside the cave. Her mother arrived with a basket full of fruit in her arms. Eve had made her the basket, and her mother had remembered to use it this morning. She, like the other adults, sometimes forgot stuff like that. Eve found it strange they could forget such simple things, but at least today her mother had remembered. Eve glanced at her brother.

"I 'minded her," he said.

Eve shook her head at her brother and stood up. "*Re*-minded her." He would get it—or he wouldn't. She had better things to do than teach him.

After breakfast, with no other chores to do, Eve refilled the family's waterskins in the river and replaced them under her father's approving gaze. Eve walked over to him and patted him on a hairy arm, careful to avoid the bare spots caused by scars. He had to have received them before she was born. "I'll be back, Papa," Eve said.

He smiled at her, and she turned and headed outside. She picked up her fishing gear at the mouth of the cave and headed for the river. She still needed to fish up her offering for the sacred tree.

*What makes us human, I think, is an ability to ask questions, a consequence of our sophisticated spoken language.*

Jane Goodall

# A Second Look     3

A mid-morning sun was shooting down its hot rays when Adam saw Eve hurrying toward the big tree by the river. *Finally!*

"But don't worry, I will be the first to go in," he told the gang as Eve stepped closer; he knew she could hear his words now. He had already let the group know if they didn't like what they found, he'd take the plank down himself. "And that's how it's going to be," he concluded. "If I don't like it, no one is going to go. And I'll lead the way—and that's final."

No one argued. Not even Eve.

Soon—to his own irritation—he found himself stumbling over his words, despite the fact Eve wasn't even interrupting him. She simply lowered her big blue eyes. He plowed on. *She's buying all this?* He wondered to himself, somewhat surprised.

Suddenly she agreed with him. "For such a daring adventure, a real, brave man is absolutely needed to lead us."

Adam stood up. Absolutely, he could do this... He was a man now, not a child. He didn't wait to see if the others were following or not, but boldly set off toward the cliff. Without looking back, he tried not to doubt himself. The rest would follow him. And they did.

As he ran, Adam was also pleased to find no one even tried to race ahead. Especially after he had laid down the law with them at the tree.

But as he neared the cliff, it seemed to loom up. Doubts began to creep in. What had Eve been up to at the tree? A sudden attack of common sense? It seemed so then, but now Adam wasn't so sure. Maybe she had looked down to cover a smirk. It didn't seem so then or even now. Adam, however, couldn't help but feel Eve was up to something. It was like she was using him somehow.

She was running right behind him. For a moment it almost felt like she was driving him on, like she, not he, was leading. *Who is in charge here? Me?* Adam wondered. Eve was clever like that, but surely, he was in charge. *My idea from the start*, Adam told himself. *I convinced everyone else, before she had even arrived at the tree.* Regardless, it was too late now to worry. He was committed.

Committed or not, his doubts mixed with foreboding under the frowning cliff-face. The tall gray wall seemed to have grown unnaturally high up into the sky as he and the gang approached it. This was an evil place for sure.

Still, as he moved amongst the beautiful flowers blooming along the path, it was hard to believe something so evil could exist. The bees buzzed lazily in the warm sunlight. A cloud of butterflies exploded from the mud at the base of the cliff—the cliff which held the crack. Monkeys chattered; birds sang; a gentle breeze ruffled the leaves. This was paradise, and it seemed to be calling him away from the menacing crack in the face of the cliff, even as it taunted him.

Adam wanted nothing more than to turn away from the wall of gray and head back to the valley. His feet began to feel heavy, and he began to slow.

"The best way to climb up is just ahead." Eve breathed her hot words into his ears.

Adam's feet only felt heavier, but with her right behind him he had no choice but to begin the climb. Slowly and carefully he selected his toe-holds and sharp, jutting hand-holds. When he finally arrived at the ledge, he sat with his legs dangling over the edge. A strange feeling of exhilaration washed over him as he caught his breath and waited for the others to climb up and sit next to him.

"Great view from up here," Monkey said, sounding nervous. Adam glanced over in surprise. The skinny boy was the first to join him. He had shot up the cliff, despite his fear of what they might find in the forbidden place. *Showing off for Eve.*

"It is a great view from up here," Twig said, correcting him as she pulled herself onto the ledge. That was Twig.

Adam laughed and yelled down to Eve and the others. "Twig's correcting our grammar, even up here!"

"What?" Eve asked, poking her head up.

"I was just saying how you can see a bit of the river and the Tree of Life from up here," Twig said. Adam scoffed. That hadn't been what she was saying at all.

Eve pulled herself up and dangled her feet. "I just hope it cannot see us! Sometimes I worry it sees everything!"

Adam glanced at Eve. "Really?"

She turned away. "Just to be safe, I gave it an offering this morning," she said. "You know, just in case."

Adam heard himself grunt. "Hmm. That works?" he asked. Worried he was scowling, he wiped his face and mouth with this left hand.

"I don't know," Eve said, finally glancing at him. "But it can't hurt, can it?"

Adam felt his scowl deepen. "Good thinking," he said. He tried to smile, but felt himself scowling.

*Good thinking? What on earth would Eve think of that comment?* He wasn't even sure what he meant. He decided she had actually been clever.

"Twig," Eve said. "What's that word for when you say something is good, but you don't really mean it?"

"Ignorant?" Fish offered.

"You're ignorant, Fish," Monkey said. Eve ignored them both.

"Sarcasm," Twig replied.

"That's right; *sarcasm*," Eve repeated. She glanced at Adam.

*Yup.* He could see she didn't believe him.

"Language is too limited for us to effectively communicate some things like humor," Twig continued. "That's why we have things like facial expressions."

"Thanks," said Eve. "Thanks. Yes, facial expressions like a frown. Thanks, Twig."

Adam had heard the lecture before and was glad Eve cut it short.

"You are welcome," came Twig's prim reply, oblivious to Eve's sarcasm.

Eve looked over at Adam again. She let out a sigh. She was waiting—waiting for him. He stood. "Alright gang," he announced. "It's time to move."

Hesitant heads turned and looked up at him, but one at a time the gang stood and followed single-file along the ledge. When Adam glanced back at Eve, her blue eyes met his. He smiled, but struggled to think of something witty to say. Nothing came to mind. He couldn't understand it. He was witty with the other kids, but with her, he often found himself tongue tied.

"This is fun," she said.

"Yes," Adam replied in a low whisper. "If being scared to death is fun."

"Yes, I—" Art said, "I think, ah, I think I need to go take care of some—um—some business. Yeah, you guys go ahead."

Adam laughed. Art knew how to be witty.

"Not a chance, you mouse!" snapped Fish taking Art to task.

"Yeah, Mouse!" Adam said, still laughing. "We need you to record our little adventure on the cave wall."

"That's probably not the best idea," Eve said. "My dad would probably kill us if he found out we were up here exploring."

Fish and Monkey chatted nervously as they continued along the ledge, their backs to the cliff-wall. Their chatter seemed to give them courage. It seemed to help keep their minds off the steep fall and the terror that lay ahead.

Adam reached the platform and stopped. He looked back.

Eve nodded. "As I left it," she said.

Putting a foot tentatively on the shaky bamboo, he looked at the ground far below, then back at her. Though impressed she managed to place the platform all alone, he worried it was far too rickety.

"I hope this will hold me," he muttered under his breath.

Art, the heaviest one in the group muttered, "Me too."

Adam shook his head as Art shuffled to the back of the line, squeezing by each of them, despite the narrow ledge. Not afforded the same luxury, Adam steeled his nerves and stepped out onto the platform. He clenched his jaw as he took three careful steps forward. Turning, he stepped off the bamboo poles and entered the crack.

His eyes fixed on the cold, dark shadows ahead. Eve put her warm hand on his back. He stepped a little further in. Reluctantly, he let himself be pushed further and further in. Soon the whole gang was inside.

With a deep breath, Adam started up the slope. No one spoke. No one made a sound as they crept over the loose rocks. When Adam reached the large boulder, Eve touched his arm. Adam glanced back at her, and she mouthed the words, "This is it."

Adam slowly pulled himself up, and peered over the boulder. His heart pounded, afraid of what he would see. When the evil thing came into view, he let out the breath he had been holding. The skull was indeed a fearsome sight—but it was not nearly as terrifying as Eve had been portrayed the day before.

*Silly Eve*, he thought as she climbed the rock and peered over his shoulder. Perhaps her surprise had been a large part of her fright. But knowing what was coming had made the skull a lot less scary. Adam climbed the rest of the way over the rock.

Eve joined him and the others followed. They all jammed together in the narrow passage to get a better look. Adam reached out and picked up the skull. Everyone drew back. He held it up, perched it on his shoulder. "It looks like it was about our size, but *real* ugly."

"Clearly not one of us," Eve said.

Twig took the skull from Adam. She was the resident know-it-all, and just had to make a more accurate assessment. "Protruding jaw—a colossal version of our monkeys—and sharp teeth. Probably eats meat right off the bone, whatever it is. I'll have to make up a name for it."

"You do that, Twig," Adam mumbled, turning to peer deeper in the crevice.

"And look at this," Fish said, holding up a bleached leg-bone. "Really big bones!"

"Let's keep going," Adam said, pushing past Fish and his bone, hoping to forestall another lecture from Twig where she would give the bone a stupid name. She claimed it wasn't her fault she was like a hundred times smarter than everyone else.

Adam pointed out fresh dirt and some half-buried tufts of grass mixed with the loose rock ahead. Eve glanced up. "It must have come down from a recent collapse from above," she said.

"If there are any more bones, they are likely buried," Adam surmised as he stepped over the loose soil on the crevice floor. Ahead, the crevice narrowed as it curved. "And that's the end," Adam said, finding it now too narrow to go any further.

"Seriously?" Monkey asked.

"That's it?" Art said and turned around. "Well I guess since we are done, we should head back now, yes?" He started walking back down the slope.

Adam turned around, and looked at Eve. "Wait a minute," Eve said, gesturing at the skull before he could go five steps. "If this skull is from a creature about our size or bigger, how did it get in here?"

That stopped everyone. They searched again. No way it came from deeper in the crevice. One-by-one their gaze turned up. Fish pointed up at the blue sky, brilliant above them. "From the sky, up there?" he asked.

Adam scoffed. "You think it fell from the sky?"

"What about these tufts of grass, still alive?" Fish said. "Maybe we haven't explored the whole world like we thought? Maybe it *lived* up there?"

"You think there is more *world* up there?" Eve asked excitedly. Adam had never considered this, but remembered Eve mentioning the idea once before. At the time he had chalked it up to Eve daydreaming again, but now faced with a real possibility of it being true he also wanted to know if there was more to the world than just the valley.

"So we haven't explored the whole world?" Monkey asked nervously. "What else do you think could be up there?"

"Good question," Eve said. "Maybe our world is a little part of a much bigger world."

"Hmm, I have always wondered where all the water comes from in the river," said Fish. "And all the big logs that sometimes wash down."

"How about you go up there and take a look, Fish?" Adam asked.

"No! No way," Fish retorted quickly.

Adam nudged Monkey. "How about you? You think you could climb up there, Monkey?"

Monkey frowned and Eve answered for him. "Oh no, it looks *way* too steep," she exclaimed.

Adam glanced at her. Eve stared at him, wide-eyed and then touching his arm winked at him. She was up to something. He scratched his arm where she had touched him. It seemed she was always up to something.

*Vanity and pride are different things. Pride relates more to our opinion of ourselves, vanity to what we would have others think of us.*

*Jane Austen*

# Up into the Blue  4

Monkey found himself nodding at Eve. As the nimblest climber in the group, this was his chance to really impress her. "I might be able to," he said, not knowing what he was thinking, agreeing to climb up the crevice. But this was his element. He'd look a fool if he didn't even try. This way at least he could be the center of attention.

He checked the width of the crack as he worked his way deeper into the crevice. With all eyes on him, he put a foot and a hand on one wall. He put his other foot and hand on the other side of the crack. Splayed out, he started to climb. But, three feet off the ground, he slipped back down. *This isn't going to work. Bloody bones, Monkey, you want Eve to think you can't do it? Or even worse, that you are afraid?*

"Just testing," he said.

Her face was lined with concern and her eyes were wide and caring. She smiled. "It's okay if you can't do it." He had to get up top, somehow! Determined to try again he put his back against the wall, and his feet on the opposite side. In this position he ascended and didn't slip. Half way up, he stopped a moment to catch his breath.

"What's the matter?" Adam called up to him.

"Catch me if I fall," Monkey called down at everyone, and laughed to see them scramble to catch him. Refreshed, he continued climbing.

"This may not be the best idea," he heard Eve say. She sounded nervous. Then he heard her ask the others, "What if he does fall?"

Adam replied. "Oh, it would probably hurt."

"Be serious!" Eve said.

"Ow! Don't punch me!"

"Don't worry, he's a monkey. Aren't you Monkey!" Adam yelled up at him.

"Yeah!" Monkey answered, afraid to look down, afraid to see how far he'd left the ground behind.

"See? He'll be fine," Adam said.

Monkey continued to crab-walk his way up, working himself higher and higher. With each step his apprehension grew. But he was pleased with Eve's concern. Nothing would stop him at this point. Finally, his head poked up and out of the crevice. He had reached the top.

"I'm there!" he shouted down to everyone.

"What do you see?" Eve asked.

Monkey ignored her as he planned a dramatic disappearing trick. She and the others looking up would see him, then suddenly he would be gone! Without a word he would disappear. Only a narrow line of blue bright sky would meet their concerned and astonished eyes.

Climbing the last bit, he put his hands on the edge under his backside. Bending his legs he pushed up and out with his arms until they were dangerously far behind himself. He could barely reach the other side.

He sat a moment, but before his arms gave way from simply holding up his weight, he jumped—not up—but backwards. For a terrifying second, he flew through the air, blind to where he was going. Then his tail bone connected with solid ground as he landed on his back. *Wham!* The air went out of him and he banged his head on the ground. Despite the pain and disorientation, he pulled his feet up and towards himself quickly, clearing the gap.

*Did it*, he thought as the pain labored his breathing. He rolled over and gazed out across the valley as he caught his breath. It had been a tough climb. Getting back to his friends, he could see, was going to be just as tough.

Monkey put that challenge aside and stood. The land around him was flat. *Big*, he thought. *So big.* Grass extended as far as he could see. Off in the distance dark shadows moved. Some kind of animal perhaps. *I hope friendly,* he thought, steeling himself, afraid they weren't. He poked his head back over the crevice and looked down at the little people below. He could see relief on their upturned faces, like happy little earthworms looking up at him.

Monkey flashed them a toothy grin. "It's big up here, really big!" He ignored all their shouted questions, and added, "I'm going to have a look around."

He pulled his body back out of sight.

## Waiting for News

Adam breathed a sigh of relief, knowing Monkey made it up safely.

"Well, that confirms that," Twig said. "Eve is right."

"Really?" Adam asked.

"Yes," Twig said. "Our world is a little crack in a much bigger world—a world we do not belong in. We should get Monkey back and go home."

"Then we can make a tall ladder from bamboo, like the ones we use to pick fruit," Eve said. "So we can all go exploring."

Eve seemed pleased with herself. Adam felt things were getting out of hand, that he was losing control. He saw it now. Eve had opened the door to the answers she sought, using him, then he had involved the whole gang. She could not wait to get Monkey's report. All of their fears and the evil skull were long forgotten. All anyone could talk about was the exciting prospect of a whole new world to explore.

Everyone but Twig. What was she thinking? What did she keep hidden? Eve seemed genuinely confused as well. She took Twig's arm and looked directly in her eyes.

"What is with you?" Eve demanded in a firm but calm voice—her most intimidating.

"This is a bad idea," Twig hissed.

Adam stepped back. "Why?" he asked, looking between the two of them. "Why don't you want to know what is up there?"

"I know enough," Twig said. "That we shouldn't go up. I can't explain. You just need to trust me on this."

"Why?" Eve demanded.

"Why not?" Twig said. "I've already told you. I don't know how much clearer I can be?"

Eve dropped her arm. "Fine."

Adam stood shocked. Eve and Twig rarely ever fought. And this argument, he could see, was far from over.

## Big

Monkey looked around before deciding which way to head. He decided to get a closer look at the animals and headed in that direction. Time passed, and he did not feel like he was getting any closer. The same grass, the same view surrounded him. The animals must be very far away, and there wasn't anything else interesting he could see. *Great bones,* he thought as he glanced around. *I am not going to be able to explore all this and still be back in time for dinner.*

After plodding on a little longer, he realized the ground wasn't as flat as he'd first thought. When he found a small drainage ravine, he clambered down to the dry stream-bed and began to explore.

As he rounded a bush, he found himself face-to-face with something new, something scary he'd never seen before. It was scarier than anything he knew; it was scarier than anything he'd ever even dreamed of.

Razor-sharp teeth filled its snarl. The creature's teeth were huge; they were hideous. And its evil eyes were a piercing yellow. Black-spotted gray fur rose on the thing's back. Monkey wasn't sure who was more surprised, him or it.

He jumped and hurried around the nearest bush. He tried to scramble back up the slope. The hyena tore after him. It quickly caught him and grabbed him by the right leg with its powerful jaws.

Monkey felt himself being dragged back down to the stream-bed. Tears of pain clouded his eyes. He screamed and kicked with his unfettered foot. The hyena hesitated as the kick narrowly missed its terrible face. Wiping tears from his eyes, Monkey took aim more carefully. This time he kicked as hard as he could, striking the beast's head. With a yelp the hyena released him and backed away, growling. Monkey turned to scramble back up the ravine, but again the hyena lunged.

Turning back, Monkey kicked, missing, but the hyena fell back anyway. Monkey understood; it was a cruel but cautious hunter.

Monkey had an idea. He bared his own teeth at the beast and growled, then slowly he backed up out of the ravine. *So far so good,* he thought even though the beast followed just out of range.

Blood flowed out of the bite on Monkey's calf. *I am running out of blood and time. I gotta get out of here, and fast.*

In one quick motion, he kicked a cloud of dirt straight into the hyena's face then took off at a dead sprint, afraid to look back. The hyena howled as it gave chase. *Herraah!*

Monkey was the fastest runner in the tribe. As he ran, his mind raced even faster. He needed to figure out what he would do when he reached the crevice. He didn't want to escape only to fall to his death.

The wind was strong in his face; his heart pounded. Suddenly he found the ground rising to meet him. His legs refused to work. *What the bloody—?*

His leg was locked once again in the hyena's iron jaw. He fell to the ground and rolled over. The beast immediately released its grip and lunged for his throat. His leg forgotten, Monkey reached up and grabbed the hyena by the dirty hair on the beast's head. He held back its massive and snarling jaws as the hyena twisted and turned.

A quick slash and its bare-teeth ripped a gash in Monkey's arm. He screamed and threw the beast back. It sprawled on the ground at his feet. A solid kick, and Monkey was back on his feet.

Monkey kept a wary eye on the hyena now; and it followed more cautiously. When the hyena again closed the gap, Monkey stopped, turned, and kicked out. His kick missed but the hyena veered and circled back. Monkey didn't wait; he took off again. Blood flowed freely now from his arms and legs.

When the beast attacked again it grabbed Monkey's ankle, tugging on his good foot. Monkey kicked the beast in the face. Then gritting his teeth, Monkey forced his foot to the ground along with the hyena's head. He stomped down with his free foot on the creature's skull. His flesh tore as the beast's jaws snapped open.

Monkey ran, howling in pain. The next time, when the attack came, Monkey was ready. He faked the kick. It had the same effect and brought him a few more steps closer to his goal. *If only I had a club,* he thought as he ran, but all he could see for miles was flat grassland—nothing to use as a weapon.

Monkey could see the crevice now. His mind wandered as he tried to visualize the moves he would have to make. *I will leap over the crevice, then sit down and kick the bloody beast away... then*

*I can slip over the edge.* Then he could work his way back down to the valley—or at least to the ledge.

Suddenly, he was down again—thinking too much! "Back off!" he screamed. He was so close now. The hyena's persistence angered him. The rage which built deep within him transmuted his fear into anger. Monkey rolled; the beast's teeth closed in on his neck. He grabbed the beast by the head with both hands. As its jaws snapped shut, barely missing his throat, Monkey's rage took over.

He plunged his thumbs into the hyena's eyes. Then with all his strength he threw the beast back. It tumbled and landed in a heap. Slowly it rose and shook its head. Monkey did not turn and run. Instead he stared into the hyena's bloody eyes.

Then slowly he stepped backwards as the hyena followed him cautiously to the edge of the crevice. Now at the edge, Monkey lunged forward with a growl. The beast stepped back, afraid.

Monkey turned and leapt across the crack. With the beast on the other side, Monkey sat on the opposite side of the crack. The hyena reached across with its filthy head, snarling and snapping angrily, but Monkey was out of its reach. *Stalemate, but now what?* Monkey thought. He needed to get back into the bloody crack. But it would take some time, and he was certain if he tried, the hyena would grab his foot.

He tried extending a foot and as he expected, the beast lunged and snapped. Monkey pulled his foot back. *No good.* Time passed slowly. His vision began to blur and he started to feel dizzy. The rage which drove him was fading. His leg was a mess. Monkey could see he didn't have long.

The beast began to growl.

## Terror from Above

Adam couldn't tell how long Monkey had been gone, but to him it seemed like ages. Then again, he had quickly grown bored with everyone guessing what Monkey would find. He had taken instead to staring into the sky above—and stealing glances at Eve's eyes . . . to compare the color. He, she, and the others were sitting now as they chatted quietly.

Pandemonium broke out above. The sounds of growling filtered down the crack as a shadow passed through the bright blue above. Adam jumped to his feet. "Monkey?"

Then, to Adam's horror, a beast poked its head into the sky above them. Several people screamed. It must have been Monkey first leaping over the crack. That was all Adam could think. A mangy head appeared in the crack above. A moment, no more, then it was gone, but that was enough for Adam to see the head had huge snapping jaws. A shiver crawled up his spine.

A spindly leg appeared from the other side, thrust cautiously out into the gap.

"What's that?" Art screamed. Bev just screamed.

"It's Monkey," Adam said impatiently, but then something wet with a bit of gravel or dirt hit him in the face. He wiped his face with a hand. Blood? Panic seized him as he stared at it on the back of his hand. Another growl brought his eyes back to the sky. Monkey's leg pulled back as the beast's head lunged toward it.

"Adam . . . is . . . that blood?" Twig asked as she grabbed his arm.

Adam wiped his face with his other hand. Now both hands had blood streaked on them. "Looks like it, and maybe some spit." He pulled his hand free of hers.

"Saliva," Twig said.

"The saliva is from the beast," Eve added.

"What?" Adam asked, looking at Eve.

She had turned to stare up into the sky and didn't answer right away. Instead she slowly lowered her head and turned to look at him. "What are we going to do?" Her look scared Adam—and her eyes were definitely as blue as the sky. "Adam!"

His name—called loud—jarred him. *I have to act!* His mind cleared and he remembered the large leg bone Fish had found earlier. "That bone!" he cried, breaking his eyes from Eve's serious gaze. "Fish! Toss me it!"

Fish threw him the heavy bone. Standing directly under Monkey and the open sky, Adam pitched the bone up with both hands. It flew up without spinning. Adam was pretty good at tossing things this way. It was a method he had mastered for picking fruit before Eve had invented the ladder.  He found it difficult to gauge the height, but the bone seemed to clear the opening.  If Monkey saw it, Adam suspected the skinny boy would catch it.

## Out of Ideas

Monkey could hardly believe his eyes.  All out of ideas and energy, he expected the beast to leap across the crevice at any moment.  But suddenly a bone floated up into sight from out of nowhere.  It startled him and the hyena both as it hovered momentarily right in between them.  Then the bone fell back down.  The beast stared into the crevice, transfixed.

Monkey leaned forward, growled, and waited.  He knew this game.  Sure enough, the bone came floating back up again.  He reached out and tried to grab it.  *Bloody bones!*

His fingers nearly fumbled the heavy thing, but somehow they locked on it and he was able to pull it back just as the beast lunged forward.

He swung the bone weakly, hitting the hyena on the head.  He visualized the surprise the whole tribe would have when he emerged with this dead beast as his trophy.  The beast, however, had other plans.  It pulled back and snapped at the bone, only slightly stunned by the blow.

Monkey swung it again and again, but the crafty beast snapped at it, while avoiding being hit. Finally Monkey took a chance and threw the bone at the beast. The bone hit it and clattered to the ground. The beast grabbed it in its eager jaws.

Monkey put both feet on the wall and began to lower himself. The beast, not distracted for long, reached a paw down into the crevice. Sharp claws tore at Monkey's retreating feet. Monkey scooted down a few more painful inches. Finally he was safely out of the beast's reach.

Monkey shifted weight to his left hand, but, slick with blood, it slipped. Monkey froze and tried to breathe. He could hear the kids yelling below. *I'm not quite home yet,* he thought wryly. The idea of having to work more now made him feel all the more tired.

His mind drifted to thoughts of a little nap. The noise filtering up from far below began to grow more distant. Eve's soothing voice, however, swam through the rising fog in his mind. Monkey loved the music of it. It was soft, like the sound of falling water. It was sweet like the sound of singing birds.

Her voice grew stronger, more insistent. "One more step Monkey, only one more step!" she said. "Climb down. Climb down to me."

"Yes," Monkey heard himself say. "I'm coming down." He opened his heavy eyes and saw where he was. He wanted to close them again, but he willed them to stay open and he climbed, inching himself down the crevice, one step at a time.

"One more step, Monkey!" Eve cried. "Only one more step!"

Monkey willed his aching limbs to move. *Yes, only one more step*, he thought, obeying Eve. Again and again she directed his hands and legs as they slowly worked their way mechanically down.

"You did it," he heard her say, as arms cradled him.

"We did it," Monkey agreed weakly. Then oblivion swallowed him whole.

> We must, however, acknowledge, as it seems to me, that man with all his noble qualities... still bears in his bodily frame the indelible stamp of his lowly origin.

*Charles Darwin*

# A Broken Monkey     5

Adam lowered Monkey to the ground. Eve's stomach churned at the sight of him. "Careful not to bang his head," she said. Her skinny friend was a mess. Never had she seen so much blood before.

"Is he dead?" Fish asked.

Suddenly, everyone was talking at once. Yes. No. Maybe. Don't say that! Say what? He's not dead! Not yet, he isn't—but he will be soon. Shut up, Fish!

The group closed around Monkey as their words rushed out. He wasn't dead yet, but he was in serious trouble. Dirt began to rain down on them. The hyena peered down, scratching at the dirt, looking like it was contemplating a leap down to finish the job it had started on Monkey.

"Everyone out!" Adam shouted.

To Eve's surprise, Bev grabbed Monkey. Tossing him over her shoulder like he was nothing, she hurried out of the crevice without a word. She stepped carefully over the platform and onto the ledge.

Eve waited at the platform with Adam. She helped him hurry the others over. Twig had the skull—for later study no doubt. Eve motioned for Adam to go but he insisted on going last. He even helped guide her over with a hand on her back. When he was across, he stopped and stooped down.

"What are you doing?" Eve asked him.

Adam pushed the platform off the ledge and it fell to the rocks below. "We are all across. We don't need this anymore."

"Hey! I almost died putting that up!" Eve said, indignant.

"Monkey is dying because it *was up*!" Adam shouted back at her.

Eve stuck out her tongue at him, the rudest gesture she knew. "How are we supposed to get back up now? We can't explore without the platform." Without waiting for him to answer she stomped off. *Let him stew on that!*

"We aren't going exploring! Who knows what else is up there?" he called after her, but she did not turn back.

All Monkey had said was that it was really big up there. Then the beast appeared. Now he was a bloody mess. *Maybe the ledge was broken away for good reason.* Maybe Adam was right, but Eve was still furious. She had put the platform up. She should have been given the chance to take it down.

When she caught up with the gang, they were waiting on the last leg of the climb down, unsure of what to do with Monkey. Twig was collecting leather strips and scraps from each of them. She directed Eve to help her bind his wounds. "We need to stop the bleeding."

After Monkey was bandaged as best could be, Eve let Adam take charge of the descent. "Bev, you and Art wait at the bottom to receive him. Fish, you find a grip half way down," he said. "Eve and I will lower him to you."

When they were all in position, Adam slid Monkey until his legs hung over the edge.

Eve shook the sleeping boy's shoulder, "Monkey, wake up!" she called into his ear. "I need you to climb down."

Monkey stirred. "What?"

"Bev can't carry you down," Adam said. "You have to hang on yourself."

Monkey nodded and Adam began to lower the bloody boy down over the edge as far as he could. Fish guided his feet into toeholds.

"Do you have a grip?" Adam asked.

Monkey nodded. "Yeah."

Adam transferred his hands to the cliff. When finally they were all under the big tree. The group gathered around, asking what they should do. "I have no idea what to do," Adam stated flatly. "Twig?"

"We should clean his wounds and wrap them better with a special leaf I know."

Eve watched helplessly as Twig sent the kids out on various missions to retrieve certain fruits, leaves, and vines which she claimed would help.

"Wow, this whole disaster took only half the morning," Adam said. He refused to leave Monkey' side. He, Twig, and Eve cleaned Monkey's wounds as best they could as they waited for the others to return. Eventually the items appeared at the water's edge.

"Adam, hold him steady," Twig said.

When Monkey screamed, Adam tried to reassure him. "It's okay, you're going to be fine. Twig knows what she is doing."

"That's right, I do," Twig said. "Eve, you better go retrieve a piece of fruit from the Tree of Life."

Adam glanced at Eve in shock. "Whoa there? Fruit from the Tree?" he said. "That is forbidden. You would never make it."

Eve rose and let out a great sigh. "It's an emergency," she said.

"How can you even get fruit from the Tree?" Adam asked. "When you get close you will have to face the magic. It might kill you. If it doesn't, your father will certainly kill you for trying."

"I can't let Monkey die because of your little exploit in the crevice, convincing him to go up there all alone," Eve said. "And we all know what the fruit is for: for when you really need it. If Twig says it is an emergency, then I am not afraid. Are you?"

"But how?" Adam asked.

"I will just march up to the tree and get the fruit. It must be possible. Right, Twig? You tell him. If not for him—"

"Leave me out of your politics," Twig snapped. "I said not to send Monkey up in the first place."

Adam looked incredulous. "You want to make this my fault? You put up the platform," he sputtered. "Now you want to march up to the Tree of Life and just get a piece of fruit like it's nothing? Ha!"

"It was your idea to leave the valley. None of this would have happened if you hadn't broken the rules and sent Monkey up," Eve said. "Because of you I have to go steal the fruit and save you from having to explain away why you sent Monkey to his death." Eve added the last bit over her shoulder as she gave him a withering look, and then, satisfied he was both abashed and confused, she hurried on her way.

It was a long run, and she ran as fast as she could. On the way to the sacred tree, Eve could think of nothing but how to accomplish her task—without getting caught, and without well, whatever it was that happened under the Tree happening to her.

Years ago she had tried to approach the Tree. All the kids had at some point. All she could remember was being attracted by the smell. Then fear, horrible fear, a feeling like impending doom, washed over her. She had backed away, and the feeling passed. Others of the gang described similar experiences. She had seen men from the tribe walk close, lay down and dream, later crawling away satisfied. Once one of the hunters tried to go under the tree. He screamed, waved his arms like he was fighting some kind of enemy, then he finally fell dead to the ground. Most of the tribe watched yet none tried to help him. His bones, bleached white, still lay under the tree. And they were not alone. The bones of monkeys and other small animals were there as well. The ground under the Tree was a graveyard of the creator's making.

The idea of adding her own bones to the mix terrified Eve. But it was time to face her fears. She had entered the crevice and faced her fear. Now she would go under the tree, and pick a piece of fruit from the ground to save Monkey. Yet exactly how would depend on who was about. When at last she saw the tree, her mind was full of contingency plans no matter who might see her.

She stopped at the edge of the stream, breathing hard. Instead of splashing across, she followed it closer to the Tree of Life, staying in the shadows of the haunted pine woods on her right. Nobody would notice her here—probably. She ducked under low hanging limbs and glanced past the dense green boughs thick with needles. She could see nothing beyond.

At last she reached the head of the stream, just opposite the Tree of Life. Here she could see the water container she had made from a hollowed-out gourd sitting on the bank where she had fished earlier in the morning. *Perfect!*

She stepped from the shadows. A cold, damp breath of air, like an icy hand on her back, urged her forward. She felt like she was being watched, but saw nobody. She crossed the ankle-deep stream and grabbed her gourd. Filling it with water, she calmly walked her new offering over toward the tree. She stopped at the usual distance and casually tossed the water toward the tree.

She glanced around. Nobody was watching. She clamped her teeth tight and walked forward. She focused her eyes on the fallen fruit littering the ground. *Have to save Monkey*, she said to herself again and again. It seemed to be working.

When she smelled the attractive scent, it urged her forward. Suddenly she felt the fear, the dread of death. *You have to save Monkey.* More dread. A skull peered up at her, it's dark empty sockets leering. Suddenly, those empty eyes glowed red, and a bony hand reached for her. Her legs weakened under her. *Must! Save! Monkey!*

Instead of collapsing, she took another step. Claws reached out of the fog in her mind and tore at her. Children laughed and mocked her. Suddenly her mother was there, hitting her, knocking her down. She wanted to scream for her to stop. *Must save Monkey.* Another step and the fear began to fade. *Save Monkey.* Another step and her vision cleared.

Her eyes focused on the fruit. A piece was just a few steps away. She relaxed her clamped teeth. She had made it. She walked to the fruit and picked it up. It was soft and fuzzy in her hand. She almost couldn't believe she had made it. She tucked the fruit into the gourd, still gripped in her hand. She looked around, surprised how pleasant and peaceful it was here. She hated to leave, but remembering Monkey's cries, she headed out, stepping over the bones littering the ground.

She stepped out into the sunlight, and sauntered toward the path. She experienced no problem heading out, only in. Stealing a piece of the fruit was way easier than she had expected. But as she began to run, someone yelled, "Stop!"

Eve wheeled around. Little Red stood up from the tall grass. *Oh, how I hate pesky children!* He had been hiding. The redheaded boy grinned at her. "I saw what you did," he gloated, "And I'm going to tell your father." Even without words, he could easily get her in trouble.

"Don't you dare," Eve said. "I will rip your red hair right out!"

"I don't care," Little Red retorted. "Let me join the gang or else I'll tell! I swear I will!"

Eve scoffed. "Ha. You're too little."

"No, I'm not," Little Red countered. "I'm big enough to tell on you." He started to move towards her parent's cave.

"Wait," Eve said. He turned back, expectant. She knew she had lost. Now she had to make the most of it. "If I let you join, you're going to have to do what I tell you to do."

"Deal," he replied.

"Okay, okay, come on," Eve said. "But keep up, you little runt," she added and took off toward the big tree. She tried to leave him behind, but he managed to stay with her.

"What's the hurry? What's going on?" Little Red kept asking.

Eve ignored him, and kept on running.

As the tree grew close, the gang rushed out to meet her. "Did you get it?" Adam cried, no cool, calm demeanor now.

Eve held up the fruit. "Got it," she called. Twig snatched the precious cargo from Eve, and ran it to Monkey. They all followed. Little Red's eyes went wide full with questions. "Don't say a word," Eve warned as Twig fed Monkey the fruit. Nobody even seemed to breathe. When at last the fruit was gone, Twig stepped back. "Well?" she asked.

"Tasted good," Monkey said. He seemed to relax.

Little Red tugged on Eve's arm. "What happened to him? What is going on?"

"Hey, Art!" Eve said, searching the group.

The chubby boy stood by the headquarters tree. "What?"

"Take charge of this redheaded runt for me," she said, motioning towards Little Red. "Find him some gang work," Eve added with a wink.

"Oh yeah, no problem," Art answered smiling.

"Wait a minute, I thought I only had to obey you?" Little Red said.

Eve smiled at Art. "You tell him, Art. As our newest member, he has to obey everybody, right?"

"True, true, my friend," Art said, sagely. "And sadly, I fear I'm feeling a bit peckish. How about you Eve?"

"I can't stand this," Adam said. "Eve, tell us how you retrieved the fruit."

"Well, I ran hard," she began, wondering how she could make the story more interesting. She looked around and every eye was on her—the truth would be interesting enough.

When finished, Twig was the first to speak. "Your clear purpose to save Monkey helped you survive the test."

"How do you know that?" Adam asked as Monkey moaned and rolled over in his sleep.

"I just do," Twig said primly.

"Should we keep him here to recover or take him home to his parents?" Eve looked pointedly at Adam as he paced under the tree. "Or are we spending the night? It will be dark by the time we get home."

"No, we need to carry him home," Adam said firmly.

Eve was sure he had decided that just now, to contradict her. "His parents will not take this well," she sniped.

"Well, we will just shrug and indicate he fell from a tree," Adam explained, clearly impressed with his lie. "We can carry him into their shelter quietly—no one will notice."

"It's a long way to carry him," Eve mused.

"We can take turns," Adam replied.

Eve stood. "Okay, you win, we should go," she said meekly.

It was surprisingly easy to make Adam think what she wanted him to think and to make him do it—and just how she wanted him to.

As they left the big tree, Eve noticed the skull had been mounted high on the tree trunk—like a trophy.

A new era was dawning for the gang. In only two short days they had broken all the rules. Now they were set to deceive Monkey's parents. It was wrong, and Eve knew it. A pesky little voice in her head told her so. Eve, however, planned to ignore that voice—at least until all her questions were answered.

*A teacher is someone who takes a complex thing and makes it simple.*

Robert Frost

# A New Weapon 6

Starlight cast deep shadows in the cave where Eve and her family slept. The waterfall outside gently gurgled and a cool breeze carried the sweet scent of the flowers from the Tree of Life to Eve's nose. All was calm, and she was safe. She told herself this over and over again. She had only dreamed of monsters—monsters who lived in the high world beyond the crevice. These monsters, large and small, roamed the world outside the valley. They had sharp teeth, and no mercy. They ate children and they were countless in number, all living, gorging themselves above the cliffs. All of them could run faster than she—and none of them ever tired. In her dreams, Eve had been running, running, trying to escape, but the monsters were always faster. "And now they know we are here," Eve said to herself with a shudder.

It had been three days now, and Monkey had slept for most of it after the gang had delivered him home and slipped him into his bed without anyone noticing. Or if they had noticed, there had been no big reaction to his condition. Blue Eyes had visited Monkey and examined his wounds, but the old man did nothing about him or his condition. It was left to Twig to tend to Monkey. Each day she changed his bandages. Adam brought him food and sat with him. Everyone seemed fine with the situation except Eve. She felt responsible for his injuries. She felt bad for what happened and wrong for deceiving their primitive parents.

The rest dismissed their parents as ignorant and unconcerned, but Eve did not quite believe as they did. Her mother was like that for sure. Speech confused her, and her mother had rejected her, treating her as a misfit. But Eve felt somehow her father understood her value and trusted her not to abuse her gift. To deceive him was like stealing from a helpless baby. It was easy, but it just wasn't right.

On this, Eve and that pesky voice agreed, but she didn't know what she could do about it as the gang laid low. It was all Eve could do to keep quiet herself, and to not confess her sins to her father. Instead, she tried to stay busy. She completed daily routines as if by rote, all the while watching and waiting for some reaction, especially from her father.

Questions about what Monkey had seen and learned also distracted Eve. As they slowly learned more and more of the details, the younger children whispered pieces of Monkey's story in hushed tones. Their curiosity grew stronger as their fears faded. Eve's own desire to see this new world for herself only grew as well. But at the same time, she didn't want to end up like Monkey—or worse.

Something else was bothering her: Twig. It was uncanny how the light-haired girl knew basically everything, down to the fact that the up above was so dangerous. She knew it was a bad idea to leave the valley, and knew the fruit of the tree would help Monkey. She was smart, but something was off.

Adam was also a mystery that was driving her crazy. What was he after? At times he acted like he was the group's leader, or was it just him trying to impress her? He had to know she was the leader. And yet he did well taking care of Monkey and, well, Eve was confused—she just could not read him.

The skull also tormented her. What kind of a beast was it, and how did it get in the crevice? She still had so many questions. Now it seemed she would have to wait.

The wet season had arrived. She looked glumly out at the rain. It frustrated plans anyone hoped to make. All the gang members agreed it was best to lay low for the time being.

Finally, after over a week of steady rain, a clear morning dawned. The gang with Monkey—who was finally well enough to join them—headed to the big tree.

"Check it out, the flooding washed out the beach," Fish said, arriving at the big tree first. "And look at our place." The lagoon had drained, and the wide, lazy stretch of river in front of their tree had become a deep brown torrent.

"Yuck, there's mud on everything," Bev complained about the sticky stuff covering the ground.

Despite his injuries, Monkey began climbing the tree. "Happens every year," he said. "Let's climb up to the platform." Last year, after the rains had started, they had begun building a platform in the branches, but never finished it.

Eve pulled herself up. She had almost forgotten about the platform. It was still quite rough, but she could see in her mind an amazing treehouse. It would work better for their meetings. They would be able to talk, without all the little children—with big ears—listening.

"Okay everybody, pay attention! We have lots *and lots* to decide," Adam said, finally calling the meeting to a semblance of formal order. *Mmm*, Eve thought. *Now he is calling the meeting to order. I used to do that.* The chattering stopped and all eyes turned to Adam. "We all need to hear it straight from Monkey. What did you see up there? It's time you tell us the whole story."

Everyone leaned forward as Monkey began to tell his tale. The story sounded to Eve a lot more dramatic than the bits she had heard before—most of it straight from him.

"The one that attacked me was probably a baby; who knows what its parents will be like!" Monkey exclaimed when he'd finished.

"Parents?" Eve questioned.

"I think he means the animals he saw on the plains," Twig said.

"Yes, that's right," Monkey said. "There were hundreds of them."

"But you said you were far away," Eve said. "Too far to see clearly."

"True. They were really far away and I had nothing to compare them to for size. But they *seemed* big!" Monkey replied. He looked around at the skeptical faces peering back at him. "What else could they be?"

As the group returned to their chatter, Eve glanced around. There was fear, but mostly excitement and anticipation on the faces of the gang.

When Monkey had finished answering all the questions, the group fell silent. "What do you think, Eve?" Adam asked, breaking the silence of the group. His voice rumbled over the murmur of the river below.

"Well, one thing we know for sure," Eve began, "We are ill-equipped to explore this new world. We can't expect to hunt up above if we can't hunt Twig's Serpent down here."

"You don't hunt down the Serpent," Twig said, stiffly. "The Serpent hunts you down."

A hush fell over the group. Eve had spoken the unspeakable.

"Why the Serpent?" Adam asked.

"Nobody said anything about the Serpent," Monkey whispered. He had heard Twig's stories the same as Eve. They all had.

"But it is some kind of monster too, right?" Art asked.

"It slithers around in the grass," Fish said.

"It catches and eats small children," Little Red added.

"I've seen it at dusk," Bev said. "It's like a fog, drifting among the pine trees. I have heard it scream in the night. There is no way I will go looking for it." She turned and looked at Twig. "What about you? You haven't said anything."

Twig squirmed. "Only a fool would go looking for the Serpent," Twig said. "I cannot explain, but again you need to just trust me. Do not go in search of the serpent."

"What?" Eve exclaimed. It was as if a tree had fallen on her. "Here you go again. What on earth are you talking about?"

The tree grew silent as all eyes focused on Twig. "You wanted to go into the crevice, and I warned you not to go. Look what happened. Now you want to go looking for the Serpent, and I am warning you again. You can't and that is final!"

"Who do you think you are, saying what we can and can't do?" Eve demanded.

"I have as much right as you or Adam," Twig retorted. "At least I know what I am talking about."

Eve opened her mouth and closed it again. "I— I can't believe I am speechless. Who are you Twig? I thought you were my friend, but suddenly you are like this totally different person."

"I'm not a different person," Twig said after an uncomfortable silence. Then she added in a softer voice, "But you are right about one thing. Now that you have brought us into contact with the larger world, we are not prepared to enter it."

"There are monsters up there," Monkey said, keeping his voice low to match.

"We are going to need some supplies if we want to survive up there," Adam said frowning. "We might be on the move for many days, and we are going to need some real weapons—for Monkey's monsters."

"What?!" Twig said.

Adam ignored her and glanced at Eve. "I agree, we should not hunt the Serpent, but we are going to have to do things differently from now on, especially if these monsters decide to come down here!"

"To eat us!" Monkey interjected.

"Not without a fight!" Adam shouted.

"Not without a fight!" Fish repeated. "Not without a fight!"

Adam continued to chant; the others joined in. The gang was on a new path. Eve found herself, chanting too. "Not without a fight!" Excitement filled the air. Weapons instantly became the new priority.

"The flint outcrop my father discovered," Eve said when the chanting ended. She ignored Twig and her sullen frown. "We could chip larger knives. Make larger weapons. I don't just mean larger clubs, but clubs with knives on the end."

"I almost killed a monkey with a dart once," Fish said.

"That's great, Fish," Art said sarcastically. "You almost killed Monkey once—with a dart. Perfect."

"Not Monkey," Fish said. "A monkey."

"I heard you," Art said. "But your darts aren't going to kill the thing that attacked Monkey."

"We need ideas for weapons, not sarcasm," Eve said.

Art glanced at Twig. "Maybe we should stay here," he suggested, sounding defeated.

"I have traps and hooks, I only need to find the right kind of plant fiber to use for my line," Fish added.

"I don't want to go back up there," Monkey stated flatly. "I didn't see anything up there we need, only trouble." Bev and Twig nodded in agreement.

"But there are things we need," Eve said. "Like answers! Who are *we*? Why are we *here*? Where did we come *from*? Why are we *different*? I don't know about you cowards, but *I have to know!*"

"I agree," said Adam. "Eventually we are going to want to know more—and we need to be ready. Maybe not today. Maybe not even next season. But we still need to be prepared. And that means we need weapons, and we need to learn how to use them."

"And who knows," Twig said with an encouraging smile. "Someday one of these monsters could wander into our valley and try to kill us all."

"And eat us!" Monkey added trying to be dramatic.

Twig sighed. "We better be ready, is all."

Adam began issuing orders. He wanted a house in the headquarters tree. A real house with a thatched roof to ward off the rain. It would have a room just for the weapons. Eve didn't argue. It was a good idea.

"The room will keep little monkeys out," Eve said, eyeing Little Red. "So little paws don't touch things that don't belong to them."

"We don't need them messing with our preparations," Adam said, cluelessly. "We might be preparing for months and months. And I don't want any disruptions—window shutters—yes? Fish? You see what I'm saying?"

"I think so," Fish replied. He and Adam discussed how the treehouse would look. Then the meeting ended and the gang headed back to the caves as clouds began to cast dark shadows, threatening more rain.

"You did a good job with the meeting," Eve told Adam when they found themselves walking side-by-side a little apart from the rest of the group.

He squinted at her suspiciously. "Yeah?"

"No, really. For once, I couldn't have done a better job myself, getting everyone focused on a long-term plan. It's something our people know nothing about." She did her best to give him an appreciative smile, painful as it was.

"I am going to have to stay on top of them all," Adam said firmly. "Or in a few days they will all be back to making fish traps and picking flowers,"

"That you will," Eve said. *And I will have to stay on top of you to keep you focused . . .*

*An ax in a forest is never heard, But it leaves a trail of broken trees.*

William Shakespeare

# The Axe  7

Eve was impressed with Adam's organizational skills. True to his word, he dragged the gang to the big tree to work every day, only giving them the day off for the heaviest rain. Even then, he had tasks for them to perform at home in their caves. Everyone had a part to play; and everyone seemed to take pleasure in their tasks—or at least with impressing Adam with their results.

Nobody in the tribe had ever made anything more than a simple lean-to in the valley since the caves were already an ideal shelter. Yet Adam clearly described the structure he envisioned. He assigned tasks, and taught each person how to accomplish them.

A floor for the treehouse was made from sturdy bamboo poles tied to the tree with vines. Bev wove heavy reeds into mats to cover the uneven floor. Fish, accompanied by Art, worked on the thatch roof.

Twig, Monkey, Adam, and Eve decided to work together on the walls, including the windows and doors. As the work commenced, imaginations ran wild with thoughts of attacks from monsters and possible fortifications to prevent such attacks.

"So why do we have to do all the work?" Monkey finally complained to Eve one day. "Where are Adam and Twig?"

He and Eve were cutting bamboo.

"Good question," Eve said. Even though bamboo culms were hollow, the walls on the larger-diameter culms were hard and thick. Each cut took Eve half a morning to make with her flint knife. "Adam has been busy keeping everyone on task. But Twig—that is another issue."

"She always disappears when there is hard work to do," Monkey complained. "But not me. I am your faithful partner."

"She mumbled something about having things to do this morning," Eve said, feeling herself grow angry. "It's almost noon. I better go look for her. Someone needs to keep her on task."

"Oh no, you're not going to leave me here all alone with all the work. If you go, I go," Monkey said. He flashed her a toothy grin. Eve could not argue. He had been smiling at her a lot since his recovery. "I will make you a deal," Monkey continued. "Tomorrow, if she sneaks off again we will follow her."

"Now you are talking," Eve said. "It's a deal, provided you work hard the rest of the day."

"Agreed," Monkey said, and they returned to work, but he was not done. "It makes me wonder. When you are officially the leader, will you mate with all the men like your father does with all the women?"

"Monkey, seriously? What kind of question is that? First of all, I am not the leader..."

"Yeah right, we can all see the way you make Adam do whatever you want—"

"And secondly," Eve said, stepping on his words. "We decided not to mate..."

"Yeah, right," he interrupted again. "You girls may have decided, but I have not. I have big plans. I just don't see the harm. We can give it a go right now. What do you say?"

"You are out of your bloody mind, Monkey," Eve said. "Is this what you boys talk about?"

"Look, Eve," Monkey said. "When the leader says yes, that's it. It is how things are done."

"Is that what you would do if you were leader?" she asked.

"Hmm, if I were leader, I would have to think about it for a while, but I know one thing, I would pick you and keep you all to myself."

"And if I said no?" Eve asked, wondering just what this conversation was all about.

"I don't know. Have you ever seen a woman of the tribe say no to your father?"

Eve thought about it. She had never considered this question, and now that he mentioned it, she could not. "Of course they say no. All the time. Now let's get back to work."

Monkey started to scrape again, then threw down his blade. "This is dumb. It's too slow." He stood and picked up a stick and swung at a nearby plant, cutting it off. "Now that's what we need. But for trees."

He was right. Their cutting method was way too slow. "Find me a short, heavy branch, like a club," Eve said. When he returned with a nice, stout club, she selected her largest stone tool and started whacking the tool with the club. It cut much faster.

"That's what I am talking about," Monkey said. "If you weren't so dangerous with that, I would kiss you."

Eve ignored his big, dumb smile. "Now, what we really need is a way to mount this stone onto the club. That shouldn't be much trouble."

Monkey turned his head to the path. "Speaking of trouble," he said. "Look who is coming."

Twig walked toward them, stiff and upright as always. Her hair bounced. She looked serious. "What can I do to help," she asked.

Eve looked back at her new tool and resisted the urge to grill her about where she had been. *Stay focused.*

"Where have you been?" Monkey demanded.

"Things to do," Twig said. Her words trailed off. "What are you two doing?"

Eve explained the idea, and what she needed.

"Easy, I'd say," Twig began. "Select a wide club and cut a hole in the big end. Then chip out a double-tapered stone with a good blade at one end. The harder you cut, the tighter the stone will fit the hole."

"Yes," Eve cried; it was as if all was revealed. "It's such a simple idea. I don't know why I didn't think of it myself."

"My best ideas are always like that," Twig replied with a smile. "Though you should ask Fish about drilling the holes. They are his specialty."

The idea, simple though it was, created a whole new host of problems. The three of them worked at it the rest of the day. They made a narrow chisel and cut a hole in their limb, but every attempt to attach a bit of flint to a club failed. At the first blow, the impact would dislodge the flint no matter how she attached it.

Monkey finally stopped them and explained the angles he thought might work. His plan made sense, but the day was done.

Adam joined them on the walk home and Eve explained the new tool they were making. Twig had already called it an axe.

"You know, it would make an amazing weapon," Adam said. "A short one you could carry on your belt. Or even a long one would be quite a weapon. I will give you a hand in the morning."

"No, that's all right, Eve and I have this," Monkey said quite loudly. "This is our idea and our project."

Adam gave him an odd look and turned to Eve. "Is that right, Eve?" he said.

Monkey was right, she supposed, but Adam was good with making things, and she wasn't sure why not get all the help they could. Twig was helping and that did not seem to bother Monkey, so it must be about Adam specifically.

"I don't know," she said.

"Seriously though, we are partners in this," Monkey said. "I want to see it through, so just go do whatever it is you were doing all day while we were working, Adam."

Eve wondered if Adam would hit him. That was what her father would do if someone stood up to him, but Adam was not the leader, or so Monkey said. "He is right, Adam. He got the project started," Eve said. "It's not worth fighting about."

It was clearly written on Adam's furrowed brow it *was* worth fighting about. He looked ready to fight. More than ready.

Eve put a hand on his arm. "So how are the other projects coming?" she asked. *Are they fighting over the new axe, or over me?*

She managed to get them home in one piece, and went to bed. She wondered how her father became the leader. He had been leader for as long as she could remember. Did he fight for the job?

Would she have to fight for it ultimately? She wasn't sure she wanted it that badly.

The next morning, Monkey was waiting at her cave's entrance. He held a new, larger piece of flint in his hand. "You are up early," Eve said.

"Yep," he said. He took her hand and held her back as the others left for the treehouse.

"Seen Twig this morning?" he asked, a knowing look on his face.

"No, actually," Eve admitted, recalling their deal to follow her if she ran off.

"Come with me, I have an idea," he said, and proceeded to walk Eve down the path, still holding her hand. As they rounded the bend, he pulled her into the thick growth along the path.

"Come on," he whispered and headed back toward the clearing. They crept up and peeked through the brush.

"Seriously?" Eve asked, looking over the empty clearing. "Here?" A moment later, Twig emerged, looked around, and headed for the stream.

"What on earth?" Eve asked.

Monkey smiled, and squeezed her hand. "Yes, here," he said.

They watched as Twig again looked around, then splashed across the stream and disappeared into the haunted pine woods.

"Come on," Monkey said. He pulled Eve toward the stream, but she brought him to a stop at the bank.

"I don't know about this," Eve said. "I have never been in the haunted pines before."

"They aren't forbidden, not like the crevice and the Tree of Life, and you . . . " Monkey said, letting his words trail off.

Eve examined him closely. He sounded very brave, but there was fear in his eyes. He didn't think this was a good idea either. "I also never jumped off the top of a tree to see if I could fly. Some things are just stupid," Eve said.

He squeezed her hand again. "Come on, I got you. No need to be afraid."

His condescension flared her temper and she splashed into the stream, dragging Monkey with her, not the other way around. He smiled at her and she realized he had played her well.

Reaching the far shore, they stepped cautiously up the bank and immediately passed from the warm, sunny morning into deep shade. Quiet and stillness filled the air here. The strong smell of pine wafted over Eve, and cold air stood the hair on her arms on end. She took a few tentative steps with Monkey, their footfalls silent in the deep pine duff.

"Which way, genius," she whispered to Monkey. His face had turned pale.

"I don't see her—or any kind of path. She vanished," he whispered.

Turning first one way, then another, they eventually arrived back at the stream, having seen nothing.

"We lost her," Eve said. "Let's get back to work."

Monkey nodded his agreement. He was still gripping his new piece of flint. Eve asked about it as they headed down the path. He became more animated with it, waving it around wildly as he spoke, but gently continued to hold her hand. He only let go when they started work on the axe.

The afternoon wore on, and there was still no sign of Twig. The axe, however, had taken shape.

"I think we have it this time," Eve said, handing it to Monkey to test. "Easy. Start easy."

Monkey approached a small tree, and gave it a tap.

"Now hit it straight and square to set the stone," Eve instructed.

He gave it a harder swing. *Thunk.* It was a very satisfying sound. He swung harder and harder. Chips flew. *Thunk, Thunk.* The tree soon came crashing down.

Eve couldn't believe it and let out a squeal and Monkey scooped her up in an embrace. Being taller than her, he swept her off her feet. He swung her around, then held her very close. He looked down into her eyes. "We did it," he said smiling and moved closer yet. He seemed ready to kiss her—and not like her father might.

"We did, and it is quite amazing," Eve managed to say.

Monkey held her tight. His lips moved closer to hers. "Yes," he said softly.

"We need to show Twig and Adam," Eve mumbled.

"Forget Twig and Adam," Monkey said. Eve did not know what to do. None of this was part of her plan.

"What are you two doing?"

Twig's familiar voice cut the moment short. It was clear and accusing. Eve jumped and Monkey dropped her like a snake. They both turned and stared at Twig. She was standing just a few paces away, a hand on each hip, glaring daggers at them.

"Doing?" Monkey stammered. "Nothing. We made the axe work."

All Eve could feel was guilt. Why? She had done nothing wrong, or had she? "We were just talking about you, Twig," she said. "You should see it. Our new axe is amazing."

Monkey picked the thing up and with a single swing chopped deep into another tree.

Twig's hard gaze softened. She had to have a closer look. She wanted all the details, insisting they head back to the treehouse for a wider demonstration.

Eve waited with bated breath as the gang gathered. She had convinced Monkey to let Adam demonstrate it to the gang, so he would not oppose the idea because it was Monkey's. It had been a lengthy argument, but she, with Twig's support, had finally won.

Adam hefted the thing, then with everyone watching, Adam hesitated only a moment before he took a massive swing at a nearby tree. The flint head sunk into its trunk. *Chud!* The thud echoed up and down the valley.

A satisfied smile broke out on Adam's face as everyone cheered. But the axe head was stuck. That had not happened when Monkey used it. When Adam pulled the axe free from the tree the flint remained. He held up the handle, and looked through the hole at Monkey. "Nice," Adam said sardonically. "One good swing and it's all over." All the kids laughed.

Monkey looked crushed. He turned and walked away. If she had let him demonstrate as he had wanted, it would have worked fine. Now he was humiliated and it was her fault.

Eve stared at the axe head, still stuck in the tree trunk and sighed with disappointment. "So it's not quite perfect yet."

"No problem, I've got this," Twig said. She held up a small length of a new vine she had discovered. She had been going on for days about how it was flexible and easy to tie. "As this cord dries, it shrinks and gets as hard as a rock. We can use it to tie the axe head on."

It was a possibility. Adam knocked the head loose from the tree. "I can chip a notch here and here," he said pointing to the axe head.

Soon Twig's new vines tied the axe together. The flint and branch were one again. Twig informed them it would take at least three days to dry.

"Until then," Adam said. "Everyone get back to work."

*They fight for her whom all the world conspires,*
*To cross in love, and do each other's harms.*

William Shakespeare

# The Fight 8

It took all Adam's control to keep his anger in check. The axe was a good idea. He was impressed with what it could do, but the idea of Monkey and Eve together infuriated him. He had successfully discredited Monkey in the demonstration, goading him into storming away. *I won this round.* Adam smiled to himself. *Now I just need to end this competition.* He went in search of Monkey and found him scratching around in a nearby flint pile.

"Adam," he said looking up in surprise.

"Monkey," Adam said in reply. "Look, we are friends, and you did a great job with the axe, but Eve is mine; you need to back off."

"Says you," Monkey spit back, stretching to full height. "Eve thinks differently."

Adam fingered the axe on his belt. He did not expect a fight. The gang usually just got along, but this was different. This mattered. "Well that is just fine. Eve can decide." Adam shoved him. "In the meantime, you keep your distance."

Monkey shoved him back, then picked up a piece of flint. Adam pulled the axe from his belt. Wet vine or dry, it had a deadly hit in it.

Monkey seemed to know it as well. He stepped back. "First you steal my axe. Now you are going to kill me with it? Eve will feed you to the fish if you do."

Adam put the axe back in his belt. "Maybe she would, but I don't need an axe to beat you." He growled and rushed forward. He gave Monkey a shove, hoping to intimidate him without really hurting him but that hope was soon lost.

Monkey took his beating well, returning as many blows as he received. Then he tripped and fell. Adam pinned him to the ground. "Remember, Eve is mine," he said, standing. "Then we can all get along just fine." He turned and headed back towards the treehouse, unhappy with the outcome. He felt his lip. He was bleeding. This was not the outcome he had wanted. Not at all.

# Leadership Crisis

Eve did not see Monkey that evening. She lay in bed thinking. Adam had their axe, and she felt like this competition between them might not be about her at all. She worried it was not even about the axe, but about leadership of the gang. Poor sleep and worry drove her to rise early, dawn barely visible in the sky.

Monkey was waiting for her at the cave opening. He had a new flint in his hand, bigger than the last one. "Monkey, what are you doing here so early?"

"Waiting for you. Are you ready?"

"I guess," she said. He took her hand and headed across the clearing toward the path. "So, what is the plan?" she asked.

"We make another axe," Monkey said. "And nobody will take it away from me without prying it from my dead fingers. There was nothing wrong with our first axe—if you knew how to use it. It only looked bad because that idiot Adam didn't know what he was doing."

"You're all worked up over this, aren't you?"

"It was our axe. We made it. Then Adam took all the credit. And now he's trying to take you away from me."

Eve shook her hand loose and stopped dead. "What?"

"What what?" he asked.

Eve shook her head and tried to quell an anger growing in her. "No," she said.

"What did I do?" Monkey demanded.

*Careful, blow this and you could start a serious fight.* Eve took a deep breath and began walking again. "I agree Adam overstepped in taking charge of the new axe," she said. "It shows you how much he liked the idea, and how impressed he was with it. You know he wants everyone to have one for battle. We are all a team. Remember, we asked him to lead us in making new weapons. He is doing what we asked."

"I never asked for his help," Monkey snapped. "All Adam wants to do is build a treehouse and impress you."

Eve realized her arguments were going no place. "Look, this all has nothing to do with me. He's not trying to take me away from anyone, and for your information, I am not yours. We are all on the same team."

"That's just what Art said you would say. Everyone else can see it, why can't you?"

"See what?" Eve demanded. He gave her a look like she was dumber than their non-speaking tribe. "Seriously, I must be missing something," she said again.

"Think. Your father is the leader of the tribe, and what do the women of the tribe do?"

"Do?"

"Seriously? You can't be this blind," Monkey said. "They compete to get his attention. They try to get him to pick them."

"Pick them?"

"To mate, of course."

"Perhaps," Eve allowed, knowing Monkey was dead on.

"Among us, you are the leader, so we guys compete to try to get your attention, hoping you will pick us. And now that you picked me, Adam is insane with jealousy. He would do anything to get you away from me."

Eve took a hard look at him. She noticed the bruises. "Oh, I had no idea," she said and gave him a sheepish smile. "I was just trying to find a better way to get our poles cut."

"So?" he asked, reaching for her hand.

She pulled back. "I can accept that you believe all this, but I am not ready to accept it myself. This could all just be your wild imagination." She kept walking, keeping her hand to herself. This was not anything like what she thought being leader would be like. "Tell you what," she said, some time later. "Let's just carry on with our new axe and keep cutting poles. In three days, let's see what Adam does. Try not to pick another fight with him in the meantime."

"Why shouldn't I?" he asked.

"Because I asked you not to, and as you said: I am your leader and you want to impress me, don't you?" He had no response, and Eve felt proud of herself, turning things around on him.

Three days later when the group reunited, Monkey had his new axe on his belt. Adam appeared to ignore it as he inspected the first axe as if he hadn't been watching it dry the whole time. "Looks good," he said.

He walked over to the recalcitrant tree which broke the first axe in two. Within moments, the tree crashed to the ground. Triumphant, Adam held up the axe. Everyone cheered. Adam walked over to Eve and knelt in front of her. He held up the axe for her to take. "We needed a real weapon, and while I was organizing the treehouse, Eve went ahead and created the most useful, most deadly, most amazing weapon possible. Now we can all make them and be safe, all because of her leadership." He stood. Smiling, he took her in his arms and looked into her eyes. "Good job," he said quietly.

The hug was not a hug like one she might have given her father. This hug felt different for some reason, more like one from Monkey. All her thoughts of how to produce more axes evaporated. In a flash she realized Monkey was right. She was in it deep.

"Thank you," she said, disengaging herself from Adam's arms and counting herself lucky none of the gang seemed to notice the awkward moment. If Monkey noticed, he pretended not to.

While she recovered her wits, Adam took charge, asking the others to take a break from their designated tasks. Each was to focus on making an axe. "One for each of us—as weapons!" he declared.

Eve glanced over at Monkey. He wore a smug, told-you-so look on his face. *Bloody bones, I need a distraction.* "I am going to make a mighty axe for my father," she announced. "It makes sense.

Everyone in the valley needs one, just in case, but the leader needs a special one."

Twig predicted Blue Eyes would have no idea what to do with an axe but Adam volunteered Little Red to help him find the best flint in the valley. "Only the best for the leader," he said.

"Get enough for all the adults," Eve added, as they prepared to leave. Despite the rains, they could hardly refuse her, not with the whole gang watching.

They were gone for several miserably wet days. With each day of rain, Eve felt relieved the task had fallen to Little Red and Adam, and not to her. She spent most of her time dry in her cave carving a bamboo handle—and entirely avoiding Monkey. She wanted to try using bamboo for the axe she was making for her father. She wanted his axe to be special, but sadly, the bamboo handle she was crafting was not working well either. Days passed and she began to wonder what was taking Adam and Little Red so long. *I should have looked for the flint myself*, she thought the next day as she stood at the cave entrance, watching the rain fall. Suddenly, out of the gloom, Adam and Little Red appeared, smiles on their faces.

Adam was covered in mud. He had a heavy branch in his hand. It was covered in mud too. "Wait until you see what we found," Little Red said, unable to control his enthusiasm. "You are going to be amazed!"

Eve smiled at him and turned to Adam. He acted nonchalant. "How did that bamboo handle work out?" he asked.

"Horrible! I had to abandon the idea. It kept splitting." She stared at the muddy branch in his hands, thinking it appeared just about right for the handle she needed. "So what's that you have there?" Eve pried, despite herself.

"Come on, let's go to the treehouse and I will tell you all about it."

"The rain—"

"It's only a bit of rain," Adam said, dismissing the downpour.

Eve figured it must have been bad out there for this to only be "a bit of rain." She had been working on a cover to shed the rain, tightly woven from a grass. Now she put it on. It had been a good idea, but it never worked as well as she wanted, and in this downpour, she knew it would be largely useless. She, however, was not about to admit that as Adam and Little Red watched her put it on.

As they ran, the rain began to wash the mud off Adam's branch. A silver sheen began to show through.

Eve pulled Adam to a stop. "Adam! What have you done?" she cried. "You cut that from the Tree of Life!"

"No, no! Don't worry! Eve—it was a gift from the creator," Adam said, resuming their journey at a walk.

"What are you talking about?" Eve said. Little Red's big smile made her wonder what was really going on here.

"I wanted to help you find the perfect branch for your father's axe—just in case, you know. Then as we walked up here, I heard a crack. I turned and what did I see? This branch fell from the Tree of Life. It came right down. The wind carried it towards us as it fell. It has to be a gift from the creator. Doesn't it? It, and only it, must be suitable for the leader of our people. I can feel it. Can't you?" He held it out for her to touch.

Eve eyed him and it. Adam was not much for talking about the Tree of Life. But there it was, a branch from the Tree, clearly broken off, shining brilliantly in his hands.

"That—," Eve said, handling the branch. "That is quite a story."

"It's absolutely perfect, isn't it?"

"And wait until you see what I found," Little Red said.

Adam gave him a withering stare. "Little Red," he warned. "We will be there soon enough."

Little Red shut his mouth, but looked like he might burst at any moment, he was so excited.

Eve enjoyed his enthusiasm, and broke back into a run. "Well? Let's get going then. Last one there," she called over her shoulder, "—is a toad's wart!"

The three of them were breathing hard when they arrived beneath the treehouse. Adam motioned for Eve to head up first. After shaking out her clothes and wringing the water from her hair at the door, she climbed the ladder, and entered the dry treehouse.

The boys joined her, all smiles. Adam with Little Red's help uncovered a pile of stones from beneath a large seal skin. The stones were white on the outside, but where they had been broken, most gleamed a shiny gray. Others were almost black.

"I chipped some of these so they are sharp," Adam warned her. "They were better than any flint we had found so far."

"Are you not amazed?" Little Red asked.

"I am amazed. Yes. These are incredible. Where did you find them?"

"Of all the unlikely places," said Adam. "Along the cliff on the beach."

"I found them," Little Red said, as Adam dug in the pile.

He uncovered a stone unlike the rest and handed it to Eve. This one was special, she could see that. Its center was a shiny, transparent yellow. It shone like the sun. She had never seen anything like it.

"I got this for you," Adam said blushing. "For the leader's axe."

Forgetting herself, Eve threw her arms around him and gave him a hug. Little Red snickered, and she released Adam.

"I think the yellow flint would go very well with the branch from the Tree of Life," Adam said, recovering first from their awkward moment.

"My father will thank you, I just know it," Eve said. "And thank you too, Little Red, for your part in this great discovery. Now let me give you a hug as well." Eve moved toward him.

Little Red ducked out of the way, making a face and a retching sound. "Gah!"

Eve had them stay and get started making her father's axe right away. Adam warned that they should not stay too late, but despite his words, they worked until dusk. Little Red returned from collecting some fruit, and they ate as the light faded. After they ate, they talked about the axe and the new flint in the dark. Little Red fell asleep almost immediately.

"Adam?" Eve asked in the dark.

"Yes?"

"Do you think my dad will like the axe?" Eve asked, worried Adam would say no like Twig.

"I would like it," Adam said immediately.

"Yes, but will my dad get it? Will he care? Twig said he wouldn't even be interested."

"Oh, I see. She has a point, and I think she is right, he might not get it right away. But once he sees how amazing it is, he will come to love it. That's what I think."

"Thank you, I think so too," she said and let out a sigh of relief. She and Adam talked a little longer, but soon Adam fell asleep too.

As Eve lay awake, she listened to the boys' rhythmic breathing. And she listened to the rain outside and the river's steady roar. Maybe she had been wrong about Adam all along. He had never mentioned his own axe which he had been working on, or bragged about finding the new flint, graciously letting Little Red take all the credit. And what he just said about her dad was kind. He was different now; he was not like his old self—or the other boys. Then she remembered what Monkey had said. Maybe this was his way of impressing her. If it was, it was working. She moved her mat closer to him before drifting off to sleep herself.

The next morning, they returned to their caves, bringing their projects with them. For the next few days, Eve whittled away at the branch, trying to create the perfect axe handle. With the silver bark removed, the branch was pure white. She was sure it was superior to bamboo in every way.

"What are you making?" Fish asked. He and Bev were taking a break from making their own axes. She suspected Fish was mostly making Bev's.

"An axe for my dad," she answered and showed him the handle.

"Strange wood. Hardly even looks like wood. You really think he will know what to do with it?"

"What kind of wood is that?" Bev asked. "It's so white, I think it will get all stained and nasty."

"Well, I think he will like it," Eve said sharply, not liking Bev's attitude. The girl and Fish watched for a while longer before leaving.

It was not long before Eve was finished with the handle. She searched out Art. He was working with Monkey on their axes. She had not seen either since the big axe demonstration. Monkey jumped up and came and put an arm around her and gave her a squeeze.

Eve ignored Monkey. "Hey, Art? Can you help me out?"

"Sure, what do you need?" he answered, a sneer on his face. It made her uncomfortable. Obviously they had been talking.

"I want to decorate this axe handle for my father. I was thinking maybe a symbol for each of the gang members."

Art and Monkey exchanged glances, laughed, then laughed some more. "Seriously? He can't even talk," Monkey said. "Why waste time with symbols?"

"Look, you two, this is to be the axe of the leader of the tribe, our tribe, so I want it to look good. Now, will you help or not?"

"Sure," Art finally agreed. After a few failed attempts by him and Monkey to flirt with her, Art set to work carving the symbols meant to represent each of them.

When Eve walked away, she was unable to help comparing Monkey's and Adam's reactions to the leader's axe. If she had to pick between them now, there was no contest.

Adam helped her shape the hard yellow flint in such a way that the axe could easily chop or kill. It was sharp enough to shave with. The golden axe, secretly made from the sacred tree, and with its golden stone head was fit for a leader; it was perfect.

Eve was anxious to present the gift to her father, but had serious concerns he wouldn't like it. She kept finding excuses not to give it to him. First the rain, then because he went fishing. Finally, on a clear, sunny morning, there were no more excuses. She desperately wanted to have the gang along for support, but as most had predicted he would not like it, she decided to go it alone.

After breakfast, she took her father by the hand and led him out to the edge of the clearing. Her mother, siblings and some of their young friends looked on, no doubt wondering what was going on.

Eve pulled the axe from where she had hidden it. The small group pressed around to see what it was. *Deep breaths.* She presented it to her father. Her father looked at the object with incomprehension, his face blank. He seemed unimpressed. But then again, he had no idea what an axe was for.

Refusing to be disappointed, Eve demonstrated the axe by chopping down a nearby tree. It was small but her father nodded in understanding. Still, his lack of enthusiasm was quite evident. Cutting down trees was not a task he or anybody truly relished. Near despair, she used the axe to shave a few hairs off his arm. His eyes opened a little wider. The spooky sharpness of it impressed him—if only a little.

Impressed or not, he kept the axe in a place of honor in the cave. Eve promised herself not to speak of it again until he actually used it, afraid the gang would make fun of him because he didn't know what to do with it.

Lucky for her, a few days later her father gathered his hunters and departed on a seal hunting expedition. "He took the new axe instead of his trusty club," Eve explained to Twig, hardly able to contain herself. Waiting for his return, for the axe to prove its worth, was excruciating.

A few days later, a commotion outside dragged Eve from the cave. The hunting party had returned. Eve, curious to see what was going on, but not wanting to act too anxious, edged closer and witnessed her father and another hunter facing off. About half the tribe gathered around them. Eve pushed to the front, unsure what was going on. Near a pile of seal meat, partially cut up, her father held his axe, red with blood.

Adam sidled up next to her. "What's going on?" he asked.

"Near as I can tell, my father was chopping up the seal meat with his axe. Big Nose over there wanted his axe. I think they are fighting over it."

Adam whistled. "Wow, I have never seen anyone challenge your father before."

Big Nose raised his club and charged forward, swinging it at Blue Eyes. "Grr!"

Letting out a snarl and hiss of his own, Blue Eyes swung his axe, slicing the arm of his attacker. Big Nose looked at his arm in surprise.

Blood pumped down it, dripping off his fingers. He let out a roar, and charged Blue Eyes again. This time when her father swung, he split Big Nose's skull open. The crowd gasped, then rushed in to have a look at the dead man's wound—and at the near magical axe.

Another man tried to grab it. Blue Eyes raised it with a snarl. The man backed off. Blue Eyes began strutting around the clearing with his axe held high until everyone lowered their own eyes before him.

Gripping Adam's arms with both hands, Eve stared him in the face. "He killed him, just like that."

"He had no choice. The man tried to steal his axe." Adam smiled wanly. "You know what that means?"

"What?"

Adam's smile turned into a grin. "Means he liked it after all."

"Adam, he just killed a man," Eve said as the gang crowded around them. Most wore their axes on their belts. "Fights are one thing, but this is different. It was *too* easy."

Finally, Blue Eyes motioned to his second in command to drag the body to the river. The man took a foot and dragged Big Nose over and deposited him in the water like a piece of refuse.

"Did you see that?" Twig asked Fish, who stood next to her.

He was busy defending his axe from a youngster. "This is crazy," Fish declared, holding one hand over the axe head on his belt. He pushed the mute child away with his other hand.

It was clear the others in the hunting party wanted axes as well. In fact, all the tribesmen did. Eve noticed that the more interest they showed, the greater Blue Eyes's pride grew.

That night as Eve prepared for bed she noticed her father tucked the axe under his cover and slept with it beside him. She decided she better make him a cover or he might injure himself during the night. Still bothered by the fight, she slipped out and found Twig. They sat near the Tree of Life looking at the moonlight on the stream.

"My father carries the axe with him wherever he goes now—literally everywhere, even if just to step out for a drink," Eve said.

"It is a well crafted weapon, and that means everything to the tribe," Twig said. "Strong instincts have been hidden by living in this safe little valley"

"But he killed Big Nose," Eve said in a hushed voice. "Killed him over my axe. I feel like it's my fault."

"Oh, that's nonsense. Big Nose was a brute. No loss to the tribe. In fact, your father did us all a favor. He got rid of a real problem."

"Twig, that's horrible."

"They need to see that once in a while," she continued. "It's not horrible. It's how the tribe works."

Eve put her hand on Twig's arm and looked at her intently. "How do you know how the tribe is supposed to work?" Eve said. "You aren't just saying that to make me feel better?"

"Eve, when do I ever lie to make people feel better?" Twig said. "You are fine. Your father is fine. The axe is a fine thing. It will make the tribe stronger. Now go to bed."

After a hug from Twig, Eve crawled into bed feeling no better about Twig pretending to always know what was best, but otherwise she felt vindicated. The leader's axe was a success. The only thing still bothering her was Twig's uncanny knowledge and confident answers.

The next day, Eve made her father a belt and axe holder from seal skin. She couldn't help but become flushed with emotion at his enthusiastic response.

The axe and all its accouterments were wanted by all. Where before, the speaking children felt like unhappy accidents, freaks of nature who had no place in the social order of things, now suddenly, and basically overnight, they were recognized as something more.

Adam stepped up, and, together with Eve, he organized the production of axes for the tribe. One day while they were working, Eve stopped and stretched her aching back. It was a fine day, and many of the tribe were sitting on the bank near the Tree of Life scraping and chipping away on their own flints. Adam sat with them, teaching the group of hunters and a number of women how to chip the flint head. Eve was impressed by his patience. Her gang had invented a clever and useful object that not only provided men with a new weapon, but also provided cutting tools for the women in the tribe.

Glancing up, Adam caught Eve watching him. "What?" he asked.

"Nothing. I am just proud of you—the way you are teaching the tribe," she said. "As long as I can remember, I have never seen any enthusiasm for the things we made amongst the tribe, least of all among the men. Basically none, until now."

"Makes sense to me," he said. "Who doesn't love a good weapon?"

Eve laughed. "So true. Especially you boys."

They kept at it for the next few weeks, and eventually the tribespeople had their own axes. Yet none, Eve noted to herself, were as fine as the leader's axe with its golden flint.

Still Eve lived with an uneasy feeling. The issue between Monkey and Adam was not resolved. Axes only made their animosity more worrisome in her mind.

*Take only memories, leave only footprints.*
*The greatest treasure is in the hearts of the hunters.*

Chief Seattle

# First Hunt 9

The rains were over. The days began warming. Eve and the others figured it was about time for Blue Eyes to take his hunters to the beach to hunt seals. Adam was ready each morning, staying close to camp, his axe on his belt. He had assured her and the gang that they would be respected now that they had made themselves useful. Twig had confirmed that providing for the tribe was the key to leadership. The fair-haired girl was rarely wrong about such things. Adam certainly believed her. He clearly had staked his hopes, dreams, and reputation on being included.

When Blue Eyes called his hunters and left one morning without inviting Adam, he rushed after them and tried to join the party, but with a growl, and a hand on his axe, Blue Eyes stopped him. It was one thing to be ignored, but it was even more embarrassing to ask and be rejected. Humiliating, was what it was. Adam seemed devastated—and angry.

The issue with Monkey, was also developing. The two of them sometimes seemed like friends, though mostly they were not speaking to each other—possibly even fighting when she wasn't around. As the gang worked on the treehouse, they had taken to measuring their heights on one of the tall poles holding up the roof. Since the last marking, Monkey had grown several inches; Adam had not.

Monkey, now taller than Adam, let it be known that once he filled out a little more, he would be the strongest. "Someday, I will be the leader."

Adam had said nothing, and Eve supposed he cared little about being the leader. She had held her own tongue, but even thinking about Monkey being the leader rubbed her the wrong way and made her a little crazy. Everyone knew she was to be the next leader.

She watched as Adam gathered his things, and headed off. She ran to catch him. "I am sorry," Eve said. "I hoped my father would include you, but I guess we are just too different."

Adam scoffed and kept walking. "Whatever."

"Where are you going?"

"I am going to go hunting on my own," he said, not stopping.

"Above?" she asked in surprise.

"Exactly."

"Not without me," she said and grabbed his arm, pulling him to a stop. "I get that you're mad, but charging off alone won't do. We're a team, and if you're going, then we should all go together."

He looked at her. He seemed to weigh her words carefully. At last he appeared to make up his mind. "I don't need any help," he said.

"You don't know that," Eve said. "What if you are attacked like Monkey was?"

Adam scowled. "Okay fine, tell the gang to meet me at the treehouse," he said and walked off.

Eve hurried back home to pack. She had her work cut out for her. Somehow she had to make this hunting trip seem like it was her idea, and that it was a good idea, even though she wasn't so sure herself. She told each of the gang to pack their things for a short hunting trip, even as she worried about running off without telling her father where they were going, figuring as the true leader of the tribe he deserved to know.

They made their way toward the treehouse in a straggled line, Twig was right next to her. "This is a bad idea," she said quietly so nobody else could hear.

"Oh, don't start with that line again. I'm having enough trouble with Monkey, Adam, and my father. I don't need a fight with you as well."

"I'm just telling you, having a new weapon does not mean we're ready for what's out there," Twig said with a wave toward the distant cliffs. "Eve, you just need to trust me on this."

"Sorry, but you know that's not going to happen, Twig," Eve said. "So either stay behind, or get on board and help keep us safe, if you know so much." The girl made no further arguments, and for once it seemed she was put in her place.

As the treehouse came into sight, Eve made up her mind as to the strategy she would follow. She gave Adam a nod as she took her usual seat.

Adam addressed the gang as they lounged under the treehouse and branches of the tree. "If—" Adam glanced at Eve. She lazily swatted at a fly buzzing around her face. "If the adults," he continued carefully. "If they don't want me—don't want us—going on their hunts, then we will have to go on our own." He did a good job of keeping the bitterness from his voice.

"Not a bad idea," Eve said, glancing away towards the crevice. "We do need to try out our new axes. I'm not sure some of them are as well designed as others." She glanced away from the cliff and stared at Adam's spear.

He had an axe, but his interest was in his current weapon. He and Twig insisted on calling it a spear. It had a longer handle than his axe.

The flint was chipped to a point and attached to the end.

"This is not a badly made axe," Adam complained. "I've told you again and again. It's a deadly spear, a hunter's weapon, not an axe for cutting reeds for your mother."

"Yes, Adam. Whatever you say," Eve said in her most patronizing voice.

"Hunting sounds like a great idea!" Fish said. "We should totally go hunting. I hate to say it, but I'm bored of fishing. Me, Fish, bored of fishing? Can you believe it? All I do is fish. Spear fish, and trap fish, and—"

"And yes, Fish. You fish for fish, Fish," Adam said. He glanced at Eve. She did not laugh.

"I'm telling you," Fish said. "It's time we do something."

"I'm in," Monkey said, standing and stretching to his full height." Adam frowned at him.

"Just a short trip," Twig said. "To see what we will need."

"It would be good practice for our first big hunt," Adam said.

Eve snapped her head to him; her blue eyes held his gaze. "Yes, it would," she said. "It would be good practice. Let's do it."

Adam leapt to his feet. "Well?" he demanded. "What are we waiting for? Let's go hunting up above. Our parents haven't even done that!"

Eve could not deny Adam's enthusiasm. His eyes sparkled with excitement. And the way he held his spear, he looked like a real hunter. With it, perhaps he would be able to kill something before it got away.

Adam's sudden interest, and the idea of preparing to explore the wilds of the outer world, brought everyone to their feet, and Eve soon found herself following him toward the crevice. But as the dreaded crevice came into view, she wondered at the wisdom of this hunt.

As she packed that morning she had tried to explain to her mother, then to her little brother, that she would be going away for several days on a hunt. "Danger," was all her brother had to say.

Now Eve wondered if that wasn't the real reason her father didn't let Adam go on his hunts. The fact was, hunts were dangerous. More than once, a man had left on one of her father's hunts and come back injured—or not at all. Eve now vowed to keep that in mind.

As she left her cave that morning, she wondered—as she had many times before—how much her father truly knew, how much was locked up in his head behind his cool blue eyes. She, like him, didn't always feel the need to make her mind known.

The day was still young, and Eve, along with everyone else, was packed and ready. They followed Adam as he led them up the cliff, her bamboo platform in his hand, with Monkey and Fish carrying the ladder from the treehouse to finish the climb.

After setting up her platform again, and a ladder to the top, exhilaration like none other filled Eve as her head cleared the crevice and she beheld the vast green plains. They stretched away like the ocean. "Wow!" she said. "This is amazing."

"I told you it was big," Monkey said, smugly.

"Where are all the monsters?" Bev asked when she arrived up top last. There were no animals of any kind about. The gang, however, found a path running parallel to their valley. They followed it upstream.

The group hiked slowly, sticking close together. Adam led with his spear at the ready. Monkey walked beside Eve. Adam, possibly distracted, didn't seem to mind. He seemed to be enjoying the role of leader.

He followed the narrow, lightly-worn path. It seemed the easiest route. "I claim these wilds as our own!" he said, slamming down the butt of his spear every time they cleared some bit of brush from the path. The way he did it—and with such confidence—he seemed ready to face any danger.

The group idly chatted the day away, eating a few scattered berries they came upon. The sun swung low and the boys pulled ahead after Twig pointed out that Fish's sister was pregnant.

"Shut up, Twig," Fish said, then he, Adam, Art and even Monkey hurried forward, leaving the girls to chat by themselves.

"Your sister is younger than me!" said Eve, wrinkling her nose.

"Gag," Twig said. "But that's what happens."

"They are always pregnant," Bev said. "My mom is pregnant again!"

"What is that now? Twelve?" Eve asked. "Disgusting."

"I don't know about you girls," Twig said. "But I am much happier hiking up above the valley on an adventure, than waddling around with some man's baby inside me." She looked over the group. "There will be no babies for me, ever!" she added with some finality.

"You know what that means though, right, don't you?" Eve asked, trying to smile away her own embarrassment.

"Fine with me," Twig replied. "*It* can't be worth the price. And you can't have one without the other."

"The boys can," Bev said. "And that's *certainly* not fair."

"Well, not without one of us," Eve said.

"Not without one of us," Twig agreed, and she began walking faster. They soon caught up with the boys and together they arrived at the head of the valley.

## The Upper Falls

Adam stared at the sight. The falls which marked the end of their valley was not the end of the world. Here there was a small pond and a second smaller falls above it. Adam glanced anxiously at the low sun then back to the water's edge. "See that spot?" he said pointing. "Right there on the shore, the flat, open spot. That will be our camp." For the first time since leaving the valley, he felt some optimism. This trip was a good idea. Throwing caution to the wind, he charged forward along the cliff edge until he found a dry ravine, and they clambered down and headed to the spot, arriving just before dark.

He had been concerned they had not seen a single other living thing but birds circling overhead. Yet this place was amazing. Even without a great hunt it would satisfy them all. *Now if only I can get Monkey away from Eve.* So far the gangly boy was her constant companion.

As darkness fell the gang sat and ate. A crescent moon climbed as the sky filled with stars. "Look at all of them, up there," Bev said. "What do you think they are?" Nobody ventured a guess.

"Ah, this is the life," Adam said. He laid back and crossed his hands behind his head.

"Seriously, what do you think they are?" Bev persisted.

"How could you forget they are called stars," Twig answered with a giggle.

"Yes, Twig, but what are stars?" Adam asked.

Twig didn't know, and for a while they all just stared up at the lights.

"Did you see that?" Eve asked after a shooting star streaked across the sky. "One just ran away and died! It must be a lucky thing to see."

"Yes, lucky, for the hunt tomorrow," Adam said.

There was a long silence. Soon the sound of the falls purring gently began to lull them to sleep. Adam looked around; he was the last awake. When he closed his eyes, he dreamt of a woman. He knew he'd had the same dream before. This dream was becoming all too common. The woman had long brown hair, and deep blue eyes. Adam reached out to her, but she screamed.

He woke with a start. The scream echoed in his mind. Usually, that was not part of the dream. It seemed so real this time. It seemed almost unnatural.

He considered waking the others, but didn't. *It's just a dream*, he told himself. The gang slept peacefully as he sat listening to the falls. His eyes came to rest on Eve. Her hair was scattered and wild. He wondered if it could be her in his dream. The dream was already fading from his memory.

After sitting for a while longer, he laid back down. He was being foolish. It was just a dream. Eventually, he fell back asleep hoping—just a little—he could continue the dream. He dearly wished he could possess the beautiful woman with the big, blue eyes.

## Goats

Eve woke feeling rested and pleased with their outing so far.

"Come on everyone! Best swimming in the world!" Little Red shouted. He was striping off his clothes, not a sight she particularly wanted to see first thing in the morning. *Gugh*, she thought as his skinny naked body plunged into the clear water.

He seemed correct, however, about the swimming. The river, too shallow and full of rocks, was always moving, and the lagoon near the treehouse was choked with debris. It was also murky and algae filled. But this pool looked deep and clear. How deep Eve didn't know.

She glanced at Twig and then at Adam. "You boys stay here; we girls are going in the water over there," she said and pointed to some bushes along the bank nearby. Their leather and woven clothes fared poorly in water. While they had always swam naked as children, and never given it a thought, recently Eve and the older girls had become uncomfortable with the idea.

Adam made a face, like he didn't understand. He shrugged. "Okay."

Eve couldn't be sure, but it seemed he was acting a little strange, and Monkey's words about mating came to her. She worried Adam had the same idea. *What am I going to do with you, Adam?* Eve asked herself as she and the other girls headed toward the bushes.

Protected from the wandering eyes of the boys, she, Bev, and Twig undressed. Unlike Little Red, who had tossed his clothes on the ground, they hung up theirs on one of the bushes. Then, seeing the boys already swimming, the three of them plunged into the cool water.

Before long Eve had forgotten her apprehensions and she and the girls and boys were all swimming together. They dared each other to dive into the falls. None did for fear of being sucked under.

"Alright—fun's over!" Adam finally said. "I saw some strange tracks as we came down the ravine last night. We need to check them out."

The boys swam back to the campsite, while Eve, Bev and Twig swam back to their private beach to retrieve their clothes.

As Twig pulled on her shirt she complained about her figure, and not for the first time. "I look like a boy. It's not fair. When am I going to start to look like a girl? Why do boys like breasts so much anyway?"

"I would trade you mine for your brains any day, Twig," Bev said, sounding honest.

"Who decides what's attractive and what's not?" Twig continued.

"Well," Eve said. "Who decides what food we like and what food we don't. We mostly like the same things, but not all of us. You think fish eggs are amazing—I think they are revolting. I am sure boys are the same way with girls. I bet Art would find you absolutely irresistible."

"Nice theory, and I am sure you mean well, Eve, but no boy will ever find me attractive."

"Oh, get over it Twig," Bev scolded. "You have the finest hair of any woman in the tribe. How would you like my *mop?*" Bev shook her head, sending water all over them.

When they joined the boys, Twig walked over to Art. "Would you braid my hair for me?" He scoffed, stuck out his tongue, then ran off with the other boys. Twig scowled at Bev. "Yeah, right. The hair is a *big draw*!"

Eve couldn't help being glad she was neither of them. Today, at least, she felt good about her looks. Hearing excited shouts ahead, the three of them hurried to catch up with the boys.

They followed the pool around to the left of the falls, and found the strange tracks Adam spoke of wandering through a thicket and a small grove of trees.

The boys had stopped at a pile of rocks near the cliff. Fish said something about losing the tracks. He was on his knees staring down at the last stretch of the path. Adam was nodding as he leaned over him, spear at the ready.

Monkey scouted ahead, climbing the rocks. He called back to them. "Hey, everyone, come up here. I think I found something."

Adam led the way up to Monkey. "What is it?" he asked.

Monkey pointed down between two big rocks. "Check it out!" He pointed at what looked like fur and bones and not much else but brown smears—dried blood.

"Wow," said Adam. "That used to be an animal, I think."

Twig nudged Adam. "The bones look fresh." She turned to Monkey. "Can you fish me out a bone!"

"I'm not a fish, but okay." He bent down into a notch between the rocks, and stretching out, grabbed a hold of one.

"Here," he said, pulling it out. The bone was shattered and came to a jagged point on one end.

"Yes. Very fresh," Twig said as she examined the bone. "And look at these teeth marks." Eve could see only large grooves on the bone which had to be what she meant. The skinny girl continued her assessment. "I'd say this was killed by something bigger than the beast who attacked Monkey."

Twig sounded more intrigued than horrified. *What have I done!* Eve thought. She had felt safe here, but clearly this was not their valley. They were not safe. She had started all this with the platform and now they were at risk. Maybe the silver-leafed Tree of Life had rejected her offering and this was to be her punishment. "We have to kill it," Eve said. "Before it kills us."

Adam glanced at her, looking surprised at her reaction. "Of course, but how?"

"We track it," said Little Red.

"Do you *see* its tracks anywhere?" Eve asked.

"Maybe we can trap it," Fish said excitedly.

Eve frowned at the boy. "We want to kill it, not trap it."

"Well, we know it likes the taste of these things," said Little Red holding up the bone, saying something useful for a change.

Art glanced around nervously. "Hopefully, that is all it likes the taste of."

"So, we trap these animals I am calling goats and use them to lure the beast in," Twig said, snatching the broken bone back and waving it as she spoke. "It's a good idea, Fish." Fish beamed at her, but she didn't seem to notice. Little Red made a whiny noise, but Twig turned to Adam. "Seems Fish will get his trap after all."

"Seems so," he said, with a grin. He tapped the rocks with his spear's butt. "Now! We have a real hunt on our hands!"

The gang began to plan out Fish's new goat trap.

"We better make it plenty big," Fish said.

"And strong," Adam added, glancing at the bone.

"I saw a bamboo grove over along the river not far away," Eve suggested, unable to resist the excitement of building something new.

Even Art was on board. "When we were swimming, I saw some reeds growing along the pond we use for cords—I can get them."

"Now all we need is a plan," Twig said. "How about we build a tunnel where the path goes through the thicket? Leave both ends open until the goats get used to it, then add some doors that drop closed when the goats walk through."

It was a good plan, but Adam wasn't ready to adopt it, not until a dozen bad plans were proposed by the others. From digging pits to dropping a cage from the trees, every suggestion was considered, and then he decided to go with

Twig's plan anyway. Eve winked at Twig, who winked back.

Adam divided them up and assigned tasks gathering materials for the rest of the afternoon. "Let's get the first stakes in tonight, so they get used to seeing them."

The site they picked was in the middle of the patch of thorns. Here the thorns grew thick and crowded the path. It opened up onto the sandy beach.

"They will have to come through here," Fish said. "Look there are tufts of fur on the thorns."

As they collected and brought bamboo stakes, Adam hammered them into the soft ground with the back of his real axe. He made two rows, a few inches apart, up and down each side of the path.

By the time they finished it was dark, so the gang quickly brushed away their tracks in the damp sand, so they would be able to observe if there had been any traffic during the night, and headed back down the beach to their camping place on the knoll. Eve walked beside Adam, wondering what he would do about dinner, about sleeping arrangements, and about the new danger they faced. If he wanted to lead so badly, she could leave such questions to him.

> *A friend is one that knows you as you are, understands where you have been, accepts what you have become, and still gently allows you to grow.*

> Elbert Hubbard

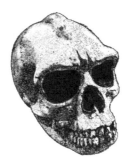

# Adam and Eve      10

"I am starving from slaving away all afternoon, and we don't have anything to eat?" Art grumbled. "Pretty poor planning, I'd say. "

Adam could not think of a good answer. Art was right—he had done a poor job of timing things.

"The stars are bright, even if the moon is just a sliver," Eve said. "I say we pick some berries." She left the open beach and struck off on her own into the thick brush and small trees that surrounded the pool.

Adam was surprised. He thought she had been walking with him because she was afraid, but apparently not. Hungry himself, he headed off after her.

"It's dark under the trees," Bev complained, following with the others.

"We should have made a cage for ourselves to sleep in," Little Red said. "Instead of a trap."

"We should have made a treehouse," suggested Monkey.

Adam scoffed as he picked. He ate and lost sight of Eve. He worried she was lying in wait, ready to jump out and scare him. It seemed like something she might do. Each time he moved forward he steeled himself.

When she didn't, and when he had eaten enough to stave off hunger pains, he called the group together, and they returned to the knoll.

Monkey began to tell what sounded like a long, scary story. "It's too late for any of that kind of thing," said Adam, cutting him off. "Tonight we will have to take turns standing watch." He arranged them in order and told everyone to remember their place. "When whoever is on watch becomes too tired, wake the next one in line, okay?"

They all nodded and spread their mats. The waxing moon was a little larger, but still a crescent. The stars shone bright as they had the night before, but tonight Adam had serious things on his mind. Something larger than a hyena ate a goat the night before—and far too close by. He suspected the scream he heard in his dream was related. He noticed the sleepers settled much closer together now. Eve put her mat right next to his. Adam lay down propped up on one elbow and watched for a while as the rest fell asleep. Fish sat leaning against a tree, his axe in his hand across his lap. He had ended up on watch first. Adam watched to see he stayed awake for a while then, turning over, fell asleep himself.

Adam awoke with the sun shining in his face. Fish lay fast asleep next to his tree. His axe lay beside him.

"Fine guard you turned out to be!" Adam said. He walked over and, standing over Fish, kicked him awake. "Everyone was supposed to have a turn, but you went to sleep without waking anyone!"

"I—I wasn't sleepy, so, I just stayed up all night," Fish said, wiping the sleep from his eyes.

Adam grabbed a handful of Fish's hair and growled. "Really?"

"I got bored. It was very quiet, and I thought I would be more comfortable laying down."

"Tell me the truth, Fish."

"Then, next thing I know, you kicked me," Fish finally admitted.

Adam let go of Fish's hair. "We could have been eaten!" he scolded. "Lucky for you, I only kicked you."

Soon everyone was awake and Fish's incompetence was forgotten. Twig mentioned checking the trap. Too excited to stop and scavenge for food, the gang took off at a run. In the lead, Adam realized before the others there were no tracks along the lake. Was this good or bad? He didn't know. He approached the path cautiously with the gang bunched up behind him. He crept slowly on, moving up the path worrying something might be lurking in the thicket. They found no tracks on the path, and none in the tunnel. Then closer to the rocks, there were fresh tracks.

Adam followed the tracks around. To everyone's surprise, the tracks turned and led back down another path to the water.

"Well that's a nuisance," Eve said.

"Let's cut some thorns and block it," Fish suggested. "Make them take the channel we want. Goats can't be any smarter than fish."

Monkey bapped the back of Fish's head. "They can't be any smarter than Fish, either."

"Right," said Adam. "No smarter than fish." He had them reinforce the walls of the trap. He helped Monkey set down canes along the ground while Fish and Bev made more uprights. Twig and Eve tied the horizontal poles to the vertical canes. After working all morning, Adam acknowledged that no single cane could be pulled out of the soft dirt, without pulling out all of them, and no two canes could be pried apart.

At noon, Adam led a hungry gang back to camp. After collecting food and eating, they spent the rest of the day swimming. There was nothing else to do but wait. It had been a good day. Adam felt he made up for his poor management the day before, and for letting the goats elude him.

The gang sat on the bank of the pool eating dinner as the water fell and the sun set. The sky was a deep red. The girls could talk about nothing else. They, Adam figured, were right, it was impressive—even if the setting sun didn't exactly take his breath away.

"This is wonderful," Eve declared, looking right at him. "I wish we could always be happy like this. Sometimes I wish nothing would ever change."

The other girls nodded their heads in agreement. Adam did not share her nostalgia. He had big plans for the future, and he was impatient to get on with them. He planned to lead the tribe some day. Then Eve would show him the same respect she showed her father. That was his plan, even if it was going to take a lot of effort to get there. When he glanced at Fish and Monkey they had wry expressions on their faces. Even Art gave him a little shrug. They probably had plans too. If they were smart they wouldn't get in his way.

"Well," he said. "I guess tonight if we don't figure out how to stay awake on watch, tomorrow there may be only seven of us instead of eight!" He looked directly at Fish.

"I didn't fall asleep, I mean—well—I am sure it must have been close to morning. I was up for most of the night," he mumbled.

"Riiight, Fish," Adam said to several chuckles. "So here is the new plan. If you're on watch, you have to walk back and forth—between that rock and that tree." Adam pointed. "You don't stop.

You don't sit down. And if you can't take another step, you wake the next person in line. Got it? This time I will take the first watch—age order, so Eve is next." She raised her eyebrows at that, but she didn't stop him to defend her claim to being older than him, like she usually did. There was no way to prove the point one way or another.

The new moon had waxed further and the shining crescent rose over the pool. As the others slept Adam walked and walked. The moon climbed over the water, and the night grew more haunting and more beautiful. His heart wanted to burst. He wondered if this was the feeling Eve spoke of earlier, of not wanting anything to ever change. His feet carried him over to where she slept. He bent over her sleeping form. "Eve," he whispered, shaking her shoulder gently.

Her eyes opened and she looked up at him. Her blue eyes were pale gray in the moonlight. "My turn already?" she whispered. "What's it been? Three trips back and forth?"

"Very funny." He pointed to the moon. "Come, I want to show you something."

"What? The moon?"

"More than just the moon. It is a perfect moon." He walked her out to the spot he had found on the beach.

She grabbed his arm. "Oh Adam, it's the most beautiful thing I have ever seen."

Her warm hand on his arm felt good—but was quite distracting. "I could have stayed up longer," he said. "But the moon got right here, with the mist from the falls glowing. I had to wake you," he said, feeling awkward.

Eve squeezed his arm before letting go. "That was sweet of you. Maybe there is hope for you after all."

He had the sudden desire to just grab her, and to throw her in the water, but a little voice of reason in his head advised restraint. "Feel like a swim?" he blurted instead. That also seemed like a dangerous thing to say, and Adam was about to retract the question when she glanced in the direction of the sleeping gang.

"Just the two of us?" she asked. Her eyes glowed in the moonlight.

"Sure, we can go over to the private beach you girls used." Adam snatched her hand. A clear vision formed in his mind of exactly what he wanted to do with her.

To his surprise, she accepted his hand and walked with him. *Is this really happening?*

He knew what he wanted, but he wasn't sure how he should go about it. Doubts crept in as they arrived at the beach. His heart began to pound. Everything was perfect save for his courage.

"You go first," Eve said, letting go of his hand. She turned her back to him. "I won't look."

*Oh no!* he thought. This wasn't the plan at all. As he undressed, Adam realized how unfair the differences between the sexes were. Even by moonlight, his *intentions* could be clearly seen, protruding in front of him. But what was Eve thinking? What were her intentions? Was she teasing him as usual?

He started toward her, her hair radiant, fringed in silver but stopped in sudden shock. He was struck by a vision of her turning toward him, looking down and pointing in disgust and laughing. *What is* this *about? What are you thinking?* Yuck! *Get out of here!*

His initial confidence shattered, he hurried down the bank and entered the cool refreshing water. "I'm in," he called, treading water silently and slowly moving further out. He faced her, never breaking the surface with his hands.

"I'm coming," she said and turned and looked at him in the water.

She hung her clothes on a bush, all the while facing him. Adam smiled, hoping she was smiling too. Then she walked slowly out into the water. She hadn't told him not to look, but maybe she thought he was looking away. Maybe she couldn't see his head in the water. Or maybe she saw him looking—and had undressed for him anyway?

*I should turn away*, he thought as she neared the water, but he couldn't. He tried but couldn't. She was the most beautiful thing he had ever seen, and her stepping out into the sparkling water was a vision better than any he'd ever imagined.

With a splash, she was in and swimming toward him. *Now what?* Adam thought. If he touched her now, he wasn't sure he would be able to stop.

# A State of Confusion

From what Eve had observed of men, romance probably wasn't on Adam's mind. However romantic a swim would be, she was sure romance was not a part of his plan. When he first spoke to her, and asked her to swim, it was the most wonderful thing she could possibly imagine. And she followed along.

Now, she wondered what she had just agreed to do. A vision of Fish's sister's protruding stomach flashed into her mind. Panic followed. That would not happen to her!

*Fortunately, I thought quickly.* She had sent him into the water alone. But when she turned and saw him out in the moonlit water, waiting for her. She again felt herself caught up in the moment. She undressed slowly, facing him, and carefully hung up her clothes, then walked into the water, picking her steps slowly, knowing he was watching. She enjoyed being the object of his desire. She swam towards him, wondering what she should do now.

Maybe she wouldn't get pregnant. *Maybe just this once,* she thought, but remembered all the births she had seen. The screams of the mother, the emergence of the baby—and the afterbirth. *No!* That must not happen to her. How unfair was the lot of women. Men had all the fun, and women bore all the babies.

"Race you to the falls," Eve said, in what she hoped sounded to him like a playful, innocent voice. Eve had to stop this without hurting him.

She dove beneath the water, and swam by the cool moonlight. The swim cleared her head. Underwater the falls thundered in her ears. The flow of bubbles over her body felt like she was floating on air. Beating Adam to the falls, she started back. He intercepted her. They stopped and drifted with the current. Each held the other's shoulder, kicking just enough to stay afloat. Adam had a dangerous smile on his face.

"You are very beautiful," he said.

## What Must Be Said

He had said it. Now he could think of nothing else to say. Eve looked into his eyes. It was a warm, loving look, but then her visage hardened. "I'm sorry, Adam, I really am. I can't. I just can't have a baby now. I'm not ready. I have too much to do. It would ruin everything. It's not you; it's me."

Water dripped from her hair but there were tears in her eyes. He reached over and pulled a wisp of hair from her face. "It's okay," he said, feeling as conflicted as she looked. "I understand. It's complicated. I can wait." Pulling her close, he kissed her. Her energy seemed to enter him and coursed through his body as they both drew closer. Adam forgot to kick, and they bobbed below the water. They came up spluttering and laughing.

Eve broke away. "Look, it's my watch," she said. "You head back and get some sleep. I will swim around a bit more and then stand watch."

She gave him a quick kiss, then dove deep and headed toward the falls.

Adam turned away and swam back ashore. He dressed with an eye to the water, but Eve was gone from view, virtually invisible in the rougher waters.

Back on his mat, he lay down. He stared up at the stars. Wrapped in thoughts, he had mixed feelings. He was disappointed because his advance had not succeeded, but he was thrilled he had not been fully rejected, only postponed. He was a man now. He had kissed Eve; and it had been amazing.

He smiled as he drifted off to sleep.

## A Secret

Returning to shore, Eve wiped herself off and dressed, thinking she had better hurry. There was beauty here, but the goat-killer was still out there somewhere. It had been dangerous for her and Adam to leave the gang unguarded so long. Dressed, but still a bit chilled, she headed for the pace tree to begin her walk, back and forth. The swim had helped clear her mind, but with each step she grew less sure, less content with her decision.

Had she done the right thing? Would Adam wait? Would some other girl take him away from her now? How long could she hold out? The non-speaking girls were more than willing, any time, any place. And they pursued Adam relentlessly ever since the gang provided the axes.

*What is wrong with me?* Eve knew Bev would have done it with Adam. Twig would have too, she figured. What was so special about her that she alone could say no? Despite her disquiet she was thrilled at the romance of the night. Adam had taken her teasing and rejection like no man of the tribe would have. The kiss had been amazing. *Why didn't I just go with the moment?*

Eventually Eve woke Twig. She had to tell someone. "Promise to never tell a soul and I'll tell you a secret," Eve said as they walked together.

"I promise." The two of them walked back and forth until she had explained all her feelings and concerns. "Wow," Twig said. "That is so romantic I cannot even imagine it." She lifted her shirt. "Undressing in the moonlight under the passionate gaze of my lover." Twig laughed and dropped her shirt. "That will never happen to me. An ugly girl can dream, right?"

"You aren't ugly, Twig," Eve said. "But the real question is, did I do the right thing by saying no?"

"I suspect you are the first woman of the tribe to ever say no to such an opportunity. So, yes, that makes you special." Twig laughed. "Stupid, but special." When Twig finally stopped laughing,

Eve was almost in tears. "I'm sorry, I shouldn't tease. Yes, I am sure you did the right thing," Twig said. "I agree in my head with you, but I doubt I would have been strong enough to have said no. But with this body, I doubt that test is one I will ever have to face. But the real question is what will Monkey do when he finds out?" Eve gave Twig a hug. "Oh, Twig, you are very beautiful, and your day will come. And, thank you, for being my best friend. As for Monkey, don't worry. He wont find out," Eve said, though she worried he and Adam would fight again if he ever did find out. She yawned. "I am tired. I think I better go to bed now. Good night, and thanks for the talk." Eve found her spot next to Adam and curled up. She was asleep in moments.

The next morning, it was another beautiful day, and the gang was excited, happy, if a bit tired. Each had taken their turn on watch. Eve was sure she had a silly, love-struck look on her face, but none seemed to notice her buoyant mood, not even Twig or Adam. Or if they did, they refrained from making comment.

Eve thought Adam looked pleased with himself. He kept them from charging off to check the trap. "Food first, today." While they ate, Eve kept glancing at him, but he acted as if nothing had changed.

After breakfast, the gang headed out to go check the trap. Goats had tracked through the open trap on their way to the water and back. Fish was ecstatic. But not Art. "Another day working on the gauntlet?" he asked morosely.

"Well, we need to put the top and the doors on," Adam said. "And the trigger mechanism to swing them closed." By late afternoon, the trap was mostly working.

Four out of five times when Little Red crawled through the bamboo tunnel, Fish's trick-doors trapped him inside. It would have to do. They swept clean the path and headed back to camp.

By the time they found food and ate, it was dark. Eve curled up on her mat and wondered what might happen when Adam woke her for her watch.

## Night Terror

*I have to make things normal again,* Adam thought as he walked back and forth. He occasionally thumped the end of his spear on the ground in frustration. When the moon finally rose, he had yet to think what to say to Eve when he woke her. He had told her he would wait but suspected one night wasn't what she had in mind. Plus, a distance had opened up between them, like they weren't the same kind of friends anymore. He had liked the way they had competed in the past, the way they teased each other. He enjoyed the friendly back-and-forth. Now it was gone.

All day they had avoided talking to each other, not knowing what to say, but he had seen her glancing his way. *You still have to find the right thing to say,* he told himself when he noticed the moon had moved. He had done more than his share on watch. He walked over and gently woke Eve.

"Hi," she said, smiling up at him in the moonlight.

He walked with her away from the others, running through the speech in his mind. "Eve," he said, jumping to the best part. "Last night was incredibly special and I will always remember it, but if we plan to wait, I hope we can enjoy just being friends like we have always been." *There, done.* He let out a sigh of relief. That hadn't been too bad, and he got it out of the way without messing any of it up.

"Of course," she said with a laugh, "And we can even be special friends—when no one is looking."

Hand-in-hand, they walked along the shore for a while. It felt good. It felt natural, the way things should be. The soft moonlight made Eve seem more than real, like an amazing extension of himself, or he, her. This was something new, something their parents did not do. He took her in his arms and kissed her again, this time without almost drowning.

Suddenly the night was shattered by a death cry coming from the direction of the trap. Adam and Eve both froze and focused on the source of the sound. Snarls and the panicked sound of bleating split the night.

"The goats?" Eve cried.

"Get everybody!" Adam yelled and sprinted, spear in hand, toward the cage. As he ran Eve shouted over the snarls to the gang.

The door of the trap facing the lake was down. Goats were trapped inside. The sound of their terrified and frantic noises rose the hair on the back of Adam's neck. Yet it was the leopard, snarling as it batted at the far cage-door which filled his stomach with icy dread. The beast struggled to disentangle an injured goat from the door.

Suddenly its huge luminous eyes stared at Adam, and he froze, his spear a well-rooted tree beside him. The large cat hissed and again batted the door. The door swung in as the frustrated cat tried to rip the goat out. But the door was hinged on top and only swung inward—so the trapped goats could not escape. The cat snarled and showed its huge teeth. The rest of the gang arrived, and pressed forward. As their numbers grew, the leopard perhaps decided it was time to claim its kill. It lunged forward and pushed the door open with its head. It sunk its teeth into the goat and ripped it out, twisting and smashing the door. A brief moment later the leopard and goat were gone, vanished into the night.

"Did you see that?" Fish said.

"Did you see those eyes?" Twig cried.

Adam shuddered. "And how about those teeth?"

The remaining goats moved toward the broken gate. *Baaa,* they bleated. Suddenly, Fish clambered over the top of the cage, and secured the broken door, glancing nervously over his shoulder as he worked.

"Wait. Don't we want to let them out?" Monkey said as Fish finished pinning the broken gate with the leftover canes.

"Why would we let them go?" Adam and Eve asked at the same time. They shared a look and a smile.

"Didn't you see that thing?" Monkey asked. "Those teeth were huge. It's claws—it's going to be back for more goats and maybe a few of us—one little goat isn't going to satisfy it."

"Exactly," Twig said.

"So we can kill it?" Eve asked. "Wasn't that the plan?"

Bev turned and stepped closer to look at Monkey. "You're not afraid are you?" she asked over the bleating of the goats.

"No, not at all. I'm just being cautious."

"Maybe we should take these goats back to the village," Eve said. "They won't believe their eyes."

"Good idea," Twig said, "We should really get out of here."

"We did not come here to run away," Adam said, not wanting to lose his leadership over the hunt. "I think we should keep them. We can take them back to the village in the morning, but we better have two of us standing guard here all night. The rest should be ready to spring into action if the leopard comes back."

"I guess we can just sleep here on the shore," Eve said cautiously, her voice barely audible over the goats. *Baaa.*

"Yes," Adam agreed. "That way we can be sure to protect our prize."

"I'll tell you what a real prize would be," Eve said. "The leopard's fur. A cloak made of it would be amazing."

"Good luck with that," Fish said.

He and Adam stayed and guarded the cages while the others retrieved their things. In their cage, the goats continued their noisy protest. *Baaa!*

After moving the campsite to the beach next to the trap, it became clear no one was going to get much sleep. The goats bleated incessantly all night long.

By morning, Adam was ready to kill the goats himself. He had the gang make harnesses and collars and a short leash for each of the goats, which turned out to be one mother and two nursing kids. After several false starts, eventually they were able to walk the mother goat around and the kids stayed close, their leashes superfluous. Fish took them to the water and they drank. At last the bleating stopped. Adam had Fish tie the doors of the trap open, so it could be used again, and then they set off on the long walk home.

On the way home Adam tried not to think about the dangerous predator who could be watching them right then, waiting to spring. The fact that he was walking along with its prey didn't mean he couldn't actually be prey himself.

When he and Eve fell a little behind, he—in a hushed tone—explained his misgivings to her. She laughed. "It's nothing my father can't take care of."

Adam's feelings for Eve's father were mixed. It was clear she thought the world of Blue Eyes, but was that because he was her father. Or because he was the chief? Adam felt Eve placed far too much faith in the man, but Eve had missed the whole point. It was not about Blue Eyes or killing the leopard. "But what else is out here?" he asked. "They could be climbing into our valley right now?"

Eve stopped, a sudden look of horror on her face. "Do you think we let a leopard in? The ladder has been up this whole time."

"I think it is unlikely."

"Ah, yeah, and even if one did get in, it would be alone and not be able to make more. Two would have to find their way in."

With the rest of the gang out of sight, Eve took Adam's hand as they resumed walking. He smiled over at her. "Oh, Adam. I am so eager to explore further, to discover the truth. How can I think about anything else when we keep learning that outside our little valley there are so many amazing things."

Adam considered her words. "You mean others like *us* maybe?" he asked.

"Oh, yes," Eve said. "I'm so glad you understand. How could I sit around my cave having babies when I don't know what is out here. I want you with me—I can't imagine leaving the valley any other way, but *us*—you know—that kind of *us*, will have to wait."

Adam felt his heart sink. There were many things he could imagine, not the least of which were the big teeth of the leopard. He honestly had no desire to see those again. But he wasn't prepared to give up on winning Eve. If she wanted to explore then he promised himself he would lead the way. Monkey could have her over his dead body—a likelihood out here, one he tried to ignore as he puzzled out how to lower the stupid goats down the ladder.

*If some animals are good at hunting and others are suitable for hunting, then the Gods must clearly smile on hunting.*

Aristotle.

# The Big Hunt     10

Outside the treehouse window, dark clouds threatened heavier rain. The wet season had arrived again. The gang had just made it under cover before the first drops began to fall. Adam turned from the window and sat, joining the group on the floor. It had been a year since they had first discovered the bigger world, and he felt pleased with the progress they'd made. "This year we finished the treehouse, trapped goats, and watched them grow and multiply—"

Fish held up a leather bag full of fresh goat milk. "And discovered how to milk them," he said smugly as he took a drink.

Adam continued. "Yes and milked them. We have also made new weapons—better weapons." His first spear he had replaced with a more balanced one of Eve's design. "And still we have yet to see a leopard or any other new animal. None made it into our valley." The gang began to talk all at once about how vicious and dangerous they were. Adam quieted them with a raised hand.

Lowering his hand, he was about to continue when Art made a fuss. "Hey don't guzzle, Fish. Pass it," Art said. The goat's milk had been a hit not only with the gang but with the rest of the tribe.

"Yeah, we all feed them," Bev said. "Share and share alike."

"None of you cared about tasting the milk. You would never have thought of drinking it if it weren't for me," Fish declared stubbornly, continuing to drink.

Adam felt his hackles rising and glanced at Eve. She gave him a knowing smile and winked. "Now, Fish," she said. "We all helped, and all like it, so be nice and share." She flashed him a winning smile and Fish relented, handing over the skin.

Adam shook his head. Nobody could say no to Eve, it seemed. "The tribe likes it too and I have noticed them helping with the feeding. Not all are interested in eating them now." Adam said. "We will have to share with them too."

"The old girls pregnant, I think," Fish said, warming to his favorite topic, a white mustache on his face. "She is looking fat—we'll have more little ones and more milk soon."

"Getting back to what I was saying," Adam said, not letting Fish distract him. "If we are going to go out into the wilds above, we should do it as soon as the rains stop. The prairie will be green then, and there will be plenty of water to drink. But—" He raised a finger. "—we are going to need to be prepared." He began listing everything they would need, starting with food for a week. He did his best to make the task sound both dangerous and difficult, almost hoping Eve would decide against going hunting in the dangerous highlands above the crack.

It wasn't that he was afraid. *I am just being smart.* It was dangerous up there, and there was nothing they needed from there. But as Adam looked around at their eager faces, especially Eve's, he could see they would not be dissuaded. They all had good axes, and many had spears, and Adam found that, for the most part, they felt overly confident they could deal with any danger. The gang was restless and eager to go. He would have to lead them.

"Plus some good ladders for the whole way up," piped Monkey at the end of his list.

"Good. Yes, ladders, especially since we'll be carrying meat back. And speaking of meat, we need to learn how to hunt big game. I am serious about reviewing our weapons. These new weapons are only useful if we learn to use them." There were several groans in the group as some began to complain, but Eve nodded approvingly. "Okay," he said. "Getting back to the upcoming hunt, the plan is to go after the big game. So, weapons training, and enough food for a week—"

"Speaking of big game, maybe we should practice more with spears," Eve said, looking at the array of new ones stacked in the corner.

Eve had worked out the details of their improved design. She had made them much like Adam's spear, except with the flint blade more securely mounted at the end of a lighter shaft. They were for throwing. The axes were only for chopping down bamboo or defending themselves. The smaller knives each of them carried were for cutting and butchering. The spears were actually pretty easy to make compared to an ax, and Adam lifted the one she had made for him, balancing it in his hand proudly, then jabbing it at an imaginary beast in the corner.

"I made them to be thrown," Eve said. "I know it is harder to learn to throw, but if we run into something fierce, we may not want to walk right up to it." She demonstrated how to hold the spear for throwing, hefting one over her shoulder.

Adam hefted his own the same way. *Might work*, he conceded to himself. He personally preferred the idea of stabbing at arm's length. It gave him more power, and more control.

But Eve had a point. "Every break in the rain, I want to see everyone practicing throwing spears and play fighting. Our accuracy could mean life or death," he said, knowing that he would end up practicing twice as much as any of them. He had to be the best.

Monkey lifted his axe off the floor where he had it next to his reed mat. "I don't need to spear nothing! I'm going to sink my axe into the head of that monster that came for me."

Twig scoffed. "Gah! Anything," she corrected him. "I don't need to spear *anything*. And we are calling the beast that bit you a hyena."

"And besides speaking like a child, you throw a spear like one too," Adam snapped.

"It's dumb to waste time fooling around practicing," Monkey complained. "We are ready to take on anything that might come along." Monkey stared Adam in the eye—as if daring him.

Adam growled under his breath and pointed in the direction of the skull. Someone, probably Art, had mounted it on the wall in the treehouse.

"So you are ready for anything? That beast will fight back, and make your little hyena look like a goat," Adam said. "Our accuracy with spears could mean life or death and none here want to die, do they?" There was no more complaining about practice. The skull did look like it came from a beast which would fight back—and savagely.

"There's only one more thing," Eve said. "We have to tell my father where we are going when we leave."

"What? No!" Adam said, confused. "This is our hunt. There is no reason why your father needs to know anything about it."

"He's the leader of the tribe, and nobody does anything without his permission," Eve insisted.

"We did last year," Monkey piped up.

"That was different. This is a real trip."

"But, but . . . " Adam glanced around at the gang. None of them wanted to help him. Not with Eve giving off her most serious, *don't cross me*, look.

"We'll talk about this later," he said, not wanting to tell her no again, not out right, not in front of the gang.

Their relationship had grown since their time at the falls and the look in her blue eyes was dark as any rain cloud. "Yes, of course, we'll talk more about it—later," Eve said, ending the discussion.

As the time to leave on the hunt grew closer, the gang made leather shoes, bags for food, and new belts to hold their axes—among many other smaller accouterments—but the issue of telling Blue Eyes remained.

Adam had not been able to persuade Eve to accept his plan concerning the rest of the tribe. Most of the gang agreed with him, they also wanted to just up and leave one morning. But Eve felt the tribe should be told where they were going, her father in particular. She refused to budge from that position. He tried to reason with her. The gang were all adults by the tribe's reckoning. Eve argued back that no member of the tribe, no matter their age, acted alone. And her father was still the leader. She insisted he could not be ignored.

The day they set for departure neared; Adam pondered the problem. Finally, on the night before he pulled Eve aside. "I have a plan," he said confidently. "We will go up the ladders, and wait for you. Then you can go and tell your father we are planning to take a one-week hunting trip. This way we fulfill our obligation to the tribe—without risking anyone trying to stop us." Adam looked at Eve and held his breath.

"That works," she said. She didn't raise any new objections. So, with no more disagreements, his plan would be the one they went with. He was delighted with her agreement. This trip was already successful. In his mind victory was already won—Eve would soon be his.

But as he headed home that evening, his last night in the safety of his family's cave, Adam tried to ignore the images of all the terrible things that could happen and the untold problems the morning might bring. This whole expedition, he knew, could quickly get out of hand. In the dark, he could hear Twig's consistent warning to never leave the valley.

## The Day of the Hunt

Eve met the gang outside the caves in the clearing. They were charged with excitement.

"We'll wait for you up top," Adam said to her as she bent over each of their packs, checking their supplies again. "It will be okay, Eve, I'll personally take your pack up there for you, so you can run fast if you need to." Adam looked up. "And we'll be careful."

Eve took his hand; she did not want to fight with him, and was touched and amused by his worry. "This is the right thing to do, Adam," she said, squeezing his hand. She turned and ran back into the cave without another word. This was a new kind of compromise. She hoped to be leader some day, but she suspected Adam and Monkey did too. This time neither lost. Both she and Adam were satisfied. It might be the start of something new. Monkey on the other hand had kept growing and was clearly the biggest of them now. He practiced endlessly with his weapons, and often ran to the beach and back, just to bring her a shell or colored rock. He was not romantic and sensitive like Adam, but he was gaining power out of sheer strength. She didn't want to admit it to herself, but it scared her.

In the cave, her father was eating and Eve decided to wait until he was finished. That would give Adam time enough for his head start. The moment gave her time to consider the gang's pact to avoid the tribe's preoccupation with mating—at least the girl's pact. It had somehow held all year, but Eve knew it would not last. She feared all she was doing by maintaining her distance from Adam was fighting destiny.

At last her father finished eating his breakfast, and she approached. He nodded at her, perhaps sensing something was on her mind. His normally empty eyes sparkled with understanding as Eve explained. It was almost as if he had known this day would eventually come, as if it too had been preordained.

He nodded as she spoke, even when she made gestures to the cliff. When she finished her explanation, her father was still nodding. He stood up from his reed mat. Fruit rinds and peels scattered as he walked over to the axe she had made for him. He picked it up and stomped out of the cave.

*What on earth?* Eve wondered at his strange reaction. She hurried outside to see where he was going.

Outside, her father sounded the hunt, like Eve never heard him sound it before. *Chaw-hooo! Chaw-hooo! Chaw-HAA!* It made the hair on her arms stand on end. She hurried to catch up with him, surprised to see the older men and women come running from the caves. The men and half the older women carried weapons. She saw the look of fear in many of their eyes.

*Oh, no,* Eve thought. *I must have gotten it all wrong. Does he think we are under attack?*

Blue Eyes shook his head no to most of the men and to all the women. All but three men he sent away, disappointed. Those he picked showed no fear at all. They brandished their axes as if they relished the chance to use them. When her father pointed towards the cliff they only nodded.

Adam's father was one, as was Twig's and Fish's. They all grinned at each other, seemingly pleased to have been picked. They quickly followed her father, who was already heading across the clearing.

Eve ran to catch them.  She needed to explain to them this was not their hunting trip, but Adam's.  The four had their axes but no other preparations; they did not look back or make an attempt to say goodbye to anyone.

The last look her mother had given Eve was a sad, knowing smile.  She seemed okay that her husband had just walked away without even a goodbye embrace.  Eve still resented her years of abuse, but she was working to forgive, to excuse the ignorance and mostly she worked to not end up the same way.  She rushed to her, and gave her a hug, then ran to catch her father.  She needed to explain to them what was happening.

Her father and his men had stopped and were waiting for her at the far edge of the clearing.  Her father waved her forward.  In frustration Eve again explained that just the gang was going, but Blue Eyes and the hunters ignored her complaints, and made it equally clear that they were coming no matter what.

Her father motioned her to lead the way as if he expected this day would come for some time.  He was clearly not as ignorant as he acted.  Eve always knew she had been right about that, but she worried what Adam would say.

As they hiked towards the crack, Eve wondered about the horrible skull, and at the scars so clear on these four men coming with her.  Many in the tribe had them, but these four had the most, especially scars on their faces and arms.

As they neared the cliff, Eve realized her father didn't look like the man she knew, the man who spent his days eating and chasing other women when her mother wasn't looking. He led the three men with confidence. They also moved with confidence and strength. Her father looked taller, prouder than Eve had ever seen him before. His blue eyes flashed with an inner strength, a knowing. Surely, he knew well the dangers that had nearly killed Monkey, and if Eve was right, those same dangers had nearly killed him and the others.

He did not look afraid, nor eager, like Adam's father did. Nor was he cocky like Twig's and Fish's. Her father instead possessed a stalwart calm. More than once Eve caught him stroking his long beard. Or hefting his huge axe. Seeing him leading his warriors, Eve could not quite place the feeling she had, more respect perhaps, but she had always respected her father even when breaking his edicts. This feeling was something more like pride mixed with relief.

Imperturbable as he was, Eve was pleased to see a touch of surprise from him and amazement on his face when he saw the ladder set up on the cliff face. He was more surprised at the platform she had made to span the ledge, a ledge she suspected he worked hard to destroy.

This was the moment Eve had been waiting for. She suspected this would be his first look at this forbidden land after a long time. As she climbed the final ladder, she beheld the vast land Monkey had so accurately described; it seemed bigger than it had last year. Grass stretched to the horizon. Eve breathed deep and tried to shake the feeling of smallness as she pulled herself up and out of the crevice. Then her father and his men appeared.

Up top, her father also took a deep breath and let it out slowly, a content expression on his face. *As I guessed,* Eve thought. This was a part of him. The gang was off exploring nearby, and when they saw her and the warriors, they came, Adam at the head.

"It's okay," Eve said. "They're coming with us."

Adam acknowledged his father, and Twig and Fish nodded to theirs. "Why are they here?" Adam asked Eve quietly.

"I think they knew our plans all along—they were ready to go. Can't you see it. Look at them. This is where they come from, where we all come from. I can only imagine they must have missed it. Who knows? But, they know the dangers up here. They clearly survived it."

Recognition dawned on the gang, and Adam alone seemed bothered.

## Adam's Hunt

Adam did not know quite what to make of these new additions to his hunt. He worried Blue Eyes would try to take charge. *Look at 'em.* Each of the old men had only an axe. No food, no nothing. *At least I'm prepared*, he told himself. He figured he was still in charge and would be as long as he continued to do a good job. *Just don't lose the initiative now.*

He gathered his courage and turned. "Let's move out. We go west," he said suddenly. *I can't get lost if we go due west.* He didn't wait for anyone to say more. He headed out, making those who had set down their packs retrieve them and catch up—everyone but Monkey and the older men. They hurried along on Adam's heels.

Monkey stomped alongside Adam, his axe at the ready. "Why west, not north like last time?" he asked as they marched away from the sun.

"Because I said so," Adam told him not glancing over to his sometimes friend, sometimes competitor. He didn't want to be seen looking back despite being half-afraid the others weren't following. He worried if he did, Eve's father or one of the older men would try to challenge him.

Only when he was certain he'd heard everyone's voice behind him, did Adam dare to steal a glance back. The group had fallen in line. Blue Eyes led his men alongside the gang, while still staying behind Adam. *I'm the leader of the hunt.* Adam breathed a sigh of relief. The adventure was properly underway, and he was leading it.

"See," Monkey said of the first set of strange prints they found in a bit of mud near a stagnant pool. "I told you: monsters."

Monsters or not, the grass was green and fresh. Still water stood in low spots in the ravines they crossed. Amazingly, just like their last visit, there were no animals; Monkey had made this place sound full of creatures.

But for that and each set of prints they came to, one of the older tribesmen acted out the animal that made them, what they looked like and how they acted. The whole gang laughed hysterically when Blue Eyes' lion chased around a squealing Art. *These guys,* Adam thought, shaking his head. *They know everything.* The fear and apprehension he had felt for the last few weeks melted away. He and the gang were on a hunt with the tribe's most experienced hunters.

By dusk, the hunting party spotted a herd of grazing beasts—so many no one even tried to count them all. Adam led the group into a ravine to spend the night. In the morning the hunt would begin in earnest. There was no fresh meat yet, but Adam felt the first day had gone well.

The hunters seemed surprised when the gang began pulling out food. Blue Eyes motioned for everyone to follow him. He led them up the ravine. He and the other men showed the gang which of the various plants they found were edible. Common in the ravine was a whole section of dandelions with their bright yellow flowers. As kids Adam had liked to pick the flowerhead when it went to seed and blow the seeds off and watch them drift with the wind. Blue Eyes pulled up the plants, and wiping the dirt off the root, he ate them, flowers, greens, roots and all. Some of the plants he selected actually tasted good. Others Adam thought tasted disgusting, but he paid close attention anyway.

"The ability to eat off the land might mean the difference between life and death someday," Twig said.

"I think I will take death," Art said. "Better than having to eat more dandelions."

Adam just wanted a lighter pack. "You'll eat it and you will like it if you are starving," he said.

"Nah," Monkey said. "I think I am with Art on this one." He made a face as he chewed. Bits of the bitter dandelion greens dribbled out of his open mouth. "Gah! So yummy I think I am going to puke."

As darkness fell, Blue Eyes and the hunters prepared a safe place against the dirt bank. Laying down, they motioned for the gang to pack in tight. Adam pushed Little Red to lay down first; the rest of the gang followed him until there was little room for him and Eve. He crawled in and Eve crawled in next to him. She laid her head on his shoulder as Adam had seen his mother do on so many occasions with his father.

The gang and the others fell asleep nearly instantly. The men snored as he and Eve talked in low tones as they stared up at the stars.

"We should take a little walk," Adam finally said. Talk was one thing, but he wanted Eve so badly he felt like he might explode.

"Why?" Eve asked him. "We shouldn't even be talking; we need to sleep. We need to be rested for tomorrow."

"I want you, Eve," Adam replied. "It's been almost a year, and I have waited patiently."

"What? Now? Not now, not here, not like this."

"But why not? It's perfect."

"It's not perfect." Eve then explained the whole situation to him, yet again. Celibacy was the only way for her to avoid becoming pregnant. "If we have a successful hunt, then we can talk about this again. For now, just hold me."

"Okay," he said and held her, but his ache did not go away even though Eve changed the subject.

"What a blessing it is to have the hunters along," she said.

Adam didn't disagree. And it did make him wonder something. Perhaps something like this was a rite of passage, some part of the tribe's culture when they lived by the hunt.

"If our fathers came from here, they must have hunted like this with their own fathers. Don't you think?" he asked. He turned his head to look at Eve when she didn't reply. She was asleep.

Soon Adam's arm was numb. *I bored her to sleep,* he thought ruefully, not knowing what to do about his trapped arm. Wake her? That sounded like a bad idea, so he was careful not to move. But the numbness in his arm grew intolerable. *I have a lot to learn about this whole mate thing.* Eve's eyes, her touch, even her words inflamed him.

Adam didn't know how much longer he could fight his desires. Out here in the wild, all this talk of celibacy felt remote, distant, and irrelevant.

Finally he eased his arm free of Eve's head and blood pounded back. *Life is good*, he told himself. He was on his first hunt, and if successful, when he and Eve arrived back in the valley, he would be a man and she would be his woman.

*I will make her my mate,* he told himself, but her words were not quite the promise he wished they were, and the scary thought of losing her saw him off to an uneasy sleep.

The next morning, after everyone had crawled from the makeshift shelter, they ate the food the gang passed around. Blue Eyes sketched in the dirt with a stick. He placed pebbles in and around the sketching, then he dropped a handful of flower petals from over his head so they wafted away in the almost windless morning stillness. He pointed to himself and everyone, and motioned that they would take a downwind approach.

Art was the first to make sense of the sketch and pebbles. "This line is the ravine. And the pebbles are the herd. But why the flower petals? Who cares what the wind is doing?"

"The beasts must be able to smell us coming," Adam said, sniffing the air. Blue Eyes nodded. Adam gave him a thankful nod back. "So we definitely need to approach downwind."

Blue Eyes made a new sketch in the dirt. He used pebbles to show how the party should fan out, and how the herd would run. The plan was to cut off a laggard from the herd and kill it.

The party moved out of the ravine. The herd of wild beasts had moved further away in the night. Their party spent most of the morning circling, patently getting closer and closer, all the while making sure they stayed downwind.

When they stopped close to the herd, Adam explained to the gang how he expected things to go, how the wildebeests would run when they spotted them, and how he expected them to take out the laggards. He glanced at Eve and added, "I don't want any mistakes." His hunt had to go off without a hitch.

He turned; Adam's heart stopped—another hunter crept in the grass. A lion crouched in the green. It looked up at Adam. It pinned back its ears and glanced from him to the others, sizing them up. The deep growl froze Adam in place. *Rrrrgrr.*

Blue Eyes and his men leapt into action. They interlocked their arms like one and charged at the lion, themselves growling. *GraAAAH!* The lion turned, and sauntered off into the grass.

As his heartbeat returned to normal, Adam tried to understand what he'd just seen. "Ah, I see," he said at last. He put an arm around Eve and Fish. "Together, we look bigger. That is why the lion was afraid."

Blue Eyes nodded his head and motioned for everyone to stay low. As they resumed the hunt, Adam could not get over the initial look the lion gave him, its strange yellow eyes and huge teeth. The way it moved, so smooth, so in control had sent chills up his back. Yet it did move away, at least when it thought they were bigger. The casual way it wandered off, not afraid, just declining the fight. Smart, was what it was. There was no point to risk fighting a bigger competitor with such easy prey around to pick from.

Eve had been right to include their parents in their plans, and Adam felt thankful they had come along on his hunt. He suspected without them the lion might have killed one or all of them.

## Eve's Trial

Eve's father pointed to a single wildebeest grazing slightly apart from the rest of the herd. His hunters split into two groups and ran quietly to cut off the single beast from the rest of the herd. The gang spread out as the hunters converged on the wildebeest.

Suddenly, the beast started to run toward the herd, but then, realizing its way was blocked, turned back and headed in the other direction, right toward the gang who had fanned out to block such an escape. They were crouched, staying still so they appeared relatively benign. "Everyone stand!" Adam shouted.

The beast was enormous and Eve felt the ground shake as she stood. It was nothing like the small goats of the valley. The wildebeest paused, when it spotted them. Then making up its mind, it charged, hoofs pounding as it headed directly for Eve.

She froze, but off to her left, Adam ran with his spear raised over his shoulder ready to throw. The rest of the gang were running toward her from the right, but she knew they were too far away. The beast was charging her and it was moving far too fast for their help to arrive in time.

She wanted to run, but her feet seemed planted firmly in the ground. She drew back her spear, unclear where to aim. The spear felt heavy, unwieldy in her hands. She wasn't as good an aim as Adam. No one was.

Horns protruded from the beast's broad head. It reared, then lowered them as it pounded ahead. Eve drew back her spear, readied herself to throw it. *Or should I hold it in front of me? Should I switch to the axe?* She hadn't any idea where to aim.

"Die!" she screamed and hurled her spear. It arched smoothly through the air. The beast didn't waver as the spear hit it right between its eyes. The point stuck in the animal's thick hide. *Yes! A perfect shot,* Eve thought, relieved. Her relief quickly dissolved as the spear did nothing to slow the beast. With a shake of its massive head the spear flopped useless to the ground. It was just an irritant, nothing more. If anything, the beast charged faster.

Eve pulled out her axe. Then, waiting for death, she looked up. Adam, on her left, leapt forward and extended his whole body and hurled his spear toward the beast. His spear did not curve at all, but flew straight. It sank deep into the beast's side. To Eve's amazement, it also appeared to have no effect—the beast kept coming.

Eve swung back her axe, ready to strike. The beast chewed up the distance. Ten paces, five. She was certain she was dead, but suddenly the creature's front legs buckled and the beast crashed to the ground and skidded to a stop at her feet, its head in the dirt.

She swung her axe at the beast's hairy neck. "Die!" she cried as she swung, then swung her axe several more times. "Die you beast," she blubbered as tears streamed down her cheeks.

Suddenly, Adam was there stopping her axe with his hands over hers. She let go and wrapped her arms around his neck.

"Are you okay?" he asked her.

"You saved my life," she said. "My heart—"

"What about your heart?" Adam asked.

It pounded in her chest. She pulled Adam close and whispered in his ear. "It's yours."

When she finally pulled back, her crazy despair was replaced by relief. She was pleased to see a silly grin on Adam's face. Then the gang were all around them, slapping Adam on the back, congratulating him. When the older hunters arrived, they joined in the congratulations.

But the celebration was short-lived. Blue Eyes gave an approving nod to his daughter and plucked Adam's spear from the wildebeest's side. He gave the weapon an admiring look, then handed it back to Adam before pointing at the vultures already circling in the sky. There was no more time for congratulations. Blue Eyes pointed and motioned to the fallen beast, and hurried them to work. Her father's frantic pace made Eve uneasy. One brush with death was enough. She didn't need another. Putting away her axe, she pulled out her knife and helped with the task of skinning and gutting the carcass.

Soon vultures began landing. *How ugly*, Eve thought with a shudder. She hacked at the tough hide, ripping it off the carcass.

"Hyenas," Monkey screamed. "Hurry." He guarded the kill while the rest hacked it up. But Eve noticed something fanatical in his voice and watched as he drew back his spear and let it fly. "Die!" He growled as the spear hit its mark. He charged after it, retrieved his spear and stabbed it a few more times before returning to them. "That was long overdue."

"Everyone guard the kill," Adam ordered. He began hanging a huge hunk of meat over each of their shoulders as they stood, their backs to the carcass, staring down the ever growing range of beasts, all snarling and dodging the gang's lunging spear tips. As they finished, a number of hyenas, Monkey's monster, and other similar sized scavengers had joined the vultures and were all growing braver and braver, even with most of the gang occupied defending the kill, rather than cutting it up.

Blue Eyes suddenly looked around and indicated it was time to go. Laden with their prize, they ran for the trench where they had slept the night before. Behind them the scavengers made a terrific ruckus, as they moved in, fighting and tearing at the carcass. Eve couldn't believe they had done it, or that she was all in one piece. Their first hunt was a success. And not all the thanks went to her father. Much, Eve had to admit, rested with Adam.

*The chase ... cultivates that vigorous manliness for the lack of which in a nation, as in an individual, the possession of no other qualities can possibly atone.*

---

Theodore Roosevelt *(The Wilderness Hunter)*

# A Bigger World     11

As Eve's father was now making an effort to teach him, Adam finally saw the wisdom Eve so often talked about. The old man certainly knew how to survive out here in the wild. Adam couldn't deny it as he stared at the disgusting assortment of organs preserved during the rush of butchering. Blue Eyes sorted out all the best parts to eat, and had Adam pass them out to the group. His warriors nodded their respect to Adam, and he thought he understood the role of the tribe leader better: to provide food and women. He had seen it in the valley, but this was quite different out here on the hunt. It was more visceral.

Blue Eyes then put him and the others to work scraping the hide. The old man had scooped out the beast's brains, and Adam was afraid he would have to eat them too, but instead Blue Eyes rubbed them on the hide once it was clean, demonstrating that it made the leather soft. He then showed him how to cut the meat into thin strips and hang them to dry in the sun on a thorn bush. At dark, after gathering up all the half-dried meat and rolling it up neatly in the hide, Adam helped Blue Eyes bury it in the loose sand and gravel against the bank. Blue Eyes lay protectively on top of it. He closed his eyes. *I guess he is done for the night.*

Adam decided on two night-watchers. The scavengers were near, and he figured, even buried, the smell of the meat couldn't be missed.

"Get some sleep, Eve," he told her. "My father and I will take the first watch." Eve had been watching him all day. He could tell she wanted to talk; he wasn't ready.

"Are you sure you two can handle it out here in the wild?" she asked him, perhaps misreading his reluctance.

"We got this. Don't worry," he said, but was worried himself. His father was no Blue Eyes, and there would be creatures out at night, creatures he did not know, but the time he figured would allow him to firm up his plans with Eve.

The night was dark. The high clouds blocked the stars, and there was no moon. Adam could hardly see his hand in front of his face. He and his father watched the darkness, each with a spear held ready in hand. They paced back and forth around the sleepers

His mind had wandered far and wide by the time a thing from the darkness came at him without warning. He swung his weapon awkwardly from his hip and felt it connect. "Bloody bones, what was that? It almost had me," he gasped under his breath. His heart raced as if he had run to the valley and back.

The shape was gone, dissolved back into the slippery darkness as quickly as it had arrived. Adam's eyes darted from side-to-side. Then he stared into the darkness, pointing his spear at every imagined sound. A shadow moved. Just one at first, then more. The shadows circled just out of his range. His father stood with him, tense, but he didn't wake up Blue Eyes or the others.

*I guess we have this,* Adam thought. He lunged at the shadows when they came closer. He hit only air. His father lunged as well. The shadows leapt out of harm's way. If his father didn't see the need for them to get help, then neither did Adam. Besides, he told Eve he had this. It would be embarrassing to have to call Blue Eyes for help.

A sound behind him spun him around. One of the beasts had dashed in. It snapped at Little Red's foot. *Why on earth is his foot sticking out?* Adam wondered. With a leap and a stab, Adam dissuaded the beast. It ran off back into the night. Adam couldn't believe the gang was still asleep. But he had no more time to think. His father was lunging at another one of the canid animals. It yelped, but two others tried to sneak around him. Adam steeled himself, and gripped his spear tight, readying himself to take them both on. He stabbed one hard, but it ran off and the other turned back as well. And then they were gone. The full complement of shadows disappeared, melting back into the night.

Adam exchanged a smile with his father, and they resumed their patrol, alert and focused. But just when Adam thought he and his father had completely foiled the animals, another attack came, and with similar tactics. Adam wanted to just throw his spear and kill one, whatever they were, but he knew that would open an opportunity for the rest of the beasts to rush in. They circled, and circled, as they made their feints. Time passed. Adam's nerves began to fray.

With a low growl, a beast appeared in front of Adam from the gloom. As Adam lunged for it, he could see its eyes glowing red. He pulled back, terrified. *What evil is this?* he wondered. Several more approached, with red eyes glowing. More than anything in the world, he wanted to cry out for help, but stubborn pride held him back. He clamped his teeth together and stabbed at the red-eyed monsters. They became bolder, more determined. He could see the beasts more clearly now too. They were shaggy with bushy tails, and quick on their feet. Each had a mouthful of sharp teeth.

*What is going on?* He glanced at his father, who showed no acknowledgment of the change, but was busy defending.

"Die," Adam hissed as he stabbed out, fully focused on the agitated wolves as they stepped up the pace of their attacks.

"What is the evil glow in the sky?" Eve said. Her voice, tense and afraid, rang out behind him.

Adam's heart almost leapt out of his chest. He spun around and found Eve behind him, spear ready.

"Evil glow? You scared me half to death," he snapped and spun back to the wolves. He noticed now, on the horizon there was a glow in the sky. It was an orange-red flickering glow. It was far too early for dawn; of that Adam was sure.

Eve, now between him and his father, jabbed at a wolf. "Why didn't you wake us?" she said as another wolf darted in.

Adam lunged at it, driving it back. "This is what it means to keep watch up here, why wake you?" he replied.

Eve scoffed. "How long have they been here?"

"Since dark," Adam answered. "We aren't really in danger. They are quite cautious." He didn't explain how one would try to cause trouble on one side, and another would try to sneak in behind. "If they rushed us all at once, it would be over. But they don't."

Eve shook her head and he could see the orange in her eyes as she rolled them at him. "And the light?" she asked. "What is it?"

"I don't know," Adam said. He hadn't been able to think much about it other than it seemed ominous, the way day was struck in the middle of the night. "Fireflies?"

His father connected solidly with one of the wolves. It yelped and then they all suddenly disappeared, loping away into the strange-colored night.

Eve looked around. "That seems to have scared them off. You look done in. Let me have a turn and you can catch some sleep now."

Adam motioned to his father that it was time to change the guard. The old dog collapsed on the ground and was asleep in moments. Adam took up his father's spear and felt the tip.

"Wet, he got a good hit in on that last round. I wonder if we should go in pursuit?"

"Don't be silly," Eve retorted. "Now tell me about this strange glow."

"It just showed up not long ago. You better not do this alone," Adam said heading back to the group. "I will wake Twig to keep you company. Maybe she will have a theory about the orange glow, because I haven't a clue."

He woke Twig and all three talked softly, spears at the ready. With three spears spread over the perimeter, they were well protected, but the beasts did not come back.

Twig was very interested in the orange glow, now fading. Adam felt like plugging his ears, as she speculated endlessly and eliminated every possible cause she could think of and was still left clueless, not a state she could abide. She proposed an expedition to investigate but now even Eve squashed the idea.

Adam sleepily reminded them of the watch order and urged them to wake him up if the wolves came back. The sky was dark again and Adam lay down. He smiled to himself. He had impressed Eve with his confidence and bravery, and he could not help but enjoy seeing Twig clueless. It had been a good night.

He was delighted to see the sun when it finally welcomed him awake. Monkey reported that all had been quiet since he went to bed and had Adam repeat all the details of the wolf attack. He and Monkey circled the camp trying to find drops of blood from the beast Adam's father hit, but all they saw were their foot prints mixed with wolf prints. Those went in all directions, skirting the camp area.

"Find anything?" Eve asked when they climbed back down into the ravine.

"Nothing. No blood, and no sign."

Adam shrugged. After a quick breakfast, he announced that they would make another attack on the herd. Full of confidence, he led the hunting party west and was pleased to find the herd right where they had left it the day before. This time Adam repeated each step of the technique of the previous day, with much the same result, but he noticed, much to his satisfaction, Eve stood closer to him. All played out the same until the moment when the wildebeest they had isolated made its final decision of which way to run. This time instead of running toward Eve, it headed toward the herd—directly at Blue Eyes. To Adam's amazement Blue Eyes ran towards the beast himself.

Adam heard himself shout. "Run!" He pounded the earth, running as fast as he could towards Blue Eyes, and towards the storming wildebeest.

Adam had no idea what Blue Eyes was doing. Perhaps, after all the hours of stalking the man couldn't wait. Or maybe he just wanted to make sure he reached the beast first, so he could make the kill. Regardless of why, the old man ran directly toward the beast with his axe raised. At the last moment, he jumped to the side as his axe came down, striking the creature with a mighty blow. The wildebeest staggered, the axe sunk deep into its front shoulder.

But then the beast took off running, as Blue Eyes half-running, was dragged alongside.

"Let go," Adam shouted but Blue Eyes stubbornly hung on. Idiot. Finally, the beast stopped and swung its head at Blue Eyes. Adam could barely believe his eyes as Blue Eyes swung a leg over the beast's back. He let go of the axe and grabbed the creature around the neck. As the beast staggered and swung its head from side to side, Blue Eyes unsheathed his knife. He extended his arm under the beast's neck and slit its throat. The wildebeest took off again with Blue Eyes on its back. Blood frothed from its neck. Suddenly it staggered and fell, a triumphant Blue Eyes on top of it. The chase had outpaced the gang, but the whole party was in pursuit. Adam and Eve were the first to reach Blue Eyes. He lay sprawled next to the beast. He smiled warmly up at them as they approached. Blood flowed freely from an open gash on his side.

"He must have snagged a horn," Adam said. "Good thing it didn't get under the ribs." Eve didn't respond. She was on her knees next to her father, holding his hand, her face horror-stricken and tear-streaked. Blue Eyes motioned to the rest of the group, as they ran up, to get to work on the kill. Adam understood. Dangers yet lay ahead. "We need to get started," he shouted. "The scavengers will be here soon."

## New Opportunities

The gash on her father's chest was a hand long. Blue Eyes lay on the grass, his proud smile now a grimace of pain. Eve took Twig's arm as she stood. "You have got to fix him," she said.

Twig glanced at the carcass and the gathering vultures, then pulling off her pack, she squatted next to Blue Eyes. "This is perfect for me to try out my new needle and thread," she said excitedly.

Eve glared at the girl. "Twig, this is not the time for experimenting, just patch him up."

"We are a long walk from home. If I patch him up, he might die before we get there. He is as good as dead now. My new stitches could save him."

Eve fought the tears running down her cheeks. She hoped it wasn't as bad as Twig said. Twig would often get so focused on one of her ideas she would over do it. Eve hoped now wasn't one of those times. She watched Twig thread a fish bone needle with a thin thread. The needle was like the other needles they had made, only smaller. The hole in it was barely visible. Eve marveled how thin and delicate it was. "Just make sure you do it right," she said.

"Don't worry, I took some of that tough grass growing along the stream near the cave and scratched the fiber out with a sharp rock, dried it and wove it into this thread," Twig said as she prepared to make the first stitch. "It's not strong enough for clothing, but very fine and flexible and I think it will work well here."

"What can I do to help?"

"You can hold the skin together," Twig said. When Eve had prepared a spot, Twig tried to plunge the needle through. Blue Eyes grimaced, and Eve cringed as the skin slipped from her fingers. "Skin's tougher than you think. Hold it tighter," Twig ordered.

"This can't be right," Eve said. "Are you sure?"

"Just do it," Twig snapped.

Eve tried again. "Ready."

Twig plunged the needle in and through. Eve gasped and her father cried out. Twig made a quick knot and drew the skin together. "There, see? As neat as a new skirt," Twig said. As she pulled a second stitch into place and drew the knot tight, Blue Eyes nodded in approval.

"That looks really good," Eve said as Twig finished another. "It closed up the cut." She glanced from the neat row of stitches to the gathering vultures. "We better hurry. We can't hang around when the scavengers come."

Twig worked as the butchering continued. By the time Adam called an end to it, Eve and Twig had finished stitching and salving the wound with healing leaves. Eve helped Twig wrap his chest. Then Blue Eyes stood. He smiled wanly and tried to help carry the meat. Eve snatched it away from him.

"We got it. You've already done more than your share," she told him. He looked pale in the cheeks and there was pain in his eyes. He was just trying to put on a brave face. He nodded then turned to confer with Adam. *He is going to make it,* she told herself.

"Thanks Twig, you have done it again," Eve said. "Sorry I was skeptical."

Twig smiled. "It's okay."

Blue Eyes and Adam gestured and pointed. At last Adam announced it was time to go home. With Blue Eyes' injured, Adam coordinated with him to set the pace east, which to Eve's surprise was a fast run. Fortunately, they had distributed the meat and hide from the day before, so now with this new load, they could head directly back to the valley.

She could tell by how Blue Eye's hunters fell in line, that this was a comfortable pace for them. They had spent most of the day circling the herd because of the wind direction, but now headed directly back to the east, passing over the place the herd had been in the morning. They fell into two groups, Blue Eyes and his hunters, and the gang. Each group was tightly packed, a technique Eve could see scattered both prey and predator they encountered.

As they left the herd behind Eve smelled something new, something wonderful on the wind. "What is that smell?" she said, glancing at Twig then Adam. "It is amazing."

"Whatever it is," Art puffed. "It's making me hungry!"

"The smell is on the wind," Eve said. "We should turn into the wind and investigate."

Adam scanned the prairie. "Keep your eyes open, but I think we need to keep moving toward home."

"We are clear of the herd. The carcass and scavengers are far behind. What's the danger?"

"No danger," Adam said stoutly. "But shouldn't we get your father home?"

Her father was doing great. Twig's stitches were holding well. And all the strange happenings of the previous night—they felt like an age ago. "If you are worried about him, what he really needs is some water to drink," Eve said. "We are all out. If you care about him, and are not afraid, let's turn and investigate this new smell, while we get him some water."

Eve smiled to herself, when Adam changed course. She felt bad for having to question his courage, to get him to comply, but the smell!

Ahead, a small ravine emerged, mostly hidden. It was just the kind of place Adam might have chosen to make camp. "Look for water," he said as they skidded down the slope.

Eve hurried forward, following her nose. She pushed through some bushes and saw something like a fog curling and rising further down the ravine. The smell was stronger now. She did not hesitate but hurried down the ravine to get a better look.

Suddenly naked bodies rose from the scrub right in front of her. Eve froze. Her heart pounded in her chest. The bodies were people, but not her people. They blocked the way. She stood face-to-face with another tribe.

"Adam!" she screamed. She had never seen anyone who was not one of them. Their features were crude, if no match for the skull hanging in the treehouse. There were around fifteen of them. Each was uglier than anyone Eve knew in the valley. They were just eight paces away and she could see clearly the surprise in their eyes. Maybe they had never seen a stranger before either. "Adam," she screamed again even louder, but still could not move. Her feet seemed planted in the ground. Eve forced her gaze away and glanced back. Adam, her father, and the rest were running fast, right behind her. Adam looked equally surprised, but Blue Eye's face showed more than surprise, it showed fear. The man who had just leapt on the back of a raging beast showed fear. Eve had never seen such fear on her father's face before. She wondered if perhaps he knew this other tribe.

He made a terrible sound, a terrific war cry like she had never heard before. "Cha-*iii*-ee!" High and shrill, it pierced the air. Then turning, he ran to the eastern bank of the ravine in full retreat.

The foreign tribesmen reacted to her father's cry, and began to move.

"Run!" Adam shouted, stepping past Eve. He brandished his spear and put himself between her and this new enemy. For a moment confusion gripped the other tribe as they looked at Adam. She thought they might run away but they began picking up sticks from the ground. The sticks were bent with a string stretched across their ends.

"They have miniature spears," Fish yelled.

"A weapon?" Monkey asked.

The strangers were intent—hurrying to put their little spears together with the bent sticks. Their confidence in these sticks concerned Eve. "Let's get out of here," she yelled, turning in a hurry and crashing into Twig. "Twig, let's go," Eve cried but Twig continued to point and stare.

Eve looked, beyond the foreign tribesmen, and saw what Twig was focused on.

Bright orange and yellow fingers danced above a pile of blackened wood. The colorful fingers twisted madly out of existence as they changed into a gray fog streaming up into the clear blue sky.

"What is that?" Twig hissed, but Eve's attention was drawn back to the strangers. The first savage to recover his bow fit an arrow to the string. He began to pull back the string and aimed it their way.

"Run!" Eve screamed, shoving Twig back. Twig turned and they ran toward the rest of their group. After a single step, Twig's father staggered and grabbed his throat. Blood began to pump out around the little spear lodged in his neck. He fell, landing on his back, and laid deadly still. Eve continued to push Twig forward. A bow twanged and something small whizzed by Eve's head. *Twang*, she heard it again.

Twig stopped. The fool girl bent down to see to her father. Blood bubbled from the hole in his neck. "He's dying!"

"Twig! Run!. They will kill you too," Eve yelled. She couldn't believe the effectiveness of their little weapon, and it looked like the whole tribe had them. She and the others would never be able to get away. In another moment they would all be dead. *What was I thinking, wanting to leave the valley? This is all my fault.*

*Twang.* Another arrow flew by.

"Attack! Charge them!" Adam cried running past Eve toward the enemy. She gripped her spear, let out a cry, and ran forward to join his insanity. They were all dead anyway. There was no point in running away. Adam was thinking fast. An unexpected counterattack and the element of surprise might save them yet.

Eve saw more arrows being notched. Adam hurled his spear, sinking it in the chest of a man poised to shoot. The bow, arrow, and man crashed to the ground.

*Don't panic, don't panic!* Eve told herself as her eyes locked with another archer. He began pulling back the string of his bow; his arrow was pointed right at Eve. She threw her spear at him. It struck him in the ribs, spinning him. With a scream of pain, the arrow flew wild.

Now weapon-less, Eve glanced back, hoping it wasn't just her and Adam against the whole tribe. Her father, with a great bellow, his injury seemingly forgotten, came charging back, his axe held high. His hunters, roaring their own war cries, charged as well. Fish and Monkey, both close behind, each launched their spears while Bev, wielding her axe, screamed her own war cry to shake the earth.

Screaming, Eve followed Adam as he surged ahead, swinging his axe in wide circles, covering the last few paces before another arrow could be shot. Eve retrieved her spear as the gang, their axes swinging, joined her in pursuit.

A naked woman rose from the ground with a spear of her own. The woman bared her teeth as her face contorted in a wicked sneer. Eve sunk her spear in her chest. Fighting panic, Eve pulled her spear loose and again moved after the retreating tribe.

The gang were badly outnumbered, but surprise and momentum gave them an advantage. Little Red roared and swung his axe. It connected. Hot blood splashed Eve.

Then Blue Eyes and his hunters charged past her. With heavy axes and towering strength, they pushed the archers backward to the gruesome sounds of bones snapping. The bowman stumbled back past the fire. There they were met by the rest of their tribe, now rising from the ground where they had been resting and eating, weapons in hand. Several moved forward from behind the fire. Eve was stunned by their numbers.

"Retreat! Run. Everyone run," Adam suddenly shouted. "Run, Run, Run! There are too many of them! Retreat!" He pushed Monkey and Little Red back. The hunters understood. There were many more, well-armed tribe members coming to aid the small contingent they had attacked. There was still confusion among the tribe of archers. Some were looking around. Others with spears were trying to give chase, but tripping over the wounded and bumping into the bowmen. It gave the gang time and Eve sprinted as fast as she could toward the far bank. She scrambled up, expecting to feel an arrow hit her in the back with each desperate step.

Safely out of the ravine, Adam led the gang east, as fast as they could run. All Eve could think about was Twig's father, left behind. He looked dead as she ran by. He was or Twig would not have left him. Eve looked over the rest of their group. Amazingly, all were still together.

Twig ran beside Eve. The girl was trying to say something, but Eve kept running, her eyes forward. She didn't want to hear it. She worried Twig would blame her and her curiosity for her father's death. "Did you see the fire?" Twig shouted.

"What?" Eve gasped, not understanding.

"It was hot!" Twig said. "Hotter than the sun!" The battle had been hot. Eve had killed people, a man and a woman. She felt thrilled like never before, and at the same time, sickened. Yet she wasn't talking crazy, not like Twig. *The shock of losing her father scrambled her brains.* "And they had meat on a stick, and it was brown," Twig continued.

"Just run, Twig, or they will have you on a stick," Eve yelled, glancing back at the other tribe, now emerging from the ravine in pursuit. "Run now! Talk later!" *Hot fire?* Eve didn't have time for Twig or her new word.

# The Escape

The tribe was still behind them. Adam had glanced back now more times than he could count. He, at the head of the hunting party, led them east, trying to avoid any obstacles to give them the fastest path, but always keeping east. He worried the sun was not moving fast enough across the afternoon sky.

He and the hunting party had a good lead, but it had stopped growing. Catching him looking, Eve left her father's side and she came alongside. He figured it was her fault they were in this predicament. He should have ignored her suggestion earlier, and he resolved to ignore her now.

"What's the plan?" Eve called to him.

"We run," Adam said, not taking his eyes from the ground ahead.

"We won't get back before dark," she said. "I wonder if they will chase us after dark or give up and head back?"

*Bloody bones,* Adam thought. Leave it to Eve to speculate and expect him to have answers. He had just seen so many unbelievable things, how would he know what this tribe would do? Dancing red fingers and swirling fog, a naked tribe with weapons more advanced than his—it was all too much. "It doesn't matter what they do," he said. "We are going to keep going and not stop until I say so." He focused on picking the path and putting one foot in front of the other.

When the sun finally hung low in the west, their pursuers were still with them, but Adam figured he had increased the hunting party's lead a little. None of his lagged behind—the gang all knew they were running for their lives. With luck their pursuers' enthusiasm would fade with the setting of the sun.

"Looking good guys, we are gaining on them," Adam called back. His group looked to be in good shape. Many flashed him a smile, but Blue Eyes' face was haggard and pale, his gate strained and mechanical. Adam feared he was too tired to go much further. A worried looking Eve ran beside him. She gave Adam a little shake of her head, but there was nothing he could do but push on.

He ran, and the sun dropped low, almost reaching the horizon. The prairie was quiet; only the hoarse rasp of heavy breathing and the slap of their feet disturbed the serenity. They had gained more ground on the enemy and Adam was starting to hope the other tribe would soon have to give up.

A cry behind, whipped his head around. Fish, who had been near the middle of the group, was down in a heap and was not standing back up. Monkey shot past him, but not Bev. She stopped, and Adam stopped as well.

"Keep going," he yelled to Eve as he raced past her, back to help Fish.

"My foot caught a hole," Fish moaned in pain when Adam joined him.

"Can you run?" Adam asked.

"Not a chance," Fish answered in a scared voice. "Please don't leave me."

"Nobody's leaving you," Adam assured him. "Bev, can you get his other side?"

She nodded and they lifted Fish between them. They locked arms behind him and they started to run. With their help, Fish bounced along on one foot. They were moving, but Adam worried it was not fast enough.

*So close,* Adam thought, glancing back to see the hard-earned gap narrow to the enemy. Refusing to give up he focused on their technique, and with each step, their speed improved. Adam realized it was still not fast enough.

Ahead Eve called a halt. Her father ran on fifty yards before stopping and coming back. The old man gestured wildly at the oncoming tribe. Adam understood. It made no sense for them all to die trying to save one person. Clearly this was not the way of the tribe, but it was certainly his way, and clearly Eve's as well. One sacrificed for the group may be acceptable to the hunters but not to them.

Adam was not sure where his sudden courage came from. Back in the ravine he had been terrified by all the unexpected dangers but had done what he had to do to save them. Now he would face this enemy alone if need be to save Fish. He was the leader of this group and would not leave someone behind to die. He would save him, or die trying.

When he, Bev, and Fish reached the group he could see Blue Eyes was angry. The old man continued to gesture toward the approaching enemy and pointed to the east, motioning them forward. Adam could not be sure what he was trying to communicate but assumed he was arguing to leave Fish behind.

Growling and shaking his head, Blue Eyes wrestled Fish away from him and Bev and tossed him over his shoulder. Everyone stood in shock as he took off running east, Fish bouncing on his shoulder.

"Let's go," Adam shouted, urging the group to follow. It was more symbolic than practical as Blue Eyes was in no shape for such activity, but Adam felt like a boy again, being shown up by an adult. He worried a moment he had lost his leadership position, but surely everyone realized Blue Eyes would have left Fish behind.

More importantly they were moving again. Their lead was secure for now, but for how long, Adam didn't know.

When Blue Eyes transferred Fish to Adam's father, he ran on at full speed, a pack full of meat and Fish over his shoulder. These old men were tough. His own father, ancient and lazy, was running all out with his load. He had a power over his body Adam had no idea was possible. They kept up the pace until dark, the old men taking turns carrying Fish plus their loads of meat.

Blue Eyes appeared to be looking around for a place to spend the night but Adam signaled no. The enemy was farther away, but still just in sight. He wanted to push on as the foreign tribe had weapons he did not understand. He had no idea if they would stop for the night or not. Instead he slowed the pace to a walk, but kept moving east under the starry sky.

Eve passed out fruit and dried meat. The gang took turns helping Fish walk as he and Bev had. The task was much easier while walking. When they stumbled across water they drank deeply. Twig took the moment to splint and wrap Fish's leg with a branch and some string from her bag. When they continued Fish could walk with just one helper.

Before long the moon rose in the clear sky. Looking back, Adam saw nobody following. Yet he did not dare run, even with the moonlight, but he kept walking, now at a faster pace. He was exhausted but pushed on. The moon traversed the sky.

"Adam, enough. We're all too exhausted to go another step." Eve's voice broke through his wandering mind. He looked around but the plains looked exactly as they had all night. The moon, however, had set. More time had passed than he realized. He looked back and again saw no pursuers.

She was right, they needed to rest. If only he had suggested it. Now that she was insisting, he would look weak if he agreed. Not as quick on his feet as he wished, he desperately looked around for a way to save face. He couldn't find one. Irritated with himself, he stopped the group and walked back to where Eve and Twig were helping support Blue Eyes. "How is he?"

"He is done in," Twig said.

Adam nodded. "We can sleep until dawn."

One-by-one the gang and hunters collapsed on the ground. Eve fussed over her father, while Bev fussed over Fish.

Adam squatted next to Fish himself. "Doing better?" he asked over the snores of Blue Eye and his hunters.

Fish smiled and nodded. "They don't waste any time getting to sleep, do they? They just lay in a pile and sleep like the dead."

"Let's hope not," Adam said.

"Thanks for saving me today. I am doing better now. I should be able to walk tomorrow."

"No problem," Adam said, standing. "Now get some sleep." He glared over at Eve, but she was still fussing over her father.

Adam lay down and was asleep before he had another thought. When he woke, it was quiet. Streaks of dawn colored the sky. Eve was kneeling over him, gently shaking him. She smiled as he rubbed his eyes.

"I stood watch. Nobody in sight," she said, anticipating his question.

"Let's hope they gave up," Adam said. "I would love to change direction this morning to be sure we lost them, but then we might not find our way back home."

"I'm not worried," Eve said "You did amazingly well yesterday. I'm so proud of you."

Adam felt his strength and confidence return. He still had concerns about the enemy, concerns about where they were. He had not been as careful as he should have been navigating in the dark. He was encouraged and decided to keep those worries to himself. "Thank you."

"You know it made sense, leaving Fish behind. It was the logical thing to do, but I am glad you are not like that," Eve said, squeezing his hand "I think a good leader has to be always willing to take chances to save his people, even if it means risking his own life."

Adam sat up feeling all but invincible. He had not talked with her about what she had said when he saved her life, but he had not forgotten a word of it. "I would gladly give my life to save you," he said.

Bev sat up, a huge smile on her face. She nudged Twig beside her. Snickers rippled through the gang. Adam blushed. They were awake, but laying quiet, listening, and now they stood stiffly, stretching, smiling and nodding at Eve, still holding Adam's hand.

Adam leapt to his feet and got them packing. Fish was able to hobble along with just a little support. With no enemy in sight, Adam decided to walk, not run. He kept the pace brisk, determined to stop only for water.

As the day passed, Adam watched for any sign of the valley, but he saw only grass. He tried to work out how far they had traveled, and felt he should see the valley soon. A knot formed in his stomach, and his jaw ached from clenching his teeth. He tried not to think what would happen if he was lost. The sun made its way across the blue sky, and still nothing but endless grass greeted them. By mid-afternoon, Adam was sure they had missed the valley and were hopelessly lost. He wanted to ask the others what they thought, but could not let them know his concern. He just put one foot in front of another.

Suddenly Eve let out a shout, "Yay! We're home."

Adam glanced up. It was true. He could see what could only be their valley on the horizon. He felt like jumping for joy, but determined to act cool. He sidled up to Eve and took her hand and squeezed it as they approached—just this once. She looked up in surprise and he smiled. He had done it. He had gotten them home safely.

As they neared the valley, he realized he had missed the crevice, arriving near the top of the valley, closer to the falls. It was a stunning sight, and brought back fond memories of their first visit. Mist rose, creating colored bands in the sunshine.

Adam nodded upriver. "I wonder what's above these falls," Adam said to Eve. "More falls?"

A smile broke out on her face. "We should find out," she said, "but not on this trip. We have too many injuries, and too much to carry."

Unwilling to argue, Adam led them back to the waiting ladder. He brushed away their tracks near the crack, then he had the ladders pulled down behind them.

Adam felt like a returning hero, leading the intrepid explorers into the village. As the Tree of Life came into view, he looked for some acknowledgment, some recognition of his safe return, but the tribe noted the party's presence with little excitement. Then Adam remembered Twig's father. He had almost forgotten the silent hunter. What would Twig's mother do? Would she blame him?

But then the women came out and divided the meat, squabbling as usual as to who got what, just as they did when the hunters returned from a seal hunt. Twig's mother was right in there with the rest of them.

"No celebration?" Monkey growled. Adam was glad someone else noticed.

"I'm just happy to be off my foot," Fish said, flopping down.

"This must be normal to them," Eve said, standing close to Adam and Twig. "Even after so many years of idleness, this is still normal, I guess—the hunt and the dangers."

Twig remained silent and Adam found her mood depressing. She was clearly still mourning her father's passing. People did not die often in the valley, at least very few that Adam could think of. All the kids assumed they would live forever unless they did something stupid. Now they had done something stupid, but it was Twig's father who had not come back. The tribe didn't seem to notice—only Twig's mother. She looked around the group and had tears in her eyes when Twig confirmed he was not coming back, but then she wiped her face and made sure she received her share of the meat.

Adam's spirits revived when the younger speaking children discovered they had returned. They pressed around asking questions and begged for the whole story. Not satisfied with just once, they wanted to hear the story again and again. Soon most learned it by heart.

The next morning Adam and Eve were outside her cave. Several of the children were arguing on the stream bank near the Tree of Life.

"I want to be Adam," one boy yelled,

"No!" another yelled. "I want to."

Two of the girls squabbled as well. "You be Twig, I want to be Eve."

"I don't want to be Twig," the other complained.

Adam looked at Eve. "It is strange to see the kids play acting our adventures."

"It's kind of scary in a way. I am not sure I like being copied by a bunch of children."

"Well, we are going to be, so we better get things right," Adam said with a laugh.

A new sound reached them. It was not a happy carefree sound of kids playing. Eve suddenly looked serious.

"As if any could replace him!" Twig was yelling at her mother. She was angry. Her raised voice reached them all the way from her cave.

"What is wrong with her?" Adam asked Eve quietly.

"I bet Twig's mother is being friendly with the other men."

"So quick?"

Twig's screaming stopped. She came flying down the path from her cave. Seeing Eve, she fell into her arms sobbing. Eve tried to comfort her. "We are just different from them, Twig. Your mom is not bad, it's just their way."

Twig continued to cry and Eve looked over her shoulder at Adam. He stood helplessly by. Eve shook her head, and he remembered when she wished nothing would ever change. He couldn't help but feel that from this day on, nothing would ever be the same. Everything had changed again, forever.

> *To bring peace to all, one must first discipline and control one's own mind. If a man can control his mind ... all wisdom and virtue will naturally come to him.*
>
> *Buddha*

# A Better Weapon   12

*Chawhooo!* The call reached Eve in her cave. It sounded like her father. *Chawho-a!* There it was again. *What is this?* Eve wondered as she gathered with the rest of the tribe. *An attack? No.* She couldn't tell if this was an old tribal ritual or something new. Blue Eyes was standing in front of the Tree of Life, motioning for the tribe to gather around.

It was the first evening with a full moon since the big hunt. Eve pressed in closer. Up until then, she and the others had been busy dealing with the meat and skins from the hunt—and with the injuries. Eve had to admit herself she had been avoiding Adam, now that he acted like she had promised something she had not. Now she wondered what her father had in mind. She had never seen anything like this before, but then again, there had never been a hunt outside the valley before, not in her lifetime.

While the tribe watched, Blue Eyes held up a piece of meat from the hunt, then tossed it under the sacred tree. He then lifted a gourd full of water and threw out a water offering. Eve had seen this kind of worship before, and had done it herself, but when Blue Eyes motioned for Adam to join him in front of the tribe, she was surprised. Her father bowed his head to the tree, then had Adam do the same. Blue Eyes turned and faced Adam, and bowed his head to Adam. Eve was confused. Was this some kind of affirmation of his hunt's success?

She was stunned when her father motioned for the entire tribe to bow to Adam. There was confusion among the tribe. Eve was pleased for Adam that he was being honored but it rankled her to bow to him. What did the act even mean? She tried to tell herself she didn't mind Adam being singled out for this distinction, for this honor. *Be pleased for him,* she told herself.

Her father again motioned for everyone else to bow to him. First his hunters bowed and then the rest followed. They all did, all but Monkey and Eve. She couldn't believe her father was making Adam the new chief if that was what this was. It wasn't fair. Wasn't she the oldest? Wasn't she his daughter and didn't she have blue eyes? And didn't she first overcome her fears and approach the tree? If the tribe needed a new chief why not her?

Instead of bowing her head, she glared at the two of them—and at the Tree. Her father glared back before ripping his blue eyes away from her.

For a moment Eve considered marching to the front and braving the Tree for them all to see. That would stop all this. The tribe would be stunned; her father would be amazed. But there were problems with the idea. She did not know for certain what the reaction would be. And it might not work. It seemed important to her that she approach the tree with a clean heart. Her motives needed to be unselfish and pure. To approach to show off to the tribe—that might backfire, and her bones might be added to the bone pile.

Blue Eyes proceeded to do a bit of a dance which the tribesmen responded to by swaying and nodding. Perhaps this was how leadership was passed down. Eve didn't know. The specific symbolism she did not understand, but she got the idea well enough. Adam was a mighty hunter who provided for the tribe, maybe not chief yet, but when the time came, who knew?

Throughout the ceremony Adam looked like he was in a daze. At times he glanced at her. His expression was that of embarrassment. It appeared this had not been his idea. Adam was far too young to be the leader; plus her father would lead for many years to come. What she couldn't understand was why he thought he needed a successor now?  Perhaps with Adam installed as her father's successor, no one would challenge him once he was dead.

*That's it, he is just setting up the succession in case of an accident.  Perhaps his near miss with the beast made him realize he could die, and the tribe would be in disarray.*  It made sense even if Eve didn't agree with it and even if her father picked the wrong person.  And what of Monkey?  She thought of Big Nose. He had rebelled, and became fish food.  Was that to be Monkey's fate as well?  He also had refused to bow.

The ceremony ended and everyone filtered back to their homes in the moonlight.  Monkey caught her eye and smiled.  He might have even winked.  Eve hung back for a moment trying to decide if she should protest her fathers actions or ignore them.  As she walked alone into the cave, her father acted like nothing had happened, already busy with her mother in bed.

Eve sighed and lay on her mat.  She wondered what Adam was thinking now.  She guessed by the puzzled look on his face, he didn't understand what exactly was now expected of him either.  But he kept glancing at her during the ceremony.  If he was thinking what she suspected he was thinking, the poor fool was in for a surprise.  A big surprise.

The next day the gang still had much to do, from drying meat, to repairing torn clothes, to taking care of medical needs.  They all agreed to meet mid-day.  They had not had a chance to meet since the hunt and there was so much to talk about. Eve was thrilled when at last enough work was finished for the gang to drift away from the settlement. She and Twig were one of the first to reach the treehouse. All but Adam had arrived by mid-day, as agreed and the gang was sitting around talking when Adam swaggered in.

Monkey bowed mockingly. "All hail the new chief."

Eve looked at him closely, wondering what he was playing at. He was the only other one who had not bowed. He was setting Adam up for something, she suspected. Adam nodded his acceptance and sat against the tree, a big smile on his face.

"If you get to have all of the women now," Bev said, sauntering around Adam, thrusting her hips provocatively. "Start with me." Everyone found that extremely amusing and laughed loudly.

Twig, still laughing, threw her hair back, batted her eyes at Adam and said, "Me next." Eve squirmed in her seat on the log and felt herself turning bright red in the face.

Adam lay his head back against the tree's trunk. "Yes," he said, smiling. "I will—after all the other women in the tribe. I will need to make up a schedule. You girls will have to wait your turn."

Adam wasn't funny yet everyone laughed uproariously as if he were more than hilarious. As the joking continued, they laughed harder. And though it was only jokes, Eve felt there was something more to it—a nasty truth lurking in the racy banter. She didn't like it.

She glanced at Monkey. He was not laughing either, but looking right at her. Many things had changed overnight. Maybe the dumb women of the tribe would favor Adam with their attention even more now. For any of them to have his children would be an honor.

Eve's stomach twisted at the thought, and she wiped at her eyes. *Only dust!* she told herself viciously. She hated Adam. The thought of him being with another woman made her blood boil.

"Enough silly talk," she interrupted loudly. "Adam's mating plans are hardly important now, not with savages possessing weapons and magic we don't understand." She put enough heat into her words to cut the banter off dead.

Twig swallowed. "I am calling their magic fire, because of how hot it was, like the sun.

"And the smelly cloud?" Art asked.

"That's smoke."

"Okay, good—"

"Their weapons are bows and they shoot arrows."

"Thank you, Twig." Eve said and waited to make sure the skinny girl was finished. "If they have them, so can we. Ideas?"

Twig had some, of course. And when she spoke she spoke as if she didn't trust the others would believe her. Then again, Fish didn't.

"The gray powder you are calling ash, I saw it, and the fire also. The fire is an animal. How else did the flames move—they were dancing."

"No. Wood turns to ash when it gets hot," Twig reiterated.

Fish scoffed. "Nonsense. The flames eat the wood to make the ash if anything."

"That's stupid, Fish."

"It's not stupid. What if the flames are like the glowing bugs at night? Did you think of that?"

Twig was stumped. "So we don't know if it was an animal or not," Eve said.

"It couldn't have been an animal," Art said. "I could see right through the flames. Couldn't do that if they were animals."

"You can sort of see through the glowbugs," Fish said stubbornly.

"You just don't like being wrong, do you Fish," Twig said. Eve wondered at the girl. If anyone hated being wrong it was her.

"Not true," Fish said, but he brooded behind folded arms after that.

"What I saw was the meat," Art said. "I think they were using the fire to dry it."

"But fast because the fire was hotter than the sun," Twig added.

"So how do we make fire ourselves?" Eve asked, ignoring Fish. If they couldn't make fire, then they couldn't, but Eve wanted them to explore every idea. Better to try and fail than to not try at all. There was a pause as everyone thought.

"We need to get the wood hot," Adam said slowly and deliberately. He seemed to strain himself with the depth of the thought.

"I think you got the whole thing backward," Eve said. "The flames make the heat."

"No," Twig said. "It's possible . . . Adam what exactly are you thinking?"

Eve seethed. She could murder Twig, kissing up to Adam.

Adam demonstrated, and Eve was forced to accept he might be right. When he rubbed two sticks together they did get hot. But she felt a perverse joy when the sticks didn't magically burst into flames.

"See, they get hot," he said, as stubborn as Fish. "I think if you got them hot enough, they would make flames." Soon everyone was rubbing sticks together, rubbing them on rocks, rubbing them on leather, and although they clearly warmed, they were not hot like the sun. As their enthusiasm faltered, Eve called them back together.

"Okay, let's put the fire problem aside for a moment. Bows and arrows. Think of everything you saw. I'll start. The arrows looked like mini-spears."

"They had feathers on their tails," said Monkey.

"I didn't see any feathers," Eve said.

"Yeah," Little Red said. "Don't say they had feathers."

"Why not?" Monkey demanded. "They did have feathers!"

"Now Fish is going to tell us they were birds," Little Red said.

Fish scowled. "Not funny, Little Red. You have feathers for brains."

"The feathers, Monkey—tell us about the feathers," Eve prompted.

"Well, there I was—"

"The short version, please."

"Yes," Monkey sighed. "I had to jump over Twig's—uh—over the body. I—uh looked down. Um, so, out of the gory, bleeding, uh, I saw the end of the stick—the arrow—sticking out of his neck—it had feathers on it. Um—I'm sorry Twig."

The girl had started crying and it took several moments for her to regain her composure. After all the stuff she had said earlier about wanting Adam, Eve had a hard time feeling sorry for her.

"Enough about the arrows; what about the bows which launched them?" Eve looked around the group. *This is more like it,* she thought. She was back in charge. Adam smiled at her. Her face flushed from embarrassment. She could still kill him.

Fish, with Twig incapacitated from grief, spoke up. "I could make one of their bows, no problem," he said. "It's just a bent stick with a string between the ends. I stumbled over one on the ground as we escaped. I should have picked it up, but didn't think of it at the time. If we ever see fire again, we should try stealing one of them too."

Twig shook her head. "It's not an animal."

Eve, however, gave him a big smile. "Quite understandable, Fish," she said. "Perhaps you and Monkey can help us make some bows and arrows." Finally something they could actually do. "Let's do this," she said and stood up. The rest followed her to their feet, eager to get to work.

By late afternoon, little arrows were flying around under the tree.

Adam's bow broke in two as he pulled on its string. Little Red shouted. "Everyone shoot Adam! He's defenseless!"

A cloud of arrows sent Adam diving behind the tree for cover. He emerged, poking his head out first to make sure they were done. "These are worthless," he announced and Eve remembered she was still annoyed with him.

"No, they are not." Eve fixed him with a cold stare.

"The arrows don't fly straight, and even if they did our bows are too weak to hurt a flea."

"We can fix that," Eve said. "We did well for our first attempt, Adam. What do you think the feathers are for?"

"I don't know," he replied cautiously. "They help birds fly, don't they?" He looked around the group for support. "Maybe they help the arrows do the same?"

On the way home, Eve walked slowly with Twig as the others ran ahead. "Vision," Eve told Twig. "That's the biggest hurdle."

"I don't know what you mean," said Twig.

"To innovation. We saw how the bows and arrows worked, but not the fire."

"I'm sure we will figure them both out."

"If someone named Adam doesn't screw everything up first. Him saying bows are worthless. And lining up the women. I—uh—" Eve sputtered.

Twig laughed. "You have it bad."

"No, I don't," Eve said. "I don't even know what you are talking about."

"I am going to call it *Eve Sickness*."

"No, you won't!"

"No. I got it. *Love Sickness*," Twig said. "And you got it bad."

Eve scoffed. "I'm not in love. I could strangle him. And it is not a sickness. It's his mind that's sick."

"So, so, bad."

"Just drop it, Twig," Eve said. "There are more important things than silly boys. Like how to make the bows and strings stronger."

"So, so bad," Twig said, clucking her tongue. "Any other symptoms? Tingling? Do you hear ringing in your ears?

"Don't be ridiculous," Eve snapped. "Now, what are your ideas for a better bow string? Tomorrow I want to have the best bow."

To Eve's relief Twig let the whole love sickness thing go and elaborated on the many ways they could improve both the bow and the arrow.

Eve and Twig reached the main path and turned toward the cave. "Eve, can I talk with you?" a deep voice behind them said.

"Adam, you scared me," Eve said with a start. Adam stepped out from behind a tree. Eve glanced at Twig, who rolled her eyes, and said a quick goodbye, before running, to catch up with the others, calling over her shoulder, "Don't do anything I wouldn't."

Eve watched her leave before turning to look at Adam. "Walk with me out to the ocean," he said.

"Why? What's out there?"

Adam shrugged. "Um—the sunset? We could watch it set."

"I don't know," Eve said. A voice in her head told her to run and catch up with Twig and the others. Instead she smiled and shrugged her shoulders, wondering if her curiosity was getting the better of her again. Twig wondered at all the things she didn't understand. Eve had an even longer list. Sun, fire, Adam, Monkey, her own mind; everything was confusing now. If only she could see what made them work.

"We can make it there in time if we hurry," Adam added. He took her hand in his and her heart raced. She didn't resist as he pulled her down the path towards the ocean. He started talking about a better type of wood for making bows. He went on and on, but finally noticed she was not talking. "What's the matter, Eve? You seem—"

"Upset?"

"Confused?" he weaseled.

"I am a little confused, but I know I am *more* than a *little* upset," Eve said. "So don't get it wrong. I am upset."

Adam stopped. "At me?" he said.

"Are you totally clueless, Adam?" she said. He hitched back as if stung or slapped, but Eve continued. "Thinking I would like the idea of you with other women?" Eve felt so stupid. She shouldn't have said that. She pulled her hand from his, and ran. *Twig was right.* She did have something wrong with her. She just knew it.

She ran. But as she ran, she ran towards the beach. She tried to think what she should have said, but all she could think of was how big a fool she had just made of herself. The only succor was it hadn't happened in front of the gang. Yet it was small comfort if Adam decided to tell them.

Through her tears, she saw a log half-buried in the sand and sat down on it. The red sun behind her turned the sand a deep gold. The sky was starting to show color—promising ever richer ones to come.

Her shadow stretched out far in front of her.

"What should I do?" she sobbed to herself, then stiffened as a tall shadow approached, Adam's. Part of her had hoped he had not followed, another part was thrilled to see his shadow closing. When he sat down beside her, he put his arm around her, and their shadows merged.

## Romance?

Adam had brought her here to the beach, and the sunset was perfect, yet she was crying and now Adam didn't know what to say. Perhaps, something funny, to cheer her up? She had not bowed when the village had bowed. He desired an explanation for that but didn't know how to ask. Maybe a joke about her and Monkey being too stiff to bow? "Eve?" he asked gently.

Making no attempt to hide her tears, she looked over at him. "Yes?"

The joking went out of Adam as he looked into her wet, blue eyes. He realized this was important; he needed to say the right thing, now, more than ever. "I only want you," he said, and glanced away feeling foolish. This was no way for the leader of the tribe to speak. Blue Eyes himself took way more mates than just Eve's mother. Why should he have to behave any differently? Was he not the top man now? The Hunter? The Provider? Would his children not make up the next generation?

"Don't lie to me, Adam."

He felt Eve's blue eyes on him, boring into him. He dared not look at them. Instead he stared out over the glowing water. He was chief. *Be strong,* he told himself. He turned to her and smiled. "I want you to be my mate," he said. "But I still have to do my duty."

"Duty?" Eve exploded, squirming out from under his arm. She glared at him, and he felt foolish, regretting his words, but his pride would not let him take them back. "Your duty, Adam?" she demanded, and he wished to tell her how beautiful she was, even angry. How smart! How strong. How he adored her. "Eve—"

"Don't Eve me!" she shouted at him, and shoved him off the log. "Go! Go do you duty without me! Not now. Not ever!"

"But, Eve—"

"Don't Eve me," she shouted at him. "You are nothing but a silly boy. Too afraid to even pick the fruit from the Tree of Life." She marched off back home without looking back. He watched her go over his shoulder until her silhouette, head held high, disappeared into the golden sunset—she never looked back. Finally, when he was convinced she was not coming back, he rolled over and stood, brushing the sand off, then, shaking his head, he sat back down on the log. "Women," he muttered. "Who can understand them? Who needs them?" He had offered Eve the top place in the village. She would be respected by everyone and they would take care of her children, bring her food and treat her with respect, even the men would! And she was mad? Angry at him? It made no sense!

"I won't be beaten by her," he shouted angrily. A flock of seagulls burst into flight. Standing, he started home. Life didn't have to be this complicated. Why couldn't Eve see that? The moon came out, and he remembered her falling asleep in his arms. More than anything he wanted her; he had to have her. He just needed to show her the foolishness of her resistance.

As he walked up the path, a small group headed his way. *Who could this be?* The gang had all gone back, and Eve had been alone. Something was wrong; nobody should be here. Adam slipped off the path.

The moon was bright, and he could make out three figures. He did not recognize them. As they drew closer, he saw they were naked—and definitely not of the tribe. Adam's heart beat triple-time and when he reached for his axe, found he had not brought it. *Bloody bones!* Alone with no weapons, he didn't know what to do.

He was still at the edge of the beach, and the savages were closing. He dared not move; he tried not to even breathe. He saw the three more clearly now. One was a woman. Two were males. When they reached the sand, they stopped. They sniffed the air and turned back.

*Not much interesting here*, Adam thought in agreement. He followed them as they walked away. They had bows slung over their shoulders. The other tribe had tracked them into the valley. They must have seen the crevice, and with so much green in the valley they followed the party down. Adam wanted to run for help, but did not dare lose them.

At the crossroad, between the treehouse and the crevice, they stopped, and laid down on the path. Adam waited. Nothing happened. They were tired, he figured. Very strange indeed.

Adam wondered about Eve. Had she managed to pass them without noticing? He tried to think back. She knocked him down and took off running. How long had he sat? He looked around, suddenly expecting to see her body along the path. Panic gripped him. It was dark when he left the beach. Was it long enough for her to have passed this point before they emerged from the crevice? He hoped dearly it was.

He crept a little closer. At least one of the men was snoring. Adam did not know what to do. He worked his way toward the treehouse, and found a place to watch from. As he sat, he tried to think. What could he do if he went back to the caves? Maybe he could gather the gang and have them get their weapons, but they kept them in the treehouse.

He considered going to the treehouse alone and getting his axe and spear. He could kill them in their sleep. He visualized the process. The first one would be easy, but then it would be two against one. And if he failed, there would be nobody to warn the tribe. It was too risky. He had no good plan.

*Oh, if only Eve were here.* He was not good at this kind of planning. Just no good at all. He was about to head to the treehouse when another worry struck him. If he raced back and led everyone there, but the savages were gone, he would look like a fool. Nobody would believe him. They could wander off in any direction. Whatever he did, he could not lose track of the invaders.

Better to risk the three-on-one, he decided as he crept back to the treehouse for his weapons. It was dark under the trees, and he had a horrible time of it. That worried him.

When he returned, he watched the savages sleep. He considered creeping up and attacking, but fear stopped him. He was no hero, he could see that now.

When he woke, the sun was well up. He could not believe he had fallen asleep. He sat up and peered at the path. Empty. The savages were gone.

"I cannot believe what a fool I am," he muttered to himself as he raced up and looked around. He saw no sign of them, no blood nor Eve's body. He ran to the beach. Nothing. He ran to the crevice. Nothing. He ran to the treehouse. Again nothing. He headed toward the settlement as fast as he could. He met the gang on the road.

"Have you seen Eve?" he asked the moment they were in earshot. She was clearly missing from the group, and so was Twig.

"She and Twig went in search of better wood," Fish said. "What is all the excitement?"

Adam told them all what he'd seen, then grilled them again for details. Yes, more than one of them saw Eve and Twig heading toward the falls to look for the best wood to make a bow.

"And you saw no savages this morning?" Adam asked again.

"Just one. A real wild one. He's running around waving all his weapons around," Monkey said with a laugh.

Adam glared at him. It was just as he feared. They didn't believe him. But he knew what he knew, and he hustled them along to the treehouse to get their weapons. "We will just have to search for them," he said, brooking no dissent. "I don't care if any of you think this is funny. I saw what I saw."

Monkey threw up his hands and that was thankfully the end of it for now.

*The heart has its own language, which speaks to the heart alone.
And the greatest love letter is written with tears, not ink.*

*Molière*

# Bow Making 13

Twig was a friend, but sometimes—and this was one of those times—Eve wanted to strangle her. Not as much as she wanted to strangle Adam, so proud and sure of himself, talking about his duty, but still; the skinny girl kept trying to analyze her, and not him!

"Twig," Eve finally said. "Let's assume that the problem is not me. Okay?"

"Okay," said Twig, not sounding convinced, but true to Twig-form she was able to mostly make the leap. She was a good friend in that way at least.

The two of them had left the settlement early. After telling Fish they would be gone a few days, they packed a few things and headed up the valley to a marshy area near the lower falls to cut samples of wood which might work for making a better bow.

Eve hardly noticed the day slipping by, the two were in such deep conversation.

"Twig, I will tell you," Eve suddenly said, stopping in her tracks. "We are different. We are special, and we don't do things the same as the tribe. Agreed?"

"True enough," Twig said.

"So, I am not going to put up with any man touching me, then touching any other woman, speaking or not. That's it. That's the deal. If he wants me, then no other," Eve blurted. Her words tumbled out. "If he so much as touches anyone else, I will kill him in his sleep."

"So that's what this is all about?"

"Adam said he wanted me to be his mate, but he would still have to *do his duty*—and he said it with a smirk on his stupid face. I shoved him off the log we were sitting on and told him to go *do his duty* without me." Eve looked over at Twig.

The girl was biting her lip. "So you shoved him off the log?"

"Right on his back side."

Twig broke out laughing. She kept laughing until tears streamed down her cheeks. "Oh, would I have loved to have seen that," she finally choked out.

Eve smiled, but did not think it was that funny. Maybe Twig was trying to cheer her up. "I don't know this plant, let's check it out," Eve said of a blue flower growing along the path. She hoped to distract Twig. She cut down a few stalks and tried to scrape away the fiber from them with her knife. "This is not working."

"Hang on, look at this?" Twig pulled some dead stalks, rotting in the soggy ground. She stripped away the rot and held up a handful of fine strong fibers. "Now, these look promising."

Sitting down along the river, they began to gather and strip away the fiber. "I see things are certainly going to be different when it comes to women," Twig said, returning to what seemed her favorite subject. She wove a bit of string from the strong fiber. "You know you are the first, and what you and Adam do is what everyone else will probably do afterwards."

"Well, then none of us will be doing anything, because there is nothing on earth he could do to get me to look at him again, especially if he ever starts running around *doing his duty*."

Twig rolled her eyes. "Perhaps we will be the first and the last generation of speakers."

They worked until dusk, then gathered some food and set up camp. As the stars blanketed the sky, they talked about their new discovery, flax, and the promising results with the string they had made.

"So you are done with Adam?" Twig asked after a long silence.

"Why? Do you want him?"

"Only if you don't mind," Twig ventured, her voice tentative.

"You can have him," Eve huffed, but saw his goofy smile in her mind and she wished she had not said that. She lay down. Instead of thinking about Adam, she plied her mind on bow making.

The next morning they moved north, and began sampling the small trees growing along the river. They were strong and flexible. Twig never mentioned Adam again, and Eve put Adam and their horrible night at the beach from her mind.

"I really like this one," she said, hacking at another variety of tree. "Look, I can bend it all the way to the ground and it doesn't break."

"Promising," Twig said. "Seems strong, and it should only grow stronger as it dries."

Eve threw herself into the work. The days sped by. The willow wood proved to be a great choice. They made bow after bow, each longer than the last. They finally decided that the longer the bow, the better. Each would need to match the shooter, and clear the ground when the shooter's arm was straight out. The flax string was strong and flexible, even when dry, and as the willow bows dried, the stiffer they became, while still remaining flexible.

The arrows, however, needed a straight shaft which was very stiff. None of the wood they found worked so they focused on various reeds, finally settling on one which was strong, and grew in the right size. It dried stiff and straight. They carved a seal bone for the point and slit the tail and inserted a split gull feather for fletching. They practiced each day, and the bow became a real weapon.

"I think the time has come to show the gang what we have done," Twig said.

"Ha, let Adam figure it out if he's so smart," Eve snapped without thinking.

"I've put up with your little temper tantrum for days now, Eve," Twig said. "You're acting like a baby. The gang is our family and I miss them. Now let's go."

It was late in the day when they neared the settlement. Eve was surprised to see Little Red fishing along the river.

"Hey, there you two are!" he cried. "We looked everywhere for you!" He ran to meet them. "Where have you been? You have missed all the action. What's that over your shoulder?"

"It's a real bow," Eve said. She ignored Twig's hard stare. "One that actually works." Little Red's eyes grew big as she unslung it from her shoulder. "The rest of the gang make any progress?"

"No. We've had no time for bows. We've been too busy chasing savages all over the valley. Adam's been working us like goats. I finally snuck off to do some fishing."

Eve looked over at Twig in shock. "Savages?"

"Yeah, Adam said he saw them," Little Red said. "Monkey says he imagined them."

"Savages here? Not likely," Eve said.

"Little Red," Twig said. "Pass the word. We will have a meeting at the treehouse in the morning and we will show everyone how to make bows and arrows."

Little Red wouldn't leave until Eve demonstrated the bow by sinking an arrow into the bole of a tree on the other side of the river. Little Red squealed in delight, plunged into the water, and crossed to retrieve the arrow. He took it and ran for the settlement.

"That's just great," Eve said. "He stole it."

Twig turned to Eve, hands on her hips. "We'll see it again tomorrow," she said. "Or do I have to do this alone?"

"Don't worry," Eve said and put the bow back on her shoulder and set out for home. "I'll come in the morning, you don't have to get so huffy." Twig let out a sigh, and followed.

*Savages?* Eve did not believe a word of it. Savages in their valley? They couldn't be. Adam was up to something. Eve approached home cautiously, just in case, but found everything as it had been, no sign of savages or slaughter.

Monkey appeared from his cave. "I heard you were back. Adam claims to have spotted three savages on the beach the evening you guys were out there. He has had us searching everywhere but we have found no sign of them."

"Umph," Eve said. She had seen nothing, but now the idea ran a chill up her back. The idea she could have run into three savages the night she left the beach alone was frightening. She thanked him for the news and showed him her bow. Monkey said he was impressed and that he could not wait to make one. Exhausted, Eve sent him home then headed for bed.

The next morning, Monkey was waiting to escort her to the treehouse. With a laugh he explained Adam had been sleeping there—and keeping watch for his savages. She had him recount the story, but it made no sense to her. Adam had stayed and watched them that first night, but he fell asleep and they had vanished when he awoke.

"What a stupid story," Eve said.

"I know, right?" Monkey said.

Adam was, however, there at the treehouse. He was whispering with Fish, but Eve ignored him and she pulled out her new bow. Twig took charge, explaining every detail.

Eve set about putting the string on. As the bow dried, it was harder to do each day, and she didn't quite get it on the first try.

Adam jumped to his feet and offered to help. Eve shrugged him off and managed to get the loop over the carved end of the bow on her next try. She set up a target, a plump melon at twice the distance they used for their spears. Eve stood under the tree and pulled out an arrow. Twig pointed out its features, then nodded. Eve drew back the bow.

She let the arrow fly. *Twang!* The bow sang a strong, resonating sound, the same sound of the other tribes' bows. The arrow passed though the melon, perfectly centered, and thudded into the coconut tree behind it. Eve sunk two more arrows into the center of the melon so none would think it was a lucky shot. The questions began. Eve did her best to answer them. Adam stared at her, a big smile on his face, as proud as he could be. *Ugh.* Eve ignored his questions, but Twig answered those herself. She stood close to him, her hand on his arm.

"Can I borrow your bow, so I can copy it?" he asked as the group broke up.

"Sure," Twig said with a wink. Eve couldn't believe it. "Here, take a few of these arrows as well," Twig added, pulling them from Eve's hand.

Over the next few days Eve didn't see much of Adam but when she did run into him, she noticed his fingers looked raw and bloody. *Hurt himself trying to make his own bow. Hope it hurts. Serves him right,* she thought and nodded. When the gang were together, Eve ignored Adam. When he spoke to her, she did not answer. But he did not react; he addressed her politely and tried to be helpful, doing much of the work making the bows for the others. Over the next few days, Eve didn't give him another thought as she and Twig made several trips north to collect more flax, willow wood, and reeds. She busied herself perfecting the design of both the bow and the arrows, and helping teach the rest of the gang how to make them. What happened to her original bow, the one Adam borrowed, Eve did not know.

There was no further talk of savages, but Adam still slept at the treehouse. One evening Adam walked into the settlement and called all the tribe out of the caves, not unlike her father might have. He led the tribe across the field to the edge of the woods, where the monkeys chattered incessantly. Eve thought to stay in the cave, but her curiosity overcame her. She had to see what Adam was up to. He had her first bow slung over his shoulder.

"He's got my bow," Eve hissed to Twig who stood next to her watching Adam.

Twig shrugged her skinny shoulders. "We weren't using it," she said.

Eve clenched her fists, and watched with the rest as Adam removed the bow from his shoulder and inserted an arrow. He held it high and turned, showing them all how it was done. Then he drew back the arrow, and pointed it up into the tree.

*Oh, my, what is he thinking?* Eve suddenly wondered in concern. He was shooting at some monkey way up in the trees, a nigh almost impossible shot. To attempt such a thing in front of the whole tribe; they would laugh for sure, when he missed. He would be disgraced. She tried not to care, but she did.

Without warning Adam released the arrow. With a *twang*, a monkey fell from high above, the arrow through it. The tribe gasped in awe and began to cheer. Even Blue Eyes looked proud. With a cry of glee one of the youngsters ran and retrieved the dead monkey, carrying it through the crowd for a closer look.

Eve was impressed—more than impressed. She was amazed. "That was an impressive shot," she said to Twig. Adam was a better shot with her own bow than she was, and only after a few days of practicing. He was supposed to be making his own but instead he must have been practicing with hers day and night.

*I'll have to practice more,* Eve thought as Adam shouted for everyone to be quiet. He walked straight at her. "Eve," he said loudly. He grabbed her hand and pulled her out of the crowd. "Eve, here, designed and made this new weapon." He pumped the bow over his head and the crowd cheered. To her surprise and confusion, he gave her back the bow, bowing his head, giving her all the credit for designing and learning how to make the new weapon. "She can teach us all how to make and use them!"

Eve flushed from embarrassment. She could kill him, but instead she smiled politely and nodded to the tribe. She sought her father in the press. He looked proud.

"What do you think you are doing telling everyone I will train them all?" Eve hissed at him while she smiled at the congratulating tribe.

"I thought you would be happy to?"

"I am, but you should have asked me."

The tribe dispersed, a dead monkey richer. Eve followed the last of them home across the field, flushed and confused.

"I just wanted to make you proud," Adam said on her heels.

"And you did."

"You did an amazing job on the bow," Adam said. "That's the only reason I could make the shot."

"That bow is junk, compared to the new ones I am working on."

"Well, I could never have figured it out like you did—the string alone is beyond anything I imagined."

"You shot it well. I could not believe it when you aimed way up in the tree. My heart stopped. It was an amazing shot. Go ahead and keep it," she said, handing him back the bow.

"Thank you, Eve," Adam said, and turned toward the path to the treehouse. "Good night," he called over his shoulder. He was still sticking with the savage story. It made no sense, unless true.

As she walked to her cave, Monkey rushed up to her. "Eve, have you seen Art?"

"No," she said. "Why?"

"I cannot find him anywhere," Monkey said. "He has disappeared." There was real concern in his eyes.

"So when was the last time you saw him?" Eve asked, thinking back to Adam's shooting demonstration. She had not seen Art.

"I am not sure," Monkey said. "I can't remember seeing him yesterday at all. Eve, I am worried. It is not like Art to miss a meal and he is not like Twig to go wandering off."

"Come on," she ordered and raced into Art's cave. She counted the kids—all there—and moved on to the next.

"Bev, are you sure?" she asked when the count came up short with Bev's family.

"Of course I am sure. I know my brothers and sisters, and my little sister is missing."

"Bloody bones, this is serious. We are being hunted," Eve said. The growing crowd looked on, unable to understand what was going on. They looked confused by all the racing around and counting. Eve had the gang together now, all except Adam. All were looking to her for direction. She looked around at their scared faces. She was in charge but she didn't know what on earth they should do. It was late and the light was all but gone.

"Okay everyone, don't panic," Twig instructed in a calm voice. "All of you get your families back to your caves. We'll be safe there. I know it might be hard, but try to encourage your family members not to go out alone. We can organize a hunt in the morning."

Eve had to agree with her instructions. It was the right thing to do and say. She went back to her cave and felt her way to her bed.

The darkness complete, she thought about Adam, alone at the treehouse, guarding the valley, still watching for the three invaders. Eve had not talked with him about such an important issue, and all over a stupid argument. Now Art was missing, maybe even dead. Adam must have been so frustrated as he had seen invaders and nobody believed him. Why, suddenly became clear. Monkey had been discrediting the whole idea, and all because of their stupid competition over her. It made her blood boil. Boys were so stupid.

Eve wondered if perhaps she should let her standoff with Adam end. He was not *doing his duty*, in fact he appeared to be ignoring the other girls. She was not the leader, but had been honored by Adam, who was acting like the tribe's leader, but after tonight it was clear Twig was in charge when it mattered. No one had won or lost. Perhaps her relationship with Adam was manageable now. It was no longer about her, but about her duty to the tribe. They needed leadership which worked. People were maybe dying, and she, as Blue Eyes daughter, needed to do what was needed to fix it.

As she lay on her mat, she began to cry. She had not led well. She had lost Art and Bev's little sister. She might even have lost Adam. The tribe was in danger, and all while she had been playing games. She needed the whole gang together, and focused on this new threat.

*Love is a promise; love is a souvenir,*
*Once given never forgotten, never let it disappear.*

*John Lennon*

# Growing Up     14

The next morning Eve called the gang together beside the Tree of Life. After such a crazy and confusing night, it was clear to her what had to be done. "Twig, I want you to stay here and organize the whole tribe to make bows and arrows. Without them, we are at great risk against a better armed enemy. Monkey and I will go find Adam. The three of us will find these invaders. I have a fine bow, and quite a few arrows, and so does Adam. Monkey, you are a master with the axe, and Twig can make you a bow as soon as possible. Fish, Bev, Little Red, keep together, and do what

Twig says. No sneaking off to fish," she said, giving Little Red a stare. "We are under attack."

Twig nodded her agreement and immediately began organizing the whole tribe to make bows, strings, and arrows.

Eve and Monkey packed a few things and said goodbye. She pulled Twig aside. "Thanks for doing this, could you also do me a favor? I want to make Adam the very best bow possible. He has my old piece of junk. Can you keep an eye out for the best possible wood and save it for me?"

Twig smiled. "I see, for Adam, yes, I can do that."

Eve took off down the path, running hard, visions of Adam's naked invaders popping out from behind every tree. The more she imagined the faster she ran. Monkey could barely keep up.

They met Adam near the cross roads. He looked alarmed. "What has happened?" he asked as they ran up.

"Art and Bev's little sister are missing," she gasped. "Have you seen anything?"

"No. I have been watching the paths around here. Nobody has come or gone."

"Really? How do you know?" Monkey asked.

"I have set little trips across all the paths, so if anyone walks by, they will knock them down. I just checked all of them this morning. Nobody is moving around down here."

"What a great idea. We need to set up some around the village," Monkey said. Eve was pleased to hear Monkey say something positive and not deride Adam. Yet the idea had problems.

"The tribe is all over that area," Eve said.

"We can set them each evening," Adam said. "We can set them off the main paths, in likely places an invader would walk. Clearly they are not using the paths near the settlement or someone would have seen them."

"Sounds good," Eve said.

"In the meantime, I think we should make patrols around the settlement, creeping up on likely hiding places, ready to strike." Adam and Monkey agreed and Eve took off running. Though the boys chased her, all her ideas of romance seemed silly now.

As they searched near the settlement, the three of them broke off the main path and began a slow, silent search. As time passed, Eve could see that Adam's confidence was waning and desperation was setting in. Meanwhile, Monkey, who had previously been supportive, now had a smug look on his face. Despite their efforts, there was still no evidence of the savages.

It was true that Art and Bev's sister were missing, and Eve's first thought was that they had been eaten by the savages. But as she continued to search, other possibilities began to enter her mind. Her thoughts were interrupted when she spotted something on the ground, causing her heart to stop.

"Look," she whispered, crouching and pointing. The boys dove for cover and stared intently. They waited, while Eve scanned the thick growth around them, listening intently for any signs of danger. All she heard was the familiar sounds of passing bugs and singing birds.

Monkey broke the silence. "What? I don't see anything," he said. The boys looked and shrugged.

"There, on the ground," Eve said, pointing.

"I don't see anything," Monkey said and stood.

"Look at that banana peel," she said.

"So?" Monkey asked, confused.

Eve shook a finger. "It's peeled from the wrong end."

"So?" Monkey asked again.

Adam smiled knowingly and pulled a banana off a nearby tree. He peeled it from the bottom, not the top. "Hey, will you look at that? Even the little strings stay with the skin. Why don't we peel it that way?" he said.

"Because we aren't savages?" Monkey replied. "This just might be the first evidence I have seen they are here, or maybe one of our tribe decided to peel a banana from the wrong end."

Adam gave him a baleful look. "No way, I told you they were here and this is the proof!"

"This is no time to argue," Eve said. She grabbed a banana and led them forward as she ate. When it grew dark, they returned home to protect their families.

It was in the dark of the night that Eve felt most vulnerable. These three savages were very clever, staying out of sight for so long and leaving no evidence but a banana peel. Her mind went to Art, her friend and part of her family, missing. Just yesterday she couldn't imagine how he had disappeared without a trace, but tonight, a chill ran down her spine. Could they have eaten him? Waves of nausea swept over her, and she cried for morning's light.

They repeated the pattern in the days which followed. Observing and creeping around, they set trip lines, and although they found more signs of the savages, they saw none. One evening, a tribeswoman screamed then staggered into the clearing. Eve raced to meet her. Two arrows pierced the woman's belly. She could not explain where she had been other than to gesture at the path. Eve organized a response. She directed Twig to care for the woman. Then she, Adam, and Monkey raced down the path. They followed the trail of blood.

"Here," Monkey called. "I found one of our baskets. She must have been picking fruit."

"A new trail starts here," Adam said, sweeping the grass with his bow by the last light of the day.

"Spread out, but be careful," Eve said, and they began their search. Darkness arrived quickly, but there was no sign of the attackers.

"They did it again," Monkey complained as they walked back to the caves. "You know, we only identified Bev's sister as missing because Bev counted her family. There could be others of the tribe missing, and there probably are. They are picking us off one at a time!"

Eve shared his frustration. She slept poorly that night. She kept seeing that poor woman in her mind. And if it wasn't her, thoughts of Art intruded as she tried to work out what they could do differently. She could think of nothing. As the days passed, the tribe made bows and arrows, and learned to use them, and she, Adam, and Monkey continued their patrols.

Each evening, more bow parts sent by Twig appeared in her bed. She spent the early part of each night working on Adam's new bow by firelight, while keeping watch. It kept her mind occupied, and was better than thinking about their enemy and wondering who would be eaten next, for surely they were eating them. During the days, she covertly collected materials to decorate the bow with colored string, dyed with various fruits, barks and roots with strong colors. At night, she wrapped the string ends tight and made a woven hand grip and arrow rest. Then she wove a matching quiver from split reeds with bits of matching colored string. Finally she added a strap.

For the most part Twig kept the gang busy making bows for the tribe, but when they were alone, she pressed Eve for details of what was happening with Adam. "I think we will figure it out eventually," Eve said with a smile.

"What's that supposed to mean?" Twig demanded, but Eve shrugged off the question. She wasn't exactly sure herself. She guessed Adam realized if he were to mate with other women, he would lose her forever. He must have decided she was worth waiting for, something she did not honestly expect would happen. She took strange pleasure knowing he was not *doing his duty.* When a dumb woman showed interest in him, as they did each evening when they returned, or even when Bev and Twig each took a run at him, he brushed them off, making it clear he wasn't interested. He was not rude about it, but he made his intentions perfectly clear.

"Where are they? This is getting ridiculous," Monkey declared one morning, after a youngster ran into the clearing with an arrow in his arm.

Eve had an inspiration. "What is the one place we haven't looked?"

"We've looked everywhere," Monkey said.

"We have seen where they have been collecting food, and seen where they are attacking us," Eve said. "But where could one hide, a place we never go because there is no food?"

"The haunted pines?" Adam said. "Of course. Nobody goes there since there is nothing to eat. They must keep coming back to our side of the stream for food. It is also scary over there."

"What do we do about the serpent?" Eve asked.

"If it hasn't killed them," Adam said with a shrug. "Maybe we will be lucky too."

Monkey looked thoughtful. "Or maybe it doesn't like to eat savages."

They headed away from the clearing. Crossing the stream, they entered the dark foreboding pines. Eve found herself holding Adam's hand.

They had a mission now, but it was still such a strange and mysterious place.

There was the rustle of leaves nearby. They all jumped, staring in terror. "The serpent," Eve whispered. There it was again—a bird scratching in the thick duff. She let out a great sigh, and they all smiled at each other.

As they worked their way closer to the village, Eve spotted movement. Not a bird this time. Her heart pounded. Savages or the serpent? Both would be trouble, but feeling powerful behind her bow, she continued forward. The boys followed, bows drawn and arrows notched. Adam and Monkey spread out. Monkey had been working hard with his new bow to catch up with their skill level but Eve wanted to get close enough that even he could not miss.

As she crept silently forward, her footfalls lost in the soft pine duff, Eve's hands started to shake. Savages squatted at the edge of the pine canopy observing the settlement. Eve was in range, and knew Adam would be good, but she hoped Monkey could hit something. This was different from shooting a melon. There were two males and one female. Catching Adam's eye, Eve nodded. Monkey looked over and nodded as well. They were all ready.

Eve drew back her bow's string, wondering if she could kill like this, without warning. It was different than last time, in the heat of battle. She remembered Twig's father, a shot to the neck. She adjusted her aim and took a deep breath.

She released her arrow. *Twang.* Adam and Monkey's bows sang as well. *Twang, Twang.* Eve's arrow missed as the savage spun toward her. Adam's arrow, however, hit the woman in the side. Monkey hit an arm. "Great Bones, another arrow or pull out our axes?" Eve asked, worried the savages were going to charge and kill them.

"Another arrow," Adam cried, already drawing back his bowstring. Eve fumbled with her arrow, notched it, and drew. She looked up; the savages, running fast, were nearly on her.

She released another arrow. *Twang.* This time she hit her target. Adam and Monkey both shot again. Then the time for the bows was over. Adam pulled his axe out and met Eve's male a few steps in front of her. He went right down, the fight already out of him. Monkey smote the other male, trading mighty blows. The female slowly dropped to the ground clutching an arrow in her chest. Then as suddenly as the fighting started, it was over.

Monkey pumped his bow over his head, and let out several hoots, as he stomped around his victim. "Yeah! Who is the best? We are!"

Eve cried quietly as Adam held her. She had panicked.

"You did what you had to do," he said gently. "We are all good now."

He held her for a while. Finally she wiped her eyes and smiled. "You have saved me once again."

When they dragged the three bodies across the stream, the whole tribe looked the savages over. Eve stood by Adam, holding his hand. She had enough of the secrecy. It was time everyone knew. Blue Eyes gave each of the bodies a solid kick before pulling the arrows from them. With a smile and a nod to each of them, he returned the arrows to their owners. How he knew whose arrow was whose, Eve had no idea. Men paid attention to those kinds of things, was all she could guess. Her father motioned then to his hunters to dump the bodies in the stream.

Twig and the rest of the gang waited impatiently. Eve gave them a quick explanation, then turned back to Adam. "Do you think we will ever find Art?" she asked.

"I am sure we would find what is left of him if we searched the pine woods," he said.

"We should just leave him then." Twig said "It is a good place to rest, and we should not disturb him."

Eve, exhausted from all the stress of the day, did not feel like arguing. She wondered at Twig's reasons, but it was getting dark, so she said goodnight to Adam and headed to her cave.

Twig followed and sat next to her on her bed. "So how is the bow coming along?"

Eve pulled it from under her covers and let Twig have a look. "Almost done," Eve said. "Now that this whole savage thing is over, I should be able to finish it tomorrow."

"I saw you had flowers in your hair the other day. From Adam?"

"Yes," Eve admitted.

"I am going to have to come up with another word for this ritual between you and Adam," she said.

"What ritual?" Eve asked innocently.

"It's like a pre-mating ritual. He brings you flowers, and you are making him this amazing bow."

"It's for the new chief," Eve said, suppressing a smile.

"Who just happens to be Adam and I see you two smiling at each other all the time, and holding hands right in front of the whole tribe."

"I don't know what you are talking about. There is nothing wrong with smiling."

"I guess I know what will come next," Twig laughed. "You're both acting like you have eaten too much of the fruit from the Tree of Life. We will all be glad when you just get on with it."

Eve laughed and put her hand on Twig's arm. "You are so right. It is quite ridiculous, but I can't help it. I feel silly most of the time, in spite of the savages. When I get the bow done, I think it will be time," Eve said smiling. "Or so I hope. Who knows what he is thinking? Men are so brain dead!"

Twig laughed. "Well, if you still don't want him, let me know," she said with a wink.

That night Eve again wondered at Twig. How did she know so much about the fruit from the

Tree of Life?  How would she know how you act when you eat too much?  It was all very strange, and yet Eve had something far more interesting to worry about.  Tomorrow was the big day.  She was giving him the bow in the evening.

## Adam's Preparation

Adam was chatting with Eve about the savages when she asked, "What do you have in mind for dinner?"  They had taken turns collecting food during the crisis; today was his turn.  Eve had never asked about what they would be eating before, and he found the question strangely put.  Her look was even more alarming.

"Something good?" he asked cautiously.

"You could bring us dinner out on the beach—just the two of us.  I think with these clouds, there should be a great sunset tonight," Eve said, nodding at the sky.  It was streaked with windblown clouds.  "I have a surprise for you."

"For me?" he asked.  "You're not going to hit me again, are you?"

She smiled sweetly.  "Who me?  Hit the big chief?  Never."

"Okay, let's meet at the treehouse.  I have some things to do . . . " he said awkwardly, unable to think of a convincing excuse to get away.  There was something about her that made it impossible to hide the truth, so he took off at a run before she could ask him what things he had to do.  He had a lot to do. First, he needed to gather a good meal. Then he needed to finish a knife he was making for her. He had a long way to go and he was unsure if this was the right kind of gift. He needed expert advice—he sought out Twig.

"I need to ask you something," he said to the skinny girl.

"Okay?" she answered. "About what?"

"Not here—come with me," he said and led her to his cave. Outside, he uncovered a hidden bone he had been rubbing on a rock to form the knife. He showed her what he had so far. He had spent all his time on the handle and had carved some designs into the end of the bone.

Twig made a face. "So, what is it?" she asked.

"It's supposed to be a knife," he answered, feeling downtrodden.

"You still have a way to go."

"I need it done by tonight," Adam said. His enthusiasm for it was sinking fast.

Twig blew out a breath. "Tonight, why tonight?"

I want to give it to Eve. We are having dinner on the beach and . . . " Adam stopped himself. "It's impossible isn't it?"

"Well this part you have finished is really nice," Twig said pointing at the carved end. "Why not cut it off here and put a hole in it and she can hang it around her neck."

Adam scoffed. "What? Come on Twig, I need help here."

"I am helping, but you're not listening," she replied.

"Well what would it be for?"

"Nothing, just because you love her," Twig said.

"That's stupid. She would laugh and throw it away. It's useless."

"Trust me," Twig said. "Make it pretty like a flower, tie a few nice shells on the string and she will love it."

"But what would it be?"

"I don't know, I will have to make up a new word for it. It can be like a symbol of your love. How about that?" she said. She was clearly enjoying herself.

"I will give it a try, but I think it's a dumb idea," Adam said. "If she hates it, I'll tell her it was all your idea."

"And if she loves it?"

"I will take all the credit, of course," he said.

Twig laughed. "Sounds like you have it all figured out."

"With your help," Adam said. "And, Twig, thank you. Now I have to get busy. We are eating on the beach tonight to watch the sunset."

Twig shook her head and giggled.

"Oh, and Twig—don't tell anyone about our plans, okay?"

She agreed and left him to his work.

## Eve's Preparation

Eve, now free from Adam, finished her bow and set out to look for Twig in the afternoon. It was a relief when she saw her emerging from the woods, herbs in hand. Eve had been working on her hair, braiding part of it and pulling it back. Eve needed to know what Twig thought of her new style, so she asked her excitedly, spinning around to show it off.

"It's great," Twig said, making a few adjustments. "So, tonight's the night?"

"Yes," Eve said. "I am off to the big tree now. Can you do me a favor and keep the gang away this evening?"

"Only if you promise to tell me everything. I suspect I will need a number of new words before you two are done!"

"Yuck, that's disgusting," Eve said and ran towards the big tree, waving over her shoulder to Twig. Eve retrieved the bow and quiver then ran them to the beach. She hid them in the sand in front of the log she and Adam had fought on last time. Then she ran back to the treehouse as fast as she could. She burst into the clearing, gasping for breath. Adam stood under the tree waiting, looking anxious, a woven reed bag over his shoulder.

"I was afraid you had forgotten," he said.

"Hardly, I just felt like taking a run," Eve said, sounding stupid to herself.

He took her hand. "Shall we go?"

They walked fast. Eve kept the conversation going about nothing. She couldn't believe how nervous she was. The idea of silence was terrifying, so she kept on about how nice the day was.

They arrived on the beach well before the sunset. As Adam spread out the food, Eve relaxed. There was something magical about sharing a meal, even when nervous. She explained her ideas about that; he listened and then, the meal was finished. "Thank you for making dinner," she said. "It was very good."

Adam opened his mouth, but no words came out. He closed his mouth and Eve could feel the same tension she had felt last time they sat here on the log. She felt she needed to resolve it. She needed to fix what she had said last time, but didn't know how. Seeing Adam also struggling was a relief. Maybe he wasn't so sure of himself after all. Maybe he was as nervous as she was.

## The Question

"It was my pleasure," Adam finally managed to say after a long pause. He couldn't think of what else to say sitting here next to perfect, beautiful Eve. She turned his mind into a fog with her sky-blue eyes on him. He stared at his feet in the sand. This wasn't going well. He'd led a hunt and killed a wild beast. He'd battled with savages, but just knowing Eve was looking at him robbed him of his courage. *I can do this*, he told himself, and glanced up at her. She seemed to be enjoying his bewilderment. He wanted to run away, but then, out of the fog, he suddenly remembered Twig's last words of advice. "Your hair looks very nice," he said.

To his surprise, she smiled sweetly. "Thank you, I braided it just for you."

He glanced back down. *Wow.* Twig was correct about that. Maybe the necklace wasn't stupid either. With new courage, he continued still looking at his feet in the sand. "I have something for you, a token of my love for you, if you will accept it." He glanced at her. "I'm sorry for what I said last time we were here. I was wrong. If you will have me, I would like you to be my only mate for life. I promise to worship you, like I do the Tree of Life, always. You are beautiful and smart. I'm not worthy of your love, but will do my best to make you proud of everything I do."

He took a deep breath and, with shaking hands, he pulled the necklace out and put it over her head and around her neck. His head spun and time stood still. He finally worked up the courage to bring his eyes to meet hers.

She was crying. *Oh, no,* Adam thought, *I have blown it again. I am going to kill Twig. Her and her stupid ideas.*

But then Eve smiled and fingered the necklace. "Oh Adam, I love it. It is so beautiful. I will always treasure it. I would be honored to be your mate and I promise to obey and respect you as my chief. I have always loved you and always will. I also have something for you."

She dug around in the sand and produced a bow and quiver full of arrows. He stared at the intricate details, and fine workmanship. "Do you like it?" she asked.

"It's amazing. I have never imagined anything so incredible. I cannot believe you found the time to make this without me knowing." He stretched the bow and shouldered the quiver. "You are amazing," he said. "I love you."

"Twig says we are married now, another of her new words. It means we are exclusive mates for life. I like the sound of that," she said, still fingering her necklace. "I love you, too."

"You will be the envy of every woman in the tribe," he said.

"And not just because I am married to the chief, but because a man loves me enough to make me this thing, this necklace which has no function at all but to declare his love!" she said proudly.

Adam set down the bow and took Eve in his arms. As the sun dipped below the horizon, he kissed her. Twig was so smart. He couldn't believe how well the evening had gone so far. Soon, the brilliant orange sky began to fade to gray.

Adam and Eve slipped to the sand in a loving embrace. Joy, contentment like Adam never thought possible flooded through him. They had both grown up living in cramped quarters. They often witnessed the animal act of reproduction. It was quick, it was urgent but appeared to end joyfully. *We are different.* It was something Eve had said, and Adam thought he understood now. What might they experience? It was a grand unknown waiting to be discovered. The night was warm, and he determined to discover it all.

The stars began to show and the moon rose over the water. He gently caressed Eve with a finger and she responded with a ripple of pleasure. She seemed to ache with desire as he did. He learned what pleased her and took his time until at last a terrible animal instinct possessed them both, and they became as one.

## Married

Eve didn't want to open her eyes, but the morning sun was on her cheeks. She had an uneasy feeling, like being watched. She opened one eye. Adam sat, staring at her, a goofy smile on his face.

"You are beautiful when you sleep," he said. "But even more beautiful when awake. And I love that look you give me when you don't approve, like right now." His smile turned to a boyish grin.

Eve sat up. "Better get used to that look, husband, because you're stuck with me now," she said, smiling herself. "What are our plans for the day?"

"I can't imagine how our ancestors got anything done, not wearing any clothes," Adam said. "When I see you like this, only one thing comes to mind," he said, taking and kissing her hand. She felt a thrill.

"And why is that?" she asked coyly, glancing away as if not interested.

"I'll show you," he said and did, and then they slept again, in the warm morning sun. When they woke, and dressed, they sauntered, hand-in-hand, back toward the big tree with the treehouse. Adam had his new bow in one hand and the quiver over his shoulder. Eve thought it looked good on him. She glanced down at the necklace, the one item that had not been removed and she determined it never would be. "What are we going to do?" she asked as they walked.

He grabbed her. "I have a great idea," he mumbled.

Later, she tried again. "I mean, what are we going to do about where we will live?" she asked as they waded into the river, holding hands for a bath and a swim.

"Honestly, I never thought about it," Adam said. "I guess mates usually move in with the man's family, but as your father was chief and has the best cave, maybe I should move in with your family."

She puckered her lips. "I am afraid I couldn't do what we just did in front of either of our families. So, if you think you might like to do that again sometime, maybe we should find our own place," she said kindly, but firmly.

"Oh, yes, I see what you mean. Well, I guess we better. All the caves are taken, but I am the leader. You pick the cave you want, and I will kill the inhabitants—it could be a good way to break in my new bow," he said, his voice full of bravado.

"Very funny. How about we live in the treehouse?" she suggested, until we can figure out a better solution. It's dry, comfortable and private."

"Well that sounds easy enough. In fact, it would not be a bad idea to keep a closer eye on the crevice. Let's get our stuff," Adam declared and they headed back to the village.

The gang saw them coming and ran to meet them. Twig had obviously given them enough information and they were dying to hear all that had transpired. Twig began the questioning.

Eve gave her a dark look. "I will explain on the way to the treehouse, if you guys could give us a hand with our things." But the boys, seeing Adam's new bow and quiver, had him take it off and show them all its amazing features. Much to Eve's delight, Twig and Bev stared at her necklace, clearly envious. Nobody in the tribe had jewelry before. The tribe's people came to see what all the commotion was about; few of the men missed the envious looks the women gave the necklace.

Eve had the gang pile their things near the Tree of Life, and then Twig had them bring out some fruit and food they had collected, including a recently caught fish. This prompted others in the tribe to bring gifts, including a skin, and some household items. It was a surprise as there had never been a marriage event before and all were very curious about what it all meant. At last, the celebration was over, and the gang loaded their things and started down the path.

Eve grabbed Adam's hand and dragged him back to where her parents stood by their cave. She gave them each a hug, and nudged Adam, and he did the same. As they hurried to catch up she glanced back and saw her parents looking pleased. Her mom had wrapped a bit of grass around her neck and was prodding her father.

"We didn't know where you were going to live, or when you might come back, so I made them wait here. Of course, they all wanted to go spy on you last night and this morning," Twig said authoritatively as if she wasn't also dying of curiosity.

"Thank you, Twig," Eve said. "I cannot tell you how grateful we are."

As they walked toward the treehouse Twig demanded a full and detailed account of everything which had happened, including their conversations, word-for-word.

When either hesitated, she reminded them, "Yours is the first romance, the first marriage and your gifts and vows are the first ever spoken, and we must learn all about them so the tradition can be followed by the rest of us and our children and their children."

"Oh, please," Eve moaned. "It was not all that well planned, but it was special." She squeezed Adam's arm, and smiled at him. Fish rolled his eyes and pretended to be shot with an arrow. "I guess we can tell you about it."

"Everything," Twig insisted.

Eve glanced at Twig and blushed. "Not everything!"

"Oh?" said a clearly disappointed Twig. "Well get started and we will see."

## A New Household

Adam smiled to himself. All this talk was a bit much, but he was pleased he had managed his part well enough, and he was not going to admit that without Twig's coaching, he would have messed it up horribly. Eve pretty much recited every word they said, to a captivated audience.

As they arrived at the treehouse, the gang started to get comfortable. Eve made an announcement. "I have a new word to add to our language, and we are starting it today. We will call it the honeymoon, because it is sweet and will be witnessed by the moon, and no one else. We will be living here and for a time, we want to have privacy to enjoy each other without wondering if Little Red is hiding behind a bush. So, from now on, the moment the sun touches the horizon, until mid-morning, the big tree is off limits, unless by invitation, for a while at least. Got it?"

"Right," said Adam. "Sun down until noon." He glanced at Eve and got the look. "Until mid-morning, the treehouse is off limits."

Adam wondered if he shouldn't have pushed harder for noon or even for late afternoon. Eve was just too beautiful. But her look made it clear he would only have her to himself until mid-morning and he let the rule stand.

Fish spoke up. "But we want to come and observe your nocturnal mating habits so we can learn."

"Best you learn that on your own when the time comes," Adam said with a scowl that ended that idea. "So, take off and we will see you tomorrow, mid-morning, no earlier."

As the chatter of the gang faded away, Adam started to plan a relaxing afternoon, but Eve had big plans for the treehouse, and instead, they spent the rest of the day getting their new home arranged. It was almost dark by the time they were settled, and Adam was exhausted, so they decided to take a swim in their private pool. It was not the afternoon he had in mind but was glad to make Eve happy on their first day together.

Eve slipping out of her clothes and stepping into the cool water. "This is so different," Eve said.

"Seems nice to me," Adam answered as he bobbed over to meet her. Their faces were just inches apart. "I could get used to this. I have a whole new understanding of the ways of the tribe." He pulled her close.

"Again? Really?" she chided. "With your vast intelligence applied to solving all the treehouse problems, I would have thought you would not have the energy."

"You're the brains—I am just the muscle," Adam chuckled.

"I can tell," Eve giggled.

Later, back in the treehouse, he complimented Eve on her idea of the honeymoon.

"It is amazing but probably not long enough," he complained. "We should have extended it to noon."

"I'm sure it will be long enough, Eve said wistfully. "It is very quiet here all alone. At the village we were never alone. I kind of miss just having people around. Meals will be kind of lonely."

"I don't miss my family at all. It will be amazing not to have to hear my father snoring all night," Adam said. "But I understand, the men hunt together, and the women prepare meals and take care of the children together. I wouldn't like to hunt alone, so we will invite the gang to join us for meals. It will be okay."

He did his best to cheer her up by helping with the evening meal. *Only married to me one day and already homesick?* he thought. If Eve showed up at home, he would never hear the end of it, and he made an extra effort to keep her mind off her family.

# Babies

Despite her initial fear of loneliness, Eve found their first night in their new home quite pleasant. She especially enjoyed the time laying on their mats, seeing the moonlight reflected off the water, making little patterns of light in the treehouse. She and Adam held hands just talking. This was something unknown in the tribe—they lay down and went to sleep in less than a blink of an eye. She and Adam had something no one else did and she loved it, but having a baby worried her.

"I guess I will start having babies now, won't I?" she asked.

"It does seem that one thing does lead to another," he answered sheepishly.

"A baby will change everything, Adam."

"Only if we let it. I am sure we can get help."

"If you say so," she said snuggling next to him. "You have a good answer for everything but it will make a big change. What have we done to ourselves?"

Adam grunted and she closed her eyes and wished him a good night. He didn't answer. He was already asleep. She let out a long sigh. Maybe some things wouldn't be all that different.

*When one door closes, another opens; but we often look so long and so regretfully upon the closed door that we do not see the one that has opened.*

Alexander Graham Bell

# To Serendipity 15

In the following weeks, a new dynamic formed among the gang and young speakers. Adam became like a father to them, the undisputed leader and Eve became their mother. Twig was their wise, all-knowing aunt and teacher. Twig was particularly frustrated with the lack of progress they made on fire. "If naked savages can make it, we should be able to make it as well!" she declared on more than one occasion. But despite her efforts, no progress was made.

One day, not much different than any other, they were busy around the treehouse, Eve was helping Twig teach the younger children, a task that was taking an increasing amount of time, Little Red and Fish were making new fishing poles; Twig and Eve exchanged glances when a fight broke out. Fish had assigned Little Red the job of drilling a hole in the bamboo cane, using a sharp shell. Drilling holes was a time-consuming project so Little Red objected.

Adam interceded. "Little Red, just drill the bloody hole!"

Little Red sat down in disgust and took one of his arrows, and, putting the point in the start of the hole, held the other end with a piece of leather. Then he looped the string of his bow around the arrow and drew the bow back and forth spinning the arrow first one way, then the other. It cut right through the bamboo, raising a little pile of dust.

"But what about the dumb children? Should we try to teach them anything?" Eve asked Twig, ignoring the boys. But again she was interrupted by their loud voices.

"You pushed too hard. It was working but now you broke an arrow, you dumb nut," Fish exploded.

"I'm a whole lot smarter than your dumb looking face, look, it will still work," Little Red said. He pressed harder and sawed back and forth with his bow faster and faster. "See, it's done," Little Red cried a few moments later. "It would have taken you all day."

One of the children Eve and Twig were teaching asked a question, but Eve shushed them all. A solution to drilling holes was most welcome.

Fish scoffed and grabbed up the pole. "Let me see." His hand touched the black hole in the bamboo pole. "Ow, bloody bones!" he bellowed, dropping the pole.

"What is it?" Eve asked as he stood grabbing his hand.

"It's hot," Fish said. "What do I do?"

"Hot?" Twig asked, jumping to her feet. "Put it in your mouth. Quick."

He complied then just as quickly she snatched his hand and had a look. "It's blistered like when you use your axe too long."

"Will it ever heal?," Fish cried, holding out his hand for the rest to see, but the gang ignored him and gathered around Little Red.

"Do what you were doing again," Adam told Little Red as the gang pressed closer, watching. "I think you're onto something."

Adam handed him a piece of bamboo. Little Red made a starter hole with his shell, then he began sawing with his bow string around the shaft of his dull arrow.

"Faster," Twig told him, but Little Red suddenly stopped. He pulled his hand from the top of the arrow where he had been steadying it. "I can't. The leather is too hot," he said, showing his palm. Twig touched it.

Fish dunked a scrap of leather in the river and handed it to him. "Push with this."

Little Red took the leather and with it to protect his hand, he began spinning much faster. A wisp of smoke rose from the bamboo where the arrow pierced and blackened it.

"Smoke!" Eve screamed. She could smell it in the air, a new smell in their valley.

"Is it hot?" Twig asked.

Little Red stopped.

He touched the black arrow tip, gingerly. "Hot," he declared.

"Everyone, try different kinds of wood," Adam said. "Let's see what we can do."

In no time the whole gang was spinning different kinds of sticks into different kinds of wood. The area around the big tree was soon thick with smoke. Twig and Eve worked together. Eve pressed down on the arrow, and Twig worked the bow. Twig had found some dry fluffy stuff from a seed pod and put in the hole in her block, a soft dry wood. Suddenly the fluff glowed red and burst into flames.

"We did it!" she screamed in delight and the gang pressed around, but the fire promptly went out. But the initial success sent everyone racing around for similar things that might burn. After plenty of choking and coughing, a reliable method was found. Adam made a circle of stones as they had seen on the hunt. A fire burned in it in no time.

"This is amazing. Feel the heat," Eve exclaimed, holding her hands as close to the fire as she dared. Eve glanced at Adam. He smiled and they hugged each other.

"Hang on everybody." Fish ran to his traps and came back with a fish. He cleaned it and stuck it on a stick then held it over the flames of the crackling fire.

"Oh my, that smells so good, let me have a taste," Bev cried.

"No, me first!" said Little Red. "I found the fire."

"I think we all helped, don't you?" Eve said.

They divided the fish.

"Let's cook everything," Fish cried and started gathering food.

"Water does not cook very well," Monkey observed as he put the fire mostly out in a big cloud of steam. Fish called him an idiot but it did turn out to be the best way to kill the flames, which Fish finally agreed was not actually some kind of animal.

As darkness fell, they kept on. They could see by the fire light. They cooked things, lit sticks on fire and twirled them around and threw them out over the water. Then Little Red wrapped an arrow with bark, lit it on fire and launched it high in the air. Having never seen anything so amazing, members of the gang leapt for joy and applauded.

The next morning, the gang refined their fire lighting method. It was still a two-person job, but Eve could see how it could be done alone. They used two wood blocks, a hard wood on top and soft on the bottom to hold a soft wood stick which they spun. The key seemed to be to prepare a little slot alongside the primary hole in the bottom block, in which the fine wood dust and eventually the first ember would be contained. Once glowing, one could carefully transfer the heat to dry shredded bark. With a bit of blowing a fire blazed. With the right materials, it was quick and reliable.

"Alright gang," Twig announced. "Let's go show the villagers how to make fire."

"Why?" Little Red asked.

"Because fire is too important for us to hoard," Adam replied. "Don't you want your mother to cook your food?"

"Yeah, I guess so," he conceded.

Adam led the gang back to the village for a demonstration. Eve tried to evaluate her feelings as they walked. All her ideas were muddled up. She had been so sure all that mattered was leading the gang, and now, their biggest discovery was about to be shared with the tribe and she was not even consulted. Twig led the procession, her hair thrown back and head held high. Eve gave her a critical look. Who was really in charge? Twig? She sure looked like it. *So bloody smug.*

At the settlement, Adam directed the making of a rock circle and gathered dry wood as the villagers crowded around to watch. Blue Eyes arrived with his axe. He glanced around like he was looking for savages.

Eve smiled at him and pulled him down to squat next to her. The confusion in his eyes turned to pride as Adam spun the stick and Little Red prepared the tinder. Everyone watched the stick spin, and gasped at the first puff of smoke, then gasped again at the first sign of flames. Once the fire was burning hot, Eve cooked a piece of meat. The whole village pressed closer, and began roasting various foods stuck on sticks.

The gang taught their families how to start their own fires and how to put them out with water. Eve was grateful the valley was lush and green. She worried if dry, they would have burnt it all down. Little fires were burning everywhere.

Adam found Eve and took her aside, coughing in the heavy smoke. "This is crazy stuff," he said with a smile on his tear streaked and blackened face. "But we have to do something about all this smoke."

"They will settle down eventually," Eve assured him. A group of children ran between them with burning sticks.

Adam coughed again. "I think I have an idea, but we need to head back to the treehouse to try it out."

"Now?" Eve asked. "Surely it will keep until morning. It's late, let's just stay the night."

"I guess we could stay," he said and broke up two other children, poking each other with flaming sticks.

"We can go back in the morning. You know our world will never be the same after this. This is a big discovery and a special night," Eve said, ducking as a burning torch flew overhead, showering sparks down on them. "We probably haven't found out half the things we can do with fire yet."

Adam rolled his eyes at one of the firecrazed children. "That's for sure."

When they arrived back at the treehouse, Adam began to collect stones from along the river. When he caught her looking out the window at him, he smiled up at her.

Eve pictured children of her own, playing along the river. This new life, this new reality with Adam and soon a family made the sadness of her loneliness disappear. She felt her belly. She couldn't tell if something was growing within her yet, but she knew it was just a matter of time. She worked on her sewing as Adam toiled. When she stole glances at his creation, she wondered what it was exactly, something to do with fire and with smoke. His stone box was taking shape just beyond the branches of their tree.

## The First Stove

"Ready for a demonstration?" Adam shouted. He was determined to solve the smoke problem and had worked all morning creating a head high firebox and chimney. Eve had been asking questions, but until he was sure it would work, he had said nothing. "Bring some food to cook," he called to her now.

Eve arrived with a range of foods. "So what on earth is it?" she asked.

"Just an idea I had. You see, we put the wood here below this flat rock," he explained. "Now go ahead and light the fire."

Adam waited, holding his breath as she lit the fire. At first it seemed the only benefit would be a flat cooking surface provided by the large flat rock he had positioned over the flames, the smoke still mostly wafted in their faces.

"Adam, look, the smoke is coming out the chimney," Eve exclaimed a moment later.

"The fire makes the air hot, and it rises for some reason. I figured if I gave it a path up, it would take the smoke with it." She gave him a smile like he was a genius. All the work was justified.

"The fire feels much hotter," Eve observed as she started cooking him a meal. "It's going to take a lot less wood this way," she said. "Just think of the time you'll save gathering wood." He grunted at her remark, but she kissed him several times to take the sting out of her comment. "Wait until the gang sees this, they'll think you're a genius."

"It just seemed like the thing to do," he said modestly. "I wonder why they haven't come to see us yet."

"I don't know," Eve said distractedly. "I love the shelves to cook on and to keep things warm, and best of all, there is absolutely no smoke in my face.

"I've realized that now that we've tasted cooked food, we'll be sitting around this fire every day for the rest of our lives. It's worth it to make it comfortable," he said.

She kissed him again and again. This was more like it. When they had finished eating, Eve looked at the path. "No sign of the gang."

"Probably all too full of food to walk," Adam laughed, "Oh, Eve! I have enjoyed being alone just with you."

*I have not failed. I've just found 10,000 ways that won't work.*

Thomas Edison

# Big Problems  16

"I have something special planned for dinner tonight. Be home early," Eve said a number of weeks later as Adam prepared to leave the treehouse.

"I will be working with Fish," Adam said. "Can I bring him home for food too?"

"Sure. I don't see why not," she said. She exchanged glances with Twig, then kissed him goodbye. "They are hollowing out a log, I think," Eve added to Twig, who had arrived early and was a part of the meal Eve was planning. They both had a good laugh at the idea.

"I don't know what he is up to with this log, but the guys are excited about it. I am more excited about cooking. Would you care for a cup of tea?"

Twig smiled, proud of their new discovery. "Why that would be very nice. I will heat up the rocks," she said and put a number of round smooth stones in the fire.

She and Eve had found a great way to boil water, heating stones in the fire and dropping them in a coconut shell full of water. As the water boiled, she could make all kinds of things. Twig was experimenting with new medicines and Eve with new foods. Tea was a new favorite for both of them. Twig had determined that dried peppermint leaves made the best tea and as Twig prepared a brew Eve chatted with her about all the other things they had been able to make with boiled water.

"We have come a long way in just a short time," Eve commented. "The ability to preserve meat and fish by smoking it will allow further travel on our hunts. And all the new foods we have added to our diet, especially all the tubers and roots which used to be tough and woody have added enormously to the available food supply. We have so much now we hardly need meat."

"But I still like it, even the parts I used to find disgusting," Twig said, licking her lips.

"I've been working on this new recipe. I call it soup," Eve said. "We will prepare a large bowl of boiling water, add a dash of salt water from the sea to enhance the flavor and cook many different things in it, all of them adding flavor to the water. It will taste amazing—Adam will flip."

As they collected the ingredients they talked. Eve could tell what Twig wanted to talk about, but was being careful. Finally Twig found her opportunity. "But let's talk about you. Can you give me an update?" Twig had been using Eve to study the reproductive system. She was one of the only speakers who was married, and Twig wanted to know everything about everything. Eve only told her what she needed to know, and when they returned to the treehouse, they started cooking the soup.

"Good," Twig exclaimed, tasting the broth. "How about a little more of this spice," she said, bringing out a ground up seed from a plant she discovered. "It adds a pleasing smell to anything it's cooked with." Eve agreed, breathing in its wonderful aroma.

A naked man walked into their cooking area. Eve screamed. The man carried a long pointed stick, which he pointed at Eve. She desperately looked around. With no other weapons handy, Eve snatched up her cooking knife. Twig's eyes grew big and she moved behind Eve. "Thanks Twig," Eve said. "Big help you are."

"You have the knife."

Eve tried to make a plan. The man looked like the other savages who had found their way into the valley. He would know that fire meant food, and probably came when he saw their smoke. Maybe, just maybe he was hungry and would eat the food they had prepared, rather than try to kill them. Eve pointed at the food cooking next to the fire. He glanced at it, then took another step closer to her and Twig. He seemed to be alone, a good thing—unless his friends were circling behind them.

Without turning, and keeping eye contact as she moved, Eve stepped back. She bumped into Twig.

"Get help," Eve hissed, pushing Twig back. "I don't think he wants our food."

He didn't. He took a few more steps closer and jabbed his spear at her. Eve backed up further. She reached the edge of the stream—Twig was gone. Eve held the knife in front of her, and stepped back into the water. *Oh for a bow.*

The man lunged again, but was several paces away. It was a signal. She was to respond, but she had no idea what he wanted her to do.

"Adam," Eve screamed at the top of her lungs.

The man did not seem to like the scream, so Eve screamed again, even louder, and held her ground. He shook his head like the sound hurt his ears. Too terrified to do anything else, Eve laughed at his confusion and waved her knife in his face. "That's right!" she shouted. "Come one step closer if you want to die!"

She screamed again, and suddenly, Adam came crashing into the clearing. Fish was right behind him. Adam flew forward, his axe raised high.

The savage ran into the jungle. Adam and Fish ran after him.

Out of breath, Twig arrived from the path.

"So much for a special dinner," Eve said after explaining how Adam and Fish had saved her. "Hopefully they will catch him before it gets cold." Twig just stared at her. "Don't worry," Eve added with a shrug. "He didn't touch me."

The guys were soon back, a little bloody but in good spirits. "Then *ploop*," Fish said. "Right in the river."

"Something smells wonderful," Adam called from the river bank as he and Fish washed up. "Nothing like a battle to give a man an appetite."

"What is wrong with you two?" Twig said.

"Don't worry about them," Eve said. "Men are crazy."

"These two certainly are," Twig replied testily.

"Tonight, we will eat something new. I call it soup," Eve announced as the men sat down at the table. "I made spoons to help us eat it." She passed the three of them a coconut shell bowl and a shell, its edges smooth, and mounted on a short bamboo handle. They sat with spoon in hand, waiting eagerly.

"Oh my, look at this. I see chunks of fish, roots, all kinds of things," Adam said as Eve poured him a bowl of soup. He tasted it, and rolled his eyes with a groan. "This is fantastic, a whole meal in a bowl, and it's portable too. No wonder that savage wanted to come down and get some."

Fish laughed at his joke. "I am going to have to take this idea of a wife more seriously," he declared. "I could get used to this kind of eating."

Twig blushed, and for a while they all focused on eating. The only sound was the sound of them slurping their soup. Eve felt like she was living a dream. Savages were springing out of nowhere, right into their home, and Adam and Fish carried on like nothing had happened. She wondered if this was to be the new normal.

"So," Eve said. She supposed it would be. "I have an important announcement. I am with child."

Adam looked awestruck. He jumped up, gave her a hug, and then checked her stomach. "Are you sure?"

"Of course, she's sure," Twig said. Adam looked at her in surprise. "We're sure," Twig added.

"Twig and I have been making observations and we are pretty sure. The signs are all there," Eve explained.

"Well that's wonderful," Adam said excitedly. "When?"

"Sometime after the monsoon," Twig said, in her teaching voice.

"Ah, the wonders of modern thinking," Eve said.

"A boy or a girl?" Adam asked eagerly.

Twig laughed. "Now you are asking for too much. You will have to wait and see!"

That night Adam could not stop talking about the baby. The savage attack was seemingly forgotten.

"Well, I'm glad you're happy, Adam," Eve said, sharply. "But I am the one who has to do all the work. I am the one who will suffer all the pain, and I am not sure about living here with savages dropping in for dinner all the time." She regretted the comment when she saw his hurt look.

The next morning, he was gone early, sometime before she woke. As the day passed, Eve wondered what had become of him. She recalled their conversation from the night before. She had been sharp with him, but he had never run away because of that before. Usually he simply ignored her complaining. She was in the treehouse later that afternoon when she heard him call. "I've got a surprise for you, come on down."

To her surprise Adam had a girl from the village beside him. Eve was not impressed, but even more irritated that he seemed genuinely surprised at her dissatisfaction with whatever he was up to.

"She can come every day," he explained. "To help with gathering wood."

Eve scowled. "But that is your job."

Adam cleared his throat and continued. "She can clean, and help with cooking and with the baby too."

Eve had seen the girl before but did not know her. Now she smiled submissively at Eve.

"Her family doesn't want her and no man either," Adam continued. Eve could see why; the poor creature was short, had a boy-like figure and flat chest. Her crooked teeth and out of control hair did not help.

"Oh, Adam, I don't know," Eve began and the girl gave Eve the most pathetic smile, as if she understood she was once again being judged and once again was failing to make the cut. The ways of the tribe could be so very cruel. She would certainly be among the community of women caring for the young, and under the leaders protection, but with no baby of her own, she was destined to live out her life at the lowest rank, doing the bidding of everyone in the tribe, beaten if she didn't, until she died, exhausted and alone. *The poor dumb thing.*

Eve made up her mind as Adam extolled the girl's virtues. *I won't be party to the cruelty.* She could not change the tribe, but she could change this girl's life. " . . . mate, I mean how could you be jealous, look at her," Adam said. "No temptation there—not even with a basket over her head."

"Adam!" Eve shouted. "That is so mean. How can you say that?"

"What? I'm just saying. You don't have to worry." Eve tried to cow him with a withering stare but he pulled her close, gave her a kiss, and whispered into her ear. "So, do you want her, or should I find another?"

"She will do just fine," Eve answered, intrigued by this new development.

"I don't want you to feel overworked," he said, then made his escape.

Eve took the girl by the hand and explained to her with hand signals that she was to come by every day at mid-morning and leave at sunset. She was not sure how much or if any of the explanation was understood. Eve looked around for something else for the girl to do. Adam arrived with an armful of wood. With a nod from Eve, he sent her with an axe to chop more.

"What do we call her?" Eve asked when she was out of sight.

"Whatever you want," he laughed. "Call her Toadface if you want."

"Adam!" Eve snapped. "If you treat her like a toad, she will act like a toad. How about Rosy?"

Adam laughed. "Rosy is great."

When Rosy arrived back with an arm full of wood, Eve stopped her. "Eve." She pointed to herself, then pointed to the girl. "Rosy." Eve repeated this until she was satisfied the girl understood. Eve then had her sweep the treehouse. Soon after the girl started, Twig stopped by. Eve explained the situation.

"Can you take her home with you tonight and bring her back in the morning, so she gets the idea?" Eve asked her friend. "I don't think she got a hint of what I tried to explain."

Twig readily agreed, interested in this new development as well. "And will Adam have relations with Rosy?" she asked.

"Certainly not. He said that's why he picked such an ugly girl to help, so he wouldn't be tempted. Isn't that horrid?"

Twig laughed.

Adam walked in, back from his and Fish's project. "What's so funny?" he asked, looking between them.

"Nothing," Eve said as she glared at Twig. The girl just laughed and laughed.

At dusk, Twig took Rosy and left for the village. The next morning, when they returned, Twig's face was livid and Rosy approached looking at her feet. Eve ran to meet them.

"What happened, is everything alright?"

"Everything is most certainly not alright!" Twig replied, shaking with anger. "Sometimes I just hate our people, they can be such brutes. Rosy's family did not want her back," Twig steamed. She lifted Rosy's down-turned face, revealing a black eye and a swollen lip. "Just look at what they did! Her own family. They beat her and kicked her out. She spent the night on the ground outside my place. We are as ignorant as savages! It makes me so mad."

"Calm yourself Twig, you're scaring her." Eve hugged Rosy, then sat her down and gave her some leftover meat from dinner the night before. "Adam," she bellowed. He appeared at a run from the woods. "Adam, we have a situation. Could you please build a little shelter for Rosy down here? The treehouse is too small for us all. Rosy will be staying with us full-time."

"Oh, I see" he said with a bewildered look on his face.

"Thanks, sweetie," Eve said and gave him a kiss.

"I'll get my axe," he said and set to work.

Twig stood watching, her hands on her hips. "Yes, well, I see you have everything nicely in hand here, don't you?"

Eve smiled. "I suppose I do."

## The Servant Problem

Adam wondered about the sudden change with Rosy but didn't let it stop him from doing as Eve asked. He decided to build the shelter under the tree, using one of the low branches running parallel to the ground. He cut a bundle of large bamboo canes and made a roof by leaning them against the branch from both sides. Then he inserted canes between each rafter to make a floor a foot off the ground, as it was often wet under the tree. He tied smaller canes horizontally to the roof and cut reed along the river to use as thatch. All Rosy needed to do was weave a mat for the floor, and triangular screens to hang on the ends and it would be a dry, snug place to sleep. He took Rosy out and showed her what reeds to harvest and how to weave the mat and she did the rest. By dinner time, it was done. Rosy took the warm skin

Eve offered her, and with a face splitting smile, she crawled into her new house when dinner was over.

Adam smiled at Eve. "Did I do well?" he asked as they climbed up into the treehouse.

"Yes, you did well, husband," Eve replied. "Very well."

As they settled into bed as usual, she still looked concerned. "Adam," she said. "I am not sure about this situation."

"What do you mean?" he asked.

"I mean Rosy. You saw what they did to her."

"Yeah, she is going to be all black and blue in the morning. But she is safe now, so what is bothering you?" he said.

"What we have done for Rosy was kind and has given her the possibility of a life, where otherwise she would have none. I don't see what choice we had, but it makes me wonder where this will lead."

"Ah, I see what you mean," Adam answered, having no idea what 'this' was and where it might lead.

"Some men will take advantage, and some will abuse—badly," Eve continued. "It's a problem the leader needs to deal with. Nobody else will. The dumb are multiplying faster than those with speech, and the problem will only get worse."

"Well, I don't know what to do about it."

"Well, I don't either," Eve said. "And we don't need to solve it tonight, but it's a problem the leader will have to address." She snuggled up next to him and promptly fell asleep.

*Typical,* thought Adam. *Drop a big problem on me and fall asleep. Let me lay awake all night worrying about it.* But he could see the problem.

As the speakers grew into adults, they would be far more successful than those who did not speak. The gang would logically recruit the dumb for labor. Monkey, for sure, and even Fish were growing up fast. Maybe not Fish—he only had eyes for Twig, but the others ... Yes, he saw what Eve meant. It could get ugly. If all the girls were taken into the households of the speaking men, and the remaining dumb men resented it, it could become ugly. Beyond ugly. Adam didn't want to get involved, but that was what Eve was suggesting. Monkey, Fish, and Little Red would not like it. He could hear them now. *What do you care? You already have Eve.* He considered several ideas, but not one was workable. Eventually he gave up and fell asleep.

*The LORD your God has chosen you out of all the peoples on the face of the earth to be his people, his treasured possession.*

*Deuteronomy 7:6 NIV*

# The Hunter's Camp     17

The monsoon season ended and Eve's belly was large. She could hardly believe how fast the season passed, but the rains had stopped and the ground had begun to dry. It was once again time for the great hunt and this year, nobody wanted to be left behind, including her. Perhaps she had been lucky, but the baby had inconvenienced her very little. There had been another visit from the savage tribe, this time just two of them had wandered into their valley, but they had met a group of armed hunters from Blue Eyes group heading to the beach and they were eliminated.

Adam would lead the big hunt. Blue Eyes would join him along with his followers, now a year older. Adam had added three new speakers to the gang, one girl and two boys and they would be going on their first hunt, but Blue Eyes had added seven new dumb hunters to the party, four of which were females. They were young and not pregnant, at least not that Eve could see. Each was quite attractive. Eve was not sure if her father was making a change from the idea of all male hunters, as the gang did, or just wanted women along for their nocturnal company. Either way, the trend Eve had feared was looking very real. Adam admitted he could see it too.

He of course professed no idea what to do about the issue, and threw himself into the preparations, leaving Eve to worry about the long term problems yet again. The growing population of the dumb was outstripping the speakers. Had it been wise for them to arm the dumb with weapons? The dumb children exclusively had dumb babies, and only some of the original adults had children who spoke. She had talked to Twig about this, and she shocked her by saying that Blue Eyes was the only father of speakers, and as he aged less speakers were being born. The ramifications of what she was saying was too crazy to even contemplate, and she put the notion from her mind. How could Twig know this? When she told Adam this, he had no idea. Eve figured Twig had to be wrong, but it concerned her, especially when it came to her own baby.

*Maybe her baby will be dumb too,* Eve thought in horror every time she noticed her protruding belly or felt the baby kick. It was a worry she could do nothing about.

At last, the day of the hunt arrived. Adam insisted she stay behind as the child was expected at any moment. She protested, even the morning of departure.

"I promise I will be back long before the baby comes. In the meantime you will be in good hands with Rosy," Adam told her. They both turned and looked at Rosy. The girl was now confident in her new position. She gave him a reassuring, if toothy, smile.

"But what about more visitors?" she asked. "I would be safer with you than facing some unknown number of savages alone."

Adam considered. "There has only been one visit some time ago, and with us up and about, nobody is likely to find their way to our valley. Stay in the treehouse and you could hold off a whole tribe. We have a huge stock of arrows here. I am sure you will be fine, and we will only be gone a few days—well, a week or so.

"Be careful," said Eve as she held him close, knowing he was right. "Promise me you won't do anything foolish." He promised to be careful.

"And promise me you will be back before the baby is born," Eve added.

"I promise."

# The Hunt

Adam kissed Eve goodbye. "I love you," he said and headed toward the ladders. Looking back, he saw tears in Eve's eyes. They were carefully hidden until then. Rosy held her hand, trying to console her. Adam considered staying behind too, but it was his responsibility to go. *Everything is under control here*, he reassured himself. Eve was smart and capable, and he would be back long before the baby was born.

Up top the crevice, the plains looked about the same as last time, but this year he led the hunting party north-east, following the river upstream. He led the group past the giant falls, ground they had covered the year before, and then struck out into new lands. Above the second falls the river tumbled down a shallow gorge. The land on each side of the river was wooded. The party walked at the interface of the woods and plains. Here there was no sign of the other tribe, none at all.

Twig latched onto Adam, and pointed out new sights and interesting plants, and kept saying it was too bad Eve wasn't along. Adam did not mind. He missed Eve's company too. The presence of Blue Eyes' other girls was far more disconcerting. They kept trying to interest him. Twig, ever helpful, shooed them away.

When suddenly a deer exited the woods, the hunters took after it. Before the day was over more than one type of deer was dead, shot by a hunter's arrow.

"I will light the fire," Adam told the hunting party, when they finally set up camp for the night. He had chosen a spot fifty paces from the tree line, giving them good visibility but easy access to wood. Soon a fire roared, a great quantity of fallen wood lying next to it. Late into the night, the hunters feasted on fresh-cooked venison.

Then the camp was at last quiet. On his watch Adam marveled at fire. It was as amazing as the first time he saw it. The flames raced skyward, accompanied by orange glowing embers. He jumped when the wood popped, sending up a shower of sparks, but fire had taken the fear out of the night. The normal nocturnal hunters kept their distance. The occasional pair of eyes reflected the firelight at the furthest extent of his view, but fearing the fire the eyes always moved on.

"Monkey, your watch," Adam whispered, giving him a shake.

"All quiet?" Monkey asked as he stood and stretched.

"Totally quiet. As long as we keep the fire going, I have never felt safer."

Adam stood a moment with him, the sound of the night noises only broken by the snoring of Blue Eyes' hunters.

"I don't know how they can sleep with all that noise," Monkey chuckled, but turned serious. "Do you ever worry about there being so many of them, and so few of us?"

"I do. I worry plenty, but I have no idea what to do about it," Adam said, happy at least someone other than Eve shared his fears. Yawning, he turned in.

The next morning he continued leading the hunting party upriver. The ground rose steadily and the woods grew denser. The river, when they hiked through the trees to see it, was moving faster than in their valley. It was no longer down in a gorge, but easily accessible down small embankments interspersed with short bluffs. The party moved silently now, creeping along the edge of the woods. Deer caught unaware easily fell to their bows. As the meat and skins accumulated, Adam considered heading back. He had made promises. But Twig wanted to push on. He worried about the dangers, but surely one more day wouldn't hurt as long as he kept an eye on the plains, watching for the tribe. Based on the visits they had to be close by. But so far he had not seen them.

The land was rich in game, but not much else. The grasses of the plains were taller here, almost hiding them from view. It made Adam uneasy, not being able to see well, yet so far, the hunt was a success. He felt he should turn back, but he had no real excuse so discussed the matter with Twig, who, for once, was curious about what was ahead, so he pressed on.

When the ground suddenly shook, a fear gripped him. *You are a fool, Adam.* He should have listened to the voice in his head. He glanced around frantically, but the grassy plains were quiet and still. A sound came from the trees. He swung right, his bow ready. Branches snapped and the earth shook. Something heavy was coming. A roar sent a shiver up Adam's spine.

Two giant beasts emerged from the trees. They took one look around and lumbered toward the hunting party. A third emerged, then three more. Adam had never seen the like. They were more than twice the height of a man, with gray wrinkled hides and legs the size of tree trunks. Their giant heads, floppy great ears and noses which reached the ground were strange, but nothing compared to the prominent long white curved horns or fangs coming from their mouths, longer than a man and sharp on the ends.

"Bloody bones!" he muttered. "What on earth?" As he spoke, one raised its massive trunk and trumpeted a war cry to shatter a man's teeth. It scared Adam to the core. It and the other elephants thundered towards him, shaking the ground so violently Adam thought he might fall down.

Glancing at Blue Eyes and the older hunters, Adam hoped they had a tried and proven trick to counter this enemy, but they looked equally unprepared. Adam had thought the wildebeests were large, in fact huge. They were dangerous, but they were mice compared to these monsters. He glanced around, and thought fast. The hunting party was more-or-less in two groups. The gang was together in one group closer to the treeline.

Blue Eyes' dumb hunters stood together slightly farther out on the plains.

"Run for the trees," Adam shouted. It was the only place to hide, and hiding was clearly their only option. He drew back his bow and loosed an arrow. It seemed pitifully small. He hoped it might slow the elephants down. Without even watching its effect, he ran for the trees. He was on an interception course with the elephants, but it couldn't be helped.

"Scatter and hide!" he screamed, thinking how bugs disappeared when you lifted a rotten log, each to his own hole. He and the party were the bugs; and hiding would be their only hope; and the only place to hide was the trees. The gang scattered. The hunters did as well.

All but Fish and Twig. They were between him and the stampeding elephants. Twig screamed. She was not moving. Fish turned back.

"Twig! Run!" Adam pointed, but the girl wore a mask of paralyzed fear. Fish reached her and took her hand. He dragged her toward the trees. Then she began to run. Twig broke away from Fish. To Adam's horror, she ran directly towards one of the angry beasts.

"No Twig," Adam shouted but she didn't listen. She waved her arms, charging forward. The elephant was not dissuaded and charged her. At the last moment, she dove out of the way. Her small body flew off to one side, just missing a tusk. She tumbled. Then like an ant, she was back on her feet, behind the beast, sprinting for the woods.  *Nice moves, Twig,* Adam thought as his body tingled all over.

Fish tried the same maneuver but didn't clear his elephant's tusks.  He flew high, through the air.  Adam couldn't tell if he was dead or alive.  Then it was his turn.  He dodged right and left and ran the gauntlet of swinging tusks and stamping feet, sprinted into the woods, his mind reeling.  He dove into a thicket, burrowed into the underbrush, and lay still.  Monkey climbed up a tree, and helped Twig up behind him.  What became of the rest of the hunting party Adam did not know.

There were noises close by.  He sucked in his breath and tried to freeze.  The elephants were making another pass through the woods, the ground shook amid the sound of splintering wood as they rampaged.  Then as quickly as they arrived, the beasts headed off across the plains.

Adam emerged, shaken.  He looked around at the deeply rutted paths among the trees.  This was an animal highway to the river.  In the dry season there would be even more traffic than now for sure.  Following the torn-up sod to see bodies scattered among the tracks, his heart sank as he emerged on the plain.  He ran to the closest body.  It was Fish.

"Twig," Adam called.  She and Monkey ran to join him.  Fish was alive but his leg was badly gashed.  Twig opened her bag and began working on him.  Adam moved to the next still body.  The first thing he saw was a mud strewn shock of red hair. *No, not Little Red*, he prayed. As he knelt down, Little Red opened his eyes. "Are they gone? he asked.

"Yes. They took off," Adam assured him. "Hopefully they won't get thirsty again soon. Can you sit up?"

Little Red was bruised, and his arm was hurt, but, to Adam's relief, he looked like he would live. Adam had Monkey stay with him and moved on. As he searched he feared what he might find. Bev and the three new gang members emerged from the trees, along with most of the hunters. Adam sighed—his friends were safe. He headed further from the trees to where several of Blue Eyes' hunters lay. They had not been so lucky. One male was dead. Two males and one female were badly wounded. Adam was not surprised to find they were all young. Blue Eyes, and all his veteran hunters, had escaped unscathed. Adam guessed this had been a routine encounter to them, yet Blue Eyes had no way to warn these inexperienced hunters. Those who survived this day would be ready next time. *I should have anticipated more wild beasts and been more cautious.* With trees to hide them and with close access to the river, he should have been ready, but he had been totally preoccupied with worries of the strange tribe.

Adam moved the hunting party past the highway into an area of large trees with spreading branches. The ground under them was free of brush. With camp set up under the biggest tree, he and Twig treated the wounded.

Monkey built a large fire and they all settled around it, and, with plenty of meat to eat, the talk was of nothing but elephants, how big they were, what they might eat, and how they might be killed. Adam was mostly quiet, lost in thought. This hunt, his first hunt as tribe leader, had turned into a failure. Fish and several of the tribe would not be able to walk back, and Twig did not even want to move them under the trees, but he insisted they needed them close to watch and protect.

Adam wished Eve were here. She would have the right words for Twig and for the wounded. She would know what to do to make him feel like he thought of the idea. He could see that now. Without her his mind seemed dull and blank. He was no leader without her. Never again would he take on this kind of risky operation without her by his side. In fact, as he watched Twig giving orders, it became clear she was the true leader. Adam had eventually confessed to Eve that the necklace was Twig's idea. Eve had then confessed many of her own ideas came from the light-haired girl. They both went to Twig for instruction. That was what a leader was for, wasn't it?

Doing what little he could, he organized a watch and lay down as the night noises began. Foreign sounds pierced the night, louder and more aggressive than he was used to. *Tomorrow*, he decided. *We will build stretchers and head home.* He had broken his promise to be careful, and wasn't going to risk being late. The decision made, he closed his eyes. A dream as real as day washed over him.

He was up in the air and looking down on the large tree he lay under. It was not dark; light shone all around. Nothing like it had ever happened to him before. He wondered if he was asleep. Suddenly he was on the ground looking up through gaps in the tree at the stars above. The occasional orange ember danced up to meet them. He was not asleep, but not quite awake either. He closed his eyes and it happened again. This time he was lying in the soft moss beneath the Tree of Life. A voice from everywhere called to him. It was the voice of the creator.

"Adam," the creator said. "Stay here and build a camp for the dumb and remain separate from them. You are a special chosen people who must remain pure."

Then he was floating up into the sky, up the valley and falls. Suddenly he was back looking at the large tree he was under, but this time, he saw a large treehouse in it. A great fence around it contained a huge village.

The fire popped. *Ckak!* A cloud of embers rushed to the stars. Adam shook himself and sat up, looking around. The watch, one of Blue Eye's dumb men, was sitting quietly by the fire. The wounded slept restlessly. Everyone else was asleep. As he looked beyond them, Adam saw the village in his mind, superimposed right in the woods, right here where he lay.

*What has happened to me,* he wondered. He wished Eve were here, he would have asked her, but Twig was the real thinker in the gang. She always had a theory about everything. He thought hard about the long discussions the gang had so many times about what Twig had said about the creator, but he could hardly remember. If only he knew her secrets. She knew things that the rest of them didn't know, but rarely divulged them. Instead she spoke of her senses, her intellect, and the world around her. Of course, she had theories, and they usually made good sense. She was sleeping nearby. He crawled over and reached out to wake her.

He didn't want to wake her, not after this crazy day. She had worked so hard to patch up the injured, but he had a strong feeling his vision was from the creator. After all, it began under the Tree of Life. None of the gang ever had a vision from the creator before, but it made a kind of sense. Their parents would not understand a message if they heard it, and up until now, the creator likely considered them children.

"Twig? Are you awake?" he finally whispered. He wouldn't wake her, but just in case he would see if she was already awake.

She stirred. "What, my watch already?" she asked groggily.

"No, but since you're awake, can I ask you something?"

She rolled her eyes, and sat up. "Seriously Adam, a question, now?"

"Come on, let's not wake everyone," he said and they walked toward the river, being sure not to stand too far from the fire.

"I know you have thought a lot about us and the creator, and everything, but I am afraid I have forgotten much of what you had said. Can you give me the short version, sort of, just your conclusions?"

Twig smiled and stood a little closer, "You really want to know or do you miss Eve and want my company?"

"Please, Twig. Something very important happened and I want to understand it."

Twig spoke for a few moments about how incredible the world they lived in was, with its vast scale and balance. Light and dark, warm and cool, wet and dry. "I have concluded that an amazing creator had to be responsible for such a place," she said, "I have also studied life. I watched the ants, the caterpillar turning into a butterfly, the lizards, the fish, the birds and all the animals. I am sure you have noticed the common elements. All life is another creation and is all different, but the same. The patterns and behavior have infinite variety but all follow the same rules. All life battles to find its niche and battles to survive and reproduce. It is their purpose in life. The only exception which fascinated me is the Tree of Life. It has no seed—I checked the fruit. And no new shoots come up from the roots. I even tried to grow a tree from a cutting. It has to be a special tree of the creator."

"Wait a minute, you cut a branch from the tree?" Adam interrupted. "How did you get to it?"

"A storm blew off a branch. So anyway, everything else followed the pattern, until I started to evaluate us. We are different, too. We are clearly animals and do all the things other animals do, but we hear voices in our heads, all the time, telling us to act in a way different than our animal desires. It makes for a conflict and we must choose. The dumb do not hear this voice. No other creature I have seen suffers this conflict."

"So what is our purpose?"

"Good question," Twig said. "Our purpose seems to vary from person to person. I think we might each be given a special purpose from the creator."

"Makes sense," Adam said. "So, what about the creator?"

"We can talk, reason, visualize, and empathize, but the truly exceptional thing about us is this ability to know right from wrong, and we are free to choose. I call this voice the voice of the creator."

"Yeah, I get that, but this is different," Adam exclaimed. He had heard a voice in his head as well, but it was nothing like Twig's explanation.

"Adam, what are you talking about? Are you wondering about what to do with the dead hunters?" she asked in her patient-with-idiots voice, like he was Fish or Little Red.

"Dead hunters? What? Oh, yes, that is another issue we need to talk about. I don't think we should eat them. But back to my vision. Does the creator actually speak to us?"

"What vision?"

"I don't know exactly, but I am under orders from the creator. I need to obey his mandate. I am the tribe's leader, but I also have a leader. It's a relief and a comfort to know the gang is special, and that we were created for a purpose."

"So, what was your vision?" Twig demanded.

Adam yawned. "I am too tired; we can discuss the details in the morning. But since you are convinced there is a creator, you cannot rule out the possibility I was given a direct order, right?"

"Well, I guess that is true. Clearly we speak, and learned from somewhere. But as to your vision, I really need ... "

"Good enough for me," Adam said and gave her hand a squeeze. "Good night."

He lay back down, his mind clear. The next thing he knew it was morning. He jumped up and hustled around and fixed breakfast. As they ate, he announced his new plan. "This is a fine place to set up a permanent hunting camp. It's clearly on an animal highway to the river and should be able to provide us with meat and skins year round. We will stay and give our wounded time to heal. We begin by building a treehouse."

"Seriously?" Monkey said, incredulous.

"You aren't arguing with me, are you?" Adam demanded.

"This seems a rash decision, is all."

"Nothing rash about it. It makes perfect sense, so let's get to work," Adam said, not knowing if he dare share his vision, but based on Monkey's reaction he was glad he didn't. Twig, however, smiled and nodded as he spoke. The rest of the gang had noticed her agreement, and that seemed good enough for them.

Before anyone could object, Adam stood and began to organize them. He sent Blue Eyes and his hunters out for even more meat. By the time they returned Monkey was already high up the tree. He had identified the best place for the treehouse.

Bev had appointed herself caretaker of the sick. Adam brought Twig with him to scope out the area. They searched for plants, medicines, bamboo, reeds, and everything else they might need to build a settlement.

"Tell me about your vision," Twig said when they stopped along the river for a drink.

Believing she was sincerely interested, he told her everything word-for-word. "But I am also concerned about the delay. I promised Eve I would be back before the birth. You know her temper. Last time I crossed her, she knocked me off a log and did not speak to me for a month."

"What was that about?"

"Who knows, nothing important, nothing as big as this," Adam said. "But I wonder if I am doing the right thing by staying."

"If it is indeed the creator's wish, we must obey. But I am not clear what the *separate* part means."

"I don't know either," Adam answered. "Does it mean we should separate completely, so that they live here and we live in the valley? Or does it mean we should not mate with them?"

Twig looked thoughtful. "Hmm. I can't see you kicking your parents out of the valley, or mine either, but it does make sense to not breed with them. We are different and want to stay that way." They talked a bit more about it before Twig said, "If you want my advice, keep the *separate* issue quiet until you are sure, but to be safe, we can't let anyone breed with a non-speaker."

"Good advice," he said. "I will follow it as always." He gave her a quick hug and they moved on. Adam suddenly stopped. "And the dead bodies?"

"Well, we can't leave them laying around or they will stink, and animals will come and tear them up. We could toss them in the river, but that might worry people who see them floating through the valley. We could try burning them, but the dumb might think we are cooking them, so I guess we better bury them." Adam nodded and took care of the dead hunter.

The wider work on the settlement began slowly, but eventually each member of the hunting party found a role and things began to happen. Fish, under Bev's continuous care, became the stationary foreman. He directed the wood cutters, rope makers, and thatchers. Soon the treehouse began to take shape. There were unknown dangers here and Adam pushed them along until finally the wounded could be moved into the completed house. Fish, from his new vantage point continued to direct the work, and with Bev at his side, he grew stronger each day. Blue Eyes and his lieutenant took a small party of hunters out and returned with fresh meat each day. A smoking area for the meat was erected and a processing operation was organized for the skins. At last, Adam began the task of building a palisade fence around the area, the last piece of his vision. He outlined the task and his schedule. He was desperate to return to Eve, before the baby was born.

"Adam, you are pushing Fish too hard," Bev said one day. Fish looked embarrassed by her interference. As far as Adam could tell Fish was growing stronger everyday.

"I'm fine Bev," Fish said. "It's a tough schedule but it's important. The elephants or something even bigger could come back at any time."

"Exactly," Adam said. He shook his head and hurried over to welcome Blue Eyes and his hunters back from a hunt. It was another successful one and they were heading to the smoke house. Adam passed Twig on his way over. She wore a worried look on her face. "Now what?"

She turned and ran toward the river. Adam considered following her, as he kicked himself for driving her away with his callous tone. *I have enough problems to worry about without worrying about Twig too.*

He half expected to see elephants pounding out of the woods at any moment. The heavy wall was the only defense against them he could think of. It had to be strong. Strong enough to stop one or more of the massive beasts. There was also the threat from another tribe and that worried him as well.

To top it all off, Blue Eyes' hunters had an aversion to doing manual labor. Only if Adam worked alongside them, did they stay focused. When he thought about Eve, he pushed them harder. He figured whatever was bothering Twig, would either take care of itself, or she could tell him about it directly. She was an adult just like him.

As the work continued Adam forgot the incident. He focused all his effort on building the wall. He was rewarded with half a dozen new logs added each day.

"Anxious to get home?" Twig asked one day when they found themselves at the river getting water.

"I can't tell you how anxious," Adam said, looking around to make sure they were alone. "I hope I am not pushing too hard but I don't feel I can leave until the wall is finished. And still I have to keep my promise to Eve."

"Yeah," Twig said. "But I think we can leave a small party here to finish. Everyone knows what to do. It's now just a matter of time."

Adam smiled, jumping at the suggestion, "Oh yeah, that never occurred to me. I am working on the gate now, once that is done, I could theoretically take off. Any ideas who we should leave behind?"

"Well, actually, if you leave Blue Eyes and his hunters and the wounded, I can stay and take care of them. You can take the rest back."

Adam rubbed his head, and thought about it. "Have you talked with Fish about this?" he asked, impressed with his clever deduction. He had the idea that Fish and Twig might become an item, at least it looked to him like that might be her plan.

"No actually, Bev is never away from his side. Things are happening between them, but if we could just get her out of the way . . . "

"Ah, so this is not about getting me back to Eve, I see how it goes. Well, when I finish the gate, I will ask for volunteers. It is dangerous here and I would not just order people to stay. You have until then to work out your plan with Fish."

Twig did not look happy about the prospect, but Adam was so excited about leaving he rushed back to the gate with renewed energy.

At last the day came when the gate was complete. That night, Adam addressed the gang as they feasted on fresh meat around the fire.

"It is time some of us return to the valley," he announced. "But someone has to stay and take charge of the camp and finish the wall—"

"Fish and I will stay," Bev blurted out before Adam had finished speaking. Adam raised an eyebrow at the girl and then looked to Fish at her side. He nodded. Adam listened to the crackling of the fire and glanced at Twig. She was looking at her hands. Had he missed something?

"We're getting married. We can make this our home," Fish said.

Adam's mind filled with confusion. "Really?" he asked.

"Yes, really. I will make a good husband, and Bev and I have grown close to each other—and to this treehouse."

Adam tried not to think about what that meant. "And you want to stay?"

"Of course," Bev said. For several moments only the crackle of the fire and the ubiquitous night noises could be heard.

"Don't act so surprised, Adam," Fish said. "I'll make a good husband."

"It's not that—it's just, I thought—"

"What?" Bev demanded.

"Nothing. I am just surprised. I am happy for you both and wish you the same joy Eve and I have," Adam said. He glanced over at Twig for help, but she looked at him like he was as dense as the dumbest of the dumb.

"You don't mind the hunters around?" Adam asked. He was the last to know that there was something between Fish and Bev and he didn't want to dwell on his ignorance. He wondered what else had been decided without him.

"The hunters seem happy in this life," Fish said as he put an arm around Bev. "I assume you will take Blue Eyes with you?" Adam felt himself frown. "To gather up their women and children," Fish added helpfully. "I thought that was the plan."

"Yes, yes of course," Adam said. He glanced around as if looking for something. He realized he was probably the only one of the gang who did not know the plan. "I guess we can start packing up the meat and skins. We should haul back all we can carry."

"Ah, yes, we have a plan for that as well," Fish said. "Every full moon I will toss a bundle of skins along with dried and packed meat on a bamboo raft, and send it down the river. Keep watch until it arrives."

"That's a great idea," Twig said. "Waiting for the first raft might be a little tedious, but once we know how long it takes, it should be no problem. We can watch from the bridge. And if you need anything, make some symbols on the bamboo. We will agree on symbols for the basic items you might need and we will send a party out with your requests."

"We can include items like weapons, tools, fruit and medical supplies," Adam suggested.

"Adam, I am concerned about something, actually several things," Fish said, suddenly very serious. "What if we are attacked by the other tribe?"

A chill ran up Adam's spine. He had almost forgotten all about them, what with the elephant attack. Then there were the injured, and the vision, then all the building, and all the worrying about Eve. He had promised to be back. It had been weeks now. "You have good fighters here, good defenses, and plenty to eat," Adam said. "There is more risk than in the valley, but we are outgrowing the valley. We must expand. Just keep the hunters busy building better and better defenses. We will supply weapons and more hunters as you need them."

"I am concerned about the hunters without Blue Eyes to control them. What if they don't listen to me? The youngsters are sullen when not under Blue Eye's gaze," Fish said.

"I am also concerned about us in the valley," Adam answered gravely. "All I can suggest is that you try to control the food supplies and hand them out in a shared meal, so they learn a dependency. They like cooked food, but don't do the job very well on their own. Do the cooking inside the fort and trade for the game they collect."

"Okay," Fish said. "We can give it a try."

"We can have Blue Eyes come up on each of the visits—that will help," Adam said.

He was so excited about finally going home he could barely sleep that night. He was impressed with his advice to Fish. Make the dumb dependent, and make them work for their food. It was a good plan, but Adam couldn't see how he could do the same thing in the valley. Food was readily available.   He felt pretty good about following the creator's edict and expanding the tribe's lands when he didn't think about the dead hunter and Eve home unprotected.

The next day thoughts of Eve and a baby waiting for him, helped him flog everyone toward their departure.  The sun was barely up when the symbols were agreed upon and all their cargo was loaded.  Then he was headed toward home, taking the remainder of the gang and Blue Eyes with him.

## Left Alone

Fish glanced at Bev. "What have we done?" They were watching as Twig and the others disappeared from sight. Bev was clacking and twirling the bracelets he had made her. To his dismay, she insisted on wearing both of them on her left arm. They were wooden bands he had carved and inlaid with fish bones. He was not about to be out done by Adam. She dried her tears.

"You are smart," Bev said. "We will be fine. We have everything we need." She sounded surprisingly confident after so many tears. She touched him on the hand. "Now come and eat. I have made you something special for our first day together."

Bev called for Scarface as well. Scarface was what they called Adam's father. As Blue Eyes' lieutenant, he was now in charge of the hunters. He came at a run. His wicked scar tracked from his hairline to his cheek. He didn't care what they called him—as long as he wasn't called late for dinner.

He understood the old ways of the tribe and Fish knew that as long as he kept Scarface happy, he would keep the others in line. Fish learned when making the treehouse convincing Blue Eyes or Scarface was the best way to get things done. Now the hunters followed Scarface as they did Blue Eyes, if with slightly less enthusiasm. Fish treated Scarface with respect even though he was officially in charge and offered lots of encouragement, modeling his methods on how Adam worked with Blue Eyes.

Rebellion was Fish's biggest fear. The younger hunters were different, just as those who spoke were different. The young dumb were belligerent, and aggressive. Scarface was equally dismayed with their laziness and obstinacy, and it was clear to Fish getting them out of the valley was a good idea.

After a hearty breakfast, feeding the hunters, Fish busied himself with arranging the first shipment. Bev tried to slow him down. "You don't want to hurt yourself."

"Bev, we have to get the first package ready by the full moon."

"Leave it to me. You need to take it easy still," Bev said. "Your injuries are healing but you are not yourself yet."

He dismissed her concern and hobbled out on a crutch. "You know, Fish," she called after him. "My only regret is to not be with Eve for the birth."

Fish stopped, turned, and made a face. "Adam was already nervous about the birth before he left. I can imagine what he would be like if there. That is a treat I am happy to miss. I bet he is hoping it will be all over before he gets back. That's what I would want. It's a messy business."

"Don't get cocky, your day will come, and it will be just you and me," Bev said.

"On that day I will do what has to be done," Fish said. "I am sure I'll still be happy to be here, in charge of my own hunting camp, my own household. I have had a hankering to get out on my own and do something, and this is it. Here I am in charge with a new wife at my side. Between the two of us, we can do anything!"

*Our animal origins are constantly lurking behind, even if they are filtered through complicated social evolution.*

Richard Dawkins

# Lure of the Leopard  18

Eve counted the days. When the first week was up, she woke and looked expectantly down the path. Nothing. She had taken to talking with Rosy. It was not very rewarding. The girl paid no attention and often fell asleep. Today Eve decided it would be a good day to clean the treehouse, and she went at the place with a vengeance. She toiled all day, and all day she hoped the hunting party would return. They did not.

That evening, her water broke and labor pains began. She managed to climb the ladder to the treehouse, but when Rosy saw what was happening she disappeared down the ladder.

"Rosy," Eve called, again and again, but the girl was gone. Eve couldn't believe it. Adam had said he would be back. He promised. Adam said with Rosy on-hand she would be fine, but Rosy had never had a baby before and probably found the whole thing too frightening. The women of the tribe more or less took care of themselves in the process, and few wanted to be involved in others'. Maybe Rosy went to get her mother. She would not be much help, but better than being alone.

"Ahhhhh yeee," Eve bellowed as a nasty contraction hit. Between them she tried to prepare the treehouse, but she had no idea what she would need.

"I am going to kill you Adam," she said after each new contraction.

Suddenly there were noises below. "Rosy?" she called. Finally the ugly girl's head appeared at floor level.

Another contraction dragged a screech from Eve and Rosy's head disappeared once again. Eve promised herself if she lived through this night, she would kill Rosy first, then Adam when he returned—if he returned.

Darkness fell and Eve was unable to see anything at all. She could not imagine anything more terrifying than having a baby alone in the dark, unable to see what was happening, but nothing she could do would delay it until morning, and there was no way she could get down and make a fire. As the night dragged on, the contractions came closer and closer together.

"Adam I am going to kill you," she growled again and again.

Finally, she felt something changing in her. She felt in the dark; things were happening. *Time to get this baby out*, she decided. The next contraction she screamed and pushed and pushed. She pushed and screamed. A pain like she had never felt before stole over her. The baby slid out of her and she shook uncontrollably.

She felt around in the dark for her baby. Eventually figuring out head from feet. She laid it on her chest before falling back exhausted. It screamed, But at least it was alive, if not very happy about it. Finally Eve got it to nurse.

There was a slippery cord still attached to something inside her. It was a terrifying prospect. She pushed and something messy came out still attached to the baby. She decided to ignore it until she could see. Dawn was not long in arriving, and it was a bluish thing hooked to her baby with a cord.

She desperately wished she had paid more attention to the many births back at camp, but all the yelling drove her away. Now she hoped the umbilical cord would fall off on its own.

Rosy's head appeared. She smiled to see the baby. She brought Eve some berries to eat. Eve could just kill her for leaving in her time of need, like Adam had, but the berries tasted good.

Eve tried to sleep, but the baby, a boy, was overly demanding. When she got sick of seeing the afterbirth she cut the cord with her knife and tossed it out the window into the river.

Rosy was a help that day, bringing her food and helping clean up the mess. Mid afternoon Eve awoke with a start. Rosy flew up the ladder and pointed down, a terrified look on her face. *Now what?* Eve wondered. She crawled to the door.

Savages stared up at her. One waved his spear threateningly. She had seen that little game and had no patience for it. Exhausted or not, she motioned to Rosy to help pull up the ladder. Fortunately the savages had not grabbed it. No sooner was it secured on its hooks, the first arrow whizzed in the door, just missing Eve. A second arrow nicked Rosy's arm. That made her mad and she picked up Eve's axe, ready to attack. Eve held her back, instead retrieving her bow and leaned out the door. She loosed an arrow. *Twang.* A savage fell to the ground. Eve let loose two more arrows. *Twang. Twang.* A second and a third savage fell to the ground. The rest of the savages disappeared before she could take out another. The baby started to scream.

"Adam, I am going to kill you," Eve growled. "Leaving me like this!"

She waited at the door, daring another savage to show her a target. She watched the three she shot die. One naked woman and two men. *Waaaa*, the baby screamed. Eve pointed to the baby and Rosy picked him up and tried to comfort him.

An arrow passed through her hair and grazed the side of her neck. *Whizz.*

"Bloody bones," she swore. "That was close."

She had no idea where it had come from and remained out of sight. Every once in a while she pivoted into the doorway, scanned the woods and pulled back.

How many were there? She tried to remember her first look. Maybe five or six, but there could have been more out of sight.

Time passed and nothing happened. She took a break from her watch and nursed. She looked over their supplies. She had plenty of arrows, Adam had insisted on that. But she had no food, and just a small gourd half-full of water hanging on a peg in the corner. She looked at Rosy and, remembering the previous night alone, Eve grabbed the gourd and drank it all down.

The day finally ended. Eve wondered what would happen next. The savages had let only a few more arrows fly as the day passed, but a fire glowed not far down the path. They were not going anywhere, and where was Adam? She could just kill him for not coming back already.

By the time it was pitch dark, Eve was in a panic. She worried the savages would climb the tree in the dark. She wondered if she should try to escape in the dark? She could not last long without water. She was already thirsty again. She paced back and forth, three steps one way, three back. She held a fussy Adamson, her name for the boy, in one arm and her bow in the other.

Every so often Eve looked out the door. Now, however, it was too dark to see anything. She made up her mind. She set her bed opposite the door, and propped herself up against the opposite wall. Bow on her lap with an arrow notched, she waited. The starlight outside illuminated the opening of the door. If a head appeared, she would see it.

Her eyelids began closing. She forced them open. She could not sleep yet, even if the baby finally was. Again her eyes started to close. Again she fought to keep them open. This battle continued until she finally heard something.

Her eyes popped open and she saw no starlight, saw nothing but darkness through the doorway. In a panic she fumbled with her bow. Controlling her fear, she drew back an arrow and shot. A cry and a thud followed the twang of her bow. She could again see out the doorway. Wide awake now, blood pounded in her ears, her breathing was heavy. *That was close*, she realized.

She wished for a solid door, but all the treehouse had was a mat, she could unroll over the doorway. If she could not stay awake, she thought to tie it in place. Then at least the noise of a savage tearing it might wake her.

The baby woke and Eve nursed Adamson again. She looked at the baby. For the first time, she felt nothing but contempt for him. Were it not for the baby, she would have been with Adam on the hunt, and she would not have lived out a night of terror giving birth. She would not be exhausted from defending herself against these savages now. Adamson did not look any different than any of the newborns of the tribe. It was ridiculous how long she would have to wait to find out if he would even talk. *Years!*

Finally the baby fell back asleep. Eve pulled the drape over the door, then stopped and pulled it aside. The fire was out, and all was quiet. She left the drape, hanging, gently swaying in the breeze. *This is it.* She decided she was getting out of here. Quietly, she woke Rosy, and together they lowered the ladder. Wrapping the baby tight to her chest, Eve climbed down, pleased to find a new body at the bottom. Four down, and who knew how many left to go?

All was quiet, and Eve waited while Rosy joined her. Eve held her axe at the ready and made sure Rosy had hers. Slowly, they crept down the path then slid off to the right, and started to ease through the thick vegetation, attempting to cut the corner between the two paths, the one to the treehouse and the main path from the beach to the Tree of Life. It was slow, difficult going in the dark.

"Waaaa," the baby began crying. Eve could not believe it. Of all the time to start, but there was nothing she could do about it. She considered smothering him, but instead, she threw caution to the wind and started crashing through the dense growth, hoping they were almost to the main path. The baby seemed to like all the motion and grew quiet, but Eve knew the damage was done.

When at last they broke from the forest, she found they were on the main path, heading toward the settlement. With a glance back, she began to run as dark shapes moved behind her and Rosy. She and the girl ran, just able to see the familiar path, but she was running slow and she was tiring fast. She had not figured on the effect of the birth slowing her down. Adam's bloody baby crying messed up her escape. Now they would die. She ran on as foot falls behind her grew closer. She stole a glance back. Only two, no, just one was following, maybe fifty paces behind, a female.

"Rosy," Eve shouted and stopped. Rosy turned and saw the woman. With a scream, she swung her axe. The savage woman dodged, and brandished her spear, but Rosy was fearless. She rushed in, swinging her axe. It was all over in a flash. The savage woman lay dead. Rosy, however, continued hacking.

"Rosy, come," Eve called, starting to move again. Rosy stopped hacking. Smiling, she joined Eve. They ran, but at a slower pace now, eventually walking as nobody could be seen behind. *Five down, probably only a few more now left to go.*

By the time she reached her parents cave, she was barely able to walk. Rosy supported her as they staggered in. She woke her little brother, told him what was happening, and collapsed on her father's mat, Rosy beside her.

She was barely aware of the passage of time. The baby cried, she fed him, people came and went, she ate and she slept. Sometimes it was daytime, sometimes night. When she dreamed, she saw a leopard, its eyes glowing. It leapt toward her, waking her. Her anger with Adam faded, and was replaced with worry. He and the hunting party were gone so long now, she feared he and they might never return.

## A Side Expedition

As the gang left the camp, Adam set a fast pace.

"What's the hurry?" Little Red asked, glancing around. "Savages after us?"

"I have got to get back before Eve has the baby," Adam answered.

"Oh, Adam," Twig said. "That apple has fallen from the tree ages ago. One way or another, you've missed it."

"That can't be. I promised," Adam said. "How do you know?"

"Eve and I worked out the timing," Twig replied. "It is too late now, so we might as well take our time."

Adam walked on, gradually slowing the pace. He was in no rush to find himself in trouble with Eve.

As they walked the grassy plain passed under his feet, his pack got heavier, and his pace continued to slow. This trip had changed everything. It felt odd to not have Fish and Bev along. It was also odd to see Blue Eyes, walking alone, without his fellow warriors.

"You look deep in thought," Twig said, stepping alongside him.

"I was thinking," Adam said, "Everything has changed yet again. The gang may never be together again."

"You're right, and it makes me wonder what will become of me," Twig said dejectedly.

Adam gave her a hard stare, but did not comment. It did not feel like a conversation which would end well.

"You have Eve. Fish has Bev. So, what about me? Am I to pick between Monkey and Little Red? No, thank you."

Adam remained quiet. *Is this what girls talked about?* he thought. *If so, I am glad I'm not a girl.*

"I only wish I could have found a leopard," Adam said, changing the subject to something meaningful. "I would love to bring Eve the hide. We spotted one several times, but they are too good at disappearing. I never got anywhere near enough for a shot."

"Oh, Adam, it's a pity. Eve said she would like a leopard skin. It would make things go smoother for you if you came back with such a prize. We have been gone much longer than expected and she has to be worried—beyond worried. I can tell you, she is going to be blazing mad."

Adam had not considered that. He had been so worried about keeping his promise he had not considered her worry. He stopped dead in his tracks. Little Red, who had been easing up closer to them plowed into him.

"Little Red," Adam barked. "Watch where you are going."

"Don't stop in the middle of the road," Little Red snapped back.

"Don't follow so closely."

"I couldn't hear from further back," Little Red said. Adam glanced at Twig.

She rolled her eyes. "You see, what did I say? Definitely not," she said, shaking her head.

"Definitely not what?" Little Red asked, looking back and forth between them.

"Definitely would not want to show up without a gift," Twig said, and Little Red laughed and agreed. Twig laughed as well.

Adam stepped up his pace and left the two of them and their cackling. *How mad will Eve be?* he asked himself as he walked along. He often remembered the day she knocked him off the log on the beach and stormed away. Try as he might, he still couldn't remember why. *If she was that mad over something I can't remember, how mad would she be about this?* Twig had never steered him wrong before, when it comes to Eve and matters of the heart. "So, Twig, can I talk to you alone?" he asked, turning his gaze on Little Red who was right next to her. Twig stuck out her tongue at Little Red and skipped up alongside Adam.

"As you command," Twig said, a big smile as she took his arm.

"Look, I've been thinking. Are you serious about Eve being mad?" Adam asked.

"No, not Eve. When have you ever known her to become angry?" Twig said mischievously, her eyes twinkling.

"Exactly," Adam answered glumly. "I think I better go in search of my elusive leopard."

"You sure?"

"No, not really. It would delay us even more, but you might be right. It would be a good thing to come back with a gift."

"You know," Twig began after some thought. "There is a way to do both. Why don't you send the gang home with Blue Eyes? You can put Monkey in charge. He would like that. This way Eve will know you are okay. We will show up a few days after them—when she has cooled off—and with a beautiful leopard skin cloak."

"We?"

"Can you sew?" Twig asked.

"Not too well, but just you and me?" Adam asked. "Will that be okay?"

"Imagine Eve if I left you out here and you never returned," Twig said. "She would kill me. And if you did get hurt, who else could patch you up?"

Adam walked a moment in silence, well aware of Twig's arm still on his. *What is she up to?* he wondered. He felt he was being manipulated. Now instead of Eve it was Twig. *But to what end?* She was making a good point, and perhaps just the two of them, rather than a whole group crashing through the brush, could creep up on a leopard. He imagined the sight, a beautiful leopard, looking up suddenly, right down the shaft of his arrow. "Okay. Let's do it," he said. He shook off her arm and turned back to the group. "We have a change in plans."

"Ugh," Little Red said. "What now?"

"Nothing for you," Adam said. "I have one last task that I need to finish. Twig and I will be delayed a few days. I want the rest of you to head home as fast as you can. Monkey, you are in charge. Be sure to tell Eve I am fine and will be home as fast as I can."

Adam signaled to Blue Eyes to go back with them. He smiled and nodded while Twig repacked. Adam was alarmed, however. The man's smile was too large. It was almost a sneer, as if he thought he and Twig were going off to be alone. The smile on Monkey's face sent a similar message, but Adam figured it was too late. He had made the announcement and there was nothing to be done about their imaginations.

When they finished swapping around the supplies between their packs, Twig made a big show of hugging everyone goodbye like they would never see them again.

"Monkey, don't forget to tell Eve, I have an important task to complete. Tell her I will be home as quickly as I can," Adam said, holding the boy by both shoulders.

"Don't worry," Monkey said with a grin. "Even if I did forget, you know she would pry it out of me."

Their final farewells said, the gang, now led by Monkey, continued along the tree line, heading for the valley.

Adam turned away from the trees to the plains with its herds of wild beasts. Where the herds were, there would be leopards. Without a word Twig, again took his arm. She walked beside him companionably and smiled when he glanced at her.

Blue Eyes' sneer flashed through Adam's mind. The old man had been the chief for years, and he had been with all the women of the tribe. *I am sure he wondered about my lack of interest, and was now pleased I was finally doing my duty. Oh, no, there is that phrase.* Talk of duty had made Eve so mad, it frightened Adam how glad he was that Eve's father couldn't talk.

*There are hunters and there are victims. By your discipline, you will decide if you are a hunter or a victim.*

General "Mad Dog" Mattis

# The Bet  19

Adam tried to put Blue Eyes and thoughts of doing his duty from his mind. He needed to focus on the hunt, but the feel of Twig's arm in his—their feet in lockstep—and the glow of her golden hair in the sunshine was a serious distraction.

Twig suddenly pulled him to a stop. "There, it looks like a large herd ahead."

Glancing at the sun Adam was shocked to see it was mid-afternoon. He was even more shocked that Twig spotted the herd before him. He had not noticed anything but her hair blowing in the gentle breeze. Pulling his arm free of her, he focused on the herd. His plan was simple. Kill one of the beasts and take enough meat for the two of them to eat for a few days, but leave the carcass. Then all he had to do was see who showed up. He would do the same thing day after day, until a leopard appeared.

The sun hung low by the time he and Twig crouched and silently approached a wildebeest which had wandered from the main herd. Adam shot his bow. *Twang.* The hooved beast staggered, pawed at the ground, and collapsed, unaware of Adam and Twig, in the grass nearby.

Twig, who had been anticipating his moves up until then, rushed forward, her knife in hand. She hunched over the fallen beast.

"Nice shot," she said when Adam caught up with her.

"Thanks," Adam said, feeling disoriented. Neither of them had said more than a few words since they had left the gang. *We somehow knew what each other were thinking,* Adam realized as he watched as she expertly sliced open the beast's hide. He had been afraid of her talking the whole way and driving him crazy, but it had been the opposite. It had been a great day and a fine hunt, almost frighteningly so. It was almost like the girl knew what he was thinking without having to say anything. She was so much like Eve in that way. The thought worried him and he hoped he and she would return home soon before he tripped up and made a terrible mistake.

"Nice work with the knife," Adam said cautiously, as he watched Twig carve their steaks.

"It will be dark soon. Do we hide nearby and watch?" she asked. "Or what do you have in mind?"

"Sure," he said and searched around while she finished up and located a small rise nearby.

"We can set up camp on that hill and keep an eye out," he told her. "But I seriously doubt we will see anything today. The leopards will be wary."

"Finished, lead the way," Twig said with a smile and blood spot on her nose.

"Hang on, you have a . . . " Adam said, reaching out and wiping the tip of her nose clean. "Got it. Better." He felt his body responding and turned away quickly.

They walked to the rise and dropped their packs. "If you go collect some dried chips, I will get a fire going and start cooking dinner," Twig said as she started hacking down the tough, dry grass.

"Deal," Adam said and hurried off to the plains. Dried animal droppings burned hot and long, the only real option for spending the night safely on the plains. It was almost dark when he arrived back on the knoll. By the end he was guided by the welcome glow of Twig's grass fire and by the smell of meat cooking.

"Wow, that smells good," he said as he piled chips by the fire. "I am ravenous."

"You're just in time. Sit and get comfortable."

The night was clear and quiet, the peace of the plains only broken by the sound of scavengers squabbling over the carcass. Of their own meal, Adam ate, and ate, until he could eat no more. He drank from their goat skin bags and sat watching the fire.

Twig scooted close. "It's been a great day, Adam," she said softly, taking his hand in hers. "It's probably one of the best days I have ever had. Thank you."

Adam considered her words. It had been a pleasant day, but certainly did not rank up there as anything special. "I'm glad you enjoyed it," he said awkwardly. "Tired?"

It seemed to him Twig started to say no, but then changed her mind. She rose to pull out their mats. Adam stoked the fire for the night, while she worked. He looked up when he felt her hand on his shoulder.

"Um, I'm sorry, Adam," she said. "It seems when we were repacking everything, your mat must have been transferred. But mine is extra big, so we can share."

Adam wondered if what she described was truly an accident. Her plans seemed all too clear now. He was determined her plan would fail. When they lay down and arranged the single skin—plenty big to cover them both—Adam turned on his side, away from her and let out a long breath. *Message sent.*

"Good night, Adam," Twig said. He could feel her stare on the back of his head.

"Good night, Twig," he said without looking. "Sleep well."

He regulated his breathing to sound like he was asleep while he waited for the inevitable interruption, but none came. Every time she moved, he expected a hand to come sneaking over, but none ever did. Finally he drifted off.

He woke a few times, tossed a few more chips on the fire, glanced around to make sure all was quiet, then lay back down. He took a long look at Twig's sleeping form and realized he might have been wrong about her. She was Eve's best friend; surely she would not do anything to hurt her. She probably was not used to this kind of adventure, not like him and Eve.

When he fell asleep again, the next thing he woke to was the smell of cooking meat. Opening his eyes, he saw dawn streak the sky above. He sat up.

"Good morning, sleepy head. Hungry?" Twig said cheerfully. She was squatting next to the fire, grilling bits of meat on a stick.

"Always," he replied with a smile, surprised that he had been entirely wrong about her and feeling guilty about having such thoughts.

He embraced breakfast with gusto. "Today let's scout the area and see if we can see any signs," he said as he chewed. Twig eagerly agreed.

The herd had moved off in the night, and the night scavengers had cleaned the carcass well, so they packed up their meager camp and headed off, arm-in-arm in pursuing a leopard farther out into the vast plains as the sun beat down on them.

They found some leopard tracks and were moving fast to catch up. "Adam, it's no good," Twig said at a little after noon. "I am trying to conserve water, but I am thirsty."

Adam, in high spirits, had not given any thought to the water situation. Alarmed, he stopped and checked his skin, then checked Twigs.

"Here, have a swig of mine," he said, handing his water over. "I have been pushing hard, with no thought for anything else but finding a leopard. I expected to find water along the way but wasn't thinking. The herd must drink, so there has to be water."

"Or perhaps they are able to operate without longer than we can," Twig said. "But what if we don't find any? Is it back to the river?"

"Yes, exactly right, but it is almost a two day walk to the river. If we keep going and find water by tonight or anytime tomorrow, we will be in great shape, but if we don't, it will be difficult to make it back to the river again."

"Oh, Adam," Twig said. "I wish we had bigger skins. Monkey's skin holds enough for the whole village. I should have tried harder to get him to trade with me."

"Good luck with that—parting Monkey from his water is pretty much impossible," Adam laughed. "But you are right. We are at a critical point. We must make a hard decision. Alone I would go on, but I can't let you take the risk. We have to call off the hunt and go back. We have to go back to the valley and suffer Eve's wrath."

Twig turned to face him. She took both his hands in hers and looked into his eyes. "Adam, you are a good man, and you take good care of me, but I can't be the reason you abandon your quest. We are in this together. Let's go on together until tomorrow night. If we find no water by then, we can turn back and crawl to the river if need be."

Admiration welled up in Adam. "You are a remarkable woman, Twig, like no other," he said. He wrapped his arms around her and held her, nuzzling his lips to her golden hair and kissed the top of her head. She turned her face up to him and kissed his cheek.

"We are a good pair, aren't we," she said. "Come on, let's get going."

For a time she led, and he looked at her slim narrow shoulders, narrow hips and thin legs as she strode purposefully after the fleeing leopard. Only her head, perhaps a little oversize or perhaps seeming so in contrast to her thin frame, was striking, with her lush main of golden wavy hair. No, it was not her body or her femininity that was so striking, it was her brilliant mind and iron will. He could see her crawling to the river, without ever complaining.

*What will become of her,* Adam wondered. Losing Fish, no one would marry her now. It seemed terribly unfair to Adam that she should be deprived of love just because of how smart she was. Even he had been afraid of the idea of marrying her. Her brain was her curse as much as it was her gift.

The sun dropped below the horizon, bringing an end to the oppressive heat. Until now, there had been no need to stop what with there being no food and no water, just dry grass for as far as the eye could see. Twig had stopped holding on to his arm since they made the decision to go on. Instead she held his hand as they walked. It was a companionable way to walk, and Adam did not mind.

"I cannot see the tracks anymore," he declared as he pulled Twig to a halt. "We have to stop. I am dead on my feet. Let's have a sip of water and sleep."

"Whatever you say," Twig said with a half-hearted smile. She looked dead tired, but dug out their mat and cover, and laid them out in the twilight. Soon, the stars emerged. Adam lay down and Twig snuggled in close to him.

"You don't mind holding my hand while we walk, do you?" she asked.

"Not at all."

"Good, then would you mind holding me close tonight. I am a little afraid with no fire."

Adam rolled over and faced her. He wrapped a strong arm around her and pulled her frail body close. "Good night," he said and reached up to kiss her cheek, but she twisted her head and kissed him on the lips instead.

"Good night, my dear," she said. "Thank you for letting me pretend you're my husband, at least for this trip. It is a wonderful thing to be married, isn't it?"

"It certainly is," Adam said, amused despite his exhaustion, hunger, and thirst. "Good night my dear wife."

As he drifted off to sleep, he was confident their little game was harmless. Eve was his wife and nothing would change that. And, Twig was certainly smart enough to know that.

Adam woke, stiff, sore, and both hungry and thirsty. Those concerns evaporated as he realized someone was running a finger through his hair.

"Good morning, my love," Twig whispered in his ear.

He opened his eyes and smiled at her. He worried he was wrong last night about this being a harmless game.

"I would have breakfast cooking for you if we had any food, but here, have some water," she said.

"No worries, we will find food and water today, or my name's not Adam," he said confidently, and climbed to his feet. Taking her by the hands he helped her to her feet. She staggered a little bit and took the opportunity to wrap her arms around him and give him a little hug.

"Thank you for keeping me safe last night," she said and gave him a quick kiss. She changed the topic to the herd, and Adam set out with renewed concerns as to her nocturnal designs.

To make matters worse the herd was not grazing but traveling, leaving a path of dry dusty ground ahead. Within the hoof prints—thousands of them—there were those of jackals, hyenas, lions, and, from time to time, those of a leopard. The whole community was on the move, but to where Adam did not know.

One thing he didn't see was any sign of the savage tribe, which was a relief. Either they knew better than to follow without water, or they were elsewhere.

"The herd is moving faster than we are, so it must be water they are after. They are not stopping to graze at all. I am sure water must be close," Adam said when Twig asked, not because he believed it, but because he knew that is what she wanted to hear. It was so unusual for her not to have all the answers like she usually did, but out here, he decided, she didn't know as much. It was nice for a change. He glanced over at her. She held his hand and walked quietly beside him.

She returned his glance with a smile. "I am sure glad you know what you're doing because our water is gone," she said. "And it feels like it's going to be another hot day."

Her confidence scared him, and he felt like a little boy again, out on a dare, and things were not looking good for him. He walked on in silence, always looking ahead for something. They passed two carcasses, only fur and bones left. The weak were dying and the scavengers were being fed.

Adam glanced at the sun. *Noon, and still nothing but dust.* But far ahead birds circled high in the sky.

"So how are you doing? Sun not too hot? Shoes comfortable on your feet?" he asked Twig as he kept an eye on the sky. At least a hundred birds circled. "I can smell water. I predict I will be able to offer you a drink in no time at all."

Twig sniffed the air. "I don't smell anything. Has the heat gotten to you? I bet you, we find no water before the sun reaches the horizon."

"I bet we do," Adam retorted, delighted with his inside knowledge.

"What do you bet?" Twig asked. A smile split her face. "What have you got I want?"

"I don't know, I don't have much, but you can have anything you want, provided you can collect it before the sun completely sets," Adam said. He was more than a little delighted with his quick thinking, putting in a deadline.

"It's a deal," Twig said quickly. "And you get the same thing from me."

A bet was a bet, and it was something the gang liked to do. Nobody would dare fail to keep their word when they lost. Adam started to plan as they walked. His shirt was starting to fall apart, he could have her mend it, or maybe give him a haircut. He smiled to himself as he walked, and she kept glancing at him.

"Pretty sure of yourself, aren't you," she finally said as they walked on, seeing nothing new. The birds had settled and the sky was empty, but Adam knew they had to be feeding on a lake or river.

"I am seriously struggling to decide between all the ideas I have for what to ask for when I win."

"Humph, that's getting ahead of yourself. Hey, is that a little herd of deer over there?" she cried suddenly.

"Looks like it, I am sure there will be all kinds of game near the water," Adam said smugly.

"Shouldn't we go shoot one?"

"Oh, no you don't. You want to slow us down so we don't reach the water until dark. I know your little schemes."

She squeezed his hand. "Adam, you are cracking up in the heat. What do you want from me so badly? You know if you asked, there is nothing I have I wouldn't just give you. I am so hungry, surely we should get dinner." But Adam walked on. Girls didn't understand the thrill of winning.

Deer, then a herd of antelope bounded away as they approached. Adam and Twig crested a hill and looked down over a shimmering lake.

"How did you know?" Twig exclaimed, jumping up and down. "A lake, I can't believe it. I could drink it dry. There are even a few trees around it for shade."

"I won," Adam gloated, but Twig tugged him toward the water. "Hold on, slow down," he told her. "This is the killing grounds, as the thirsty beasts head for the water, I am sure every predator is waiting to take what they can." Adam took his bow off his back and notched an arrow, slowing his pace and motioned for Twig to do the same. "Let's claim that small tree over there, drop our packs then carefully go fill our skins."

"Fill our skins?" she said. "I am going swimming."

"Not until I am sure it is safe. This is not our valley. Who knows what lives in the water?"

Twig stopped; her face lost its huge smile. "Oh, yeah. That's a good point."

Adam's triumph was complete. The all-knowing Twig stopped in her tracks. This was such a victory, he considered taking it easy on her when it came to the bet.

Bow in hand, Adam stopped about ten paces from the water after hanging their packs from the tree. "I don't like it. It is blazing hot, yet not one single animal is standing waist deep to get cool, and nobody but us appears to be thirsty."

"Be glad," Twig said impatiently. "Let's get some water before a pack of lions decide to come and drink."

"The water is muddy. Like a storm. Can't see a thing. Wouldn't be muddy unless something is out there stirring it up," Adam said edging closer. "And look at these tracks all over the shore. I don't recognize half of them. Clearly every animal comes to drink, but doesn't hang around."

He scanned the lake. There was a plethora of wading birds on the opposite shore, but none in front of him. But needing water they really had no choice. "Okay, you stay here, with your bow ready," Adam said. "I will leave mine on the ground and creep up and fill one skin at a time. Watch for something scary. Something is keeping the other animals away."

## Payback

Twig drew her bowstring back and waited patiently as Adam crept to the water's edge. She scanned the water as he gingerly dipped the waterskin in. When he glanced back, she felt herself smile even as her skinny arm shook from pulling the bowstring back. *Don't let him distract you,* she admonished herself, wishing she had his insane courage.

He rose and backed away from the water, full-skin in hand. Twig relaxed her bow.

"Drink all you want and I will refill it," he said, offering her the skin.

She snatched the skin from him and drank and drank until satisfied while he watched, a grin on his face. "Thank you for saving our lives," she said, handing him back the half-empty skin. "And thank you for letting me drink first. You are a fine man."

Now he drank until the skin was flat. He gave her a nod then headed back toward the water. Again, she drew her bow and guarded him. Again he made it to the lake and back safely. "So far, so good. One more and we will get something to eat," he said as he headed to the waters a third time.

"Be careful," Twig advised as he squatted and dipped the last skin in the water. "It is hard to tell with all the bugs darting around, but something like a fish is looking at you!"

Adam looked around. "I don't see anything!"

"There," Twig said, pointing with her drawn arrow. "Maybe it is just a big frog."

Suddenly the water boiled. With a large splash a ferocious creature broke the surface. It charged toward Adam.

Twig screamed. Birds took flight. Adam was in the way of a shot. Time slowed as the beast charged towards him low to the ground. The creature's mouth was full of huge white teeth.

As it broke from the water, Adam leapt to his feet and ran. The crocodile chased after him. It was long—even several paces up the bank, part of it was still in the water. As Adam grew closer, the arrow slipped out of her hand and whizzed by Adam's head. To her amazement the arrow stopped the crocodile. The beast turned as quickly as it came out and disappeared back into the water.

"Great bloody bones," Adam gasped. "I knew something had to be in there but that was no frog. It was all teeth and a tail." Stepping next to Twig he glanced back. "I see a broken arrow. You shot him?"

"Him? Her?" Twig said as she tried to calm her breathing. She was sure her face revealed her horror. "Right in the mouth," she managed to say, then added, "That sent him packing in a hurry." She swallowed.

Adam was looking at her with admiration in his eyes. She smiled as he hugged her. "You were amazing," he said. "I was scared to death. I could barely run, but you stayed cool and shot him right in the mouth. You didn't even run. You are amazing."

"No, Adam, you are the brave one, to even go up to the edge. Now let's get something to eat!"

He did not need another invitation. He retrieved his bow and skin and took her hand and headed for their special tree. "You get a fire going and I'll go get dinner," he said and then gave her a wink. "And then we can focus on my prize for winning the bet."

Twig shook her head. All men were boys.

## The Reward

The sun touched the horizon forcing Adam to hurry despite his load. He returned to find the camp neat and clean. Twig had the firewood and dried chips piled next to their mat and a small fire burning. The smoke drifted upward into their tree.

While hunting, an idea had come to him, but it would be too much to ask for a bet. It was something he wanted more than anything in the world, but he could not use this silly bet to insist on it. He flopped the small deer he carried over his shoulder down next to a tree about thirty paces away.

Twig, knife in hand, joined him. "What's the plan, great hunter?" she asked as she began cutting into the carcass.

Adam explained his plan to hang the carcass in the tree. "Most of the predators can't climb trees, right?" he said. "But leopards can!"

"Oh, I see. How very clever," Twig said. "All we have to do is lay around under our tree and wait for one to show up."

"You got it," Adam said. He hoisted the dead deer up as high as he could. "That's why I shot a small one," he grunted. "So I could get it up here."

When he finished, she took his hand and they walked back toward the fire. The darkness closed in around them.

"You are so clever and so thoughtful," she said lightly. "That is what I love about you."

*Hmm,* he thought. *She just had to say love.* He could see she didn't want to scare him or make him feel uncomfortable so he let it slide. "Now lay down and relax while I cook your dinner," she said. "Take your time and decide what you want for winning the bet."

"Anything at all? No matter what?"

"That was our deal. I don't know what I was thinking about. It must have been the heat."

"I can't take advantage," Adam said laying on the mat, his fingers interlocked behind his head.

"The deal was it had to be done before the sun finished setting. My time is up."

"Again, a man of your word," Twig said. "But since you were off hunting I will give you a little more time."

"Oh?" Adam said. "So how long do I have?"

"Let's say until first light."

"Well, what do men want more than anything during the long watches of the night?" Adam asked in a flash of insight.

"Well, I can think of one thing," Twig said. She glanced over at him and gave him a seductive smile.

"Someone to keep the fire going all night," Adam boomed. "You can watch for the leopard while I sleep."

He laughed hysterically. Twig had something else in mind and might be hurt initially, but as he continued laughing and congratulating himself, she would decide he was oblivious and conclude he had no clue what she had been thinking.

"All night?" she asked glumly.

"You are so dissed," Adam said. "I was going to have you sew up my shirt, or do some repairs to my shoes, but that would have been hard to do by firelight. I had considered a haircut, but couldn't do that without being able to bathe. Then it hit me, when you said all night long. Oh yeah, what a great idea."

"You got me indeed. I couldn't think of anything you could have wanted that would have taken all night, so thought you would be stumped," she said defeated. When the meat was done, she rubbed some seasonings on it. "Been saving this. Hope you're hungry," she said, handing him a big hunk of meat, still dripping juice.

"Oh yeah," he groaned, savoring the meat. "This is fantastic, what was that you put on it?"

"My secret recipe," Twig said. "I will tell you if you excuse me from watch tonight."

"Fat chance. I don't need to know what it is. It's enough that you know."

They both ate until full, Adam laid down, pulled the cover over himself. "Goodnight, my dear, or should I say good watch," Adam said. "Thank you for a fine dinner. Wake me if you see any action by the tree. And remember to keep the fire bright enough so you can see."

Twig scooted over to sit beside him and ruffled his hair. "Good night my love, you earned a good night's sleep." She leaned over and kissed him full on the lips. It was not a quick peck, but a real kiss.

He started to respond then pulled away, remembering his plan. He decided he did owe her something so looked her in the eye. "You saved my life today, I feel I owe you not one night of service, but a life-time of service. Thank you," Adam said. He felt that was true enough, but also felt his resolve begin to weaken.

Twig bent forward and kissed him again, this time eagerly and he could not help responding to her warm lips. Flustered, she pulled back when his hand ran over her thigh.

"We mustn't," she breathed. "Not like this, not unless we are married."

Adam froze and the blood in his veins turned to stone. She had slipped, and now her whole plan was laid bare. He could see she had planned all along to use logic and rationalization to plant the idea of marriage in his head. She wanted him to think he thought of it. He could see it now. She wanted him to go back and propose the idea to Eve. But she had slipped up. Twig had lost her head. It had to be the kiss. It was too passionate for her. She was taken over by its power. To Adam that was the most remarkable thing. Twig had lost control. It was a first, he was sure. "I'm sorry," he said. "I know I should not have done what I was starting to do. If you hadn't stopped me, I would have, with no regard for Eve, for you, for the creator, or for my vows. When the passion comes, my brain shuts off. But you said something shocking. Is that what this is all about?" He waved his arms around the campsite.

Twig laughed, a strained guilty laugh. "Nothing like this has ever happened to me before, it is scary and exciting and to be totally honest, something I don't want to say no to either, but you are right. I would regret losing my head, well maybe I would. It was the only thing I could think to say." She stood, arranged her rumpled skirt, and smiled down at him. "I will clean up and watch for the leopard. You get some sleep."

"Oh no, not so quick. Eve told me if I ever mated with another woman she would cut my throat in my sleep, and I believe she would."

"She told me that as well."

"So how do you think I could marry you?" Adam asked. "Are you planning on killing her?"

"Of course not," Twig said. "She is my best friend. Now look, you know the way of the tribe. It is the leader's job to produce as many children as possible. This idea of marriage is new. Who do you think made it up? I did. Who told Eve what to do? I did. Who told you what to do? I did. I made it up, because it seemed like a romantic thing at the moment, but I can change it, just like that," she said, snapping her fingers.

"I don't think Eve would agree," Adam said. "We said our vows. You know how stubborn she is."

Twig looked down. "You're probably right. I'm sorry. It was a passing dream, nothing more. Now get some sleep."

Adam laid down, and tried to think, but his muddled mind refused to work. Twig had been sincere, and as far as he could remember, he had never heard her say she was sorry. He believed her.

When he awoke, it was like rising from a deep pit. Someone was shaking him. A hand over his mouth kept him from asking what was going on. His memories came flooding back, and he was suddenly wide awake. Twig removed her hand and gazed at the tree with the dead deer in it.

A leopard slowly circled, looking up. Terror struck Adam. It was just like so long ago when the leopard attacked the goats. He froze that time, paralyzed with fear. For a moment this leopard stared at him and the fear returned. If he shot, it would charge, and it was fast. If he missed, he would be dead. He had dreamed of this moment for months and months, but now all he felt was fear.

Twig pushed the bow into his hands and looked at him expectantly. He took his time getting set up. He drew out his best arrow.

He mouthed the words: "On three."

Twig hesitated. "On three?"

Adam nodded. "You too," he whispered and she raised her bow. Adam prayed the beast would just run off so he wouldn't have to shoot and possibly miss. Aiming carefully, he pictured the beast's heart, and waited until it turned. Fear pushed his bow and arrow towards the ground.

"Adam?" Twig hissed.

He could not let her see his fear. He raised his bow again. The beast turned. "One, two, three," he whispered.

*Tw-wang-g.* Their bows sang out together. The noble beast spun toward them, two arrows stuck in it. It paused a moment, then started across the thirty paces towards them in great bounding leaps.

Everything in Adam cried out for him to run, but instead he pulled another arrow at lightning speed—twenty paces left. He notched it and drew the arrow back. With ten paces left, he let it go. His second arrow sank deep into the leopard's chest just as it prepared to make its final, killing leap.

Twig screamed, but as Adam fumbled for his axe, the beast fell, twitching to the ground at their feet.

"You did it," Twig said. "I can hardly believe it."

"We did it," Adam said, turning to her. "I couldn't have done it without you."

He hugged her, almost crushing her in his arms. He wanted to say more but no words would come out. *What did it mean? What strange game were they playing?* He held her and stroked her golden hair, worrying what would become of them if things were to once again grow out of hand.

With the smell of blood in the air, the scavengers began to gather. Adam pulled Twig back and looked into her eyes. No words were needed, her eyes told him everything. He was sure his did as well.

"Well, let's get the skin off him before the scavengers do," he said in a low voice. His words broke the spell and they leapt into action. "Is dawn close or is the night still young?" he asked later as he built up the fire.

"It is close," Twig said. "It was a long night of watching."

"But it ended well," Adam said. "You did well."

"We did well," she responded.

As the sky lightened, they scraped the hide and stretched it to dry among the branches of the tree. After breakfast Adam dragged the carcass to the lake and tossed it in. Then while the crocodiles fed, he refilled their skins, and rinsed the dried blood from his arms and hands.

"Sleep, my lovely wife. I'll watch over you now," he said and kissed Twig's forehead. She smiled and closed her eyes. Adam sat and watched the animals come to the lake and drink. There were no casualties. The croc's had already feasted. Other than the occasional wary glance at the fire, the beasts ignored them under their smoky tree.

> *Those who tread among serpents, and along a tortuous path, must use the cunning of the serpent.*
>
> *Thomas Becket*

# The Serpent  20

Twig finally woke up around midday. "Good morning," she said, stretching. She smiled and sniffed the meat he was cooking. Adam figured it was the least he could do after she watched him sleep all night. He had thought long and hard all morning and had made up his mind what needed to be said. He waited until she was organized and enjoyed the meal he made. "Twig, we need to talk," he began—her smile faded and she looked very serious. She also knew no good conversation began this way. "Twig, there is something I want very badly from you, and I almost asked you last night, but decided it would not be fair to take advantage of our bet. This is far too serious for that. So I am going to ask you now. I am asking you to do this for me because I am asking and because you trust me." She looked at him, a strange expression on her face. He decided to move on before she said no. "Twig, I know that you know things, things about our past, and about who we are and why we are here. You tell us what to do, but you never explain why or how you know. I need to know the secret you have been keeping from us."

"And here I thought you were after my body," she said with a forced laugh. "What do you think I know?"

"Don't fish around to see how much you need to tell me. I want to know it all. You have dropped hints, and I have a pretty good idea, but I want to hear it all from you. All of it. Does the creator talk to you too?"

She frowned, then leaned over and kissed him. "I have never told anyone my story," she said. "But I will tell you because I love you." She stood, walked around the blanket and fire before sitting back down. "This is going to take a while."

Adam nodded, and waited. "What is one more day?"

"You know the Serpent in the pines?"

"The Serpent? Sure."

"Actually, you don't," Twig said. "Because, first of all, the Serpent is not a snake or anything like that. She is an old woman who can speak just like us, and she has blue eyes."

"A woman?" Adam couldn't believe what he was hearing. "She can speak?"

"She is my grandmother."

"Twig, have you gone mad?" Adam exclaimed. "All these years, with all the stories, now the Serpent is your grandmother? What does that even mean? What is a grandmother anyway?"

Twig looked around as if seeking a way to escape. "A grandmother is your mother or father's mother, I think. Maybe she is just your mother's mother."

"But your mother doesn't have a mother. None of the tribe's women have mothers."

"Ever wonder why? What happened to them?"

Adam thought. He supposed his parents must have parents. "I have to admit I never considered the question. But you have one?"

"Some of my earliest memories are of a crazy old wild woman. She used to find me. She took me away and talked with me. I believe she taught me to speak. But it was a long time ago. I have not seen her in ages. Hadn't until we found the skull. I knew then it was time to seek her out. The nightmares. I needed to know what she knew about it."

"Why would she know?" Adam asked, completely blown away by this shocking news.

"She speaks. None of our parents speak. She was there. She knew what happened."

Adam shook his head. "So wait? You know where she lives?"

"She lived across the stream in the haunted pine forest," Twig said. "In a hollow tree."

"In a hollow tree? Right across the stream?" Adam burst out. "How can she live right across the stream, and I have never seen her?"

"When was the last time you went into the haunted woods?" Twig asked.

"To hunt the savages," Adam answered. "Before that? Never. Not really sure why. There is nothing over there and everyone says it is full of strange voices and creatures. I thought it was the Serpent."

"One day when everyone was busy, I took the skull, and crossed the stream," Twig said. She looked up into the tree above, and her expression changed. So did her voice. "The towering pines shut out the light, leaving the ground deep with needles and nothing else. No flowers, no fruit, nothing to eat. The woods stood undisturbed. As I watched I began to remember things."

Adam felt the hair on the back of his neck stand up. He reached out and took her hand without thinking. "What things?" After everything, Adam couldn't believe what he was hearing.

"As a child, my mother averted her eyes when the old woman showed up naked and looking scary. Then the Serpent would take me across the stream. She was a strange old woman, naked and shriveled, with wild white hair, but bright blue eyes, just like Blue Eyes. She spoke, and taught me to speak, and I in turn taught the gang to speak. I was afraid, but intrigued. But that is all I remember. How often had I made the trip? How long had I stayed? I can't remember. Why did the woman stop? Fear is all I have to answer that question. Whatever happened, it must have been bad."

"Go on," Adam said.

Twig blinked, shook her head, and continued. "As the branches closed behind me, the sounds of the valley faded. The babble of the stream, the splashing of the falls, even the birds and monkeys chattering in the trees on the other side of the stream were replaced by an eerie quiet of a winsome breeze, high in the trees. The air smelled of pines, heady and sweet, but musty. I remember a white butterfly, alone, strange and unnatural in the gloom of the woods. The sun did not penetrate the dense canopy. I walked, occasionally ducking under dead branches spiking out from the massive pine trunks. I walked one way, then another, wandering around, losing all sense of direction, looking for a sign, any sign of her. The trees were not as big as I remembered, but I was little then."

"Did you find her?"

"I did, but at the time I wondered if she had died," Twig whispered. "Then a shadow moved between some trees. I could hear my heart beating. It was so loud I was surprised I could even hear what came next."

"She found you?" Adam asked.

"A strange, unnatural sound best describes her cackle. It froze me in place. I called out to her.

'*Grandmother?*' Silence. I took a tentative step toward the tree where her shadow had disappeared. My feet grew into the earth, yet somehow I moved another step, and then another. The tree seemed to grow taller as I approached."

"She can make the trees grow taller?" Adam asked.

"No," Twig said. "I whispered, as I reached the tree. 'Grandmother?' Why had I never been back here? What had happened? I could not remember. Perhaps it was for a good reason. I considered turning back. I am not like Eve. I usually know when to leave something bad alone."

Adam snickered. "Really?"

Twig gave him a hard stare. "The real question in my mind has always been, *why me?* I am like everyone else." Adam choked back a laugh. "My mother is normal enough," Twig added defensively.

This time Adam could not contain his laughter. Twig stared and he realized she did not have a clue. He thought fast. "Your mother also has light hair—you are the only two," Adam said. "And don't you think it odd that you have no brothers or sisters. Everyone else does?"

Twig's face softened. "True enough," she said. "Maybe my mother is not quite normal, not like the rest of the tribe. I, of course, am normal, nothing like my crazy grandmother. Well, I am at least mostly normal."

Adam smiled at her. "Right. You're totally normal, Twig."

"Anyway," Twig said with a grimace. "I stepped forward, almost touching the tree. I took a step, then another. I peered around the tree. Then I saw the familiar split in the bark. I knew then it had not all been some fever dream. The tree was the same hollow tree I remembered. I called out again. What a strange name. Grandmother."

"A voice, sharp and cutting, came from the crack in the bark. 'How dare you disturb me.'"

"She wasn't nice to you?" Adam said. "I thought she liked you."

"I had tears running down my face by then, I was so afraid. A head appeared from within the tree, white, wrinkled. Her long white hair was even longer and more scraggly. Bright eyes stared at me from deep within her wrinkled face. A hideous, toothless grin leered at me. I sucked in my breath and tried to stop the scream, but it was too late and the view too shocking as more of her naked form emerged, horribly shriveled. She said I would look like her when I was older," Twig choked out the last part.

Adam wrapped an arm around her frail shoulders. "Twig, it's okay. You don't have to believe her."

"But she is right about everything!" Twig bawled.

"I'll shoot you with an arrow before it comes to that," Adam said, patting her on the head.

"Thanks, I think," Twig said before wiping her eyes and continuing. "'Sit, young one,' the Serpent told me. Then sat opposite me, in the door of her lair. Her eyes seemed to look into my innermost being. She asked me why I sought her. When I showed her the skull, she drew back at the sight. 'Brutes,' she hissed. 'Where did you get that? I made Blue Eyes smash down the ledge!'"

"She made Blue Eyes break the ledge?" Adam asked in amazement.

"It was she who insisted on the crevice being cut off. Before I could ask more, she laughed. No, not a laugh. It was an evil cackle. Her gaze drifted to the trees, and her voice turned inward. 'Perhaps it is time?' she said. 'The girl has found the skull, and now she has seen the truth, perhaps she should know all?'"

"She was talking to herself?"

"I wondered at the time, but she had been alone for countless years, why not talk with yourself?"

"This is all crazy?" Adam said, glancing around, half expecting to see the scary old woman peeking over some bushes.

Twig sighed. "Let me tell you exactly what she told me, so please do not interrupt or I will lose my place," Twig said, and her own eyes now stared out into the distance.

"Wow," was all Adam could say when she had finished explaining how Blue Eyes led the tribe over the plains, all while being chased by hideous human-like beasts the Serpent called Brutes. The tribe had run for their lives. The weak, the old, and the young they left for dead. The story, however, ended with Blue Eyes discovering the crevice and escaping the Brutes by entering the valley.

Adam pulled his mind back to the present, to their camp under the little tree. The afternoon was slipping by. "That's the ending?" he asked. "That is no ending place."

"That's what I said," Twig replied. "But she said she was tired. 'Come back tomorrow and I will finish the story, but only if you bring me three pieces of fruit from the Tree, not from the ground. I am too old to climb.' The old woman slowly pulled herself upright, and disappeared back into the tree. Cold and scared, I headed home."

"Brutes ate your grandfather," Adam said. "Yuck."

"Right? But did you feel like I did, like you were actually there, running for your life?" Twig asked. "I tried to tell the story exactly like she did, and that was how I felt."

"It was like I was in a dream," Adam said. "I was right there with Blue Eyes, battling Brutes."

"Sadly, at the time I was less enamored with the storytelling, than with learning all the answers I had so long sought. It explains the scars, the mating, the casual way Blue Eyes killed Big Nose, and how they knew how to survive up here. I had even more questions though. Why can she speak, but not our parents? What happened in the valley?"

"Twig, you are never satisfied, are you? I suppose you stole the fruit she wanted?" Adam said, feeling proud of her.

"Of course. I was tempted to ask Eve to help, but decided if she could do it, so could I. At dusk I managed to get the fruit. It was just as Eve described. That night I could hardly sleep, reviewing every word the old woman said. Clearly she is Blue Eyes' mother."

"But that would make her Eve's grandmother, not yours," Adam said. "But it was not Eve she taught to speak. Why?"

Twig just shook her head. "I wondered the same. I also wondered if it was my mother with the hurt leg? And what is with the Serpent's white hair? How did that happen? And all those wrinkles, and running around naked? Also her teeth."

"What about her teeth?"

"She did not have any. So anyway, I went back in the morning. 'Grandmother, I'm back,' I called as I approached the tree. 'Did you bring the fruit?' her voice, eerie and disembodied, drifted from the hollow tree. I told her I brought three. A moment later she appeared, looking much as she had the day before. She snatched up fruit as I pulled it from my pack and tucked it away in her tree, then looked up again. 'For years, nobody cared what I had to say. They discover a brute. They make a new weapon, and then they are surprised when it is used to kill one of our own. Now they want to hear what I have to say.' She began to cackle again after that."

Adam took Twig's hand. Twig looked out over the water. "She saw Big Nose die? Then what happened?" he asked her.

"I reminded her where she left off and she continued. 'The tribe climbed down into the valley but I stayed,' she said. 'The girl with a bad leg was left behind, and I helped her climb down. I spent the night at the edge of the jungle so I could watch over my son.'"

Adam felt himself drift again into the story. Some time later, Twig squeezed his hand, and he was back. The story had done it again. As Adam emerged from the story, he was surprised to find himself still sitting under the tree, still gripping Twig's hand. The sun now hung low in the sky. "And that was it," Twig said. "She told me the story was finished. And that she was tired. I tried to help her up. She hesitated, and glared at me, but finally allowed me to help. I held on to her frail body and walked her to the gap in the tree."

"And that was it?" Adam asked. "Did you go back?"

"I did, but I had a horrible sense of foreboding when I heard no response when I called at the crack in the big pine tree. I crawled in a little way, and found her. Her face was pale and drawn. She was just laying there, bits of fruit still in her hand. There was a tattered seal skin on the ground, and the woman was curled up on it. There were dried plants hanging above, and little piles of nuts and some roots, and not much else. I reached out and touched her hand. It was as cold as the earth itself." Twig shuddered.

"She ate all the fruit and it killed her?" Adam asked in amazement.

"And it was me. I killed her," Twig said, her voice filled with emotion. She turned to Adam, and he held her close. "What are you talking about? You didn't kill her."

"I brought her the fruit, three of them, and she ate them all. If I had not brought them, she would be alive now."

Adam's face fell. "I didn't think . . . I don't know Twig. I'm sorry." He held her for a while but had to know more. "Twig, what did you do with her?"

Twig wiped her eyes. "Well, I didn't eat her, and I couldn't toss her in the stream. She is one of us, so just left her sleeping in her home."

"You didn't tell anyone, not even Blue Eyes?"

"She was one of us, rejected by the tribe. Who cares what they think, and Adam, don't you get it? He is your father too. She was his mother. He obviously did not care about her, or he would not have left her alone all those years. I did, however, take a lock of her hair, to remember her by." Twig dug under her skirt and pulled out a carefully braided lock of white hair.

Adam took it and held it. There was no doubt Twig's story was true. "I've never seen anything like it."

"I wanted to keep the rest of the tribe out of there, so I encouraged the Serpent legend," Twig said, standing.

She dug out some leftover meat, and laid out their mat. She pulled Adam down next to her.

"Blue Eyes is my father too?" Adam asked, her earlier statement finally sinking in.

"I think he is the father of all of us. Think about it. You heard how things were. Blue Eyes is old, but still chases all the women. When young, he was the leader, and had little else to do."

Adam considered. "So?"

"Listen, it explains everything. We all speak, most of our younger brothers and sisters speak, but not all. More kids our age speak, fewer of the younger kids. It's him. He is the one."

"So what you are saying is that when he stops messing around with the women, or dies, there will be no more speaking children among the non-speakers," Adam said, his brow wrinkled with the magnitude of the conclusion.

"It's my theory, and it fits the facts, but I might be wrong. We must go through all our memories, our observations and see if we can find a flaw. A single case to prove the theory wrong. I think it also fits with your mission from the creator."

"So it will be up to us to carry on making speaking children in the future. It's all of our missions from the creator," Adam said, looking at Twig with a big smile. "So that is why you were planning this little event."

"Keep your pants on. It's just a theory," Twig snapped.

"Well, we learned several things," Adam said. "The 'light-haired beauty' must be your mother, and the Serpent must be her mother." Adam looked at Twig, who nodded. "And Eve's mother must be the 'not-so-good-looking-but-favorite mate.'"

Twig smiled. "So your mother and Eve's father are brother and sister."

"Which is why we are best friends," Twig declared and reached out and gave Adam a little hug.

Adam lay back and stared into the sky, as he awaited the first star. Twig was different—like her grandmother. Was that why she was taught to speak and given the fruit? Adam pictured the wizened old woman. Maybe her shriveled form really was what they had to look forward to. He wondered who taught the old woman to speak. Maybe she talked with the creator too?

"A grape for your thoughts." Twig's voice pierced his revery. He turned, smiled and squeezed her hand.

"The Serpent wasn't alone if she talked with the creator," he said. "But this is all too much for my mind to grasp. The whole business about the tribe falling sick and them dying. How could she know to save them with the fruit? It always comes back to the fruit, doesn't it?"

"It is a bit overwhelming, even now, and yes, it was the fruit that saved them, or changed them, and the fruit which made the Serpent special. It let her talk to the creator. The fruit must have made me able to understand as a child, and don't forget the fruit saved Monkey."

"But ignorant us, went blundering up the crevice, and wandered like babies into who knows what. Why didn't you tell us?"

"I did, don't you remember?"

"But not why."

"She made me promise not to tell," Twig said. "And before you ask, I had no idea why, but now that I think about it, it was probably so others would not come and bother her. After all, she could have taught all of us to talk, but she only taught me. She must have wanted to be alone. So now that she is gone, I suppose it is alright to talk about it." Twig smiled at him, curled up, and closed her eyes. Adam suspected there would be no sleep for him tonight, not with so much to think about.

By morning he had more questions and could hardly wait for Twig to wake up. "So, tell me. Who is going to be the next leader of the tribe?"

She gave him a hard look, and busied herself with rolling her mat, but not distracted, he waited, and focused on her every move.

"Now or when Blue Eyes is no more?" she asked.

"Both."

"Who do you think is the leader now?"

Her time of honest talk was clearly over. Twig was back to her old self.

"Stop playing around, Twig. Answer the question."

"The tribe follows Blue Eyes," Twig said. "We do not."

"True. Who do we follow?" Adam asked, hoping she said him.

"Eve clearly feels she leads us, and expects to be the leader of the whole tribe some day."

Adam felt his hackles rising.

"Who do you think leads us?" he demanded.

"It is pretty clear Eve leads us, but who leads Eve? You?" Twig asked, sporting a wicked grin. Adam felt this line of questioning slipping off the path yet again.

"You think I lead Eve?"

"No," she said flatly.

He had hoped for a yes, but knew the answer was no. Twig was at least being honest.

"Then who does?" he asked. He just wanted to hear her say it.

"I guess I do. I do it discreetly and kindly, but I initiate most of her ideas."

"And if I were the leader instead of Eve, you would do the same with me, wouldn't you?"

"I suppose I would. It was why I was chosen. Of all the speaking children, only I was selected to be taught by the true leader of our tribe."

"I see," Adam said. Blue Eyes had picked him to lead the tribe. But, Twig had made it pretty clear the gang was never going to be led by the tribe's leader. It didn't matter two grapes who Blue Eyes picked, the gang would be led by whoever was strongest in the gang. And whoever that was, they would be led by Twig. "Well," he began and stopped. He did not have any kind of answer. He did not like it, but guessed it was just the truth of the matter.

She looked at him kindly, pulled him close, and rubbed his head. "There, there. Don't worry about it. You lead us every time we go on a hunt."

It wasn't much, but Adam felt it was something, and for now that was enough.

*Life is ten percent what happens to you
and ninety percent how you respond to it.*

Charles Swindoll

# Home 21

They spent two more days at the lake, feasting, drinking all the water they wanted and turning the leopard hide into a cloak. They talked and laughed, but never about what mattered. As they headed home, they walked hand-in-hand. While Twig still slept in his arms, nothing happened. And yet every day his passion for her grew. Every day the tension between them grew as well.

When the crevice was within reach, their water was gone, but they had the prize. "When we reach the crevice our adventure comes to an end. We must face Eve. "

"You undoubtedly have a child," Twig said.

"I may. Eve and I are the first couple to ever be married, but you were the one who explained to us what we should do. There are only the rules we make for ourselves. We made them, and we can change them. I love you and can suggest to Eve I marry you as well."

"And if she says no?" Twig asked, getting right to the point as always.

Adam thought for a moment. "Then I will keep my vows and not marry you," he said. "But I will always love you and take care of you as long as I live, but won't be your husband, not until Eve agrees. I am sorry but I can't think of any other solution. Can you?"

"Who will ask Eve?"

"I will, once we have exchanged news. I will explain to her what happened, or, oh, hmm . . . I do not see that working at all. Please, you . . . You are the smart one, tell me what to do; I'll do it."

Twig pulled him to a stop and turned to look him in the eye. "Adam, I have had several days to think, and dream and wish, but now it is time for reality. You will tell Eve of your great love for her, and how you wanted to bring her the most precious gift in the world, and how you insisted on going after the leopard, despite the danger, and how, for her sake I came to patch you up if needed, and tell her all the details of our dangers and perils and ultimate success, and how glad you are to be home."

"That's it?"

"You might have to promise to never make such a trip again without her at your side. Say nothing of our little kissing game. There is far more at stake than just us. I will remain her best friend, and I will always love you in secret, and please, care for me in my times of distress. I fear I will grow old alone. After loving you, no other man will do."

"No, I couldn't bear it," Adam cried.

Twig, however, was unmoved, despite the tears in her eyes. "Bear it bravely," she said. "Or I will wander off into the prairie, and you will never see me again."

Her words filled him with trepidation and Adam had mixed feelings as they climbed down the crevice. Someone had removed the ladder, but the valley still smelled of wild flowers and fruit. There was a comforting familiarity at being home. Here Adam knew every plant, every animal, even if it was Twig who had named most of them. It was sad their great adventure had come to an end, but, all the same, it was comforting to be home.

As they walked down the path toward the treehouse, Adam saw Twig reaching for his hand, and pulling back. *She is not mine, not any more,* he told himself.

"Eve, I'm home," Adam bellowed as they approached. The sight of naked savages dead under the treehouse froze the blood in Adam's veins. The four savages each sported one of Eve's arrows, and the treehouse ladder was down.

Except for the buzzing of the flies on the already bloating bodies the camp was quiet.

"Eve," Twig screamed, but there was no answer.

Adam walked to the ladder, each step more difficult than the last as if he was carrying an ever increasing load. With each step his dread grew. Up top the mat hung over the door, gently swaying in the breeze. He braced himself to see Eve's body, as he reached out with a shaking hand. Pulling back the curtain he looked inside; the treehouse was empty. All their stuff seemed to be there, all except Eve's weapons. They, like Eve, were missing.

"This is all your fault," he hissed at Twig as he descended the ladder and ran past her and headed as fast as he could run toward the settlement. He could hardly think straight. Not knowing who to kill boiled the rage inside him. It was not really Twig's fault. The bodies had been there a while, and the slaughter may have even happened before Monkey arrived. In that case it was entirely his fault. His heart stopped yet again when he saw another body ahead. "Please no," he cried as he approached.

Relief flooded over him as he drew closer. The body was that of another savage, this one killed with an axe, but more than killed, he noticed. It had been hacked to bits. He tore off again.

Everything seemed normal when he finally reached the bridge and turned towards the caves.

Suddenly Monkey jumped out in front of him, bow in hand.

"Whoa there, I almost shot you coming in so fast at dusk," he said. "There are savages about."

"I saw the bodies," Adam gasped, desperately looking at the faces emerging from the woods. He recognized Little Red, but saw no sign of Eve. "Eve? Is she alright? Where is she?"

"Relax," Monkey said. "She is fine."

"I said, where is she?"

"Up at her parents cave with the baby."

Adam did not wait to hear more. He raced past Monkey and Little Red and headed for Blue Eyes' cave. Eve was cooking in front of the cave. She leapt to her feet and ran to meet him. He hugged her as she fell into his arms. Lifting her off the ground, he swung her around. They both talked at once.

"I was so worried when I found the savages and the treehouse empty," Adam said. "I am so sorry. This is all my fault. I will never leave you again."

"Yikes, you are so filthy," she declared. She looked beyond him and across the clearing. "Where is Twig? Is she okay?"

"I left her at the treehouse, she is fine."

Rosy exited the cave holding a baby. She bounced the little guy on her hip. "Adam, meet your son," Eve said. "I call him Adamson. Take a look but then get down to the stream and bathe. Your smell alone will make him sick."

"So how was the birth?" Adam asked as she walked with him toward the stream. He could not help glancing across at the haunted pine woods. Knowing what he knew now, he saw them in a whole new light.

"Oh, you have no idea. It was an ordeal. I will tell you all about it, but later."

Adam smiled to himself as he lay in the shallow stream. The cool water refreshed his spirit. The sweet smell of the Tree of Life relaxed his mind. There were no crocodiles waiting to ambush him here, no hyenas lurking in the brush, ready to attack, and no lions, nor leopards here ready to tear him apart—only one leopard skin.

He had done the right thing, and he vowed to never talk to anyone about Twig's love. She had much to occupy her time without him. There was a world of knowledge to gain, sick to cure, injuries to heal, and a tribe to lead. Just as her grandmother led Blue Eyes, she would lead him. The realization hit Adam like a rock. Twig was not one to give up and quit. She would lead, and, married to Eve or not, he would obey her wisdom.

When he looked up at Eve, all was not right with her—he could see it in her eyes. She was not smiling, but staring out across the stream. There was so much she did not know, and Twig was right. She did think herself the leader. She would not accept the new order easily. *I need to handle this carefully.*

He stood. His body dripped stream water. "Eve, I am sorry I left you. I have learned so much. I know it was wrong to leave you. Everything has changed, and . . . "

She cut him off. "I have learned much as well, Adam," she said. "There are savages still out there. We are lucky to have Monkey in charge, keeping us safe."

Her words rocked Adam. Not knowing what to say, he reflected. Monkey was in charge but only because he had put him in charge. The way she said it was odd.

Adam was about to explain, but she turned from him. "Here comes Twig," she said. "I hope she had a nice time alone with you while I was fighting for my life."

Adam frowned to himself. He could see things would be difficult for a time. As Eve went to greet Twig, he checked out the baby. Rosy seemed hesitant to give Adamson up. The little version of himself was really something to see, but he kept an eye on Eve as she and Twig talked. Both gestured wildly, and Adam was glad he was not standing between them.

As the sky turned dark, he scooted closer to the fire to keep warm. Now what? Did Eve expect him to sleep with her in Blue Eyes' cave? And what was Monkey up to? Also it seemed Blue Eyes was missing. There were more savages about and he wondered if they had got the old man. When Adamson started to fuss, Adam handed him to Rosy. Then when Eve emerged from the dark, she walked past him into the cave.

"There is some food in here if you want some," she called over her shoulder. He should have been hungry, but the knot in his stomach hid the fact. Inside the cave he took the food and tried to eat.

Monkey appeared out of the darkness. He sat down next to Adam. "So, have a good hunt?" he asked.

"Yes, but tell me about these savages," Adam said.

"When we first went to see Eve, to give her your message, we were shocked to see the rotting corpses under the treehouse. Seems they surprised her. They tried to trap her in the treehouse. On the way to the settlement we saw another—it turns out Rosy killed that one with her axe. Eve told me at least three more were following."

Adam shuddered. "No."

"We found her at Blue Eyes' cave. Her father was all fired up when he saw the bodies and sounded the war cry. He rounded up most of the remaining non-speakers and took off. Of course we had no idea where he was going. Going in search of the savages or returning to the camp we made. He never even tries to communicate. Bloody bones, I swear. I did not know what to do, so I stayed to protect the settlement. I did send Little Red to follow Blue Eyes to see where he went. What else could I do?"

"I don't know," Adam said.

"I kept a guard day and night at the bridge and waited. Eve was a mess. The kids told me she was barely alive when she arrived. I did what I could for her."

Adam punched his fist into his other hand. He was so upset all this happened when he was away. All the anger he had for Twig was back, as well as more for himself. *I knew I should have turned back from the hunt even before the elephant attack.* Now he was powerless.

"Little Red returned yesterday to report that Blue Eyes had dislodged a group of savages. Four or five of them climbed out of the valley as Blue Eyes followed. Little Red turned back at the crevice, after removing the ladders."

"That was good thinking," Adam said.

"I have stayed on watch since," Monkey said. "Just in case, but I think we are safe now."

"But for how long?" Adam said. "The savages who left may well be back with their whole tribe. We better start setting up more trip lines and start keeping a better watch."

As he and Monkey talked about their defense issues, Adam thought about Eve and how to ask what he needed to ask.

"So, about Eve," he finally said when the conversation lulled. "You say she was hurt? She looked alright."

"She had no injuries I saw, but she seemed off. Imagine being trapped with nobody to talk with. She never talked about it, but is always on edge. Sometimes she says some pretty crazy things. I do not think she is very happy with you right now."

Adam looked at Monkey closely. He was not smiling, but his eyes were. This competition between them had been going on a long-time. Adam suspected Monkey was ready to move on Eve, if he failed. "Thanks," he said. "I am about to fall asleep sitting up. See you in the morning." He headed toward the cave, then turned back. "Monkey, will you do me a favor. I plan to take Eve home tomorrow. I don't want her to see all those rotting bodies. I know it is a lot to ask, but will you recruit some help first thing in the morning and get rid of them?"

"For Eve?" Monkey said. "Sure I could."

Adam walked into the cave frowning. Eve was asleep and he lay next to her. Missing Twig's mat, he finally managed to fall asleep. The night was a blur of movement and the baby crying, but somehow he never fully woke.

When he did wake she was next to him nursing the baby. "Eve, let's go home," he said.

"Is it safe?" she asked hesitantly.

"Yes, and I want to be close to the crevice so I can make it even more secure."

She thought for a while and finally nodded. Glancing at Adamson, Adam finally understood what Monkey had said. This was not his Eve anymore. She and the baby would have plenty to say about how and when they should return.

# A Single Mat

Things felt normal for the first time since Adam was back. Eve had much to discuss with him and hardly knew where to start. She had a lot of time to think and decided to start with the hardest issue. "Adam, now that you have moved my family, the remaining tribe has no leader," she said, as they started down the path.

"Why didn't Blue Eyes take the whole tribe?" Adam asked. "Maybe we should send them off too."

"He left those not interested in going, and I guess if he could not get them moving, we won't be able to either. Regardless, we really need to solve the gang's leadership question."

"It hardly seems like much of an issue as there are so few of us now," Adam said. "Twig gave me a history on our trip, and it seems her grandmother was the real leader of the tribe. Twig said she has the same role now. She's not the one out front telling people what to do, but the one making the real decisions."

"That's ridiculous," Eve said. "I don't care who Twig thinks she is, I am Blue Eye's daughter, not her."

"You must admit, if you think back carefully, she has been using the both of us to get things done the way she wants," Adam said.

He was right, and by including himself, it did not hurt as much. "So you are alright continuing to do that?" Eve asked.

"I don't mind playing the role of leader, but only as long as you help me know what to do. I have learned that I am no leader without you at my side. I was an absolute mess on the hunt."

The anger inside Eve faded. She looked over and smiled. "You have not lost your charm, and the tribe already thinks of you as the leader. But what is this about you hearing from the creator?"

Adam told her the story. Eve was surprised and disappointed she had not had his vision also. She worried it was because she had disobeyed the creator so many times and then blamed Adam when things went awry.

"And that is why you stayed away so long?" she asked.

"I had no choice but to obey," Adam said. "But I drove everyone as hard as I could."

"Monkey did not say anything about the vision or you being in a hurry," Eve said accusingly.

"Of course he wouldn't," Adam said. "He still has eyes only for you."

Eve laughed. "You dreaming about that too?"

"Ask Little Red," Adam said. "Would he lie to you?"

"And your little hunting trip with Twig? I suppose the creator ordered you to do that too?"

Adam stopped, turned and looked her in the eye. "No, that was another matter. Twig convinced me that I should not come back without a gift for you. I fell for it. That was my fault. I should have said no."

"A gift?" she said with a smile. "But a gift is a good idea. What is it?"

"You will see when we get to the treehouse."

"I see," Eve said. "It was a special trip for a secret gift?"

"The trip was also valuable in that Twig finally told me the truth about our history and all her hidden knowledge. Blue Eyes is the father of all the speaking children, and once he is gone, there will be no more, so it is up to us to keep our kind going."

"That sounds crazy. We don't know that."

"That's what I thought, but think back. Twig explained it all to me."

"So we were a happy gang, determined to explore and have fun, then you go on a hunting trip with Twig and now Fish and Bev are married and gone off busy making babies. And we have Adamson. But what about Twig? Is she going to marry Monkey?"

"She does not want to, but she knows it is important to have children now," Adam said quietly.

"She thought she could steal you away from me?"

"No, absolutely not. Her idea was different from that. She is your best friend and wanted to join us."

Eve stopped abruptly. "Join us?" she demanded. "What does that even mean?"

"She said she would only consider such a thing if you approved."

"Join us?" Eve said again, hearing herself grow irritated. Well that is never going to happen."

"That's what I told her," Adam said, backing away. "We didn't do anything wrong. I love you, Eve. I would never break my vow to you."

Eve stomped past him and they walked in silence for a time. It did all make sense, well not exactly, what with visions from the creator and all, but if Adam did have this vision, then the rest of the story sounded believable.

"Okay, say I believe you," she said. "I will try to accept all that has happened, but you will have to be kind and patient with me. I am not quite my old self yet."

Adam promised to do his best. That Adam didn't argue and say she was herself and was just fine scared her. She really was broken if he could see it too. The birth and the battles left her in a dark place. She lost track of time until she became aware that the treehouse was ahead. She looked around for the savages as a quiet terror gripped her. The place, however, was clear.

Monkey and a group of youngsters were waiting at the treehouse. "I have set up trip lines like we discussed," he said, looking directly at Eve. "We have cleaned up as well." He flashed her a smile and she remembered what Adam had said earlier. *Surely not.*

"Thank you all so much," she said. "I really appreciate it."

"We will camp on the beach for a while to keep an eye on the trip lines if you need us," Monkey said, bowing. He rounded up the rest of the youngsters and they moved off.

"I am ready for my gift," Eve said as she headed up the ladder. Adam dug something from his pack. "It's every bit as lovely as I thought it would be," Eve said, as she rubbed the leopard skin pelt on her face.

Adam told her of the bait, and the kill as he paced back and forth in the treehouse. He made faces at Adamson in his arms.

"You weren't scared we're you?" Eve asked him.

"No," Adam said. "I had your bow and arrows to keep me safe. The leopard should have been afraid of me." He made a face at Adamson. "That's right, my son. That big, bad leopard should have been afraid of your father; he is a mighty hunter."

Eve smiled at his bravado, but did not believe him for a second. She, however, was thrilled he had taken such a risk for her. Setting down the spotted leopard pelt, she continued to unpack. *That's odd*, she thought as she shook out the last of his things. "Adam, where is your mat? Did you sleep on the ground?"

Adam stopped bouncing Adamson and averted his eyes. "Not exactly," he mumbled.

"Not exactly, what?" Eve demanded. Adamson started to cry, yet she plowed on. "You either slept on the ground, or you didn't! Which is it?"

"My mat somehow got mixed up in somebody else's pack. I don't know how it happened. It is no big deal."

"So you were *forced* to sleep with Twig, is that it?" Eve asked as the baby continued to scream in Adam's arms.

"I didn't sleep with Twig!" he shouted over the screaming baby. He stopped and stared at the baby, like it changed into some kind of little monster. "Well, we just shared her mat, that's all. Let me explain . . . "

"I know you're lying, I can see it written all over your stupid face," Eve shouted at him. She leapt up and, charging over, she tried to take Adamson away from him.

Adam turned away, pulling Adamson away from her. "I'm not lying!"

"Don't shout in his ears!" Eve hissed, narrowing her eyes. "Give him to me." She snatched him from Adam's arms. "Hush, hush," Eve cooed to quiet her baby. "Mamma's here."

She turned and stared at Adam. "I want you gone. And take this with you, I can smell you both on it." Tucking the screaming baby under one arm, she snatched the leopard cloak from her mat and threw it at Adam. He ducked out of the way and it went right out the open door. "Now get out!" Eve said, slowly and severely. "It would have been better if you had never come back!"

Adam looked like he had been hit. For a moment their eyes locked. His eyes were sad and hurt, but he said nothing. He wheeled around and climbed down the ladder. Eve opened her mouth to hurl one last insult but it caught in her throat. His kind eyes had shown nothing but hurt. The baby continued to scream as he picked up his bow and the cloak and shuffled off down the trail, shoulders drooped. Glancing at the baby, Eve considered throwing it out the door as well.

"Rosy, I need you," she shouted instead. Rosy didn't come. Eve paced back and forth. "Lost his mat, yeah right," she muttered to herself. "Just *doing his duty.*" How could she have thought he would really change? Men! And she had been a good wife. She did not jump to conclusions when Monkey delivered the message, even though he seemed nervous about getting it exactly right. And she had wondered at her father's smirk. It spoke louder now in her mind's eye than any words. But no, she did not judge, she greeted Adam kindly and listened to his stories, more lies no doubt. *Lost his mat. No idea where it went. Right!*

Eve climbed down and called again for Rosy. The girl appeared, eyes downcast, a terrified look to her. Eve handed her the baby, who immediately stopped crying.

"What's going on?" Twig's voice interrupted her.

Eve spun around. She had not seen Twig since last night and gave her a hard stare. "How could you!" Eve demanded. "My best friend. You always did want him, well you can have him. Get away from me and my house, and don't come back."

"Eve . . . " Twig began slowly.

"What?"

Twig pursed her lips as if to speak, but turned and ran off. *Nothing to say. No excuse, no explanation. Running to catch Adam, running to catch her man.*

Eve looked around, searching for an answer. *How could this have happened?* She pondered what would become of her now as she watched the river drift lazily by. The bugs hummed. The flowers mocked her from the forest. There were no answers there. And once again she was alone.

*Fishing is much more than fish. It is the great occasion when we may return to the fine simplicity of our forefathers.*

Zane Grey

# Fishing Around     22

A quick scream followed by laughter drew Monkey's attention from his and Little Red's fishing.  Not far down the beach, three naked servant girls were splashing each other with water.  Blue Eyes had left only a few servants behind when he gathered much of the tribe and returned to the hunting camp.  Since then, these three girls had been following Monkey.  They were splashing around in the water, far enough away to not scare the fish, but close enough for him and Little Red to see them.  In fact, they often glanced their way to make sure he and Little Red were watching. With effort, Monkey dragged his eyes away and turned his attention to the fishing.

"Wake up, you got a nibble," Monkey said, nudging Little Red. Monkey figured he was secretly watching the girls as well.

"I was awake, just resting my eyes," Little Red answered.

"I know you are thinking the same thing I have been thinking," Monkey said. "Ever since the excitement of the hunt and chasing savages around the valley, now just the two of us with all the kids has left me frustrated."

"I miss the action, the danger," Little Red said.

"I miss being together as a gang—a gang with girls in it," Monkey said. "Now Fish and Bev are gone, Adam and Twig are gone, and Eve is occupied with her baby."

"If it's girls we need," Monkey said. "I see three just asking for our attention." He paused to work the line. Monkey helped him land a nice fish. They dropped it in the basket, weighted with stones.

"So, how about we invite the girls over and cook some fish?"

"Sounds like a plan, but let's wait until they are done playing in the water," Little Red said, grinning.

Monkey chuckled and was just about to point out the various attributes of his favorite girl, when Adam's deep voice boomed out behind them. "How's the fishing? Have an extra pole?"

Monkey spun around. "Adam, I thought you were with Eve?" Adam sat down next to them. The girls wandered down to see what was going on. Monkey wondered what would become of his plans for the girls now with Adam here. Adam unfolded the leopard skin cloak and showed them. The girls approached. Still naked and dripping, they rubbed the cloak, taking turns trying it on. As Adam told the story of the hunt, Little Red sat listening, with a happy smile. Monkey found his eyes wandering to the girls. "So what about us?" Monkey blurted, interrupting Adam's tedious explanation about a crocodile. Adam looked up at him in surprise. "You've got Eve, and now Twig. It is not fair."

Little Red nodded at the girls. "So what's the matter with those girls? They're pretty enough."

"You're the leader," Monkey said. "So where are our women? First Bev, then Eve, now Twig. What are we to do?"

Adam looked at the girls who were fighting over who would wear the coat next. "Uh, well, that's a very good question. But you know the rules. No mixing with the girls who do not speak."

"Why?" Little Red demanded.

"Because I said so, and I'm the leader. I have had about all I can take of girls and their tricks. You two can have Eve and Twig for all I care. You just can't please them whatever you do."

"Seriously?" Monkey asked as Little Red's mouth dropped open.

"I bring Eve back this amazing cloak, and what does she do? She throws it in my face and accuses me of mating with Twig. I try to do the right thing, and I get kicked in the teeth." Adam sighed. "So why struggle? I might as well do whatever I feel like, so when I am blamed, at least there is a reason for it."

"Did you?" Monkey laughed. "With Twig? Were you that desperate?"

"Or suffering from sun stroke," Little Red chimed.

"No I didn't, but Monkey, you would be surprised. She was excellent to hunt with—the perfect companion. We walked all day and she never said a word, just watched for tracks. And Little Red, she cleaned and cooked the meat, and has some special herbs that were amazing."

Monkey gave Little Red a nudge and an encouraging smile. If the redheaded boy would take Twig, then he would have an open shot at Eve. This could all work out after all.

Adam continued talking. "And she is as brave as Eve." Adam's voice trailed off and his face clouded. "But she is sneaky. The side hunt was her idea. Look at the mess it landed me in. No, I am done with both of them."

"Speak of the skunk, look who is coming," Little Red piped up, a big grin on his face.

Adam groaned. "This is the last thing I need now."

"Let me handle this," Little Red said and walked toward Twig. "Adam is not in a good place now. Perhaps I can be of some assistance."

"Red, get out of my way," Twig snapped and shoved him aside. She had been running and was red-faced and clearly angry.

"What did you tell her?" Twig demanded of Adam.

"Nothing. Nothing at all."

Twig turned to Monkey. "What did you say to Eve when you returned?"

Adam was on his feet and turned to Monkey, with his fists balled. "Yeah, what *did* you say?"

"Nothing, I said exactly what you told me to," he stammered. "Little Red, didn't I say just what I was supposed to?"

"Blue Eyes had a smirk on his face," Little Red said. "Monkey did too."

"No, it wasn't them," Adam said, suddenly deflated. "She wanted to know where my mat was."

"Oh, yeah, the mat, I somehow ended up with it—it's at my place," Monkey said with a shrug. "I forgot to return it to Eve."

"Oh, I see," Twig said quietly. "So what do we do now?"

"*We* don't do anything. I am done with you girls. Because of you everyone is upset, and nobody is happy."

"Except those three," Twig said icily, nodding to the girls as they twirled under the cloak.

"Exactly my point," Adam said watching them play. "They are happy and carefree."

"And are probably all pregnant even if not showing yet. See how happy they will be soon," Twig said.

"Actually, the new mothers all seem happy as well," Little Red observed and Twig gave him a stare which turned his face as red as his hair.

"Look, Twig," Adam said. "You made this mess, and I have had all I can take. Do what you want, but leave me out of it." Twig stared at him a moment, turned, then headed on toward the settlement.

"Phew, that was close. I thought she might kill me," Little Red said.

"Get used to it. She's all yours," Monkey whispered to him making sure Adam did not hear.

They settled back to fishing and Monkey kept thinking about what Adam had said. *You could have both of them for all I care.* He would be happy to oblige even though he didn't think Adam meant it. He was determined to find out.

Though he waited the rest of the afternoon for Adam to make a further comment, the subject of girls and Eve did not come back up. They built a fire and cooked their fish. The three girls joined them.

"They do smile a lot, don't they," Monkey observed touching one girl's hair. "Besides my family, this is the first time I have eaten with girls who were not in the gang."

When one fed Adam a piece of fruit, he did nothing to chase them away, not like he had before.

"So are we not going to worry about keeping separate?" Little Red asked.

"Yes, we are," Adam said standing up. "I am just too tired from the trip to fight about it."

"Use my mat, if you want to. It's right there," Monkey said pointing. "I am taking a walk. I need to think."

None of the girls even gave him a glance as he stood. *Obviously I am not as interesting as Adam.*

Once out of sight, Monkey stepped up his pace and headed to the treehouse.

A baby cried as he approached. Monkey crouched in the bushes under the treehouse, unsure how to proceed. He crept up to Rosy's shelter. It was empty, in fact, there was not even a mat for her. Monkey suspected the girl moved up top while Adam was away.

Monkey hesitated. This was dangerous ground. Plenty of fights in the tribe started because a male tried to move in on another's mate. And that was what he was doing. But this was even more dangerous than that—Eve could talk, unlike the girls of the tribe. She might reject him, and tell Adam. *I had better get this right.*

## A Proposal

Eve sat nursing the baby in the moonlight. It should have been a warm, beautiful night, but

Adamson's constant whining filled her with irritation. She wished Rosy could at least take care of the nursing. Eve even thought about letting her get pregnant so she could.

The ladder creaked. Someone was coming. Eve glanced around the room. Rosy was sleeping beside her. The room was as tidy as could be expected with a baby in the house. She ran a hand through her hair, hoping it was Adam returned and not a savage. It was not the first time she had yelled at him, and he always came back.

She was not dressed. It was too hot for clothes. She arranged her blanket to reveal enough to keep Adam's attention. He was slinking back to beg for forgiveness, no doubt. She had left the door open and now peered into darkness to see his face. She turned her head down at the baby, and continued to watch the door—discreetly. *Let him wonder.*

A head appeared. At least Eve was pretty sure it was a head. If it was, it was silently observing. Eve rocked the baby and tossed her hair back. It had to be Adam, but she couldn't understand what he was waiting for. *Stunned by my beauty no doubt,* she thought with a smile. Whoever it was gently knocked on the door frame. A voice whispered. "Eve?" That was sweet of him to knock, like a stranger, but his voice wasn't quite right, Eve realized as his face grew closer.

"Monkey?" she gasped, pulling herself upright. "What are you doing here?"

"I needed to talk to you?" he said.

"Now?"

"Yes," Monkey said.

Eve tried to think, but her mind spun. His eyes were on her body. She had not quickly covered when he appeared. To do so now felt awkward. She waved a hand to the mat next to her, and waited to see what would happen next. She always covered herself when the gang was around, and felt a strange excitement at ignoring the convention.

Monkey sat and awkwardly stroked the baby's head. "He is a fine baby." He looked into Eve's eyes. "And you are a fine mother." His eyes held a look she had seen before, back when he was recovering. That seemed like an age ago now. She thought he must have come with a message from Adam, but his eyes were dead serious, admiring, as if anticipating.

*What is going on here?* Eve wondered. Monkey just smiled. He was not in any kind of hurry.

"Eve, I am so sorry for what happened with Adam. I feel like it was somehow my fault. I should have brought him back."

She was touched by his kind words and tender voice. She let her expression soften and gave him a little smile.

She put a hand on his arm. "Thank you. It is kind of you to say that."

"If you need anything..."

"So Adam did send you?"

"No, he said he was done with us all. He is going back to the old ways—heading up to the hunting camp I think."

"Really?" Eve said. "I don't believe it."

"I wouldn't if I hadn't heard him say as much," Monkey said. "I certainly wouldn't run off if I were him. After all, only you saved me climbing down the crevice. I would be happy to keep you company and help around the place. Without anyone to talk to out here now that Twig and Adam are gone, I know you have to be lonely. I am not the leader, so you don't have to worry about me being unfaithful." He stopped, and let his voice trail off.

She felt a tear run down her cheek. It splashed on the baby's head—then another. Monkey looked at her intently, as if for a sign. Finally, he glanced at the door.

She reached out her hand, and touched the side of his face, and he licked his lips. "You are very sweet and very kind," she said. "And we do have a special bond. I have not forgotten. I appreciate your offer, and I will keep it in mind, but right now I am so hurt and so confused I just don't know what to say."

"That's all right," Monkey said. "I understand." He put an arm around her bare shoulder. She let her head fall on his shoulder and she cried for a while. He felt safe to her, and she was surprised at his kindness. He did not move, but just listened as she cried. Then the baby started to fuss.

"Sorry, need to change sides," Eve said and the moment was over. She wiped her eyes. "It's late.

You can sleep here and we will talk more in the morning."

## More Trouble

Twig fell asleep exhausted. Now she awoke, startled. She reached for Adam, but he was not there. Someone else however was. She could feel their presence. Though it was dark in her cave, she could hear shuffling feet. There was movement. Was Adam coming to her, sorry for what he said? Then she remembered the savages and reached for her bow.

"Who's there?" she whispered.

A whisper reached her. "Where are you?"

"To your left, forward. I'm here."

The figure materialized and squeezed in beside her. "Tight cave," Little Red said and lifted her cover.

"Little Red, what do you think you are doing?" Twig asked, too shocked to say anything else.

He crawled in next to her, lay on his side with his head propped up on one hand, a smile on his face. "I don't think I have been in your cave, since you moved out on your own. It is hardly big enough for one. It will be a tight squeeze for two. You know, everyone calls me Little Red, but I am not so little any more. Bigger than Adam I would say."

Twig, wide awake now, gripped her bow. "Okay Red, what are you doing in here?"

"We were all at the beach, after you left, and decided to sleep there, but then Monkey walked off. He said he needed to clear his head or something stupid like that. Adam slept like the dead, but I woke up in the night. The moon is actually quite bright tonight, and found Monkey was not back. I started worrying about savages, so left to go check our snare lines. You know, the little traps that we set on the paths to see if anyone had come by, and ... "

"No! I mean what are you doing here in my bed?" she growled.

"I am trying to tell you," he said and put a hand on hers. She shook it off. "So like I was saying," Little Red said. "I checked the traps, but nobody had been by. Then I cruised by the treehouse and heard voices, Monkey and Eve. That decided it. I figured I better come find you."

"Why? What on earth are you talking about?"

"You heard Adam. It's all decided. Adam said he is done with both of you and we could have you. Monkey already got Eve so I guessed I get you. There are no others so I didn't have much of a choice, but you are better than nothing."

"This must be a dream," she said. She reached out and touched Little Red. He was real.

"Wow, that was easy," he said and put an arm around her waist. "I thought you would object."

"Little Red, are you out of your bloody mind? Do you ... " she began but he kissed her, cutting her off in mid-sentence. She gouged her fingernails into his eyes and pushed him back.

"Get out of my bed," she hissed. "How dare you touch me."

"Now that's the Twig I expected," he chuckled, rubbing his eyes and starting to worm his way out. "There is no use fighting it, Adam has given you to me. He likes the old ways better. So you might as well make the best of it."

"I think not," Twig snapped. She kicked him as hard as she could. He bumped his head and yelled as he crawled back. Unable to control her anger, Twig brandished her bow at him.

"Woah, woah! Hang on! What are you doing?"

Twig dug an arrow out of her quiver, as Little Red clambered to his feet and backed out of her small cave. She could still feel his lips on hers. They were nothing like Adam's and she felt revulsion at being used.

"Are you crazy?" Little Red protested. "Are you seriously going to kill me? For what? I didn't even do anything." He turned and ran.

Twig notched her arrow and drew it back as Little Red's figure faded into the darkness.

She let the arrow fly. *Twang.* Her arrow followed him into the darkness. *That will teach him!* she thought.

She listened for sounds of life, but all was quiet. Her hands began to shake and she collapsed on her mat and began to cry. What if she had killed him? What if his body was laying out there, right outside her cave. He was sweet and sensitive normally, and he did leave on his own when she told him to. She thought about having a look, patching him up, but felt powerless to move. What had happened to the gang, to all their plans and dreams? Everything, it seemed, had fallen apart.

## A Bad Wind

Adam, having slept like the dead, rose early. He could not believe the mess he was in. He was now alone with the three girls on the beach. They were curled up under the leopard skin. He thought hard about the night before. He had looked at the girls more than once, but had not once thought to touch them.

"Bloody Eve," he swore. He didn't want to be bound by his oath to her, but even now, he still was.

Recovering the skin, he headed down the path, off to see Eve; surely she had calmed down by now. He was just about to turn toward the treehouse when he saw Little Red headed up the road towards him.

"Where have you been?" he asked as the boy drew close.

"I have been shot," Little Red sobbed. There was blood on his shirt.

"Savages? Where are they?" Adam asked, pulling off his bow.

"No. Twig shot me," Little Red said, and showed him the wound, a scratch on his side. "But you see that hole in my shirt? Just in line with my heart. It just grazed me. Just a little to the right and I would be dead. You created a monster, Adam. Good thing it was dark."

"What were you doing with Twig?" Adam demanded. "I thought we were sleeping on the beach."

"Well you said you were done with her and Eve. Monkey went off with Eve, and I went to be with Twig, but she gouged my eyes, and kicked me, then finally shot me. I am done with her too. I see now, why you gave up."

Adam wanted to laugh—would have laughed himself sick—except the thought of Monkey with Eve turned his stomach.

"Go back and lay low. Do some fishing or something," Adam said. "Forget about Twig." Little Red nodded and headed back the way he'd come as Adam tore off toward the treehouse.

## No Monkey Business

Eve awoke to Rosy shaking her shoulder. Adamson was screaming. "What I wouldn't give to actually sleep," Eve grumbled, and with a sigh she took Adamson and cradled him to her breast. Monkey sat up and stared at her. She had forgotten he was there and had not covered herself, again.

"Does it hurt when he bites?" he asked.

"Sometimes," Eve replied. "You want to try?"

He laughed nervously. "No." His apparent discomfort amused her. For his staring eyes, however, she felt disdain. Still she did not bother to cover herself. Now she would see what he was really about. "So why are you here again?" she asked. "I was tired and upset last night. I cannot quite remember." She gave him a patronizing smile, designed to make him squirm. Monkey looked like he had been slapped. She felt a twinge of guilt, suddenly realizing how cruel she could be. She hurt people, and often enjoyed it—just like her own mother. *Was that why I tore into Adam?* She wondered if she was just as broken? Finally feeling totally exposed, Eve pulled her cover up.

"I came to offer you my services," Monkey said, stumbling over his words. "And to tell you how I feel about you."

"Thank you, I thought that was it," Eve said. "I am touched, and, well, how can I put this?—honored." She decided to see if he was staring at her breasts or looking at the baby. She held Adamson up, letting her cover fall. "Would you like to hold him," she asked.

Monkey looked pleased, and to Eve's surprise his gaze followed the baby. He reached for Adamson awkwardly. "Not sure what to do, exactly."

After she showed him how to hold and burp the baby, he bounced Adamson and Eve quickly dressed. Maybe she was wrong about him. "Am I cruel?" she asked.

"Cruel? No, not at all. You are smart and strong, and have little patience with us when we don't do our best."

"That's sweet of you to say, but tell me the truth."

Monkey delivered a huge burp from Adamson. He looked at her proudly. "You might just have a bit of a temper, but I can live with that."

"You did a good job with Adamson. I am sorry for my temper, but I am determined to learn to be kind. We were both abused by our mothers when young, I'm sure you remember, and now I find myself turning into her and it scares me. I want to be kind and compassionate, and want to raise Adamson to be kind too."

Eve always thought Monkey talked too much, but now he let her ramble on about her feelings. She had been wrong about so many things. Her mind wandered to Adam.

"Where might Adam be?" she asked idly.

"He was sleeping on the beach last time I saw him," Monkey said as he booped Adamson on the nose.

Eve sighed. "Well thank you for coming, it is nice to have someone to talk with." She had wondered if Adam was with Twig. Perhaps Monkey was covering for him, but he seemed to be telling the truth.

"I am at your service and have nothing planned today," he said. "Maybe we could take the baby for a walk? I could put together a little snack."

"Thank you for the offer," Eve said. "Tempting as it is, I am still in shock from all the happenings, and need time to think. Maybe you can drop by for dinner," she said.

*Eve, what are you doing now?* She admonished herself. She had made a vow. Now she wondered if this was how it started with Adam and Twig.

Monkey brought her the baby, bent forward and kissed his forehead then, ruffling Adamson's hair, he kissed her forehead. Bowing, he departed.

Eve sat down next to a sleeping Rosy and gently woke her. The girl glanced around. She seemed relieved to find the treehouse empty. Eve asked her to make breakfast and the girl hurried out the door.

Eve realized the only thing she hated more than being passed over as leader was being alone. She looked out the window. She feared Adam would never return. Something would have to be done.

*Your time is limited, so don't waste it living someone else's life. Don't be trapped by dogma—which is living with the results of other people's thinking.*

*Steve Jobs*

# The Creator Speaks     23

Out on the vast plains, Adam set up camp by the last glow of the setting sun. He had been traveling north much of the day. He still couldn't believe that just as he arrived at the treehouse to try one last time to patch things up with Eve, he spotted Monkey climbing down, a big grin on his face. His rage, however, had finally subsided. He looked at his hands. They no longer shook, even though his knuckles were still bloody. His world had fallen apart. First Little Red, then Monkey had been the last straw and Adam had lost it.

He had done things as they had been done in the old times. He was not sure if it was right or wrong, but it was done now. He had spared Monkey's life, telling him if he ever caught him anywhere near Eve again he would kill him. Bloody and beaten, Monkey had fled before him.

The girls would not part with the leopard skin. He could see they were going to be trouble, so he returned the skin to the treehouse, where he found his pack on the ground with his things in it. Picking it up, he took off toward the crevice with the three girls following him. At least they were dressed now. He would take them to the hunter's camp with him.

Fish would not betray him, would not do the unthinkable. As sleep came the girls pressed close to him. It was their first time on the prairie and they were smart enough to be afraid.

As Adam stared at the stars above, one flew across the sky, and he remembered Eve's comment. He had loved her then, there had been no question in his mind then. She had a temper. That was nothing new. Had he known Twig's full intent? Had he encouraged it? Had it been wrong to play their little game, even though he had resisted the act itself? The pain in his stomach, and the little voice in his head, said it was. Maybe it was wrong but he was stubborn, but so was Eve, and so was Twig. He was not about to take all the blame himself.

His mind returned to Little Red and Monkey. He had told them he was done and they could have Eve and Twig. That was how things were done in the old days. Could he really blame them for taking him literally? Some traditions were good. Others clearly did not apply to them. Even as the leader, the girls were not his to give away.

In the morning, he arose hungry. He ate what little food he had tossed in his pack, not near enough for four of them. Standing, he and the three girls headed north.

As he walked, Adam tried to think logically about his situation. He needed a plan. Being chief without Eve was not going to work. There was trouble in the valley, big trouble, what with servant girls on the prowl. Eve would know what to do. Twig would also know, but he didn't feel he could trust her not to give him devious advice.

Looking up, he saw Bev running towards him alone. Fear gripped Adam's heart and he ran to meet her. "Bev, what's wrong? Is Fish okay?"

Bev gulped air. "He is okay. He was afraid to leave the camp, so I came." She eyed the three girls.

"What is it?" Adam asked.

"We just did not know what to do. We saw another tribe, a big tribe, and they saw us. They killed one of our hunters. Blue Eyes and many of his hunters just up and left—without a word, of course. Maybe he is coming to get you, but even if he is, we didn't know what you would think of his gestures. Did you see him? He's less than a day ahead of me."

"No, I saw nobody," Adam replied. "But then again I was not expecting to see anyone."

She glanced at the three girls again. "I see."

"These three are exactly why I came," Adam said.

"They can't help us," Bev said. "We are almost defenseless in the hunting camp without Blue Eyes and the best of the hunters."

"Bev, even still," Adam said. "It is crazy for you to be out here alone."

"If you think it is dangerous here," Bev retorted. "So is sitting around waiting to be attacked."

Adam gave her a hug. "I know. I know."

"Who are these girls?" Bev asked.

"These three were causing trouble so I thought I would bring them to you," Adam said. "I had a blowup with Eve and decided to come hang out with you and Fish for a while.

Bev gave him a hard stare. "Adam, since when do you run away from your problems? Tell me what happened with Eve. Is there a baby?"

"There is. Eve called him Adamson, and he seems quite normal. He can certainly scream, if that means anything."

Bev hugged Adam. "Congratulations, I am so pleased for you, but what was the problem?"

"Oh, you know Eve. Twig and I made a detour on the way home. I finally got my leopard, but I accidentally left my mat with Monkey. Eve accused me of sleeping with Twig. Then just last night she spent the night with Monkey."

"Did you?"

"No! Of course not," Adam said. "Well, we shared Twig's mat, but I did not mate with her despite what Eve thinks."

"Sorry, but that does not sound like any reason to just up and leave, not after she has been waiting for you all this time. Your one week hunting trip turned into how many days?"

"Not you too, Bev," Adam said. "Your girls are all the same!"

"I can take these girls for you, but Adam, you need to go home and fix this. Beg and crawl," Bev said. "Then, you, Eve, and Twig need to round everyone up and come save us before it is too late."

Adam sighed. "If you insist," he mumbled, before giving her a half-hearted hug. Bev prodded the girls in front of her, and Adam began the long trek back to the valley, walking normally. There was urgency now, yet he could not feel excited by it. He was the leader now, and yet he felt no joy about it. Going back to Eve was going to be hard. Very hard. He began to run.

By mid-day, the sun was hot. Adam stepped off the path where it neared the trees and sat on a fallen log in the shade. He needed a drink and had to think. Movement out the corner of his eye turned his head.

A dark gray snake sat coiled beside him. Its flat head rose a foot off the ground. The snake opened its dark mouth, as if deciding if it should strike.

Adam did not move a muscle. He had little experience with snakes. There were few in the valley, but Blue Eyes and his hunters always killed any snake they saw—and they did so cautiously. If he had someone with him, Adam figured they could distract it as he leapt back, but he was alone.

The snake licked its forked tongue in and out as its head slowly bobbed closer. It slithered close until it was only a foot or two from Adam's bare legs. He resisted the urge to jump away and run. As he sat deadly still, time passed achingly slow. His nose itched and he could feel a sneeze coming on. He knew he must move away, but how? His hands were on his lap, holding his water skin—his own axe was on his belt, so he could not scoot down the log without moving both his hands and feet. He inched his left hand to get a grip on his axe.

Like lightning, the snake hit his leg. Adam could not believe how fast it moved. He leapt up. Swinging his axe, he knocked the snake from his leg. The blade sank into the ground, cutting the snake in half. Both halves wildly wiggled and twisted.

"Die," Adam shouted and pulled his axe up and chopped again and again until the snake was nothing but dead pieces. He collapsed on the log, and inspected his leg. It tingled. Red holes, a little trickle of blood coming from each, marked his left calf.

He tried to remain calm. He had little water, no food, and was still a long way from home. He figured he was still closer to home than to the hunting camp. He glanced at the meaty snake chunks. It had been longer than any snake he had seen before, longer than he was tall. He scooped up the chunks and stuffed them in his pack; snake was a tasty treat. He stood and started out for home at a run. He wanted to run as long as his leg would let him. *Run until I drop.*

He wondered what made the hunters so terrified of snakes. *Will it kill me? Will I have great pain?* His leg worked fine, but as he ran he started having trouble seeing clearly. His dry mouth also began to taste wrong. *Just keep running,* he told himself. When he stopped to check his leg he threw up. His leg still looked largely unhurt save for the two small wounds. Yet he could tell something was not right with him. The world spun as he tried to again run.

"I am going to die," he cried aloud when he fell on his face. He lay there, the sun on his back. He tried to breathe. A scary realization washed over him. This was what would kill him. His lungs felt like he was being crushed to the earth as if someone huge was sitting on him.

The fear of death cleared his mind. *What are my options?* he asked himself, as a rational calm washed over him. He ticked his options off in his mind. None were any good, not without breath. A peace enveloped him and closed his eyes. His life was so full of pain, and he felt an eerie calm as he let go. He had lived well and had many great experiences, but recently life had turned into a nagging burden. It was a pain he would gladly relinquish. "Thank you, my creator for the life you gave me," he mouthed the words and prepared to die.

A voice, clear and familiar, spoke. It was the voice of the creator. "Adam, what are you doing up here?"

Not the question he expected. Here he was, willing himself to breathe, but no breath would come. He was face down and dying. *I was running away.* Now, he figured, was not the time for rationalizations.

"What about Eve, and the command I gave you?" the creator asked.

He saw a vision of Eve crying and the servant girls dancing. *I was upset. I am sorry, I failed you.*

"What are you going to do now?"

*Let me live and I will beg Eve to forgive me. Together we will try to lead our people and keep separate.*

"You answered wisely. Now breathe," the creator said. "Go, pick two of my fruits. Both you and Eve must eat from the Tree of Life; only then will you be saved. Only then will the two of you become one."

Adam sucked in a touch of air. He released it. Slowly, his breathing became deeper. Eventually he raised his head and looked around. The grass waived gently in the breeze. It all looked the same as before.

"Oh, I forgot to ask. What do you mean by separate?" he asked, waiting expectantly, looking up, but there was no answer.

Finally, he stood and started to walk. Soon he was able to run again. It annoyed him that he forgot to ask his question earlier, yet at the same time, he felt he knew the answer. Separate meant separate in all ways. As he ran, he wondered if it was the snake bite making him imagine things, or did the creator really speak to him again? He had been certain he was going to die, yet he lived. Did that really happen; did the creator heal him?

Either way, it was clear the advice was good. He would go and get some fruit, take it to Eve and see if they could heal their relationship. He had never had the courage to approach the Tree, no less eat the fruit, but he would have to do it. The thought terrified him. He envisioned the bones of those who tried and failed. It was his own fault Eve had gone to save Monkey. Twig had to for the Serpent, and now he would to save his marriage. And he would have to do it alone. But he would, to save Eve, to save their marriage. They would eat it together, and he would tell her he was sorry and he hoped they would be healed. Then they could decide what to do about Fish, Bev, and Blue Eyes.

He ran slower as the day drew to an end. His leg, surprisingly, felt quite normal, but once again he struggled to breathe. He hoped to make the valley by dark. He could cook and eat his snake, then reach the Tree of Life by morning. He was beginning a new life. He would live this life differently.

With no hope but the creator's words, Adam focused on putting one foot in front of the other.

It was all he could do. The world looked strange, and the sounds of his footfalls echoed in his ears. He heard what almost sounded like a shout behind him, but dismissed it. It was dusk and he was almost home. Maybe Blue Eyes, and his hunters were returning. Regardless, Adam knew he could not stop.

He staggered on. The crevice came into view. He looked back and could see his followers in the last light of day. They were not Eve's father and his hunters. A host of naked savages chased him. *Bloody Bones, what have I done?* He had led the whole tribe directly to their hidden valley.

## Eve's Crisis

Eve waited all day but nobody came to see her. The leopard skin cloak which hung on the ladder she put away. However, Adam's pack, which she had tossed out, was gone. What did that mean? There was only one thing she could imagine: Adam had left, probably for good.

She distracted herself by cooking an elaborate dinner. Rosy kept looking at her funny. The girl didn't know Monkey would be back. As darkness fell, Eve paced, watching the path. It grew late and still Monkey had not arrived. Finally Eve broke down and ate with Rosy in silence by firelight.

She slept poorly, waking up at each sound outside. Nobody appeared. The next day she felt angry and betrayed, then finally sad. She had driven away everyone she loved, her husband, her best friend, and even her gangly admirer didn't want to see her.

The next day dragged. Another lonely dinner brought despair like she had never felt before and she fell onto her mat and cried.

"I'm a fool," Eve wailed when she could take the silence no longer. Since Adam had been gone she had taken to discussing things with Rosy. The girl wasn't much of a listener, usually falling asleep. "I still love him dearly, and miss him terribly. But I cannot live with what he did," she concluded. Rosy began to snore.

Eve turned her attention to the only other one awake. The fussy baby who would not nurse, who would not sleep, and who would only be quiet when she paced the floor. He was a little version of Adam. The two of them were the cause of all her trouble. The realization washed over Eve like a wave. If not for her pregnancy, she would have gone on the hunting trip and none of these bad things would have happened.

She stared at the squirming baby. He would always be a reminder of Adam. He would remind her of Twig and Adam together.

Eve headed down the ladder, into the night. Dark thoughts entered her mind. With no clear path ahead, her feet led her towards the ocean. The stars shone bright and the moon revealed the way.

There could be no evidence of what she planned—and she would need a convincing story—an accident or fever. Other babies in the tribe had suddenly died.

The sand was cool on her bare feet, and the drone of the surf was a comforting sound. She had taken Adamson swimming in the river before. It would be a painless way to go.

She stopped at the infamous log where so much had happened. Undressing, she folded her clothes neatly. Adamson lay on the sand watching her. Picking him up, she walked toward the surf.

Cold water swirled around her ankles, then around her knees. She stopped. The moon reflected off the water. It was a beautiful sight. It was a silvery pathway shimmering before her, calling to her. She had never swam in the ocean, only played in the waves. It looked like it would be easy to just walk out past the waves. Maybe she and the baby both could just float away. It would end the madness.

The water swirled around her waist. The cold water made her stomach cramp and she cried out. Determined to proceed, she laid back into the water. She kicked and paddled with one hand, holding Adamson to her chest with the other. Waves washed over her head. Adamson spluttered but did not cry. He liked the water.

Eve swam on. Beyond the break point, each wave lifted her gently and eased her back down. She stopped swimming and rested. She felt strangely buoyant, and she wondered if it was the creator lifting her and Adamson up. She pondered the thought as she let Adamson go. He bobbed and splashed. Eve turned away and began to swim for shore.

Something brushed her leg and it made her jump. The story Adam told of the crocodile flashed into her mind. Terror filled her.

"Adamson," she cried, turning back. He still bobbed in the water. Something nipped her thigh. She kicked and paddled as hard as she could toward him. Grabbing him, she kicked for shore with all her strength. No hideous beast was going to eat her baby!

As she staggered up the beach breathless, Adamson started to whimper. She held him close. "It's all right," she said softly. "I have you. No monster is going to hurt you."

She walked to the log and sat down. Gazing up into the sky, she realized she was broken. Was there a cure? The only thing she could think of now was eating the fruit of the Tree of Life.

Adamson whined.

"You're hungry now, aren't you," she said half to Adamson and half to herself. "Worked up an appetite swimming?" A giant star streaked across the night sky and faded away. "It is a sign, Adamson. It is a good sign. The creator has spoken."

The next day she was up at first light. The sun was well up by the time they set out for the settlement—so much stuff to pack. Rosy walked several steps behind her carrying the baby. Eve had made up her mind to repair things with Adam. They had both been stubborn. But all this waiting was not fair to the baby or her. She was stuck alone with a fussy baby, while Adam was off having fun with the gang. Of course he could outlast her. She wondered what she would say when she found him.

"I miss you and changed my mind," she said as if talking to Adam. "It's okay for you to sleep with my best friend."

Eve felt like screaming, she was not going to say that. After she tried out a few more lines she realized she should have just trusted Adam. She had no proof he slept with Twig. *I am sorry I did not trust you, Adam. I should have believed you. I do now.* She stopped so suddenly, Rosy plowed into her back.

Eve laughed and kissed Adamson and a surprised Rosy. It was the truth. She should have trusted him. It was the right answer, honest and heartfelt.

As the sound of children playing reached her she felt that old revulsion, felt the old pain. It was time to let it go. *It's time to let it all go. She could not change the past, only her own attitude.*

She walked purposefully across the meadow toward the Tree of Life. She would pick the fruit, and take it to Adam. They would eat it together and see what happened. It was time.

*Then God said, "I give you every seed-bearing plant on the face of the whole earth, and every tree that has fruit with seed in it. They will be yours for food.*

*Genesis 1:29 NIV*

# A New Beginning     24

As Eve approached the Tree of Life, Little Red came running to meet her. He looked terrified. "Have you seen Adam? Have you seen anyone?"

"No, we just arrived," Eve said.

"I can't find any of the gang. Not one."

Eve stopped. Adamson was getting fussy. "Here, sit with me beside the stream while I feed the hungry one."

"We have no time to sit. Everyone is gone."

"Settle down. Tell me everywhere you have looked."

They sat and Little Red listed everyplace Eve would have looked. "Adam's mat is missing, so is Twig's. Even Monkey's is gone."

Eve felt her anger rise, once again, then took it in hand. *Trust.* "Tell me the last time you saw each of them—exactly."

"So Adam and Monkey disappeared first, some time the night before last. I saw Twig heading north this morning."

"So she is not missing, just traveling up to the falls, to collect herbs as she often does. I saw Monkey early yesterday morning," she paused, hesitant to admit what almost happened. "So you see, nobody is missing, just going places." She smiled at Little Red. She used to hate him for being carefree and having grown up without the pain she suffered, but now seeing the concern in his face, his red hair flying everywhere and a little red beard starting to grow, he was not that little any longer. He seemed taller every time she saw him.

"Let's go start with Twig's place," Eve said, rising and handing Adamson back to Rosy. They walked the short distance to Twig's cave.

"See, she is gone," Little Red said as if afraid she had not believed him.

"More than gone. She has taken everything." The thought sent a shiver down her spine. *Twig gone? Like really gone?* With a new urgency Eve led Little Red to Monkey's cave.

"See, Adam's mat is gone, and so is Monkey's."

"How do you know Adam's mat is gone?" Eve asked.

Little Red explained. Eve felt her face flush. The missing mat perhaps had been an honest mistake. What had she done?

"Would you do me a big favor, Little Red? Hike up to the falls and search for Twig. I would go with you but I want to search for Adam. If you find Twig, ask her to come back—beg her to come back for me."

Pulling back his shoulders, Little Red stood a little straighter. "I would rather not, Twig is not one to listen to me, and last time I saw her she shot me." He poked a finger through the hole in his shirt.

"Don't be ridiculous. Please go and beg her to return. We need her." He did not answer. "Thanks," she said and rose to her tip-toes and kissed his forehead. He looked surprised, flushed bright-red and hoisted his pack. Kindness worked, and she vowed to become kind, even if it killed her.

Somehow the day was nearing an end. She considered going home but did not relish the long walk in the dark. Twig shot Little Red? What on earth was he talking about?

Eve took Rosy by the hand, and returned to Monkey's cave where the three of them spent an uneasy night. In the morning she planned to pick some fruit and go seek Adam.

## Surprise Meeting

When Adam arrived at the treehouse to sound the alarm, he found it empty. With no sign of the savages, he stumbled on. The settlement was strangely quiet when Adam arrived. Struggling to breath, he approached the Tree of Life slowly. His symptoms had returned and each step was a labor, each breath a battle now. He could not think about anything but the tree. It was his only salvation now. It and Eve.

It was a fine morning, the sun was warm and the air sweet with the fragrance of the Tree, but he felt only pain and pushed on. As he approached he saw Rosy sitting by the stream holding Adamson.

"Where is Eve?" he asked her. Rosy looked up and nodded to the Tree. Eve stood on one of the Tree's many large white branches. *What on earth?* She looked so beautiful, her hair gently blowing in the breeze. Adam nodded at Rosy and began to walk towards the Tree.

As the aroma drew him in it was like he was being laughed at, being mocked. Suddenly he was being pushed to the ground. His legs gave way. Remembering his mission, he pulled himself to his feet. He was still blind to all but the mockers, who intensified their attacks. Hard-fought step, after hard-fought step he struggled to move forward. Finally, the fog cleared. He saw the tree; he had made it. He felt like shouting for joy, but his breath was ragged and he probably couldn't shout if he tried. Instead he stood and watched as

Eve collected two pieces of fruit and slipped them in a bag at her waist. She climbed down, and he caught her as she dropped from the lowest limb.

"Thank you," she said looking confused. "You're here."

"Yes," he said, eyeing the bag. "Is someone wounded?"

Eve turned and walked from the tree. "Yes," she said. "I hope it will not be too late. Will you help me?"

"Of course," he said, spinning around. "But Eve, who is hurt?"

"We are," she blurted, stopping and turning to face him, tears in her eyes.

"Us?" Adam took a step towards her and staggered to the ground.

Eve rushed to him. "Oh, Adam," she cried and bent over him. "I'm sorry I didn't trust you. I'm sorry I was so horrid."

"I am sorry too," he said, looking into her bleary eyes. "I should not have stormed off. I am sorry I let Twig talk me into going on the hunt. I should have known it would be trouble."

"Adam, your eyes," Eve said. "Adam, what is wrong?"

"Snake bite," he wheezed. "Can't breathe."

"No!" She looked around in panic. "We need to get you home."

"The fruit," he said. "For each of us." She dug it out and he bit into the sweet and spicy fruit. As they ate he ignored her orders to be still. "Don't stop me, Eve. I have to get this out." He told her his story, in short phrases. He told her of the snake bite, and then the news from Bev. He did not mention Little Red or Monkey. She listened attentively, asking questions and nodding her understanding, no criticism, no judgment.

"How is the leg?" she asked when he had finished. "How's the breathing?"

"Getting better," he said. "But there is more, Eve. I hate to admit, but in staggering back to the valley, I have led the other tribe here. I can hardly remember, but they were chasing me. I guess they probably followed me into the valley. I did not remove the ladders."

"Great bones! A whole tribe of savages in our valley?" Eve exclaimed, jumping up looking wildly around. "I can't believe it, there they are now," she cried. She dragged Adam to his feet and pointed.

He looked in alarm. "That is just Blue Eyes and his hunters," he said. "Don't panic."

Blue Eyes and his hunters approached and knelt before the tree. Eve, her arm around Adam, helped him walk out to meet them. Monkey was hanging out in the back of the group.

With every step, Adam felt stronger. He let out his best war cry as he pointed back toward the crevice. Blue Eyes leapt to his feet. He pointed as well, and cried out again and again. Many had been watching, and now returned with weapons.

"Weapons," Adam said. "We must get them."

"And where is the gang?" Eve said. "I could only find Little Red, and I sent him to the falls to look for Twig."

"Monkey is with Blue Eyes," Adam said awkwardly. "There is not a moment to lose." He motioned to the gathered group to all head toward the main path.

*Strategy,* that was what he needed. The foreign tribe might outnumber them for all Adam knew, and they had the same weapons. The thought left Adam feeling undermanned for such a battle, and as they ran, he began to worry more. If they met them now, unready, with his son along, it could lead to disaster.

"What is it?" Eve asked.

"I was just thinking this could get out of hand quickly. Maybe you should go back and wait with Adamson at the caves."

"No," she replied stoutly. "I am never leaving your side again."

"But all I have is my axe."

"More than I have, but I'm still coming. Think. If they had followed you we would all be dead. I am sure they are all eating and sleeping. Remember how barren it is above?"

"Perhaps," he said. She was probably right as usual, it was good to have her at his side. He took a deep breath. *Cured.* He was cured and he could not believe it. The fruit had worked. Glancing at his child and beautiful wife at his side, he realized it had worked better than he had ever thought possible.

When they reached the main path without incident, Little Red and Twig were walking toward them from the direction of the falls. They broke into a run when they saw the great crowd behind Adam.

"What is happening?" Twig asked. "Little Red begged me to come back, but I had no idea." Little Red eyes were as big as melons.

"The other tribe invaded our valley," Eve said. "We are off to battle."

"Good thing I have my bow," Twig said, patting it lovingly. Little Red stepped back from her.

"Okay, let's go then," Adam said and ushered everyone towards the treehouse.

"You saw Monkey?" Eve asked as they ran. "Seems to be avoiding us." Adam shuddered but didn't say anything.

"Yeah," Twig said. "He's pretty banged up. Must have run into the savages."

"Not likely. Did you beat him up?" Eve asked.

"Not me," Twig said. "It was Little Red I shot. I only missed killing him because it was dark."

Little Red, who had pressed close to the front, fell back.

"Adam," Eve asked, looking directly at Adam. "Did you beat him up?"

"Maybe," he answered and she pressed no further.

Adam fell back. Rosy was falling behind and he took Adamson from her. Spotting Monkey, he pulled alongside him.

"Sorry about the face," Adam said. "But we need to all be together now. I need you." It was not much of an apology, but it was the best he could do in the circumstances.

Monkey half-smiled. "It's okay," he said. "I'm sure I asked for it."

Adam grunted, worried he might still get an arrow in the back if they were alone in the heat of battle.

Finally at the treehouse Adam flew up the ladder. He grabbed his weapons and all the extras they stored for the gang. Eve settled Rosy and Adamson. She kissed them both goodbye then was herself ready. They headed toward the crevice. Just past the main path, they found the enemy, massing on the path ahead.

Adam had never seen such a sight. *Bloody bones!* They were a large group, all naked and armed, even the young ones. Twenty, maybe thirty he estimated. "Okay, so here is the plan," Adam said. "I want us to stick together."

"No, Adam," Twig said. "I want you to lead a group around to the left. Eve, you go with him."

"Hold on, who put either of you two in charge?" Eve said. She dragged her father forward and signaled for him to head off to the right.

Adam could not believe this. Wasn't he the leader? "We need to stay together. Now listen up," he began again. He looked around wondering who he was talking to. There were only four adults who could speak and two of them, not counting him, thought they were in charge. The youngsters looked terrified.

Blue Eyes let out the war cry. The valley was suddenly reverberating with cries as his hunters joined him. Adam watched in horror as they, axes held high, charged the enemy.

"Archers, cover them," Adam shouted. He pulled out his bow and rushed forward. He had a plan, and this was not it. Now he had no choice or it would be a complete bloodbath.

He studied the enemy's disposition as he ran. Some seemed to be falling back, but most were slipping off the path into the thick greenery bordering the path. They were planning an ambush.

"It's an ambush," Twig shouted.

"It is!" Adam yelled. "Monkey take Twig and Little Red. We have to outflank them!" Adam pointed to the right. He turned to Eve. "You are with me."

There was no discussion or arguments, and he broke off to the left as the first arrows appeared from the trees. The first of Blue Eyes' hunters fell. By the time the hunters reached the enemies in the path—the decoys—they would be gone. Blue Eyes and his men would be surrounded.

Adam crashed through the brush, circling behind the archers. Several of Blue Eyes' hunters screamed. The massacre had begun. Adam dove left, dodged right, and cleared a fallen log. As Adam drew back his own arrow, a naked man with a bow and arrow looked over and spotted him.

The man was too late. He died to the singing of Adam's bow. *One enemy down.*

A tug at his shirt sleeve—and a thud—turned Adam's head. An arrow was lodged in the tree next to him. Eve's bow sang. *Twang!* "Got him," she hissed from behind him. "Go."

Adam crashed forward. The hidden archer's body lay splayed on the ground. Another archer ahead was shooting into the ambush. *Twang.* Another savage down, then several more appeared. Eve and the youngsters drew and shot. *Twang, twang, twang.* But there were too many savages and the dense jungle made it difficult to shoot accurately.

Suddenly the savages dropped their bows and charged toward him, spears in hand. The time for stealth was over.

Adam pulled out his axe and waded into the group. They all charged toward him. Adam struggled to move with all the hanging vines and undergrowth. The battle was close and intense. Eve's voice rang out over the screams. "Die you savage!" Adam had to smile. Such fire in her.

A savage's club glanced off Adam's shoulder. The woman with the club prepared to swing again. Adam dropped her like a tree. He hated the woman for making him kill her, and hacked on in a hate-filled rage. When he broke out onto the path, there was no living enemy in sight. The path was strewn with bodies from both sides of the struggle. Only four of Blue Eyes' hunters were still on their feet.

Their side of the path was clear, but what of the other side? He stared intently at the green wall facing him and saw movement. An arrow poked out between some branches, aimed right at him. His time was up. He was standing stupidly in plain sight.

But then Twig, blood-streaked and wild-eyed, emerged from behind the arrow. Little Red towered behind her, not so little any more, Adam realized. "We got them," Twig cried in triumph.

"Sweep the trees on both sides, kill them all," Adam called. Eager youngsters scattered.

There was no sign of Monkey.

Eve rushed by him and fell to the ground next to the body of her father. The old man was surrounded by dead hunters and savages. Her fathers' dead blue eyes stared unseeing into the matching sky. He was gone. He had died as a good leader should, fighting for his tribe. Adam hesitated for a moment, then walked by her into the far green.

Monkey lay on the ground.

Adam knelt next to him. "Hey old buddy, hang in there," he whispered, but he could see it was over.

Monkey took his hand and squeezed. "Take care of her," he mouthed the words and lay still, dropping his hand.

"I will," Adam mumbled. He looked into his friend's face, smeared with blood. He reached out and closed Monkey's staring eyes. Then picking up his hand again he cried. "Oh, Monkey why? I'm so sorry."

Eve put her hand on his shoulder. "Should I get Twig?"

"Yes, get her quick."

"Oh, Adam, It's too late," Eve said. "You know it's too late."

"I know. Bloody bones, I know." he said, placing Monkey's hand over the wounds on his chest.

"My father and now Monkey too, it is almost more than I can bear," Eve said. Adam turned to her and held her. He did not know what to say. The list of his regrets was too long to consider. Eve helped him up and together they staggered back to the path and headed for the treehouse.

He suddenly had a thought, a scary one. *Keep separate* was the command and he had no idea how to do that. But right now, almost every non-speaker in the valley had been trapped in the gauntlet—and slaughtered. He thought of the snake bite, the crazy chase which brought them here, and the bungled leadership which allowed the slaughter, and he wondered, *could this be what happens when one disobeys the creator?* Had he moved the last of them out of the valley to the camp, none of this would have happened. Monkey would still be alive. Instead he'd stormed off.

The creator offered healing and life, but did the creator also offer punishment and death? Was this really the creator's way? Adam thought of Monkey and feared it was so.

"How are you feeling?" Eve asked later that evening. They were back at the treehouse. Adam could not count the places he hurt, but was not going to let it stop him from addressing the problem. He looked around. This was the time. Rosy was busy cooking a meal. What was left of the gang lounged around, waiting to eat.

"I am alright," he said to Eve. "In fact, now that we are home and together again, I feel great." He raised his voice to address the gang. "Before we eat there is something important I wish to say." Twig and the others looked up expectantly. "We failed as leaders today and when it really mattered. The future of the valley depended on us." Eve and Twig both dropped their eyes before his gaze. "I realize that all three of us had good plans. We could have dealt with the enemy without such huge losses had any one of us led and the others followed. This must never happen again. In the old days, we would fight, and the survivor would be the leader. But these are new times, and we need new ways. We need to decide who is to lead our people. I, for one, pledge to follow that leader and give my life if needed to assure our survival as a people, just as Monkey and Blue Eyes and the others did. They are the true heroes of this battle."

Done. He reached over the bloody leader's axe, and picked up a piece of fruit.

"What are you suggesting?" Twig asked.

*Here we go again, the mind games,* he thought and looked at her. "I am not suggesting anything," Adam said. "You are brilliant and insightful and would make a great leader. Eve is courageous and wise and would make a great leader. I am stronger than both of you, but am not very clever, and am probably the least qualified to lead, but I will if asked. But we must choose only one. Then in a crisis everyone knows who to obey."

"I thought Blue Eyes made you the leader?" one of the youngsters said.

"A leader is hardly a leader if others refuse to follow," Adam said.

Eve slid over next to Twig and they put their heads together, whispering intensely. Adam continued to eat his fruit. He was done with all this squabbling. Whatever they decided would be fine with him. Adamson woke and he picked him up. He made faces at the boy and slipped him a little fruit which the little guy managed to smear all over his face. Adam was not sure any actually went down, but his son had a fun time trying. Rosy frowned disapprovingly.

Eve rose, and picked up the leader's axe. *So it is to be Eve,* he thought. *So be it.* He looked at Twig, who nodded her approval.

"So it's been decided," he said, with genuine relief that the struggle was finally over. Eve smiled, a big silly smile. "You will make a great leader, Eve."

"Silly man," she said and handed him the axe. "I can hardly lead the people and leave you home with Adamson—look at the state he is in."

"But . . . " he began, but she touched his lips.

"Personal ambition is the biggest enemy to good leadership," Twig said.

"Twig and I both failed the test," Eve said. "Your humility is your strength, and we would both be honored to follow you."

"To the end of the earth," Twig added.

"Speaking of the end of the earth," Eve said, still smiling. "Perhaps you should send someone to take down the ladders."

"Done already," Adam said. "Anything else, my trusted advisors?"

"Someone should let Fish and Bev know what happened here today," Twig said.

"Little Red has already agreed to run up there with the message," Adam answered happily, certain she or Eve would think of something he had forgotten.

"Well that's all we have," Eve said. "Nothing else is wrong which a good long night's sleep won't fix."

Adam took the axe and Eve by the hand. "Shall we go wash up in the river before bed?"

After their bath, Adam held Eve close on their mat and gazed at the gleaming white axe hanging on the wall of the treehouse, next to the skull. The two glowed in the last light of the day. He felt content with his actions for the first time in a long time.

"There is one more thing we need to do," he said. Eve looked concerned. "Now that we have eaten the fruit together, we need to be as one."

Eve looked expectantly at Adam. "I feel nervous like I did on our wedding day."

He reached for her and touched her hair. "Then let's say our vows again."

She smiled. "I love you, my leader. You seem to know the right thing to say and do—most of the time. And now is one of those times."

Adam thought the same thing about her. They reenacted their wedding, minus the sunset and gritty sand. Eve pulled out the leopard skin cloak and covered them as they lay snuggled on her mat. She looked at him dreamily.

"Eve, I'm so sorry about the death of our father."

Her smile faded. "Our father? You said something like that earlier, but how do you know he was your father too?"

"I have learned many things recently, one of which is the fact that Blue Eyes is the father of all the speaking children. There will be no more like us—unless our own children can speak."

"I had wondered . . . It makes sense, but how do you know?"

"It's a long story I will tell you some time," Adam said.

Your father?" Adam asked when tears welled up in her eyes. One ran down and dripped off the tip of her nose.

He reached for her and she buried her head on his shoulder. She sobbed for a while then fell asleep. Adam imagined himself leading a trained and equipped tribe into battle, the leader's axe in his hands.

In the morning, he woke to the smell of a fire and breakfast cooking. The sun streamed into the treehouse. He stood and tested his leg and checked his injuries. He felt great. He took a deep breath—no problem. He dressed and went down.

"Just in time," Eve said. "Hungry I hope."

"Starving," he said before asking, "Are you okay?"

She set down his steaming food and hugged him. "I am sad but somehow the fruit and the resolution of our problems took away the pain. It was bound to happen to Blue Eyes one day, the way he hunted and lived. Monkey turned out to be a hero, didn't he?"

Adam smiled and started in on his breakfast. "He did," he said and took a bite. It was fantastic, the best he could ever remember eating.

"You know, I was thinking," Eve said. "You are officially the chief now and it is your duty to help grow our tribe." She spoke between bites.

Adam stopped chewing. "No, never again will a chief have that duty. We will lead our people. You and I together. No more chiefs. The axe can hang on the wall until needed, our wall."

Eve smiled and watched him eat. "Oh Adam, it is a perfect solution, it's everything I ever wanted, and all rolled together. Only one part remains unresolved."

"Unsolved?"

"Twig." As if she was a mind-reader, Twig came down the path and walked up to the table. "Hungry?" Eve asked, jumping up.

"Actually starved," Twig said in surprise.

"Sit down and I will get you some food. I am so sorry I yelled at you and accused you. You are my best friend—and the smartest person in the world. I should have trusted you."

Twig looked shaken. The color drained from her face. Adam was quite surprised to see her caught off guard, and had no idea what might come next. He hoped they had patched things up, but perhaps it was just a truce for the crisis.

"Eve, I am sorry too. You were right, I wanted to lead. I wanted to be loved. I wanted Adam too, but he would not be tempted. He loves you too much. Please forgive me for my despicable ways. It will not happen again."

Adam packed the last of his food in his mouth in case he had to make a quick get-away. He looked at Eve and expected to see Twig's food flying across the table at her, but Eve just smiled.

She served Twig her breakfast and sat down. "He is quite wonderful, isn't he?"

"But there is still a problem," Adam said.

Twig looked up in alarm. Eve looked at Adam and nodded. "The issue of *separate* is still on the table."

"I asked the creator for more detailed instructions, but he did not answer," Adam said. "Eve and I will lead now, together, and with you as our advisor, we may have a chance to get it right. There is much trouble in the valley and we will need our best minds working together on the problems. There are children to teach, sick to heal, tribe problems to settle. So much to do."

Twig smiled and took a bite. "This is great, I could eat this forever. I am glad to be your advisor. I am also glad to see you two are happy together."

Adam looked at his empty plate. Eve smiled and took it back for more. Rosy appeared with Adamson. Their son was hungry as usual.

Eve rolled her eyes and scoffed as she took the hungry baby in her arms. "One of the leaders or not, seems like I still have to eat last."

*Horizontal Gene Transfer was first demonstrated when DNA from one bacteria was taken up by another.*

*Griffith's Experiment, 1928*

# Author's Footnote

Evolutionary biologists have demonstrated living things are subject to random mutations, and that each mutation makes a species more or less fit to survive in its environment.  One of the more significant trade-offs in brain function is instinct vs intelligence.  The longest surviving and most successful species on our planet are bacteria and a host of insects which have virtually no intelligence, and operate entirely by instinct.  Fish, reptiles, and many mammals, all have some intelligence yet they still seem to primarily favor instinct over intelligence.  From bacteria to bugs, from birds to bison, all are born knowing what to do to survive and have little *capacity for innovation. Not surprisingly, some of the most intelligent species like apes and dolphins are now threatened, even endangered.*

*Some believe an intelligent God created and set in motion this most amazing and prolific thing we call life. Others believe it simply happened. Either way, DNA analysis and the fossil record gives us a pretty clear idea how life came to be what it is today.*

*Even though evolutionary change is slow and incremental, it is relatively easy for the natural mutations within a species to vary its size, either larger or smaller, with the size optimized by a fitness for the environment. For this reason, brain size optimization is likely to have been accomplished long ago among all of the more intelligent species.*

*The brain uses a lot of energy and unless a larger brain provides a substantial advantage to survival, it will be selected against during times of stress. Instinct stores survival instructions much more effectively than a larger, more intelligent brain which must learn them again and again with each successive generation.*

*Human-like creatures seem one of nature's many experiments. For three-hundred-thousand years at least, hominids wandered Africa, making stone tools but barely surviving. From the evidence available to us, they were a bit more intelligent than their closest relative, the chimpanzee. Despite having the highest intelligence of all the animals, they barely survived.*

*These hominids lived in small groups. They cared for each other and for their young like other apes did. But they made greater use of sticks and rocks, even learning how to sharpen stones by hitting them together. Their sharpened sticks and stones they then used to hunt and to butcher their kills. Several competing species came out of this experiment, each with varied intelligence and varied physical adaptations, each with dramatically different cultures.*

*Out of this experiment came at least one tribe like the Runners. This tribe lived in a hard world. But by evolution's accident they had found a niche to survive—a small and dangerous niche though it was. Unlike their ancestors who lived in trees, the Runners' feet could no longer grasp branches, but instead they stood upright. And they could walk—or even run all day.*

*Their eyes focused forward like other predators—they were built like hunters—but the Runners lacked important accouterments. They had no sharp teeth, no claws, no heavy tail, no venom. These pathetic hominids were also the slowest sprinters of all the mammals. Even the lumbering hippopotamus runs faster. Not only were these runners not granted the tools of the trade to kill their prey, they also could not catch them easily. And as prey themselves they were equally handicapped, not only by a lack of speed, but by a lack of camouflage, a lack of armor, and a lack of the ability to fly, climb or dig. Another detriment was their thin, fragile skin which was poor shielding against environmental extremes. They had no fur for warmth nor for protection from the sun. Nor did they have the ability* to store water. Fortunately they had no need to hibernate, because they were unable to do that either.

Their senses were also marginal. They could smell, but barely. They could not track like a dog or smell an enemy before they were seen. They could taste, and while taste gave them pleasure while eating it often misled them, encouraging them to eat food which made them sick. They could see but not like an eagle or at night like a cat; they could hear, but not as well as other predators.

Their biggest weakness was a terrible curse: a long and debilitating pregnancy followed by the need to provide intense care for entirely helpless offspring. This horrible handicap kept their numbers down and few children lived long enough to grow into adulthood which they needed to produce another generation.

Yet somehow these runners managed to survive living on the plains of Africa and for years and years they developed their rather unique strengths. First of all, opposable thumbs allowed for a fine degree of dexterity. They could use tools to compensate for their lack of natural defenses, and their unusually large brains allowed humans to consider and comprehend large, complex multi-step processes. The idea of breaking off a branch and carrying it over to a food source to hit it on the head was revolutionary. No other animal could do this. It is this leap of intelligence that sets humans apart from the other animals. It allowed them to survive.

The final big innovation? Humans had the endurance to outdistance every other land-based animal. This particular ability was the result of the capacity to store fat with a high energy density and quickly convert it to energy. And the uniquely human use of sweat glands on their fur-less skin allowed them to regulate their body temperature. That granted them the ability to stay cool as they ran throughout the heat of the day. While lions lay panting in the shade at noon, humans could still run. If they stayed on the chase, humans could literally run a gazelle—which could sprint three times faster than them—to the ground, exhausted. When the gazelle fell, the humans could simply club it to death and hack it up with a sharp rock to eat. Crude? Yes, but something entirely human. And that was how they survived.

Diverse hominid creatures ranged the continent of Africa and some migrated into Europe and Asia. They ranged in height from four-feet to six-feet tall and from a hundred pounds to over three-hundred. Some were ape-like in features and actions, others more human. All used simple tools. But that was the extent of the similarities. The big differences were in intelligence, strength, and culture. Tribes sometimes joined together, blending these characteristics. Some tribes eliminated others, but generally they simply found a way to live in peace. Battle strategy was one of the more important factors in deciding who lived and who died. Tactics were surprisingly sophisticated for such primitive societies. Natural selection saw to that. It can be a very long, slow process in many ways, but in battle, poor tactics quickly resulted in the end of a family line. Those who gained the *advantage had a triple benefit. They lived, they had an abundant food supply, and fewer males competing for breeding rights.*

*The Runners, or the first to develop a crude ability to visualize, considered a probable outcome before taking a future course of action. Imagining a poor outcome allowed another option to be considered. Animals and many of the hominids did not have this same ability. They saw danger, or food, and reacted.*

*In the book, despite the previous success of the Runners' strategy, they are now threatened. A new enemy has evolved among them, another hominid runner survived by finding and preying on their evolutionary kin.*

*These are shorter in stature, stockier and much stronger, and covered in heavy hair—more ape-like in appearance.*

*Countless generations had balanced the needs of prey and predator allowing them to coexist and survive in an uneasy relationship, but humans and their hominid kin were a disturbance, a disruptive force on the continent, sometimes breaking the delicate balance. Predators would usually only cull the weak, keeping the prey genetically strong and healthy, thereby limiting the predator's source of food and thus their numbers, an endless cycle for maintaining balance on the plains. Migrating with the herds, preying on their weak, competing with the other predators, some humans found the same kind of balance. But the evil genius of human intelligence was the ability to innovate in the art of killing* without a prerequisite instinct to temper the slaughter.

And why temper the slaughter? Why not kill everything and move on? It was evil genius—human intelligence made killing an art form.

Tribes would grow in size. Whole herds of plains animals died as humans developed skills to kill faster than the herds could adapt. Finally, with food scarce, the humans would starve or move on. Their greed threatened their own existence. Under this kind of stress, disease also played a role. Viruses and bacteria staked their claims. The future of this particular experiment was by no means assured, until something happened. Something special.

Retroviruses are viruses which can enter a cell and insert its own genetics into the host. This can cause the cell to change its function. For example, instead of producing an original protein the cell may now produce modified versions—as the insertion is not always clean. The cell may make copies of the virus and spread. This spread may drag foreign genes in a horizontal transfer of genetic material from cell to cell, host to host, species to species.

Around 10% of human DNA appears to be such foreign retro-code. That's a huge amount, when you consider that there is only around 1% different DNA between humans and chimpanzees. Experiments with fruit flies suggest that large evolutionary leaps could be due to retro-code.

Human DNA analysis offers us a picture of our original ancestors, revealing that all humans descended from a small group, as few as one hundred *who left eastern Africa for the north about 50,000 years ago. From an evolutionary point of view, 50,000 years is not very long. It's just long enough for humans much like us to have differentiated ourselves by subtle feature changes, eye, hair, and skin color. Those one hundred original ancestors would blend into a crowd today and not look, or if raised in our culture, act significantly different either. These Cro-Magnon men were us, so like us in fact that scientists no longer prefer to make the distinction, as none exists.*

*So, the human characteristics we exhibit today which so drastically differentiate us from the animals did not evolve in the last 50,000 years. Those changes were too profound, and the evolutionary benefits they brought, which sometimes appear of dubious benefit, could not have driven the species to change that quickly. A dramatic, sudden change—a punctuation—much better fits the evidence that those few people managed to do what they did in such a short time. Those intrepid few, and their progeny, populated the entire earth, including the Americas, Europe, Asia and Australia, as well as reconquered Africa. They completely eliminated all their humanoid competitors on three continents, and they did it all within 50,000 years, which geological evidence shows also included a major ice age.*

*It is a remarkable, almost unbelievable accomplishment. And it all began with a dramatic and improbable mutation in a primitive tribe of hunter gatherers who ran naked across the plains of Africa. It was our unremarkable Runners. The retrovirus ran out of control. It duplicated itself and inserted a dramatic new DNA first in thousands, then millions, and finally billions of cells.*

*Where did it come from? Maybe the chattering monkeys? Maybe the strange white tree? Or maybe straight from the hand of the Creator? Whatever the source, it was clear that something special had evolved in this protected valley and because of it, the human race would never be the same again.*

## *About the Author:*

*Lawrence Stanley works as a scientist and engineer and has struggled all his life to reconcile his knowledge of geology, astronomy, biology and genetics with his religious heritage and personal experience. He undertook a quest to find the answer, even if it meant losing his faith, or turning his back on science, depending on what he found. He has studied many scientific and sacred texts. His startling conclusion is with a little imagination, both are correct ways of looking at the world. They are in agreement and complementary. He undertook writing a series of novels, designed to entertain, and perhaps to heal the wounds resulting from centuries of condemnation on both sides. The world has too much hate and suspicion. That changes today.*

WWW.LAWRENCE-STANLEY.COM